R

HEART
QUEST

HeartQuest brings you romance fiction
with a foundation of biblical truth.
Adventure, mystery, intrigue, and suspense
mingle in our heartwarming stories of
men and women of faith striving to build
a love that will last a lifetime.

May HeartQuest books sweep you
into the arms of God, who longs for you
and pursues you always.

A Victorian Christmas Quilt

CATHERINE PALMER

DEBRA WHITE SMITH

GINNY AIKEN

PEGGY STOKS

Tyndale House Publishers, Inc.
WHEATON, ILLINOIS

Visit Tyndale's exciting Web site at www.tyndale.com.

Designed by Melinda Schumacher

"Lone Star," "Log Cabin Patch," and "Crosses and Losses" edited by Kathryn S. Olson; "The Wedding Ring" edited by Anne Goldsmith

Unless otherwise indicated, Scripture quotations are taken from the *Holy Bible,* King James Version.

Scripture quotations marked (NLT) are taken from the *Holy Bible,* New Living Translation, copyright © 1996. Used by permission of Tyndale House Publishers, Inc., Wheaton, Illinois 60189. All rights reserved.

Library of Congress Cataloging-in-Publication Data

A Victorian Christmas quilt / Catherine Palmer . . . [et al.].
    p. cm.
  Contents: Lone star / Catherine Palmer—The wedding ring / Debra White Smith— Log cabin patch / Ginny Aiken—Crosses and losses / Peggy Stokes.
   ISBN 08423-7733-6 (hardcover)
   1. Christmas stories, American. 2. American fiction—Women authors. 3. American fiction—20th century. 4. Christian fiction, American. 5. Quiltmakers—Fiction.
6. Quilting—Fiction. 7. Quilts—Fiction. 8. Women—Fiction. I. Palmer, Catherine, date
PS648.C45V52   1998
813′.54080334—dc21   98-20563

Printed in the United States of America

04   03   02   01   00   99   98
7   6   5   4   3   2   1

CONTENTS

Lone Star

CATHERINE PALMER

CHAPTER ONE

LONDON, ENGLAND
DECEMBER 1886

Howdy, mister." Star Ellis snipped off a length of cotton thread and laid her diminutive swan-neck scissors atop the piecework on her lap. "Colder than frog legs out there, I'd say."

"I beg your pardon?" The gentleman entering the coach paused to appraise her with a pair of eyes the exact shade of a Texas bluebonnet. He took off his top hat and sat down on the leather seat facing hers. "Did you mention amphibians, madam?"

"I was talking about the weather. Polite conversation, you know." Shaking her head, Star threaded her slender silver needle. As the passenger coach began to roll away from Victoria Station, she picked up the length of bright cotton diamonds she was stitching together and began to work the needle back and forth through the fabric. If the only other traveler on this journey couldn't grasp the rudiments of good manners, so be it. She didn't have much of an appetite for talk anyway.

Weeks of steamship travel from Houston to New York to London had frayed the edges of her patience. Star had never had much patience to begin with, and her current circumstances left little room for feminine niceties and grace. Back in Texas, terrible blizzards had descended on her father's cattle ranch for the second winter in a row. Ahead on the frigid moors of northern England, a British aristocrat—a total stranger—waited to marry her. The first calamity had pushed her toward the second. She was trapped in their midst with no way out.

This would be her first Christmas away from home. The carriage driver had decorated his rig for the season, and his efforts at festivity were consoling. He had tacked a sprig of mistletoe over the door, and he'd tied garlands of fragrant pine twined with red ribbons on the window frames. All the same, memories of the Ellis family fireplace hung with bright knitted stockings, the cinnamony scent of hot apple cider bubbling on the stove, and the chatter of brothers and sisters threading popcorn into long garlands made Star's heart ache.

"Excuse me, madam, are you mending?"

She lifted her head as her traveling companion's voice penetrated the cloud of gloom and irritation swirling through her. "Mending?" She picked up the carefully stitched fabric on which she had labored for two months. "This is a quilt, buckaroo."

"Bucka-who?"

"Quilt, quilt, quilt." She thrust out the piecework. "I declare, you act as if you've never seen a quilt."

"Haven't," he said, tugging off his kid leather gloves and leaning forward, elbows on his knees, to examine the fabric. "Has this *objet d'art* a purpose, or is it merely decorative?"

"Both, I guess. You lay it across your bed like a blanket. Or you hang it over the window if your shutters won't keep out the cold. You wrap it around your shoulders in the wintertime. You bundle up your newborn baby in it. You spread it under a tree for summer picnics. And if worse comes to worst, you cut it up and feed it to the fire when there's no wood around for chopping. It's a quilt."

"May I?" Those blue eyes pinned her. "I'm fascinated by primitive handicrafts."

Star reluctantly surrendered her patchwork to the man. *Primitive?* She could teach this British tenderfoot a thing or two. After all, who was the best quilter in the whole county? Who had won the blue ribbon at the fair last summer? Whose quilt went for twelve whole dollars at the harvest auction? She watched the man holding her fine piecework up to the light from the coach window and studying the tiny stitches.

"Intriguing," he pronounced. "Calicut, I'd say. The fabric."

"Calico, you mean."

"Calicut, actually. It's a port on the west coast of India. They export inexpensive cotton fabrics in little prints of flowers and such. You've a selection of Calicut cottons here in your quilt. This yellow one I'm sure of, and this blue, as well."

"The blue patch is from my granny's best bonnet, and don't try to tell me it's cheap. I happen to know Grandpa brought the bolt all the way from Abilene when he came back from his last cattle drive right before he died. We made Granny's bonnet, a skirt for my sister Bess, and a tablecloth out of that bolt of blue calico. Granny wore the bonnet to Grandpa's funeral, and everyone said she looked as pretty as a picture, even though she'd been crying her eyes out for three days."

"Good heavens."

"Give me that, please." She took back her quilt. What did a man like him know about fabric, anyway? "I've been sewing and piecing all my life. Mama taught me how to use a needle when I was knee-high to a grasshopper, and she says I have a way with cloth."

"Knee-high to a what?"

"To tell you the truth, I think it's all in the colors. Before I start to cut the pieces for a new quilt, I work with the fabrics, arranging them this way and that, until I'm sure they're just right. Some gals will put any old colors together, but not me."

"I see."

The corner of the man's mouth was twitching, and Star had the distinct feeling he was trying not to laugh. She shrugged. Let him mock her. This wasn't the first time she had felt alone and awkward since leaving the ranch. It wouldn't be the last. By the following evening, she would be cooped up in a stone manor house with portraits of dead aristocrats hanging on the walls. By Christmas she would be betrothed to the son of her father's business partner. By the new year, she would be a married woman far from the loving support of home, family, and friends. But she wasn't completely alone. Long ago she had entrusted her life to Christ, and now she would have to depend on him more than ever. Though she knew she was far from perfect, Star believed her Creator had a good plan for her life. Oh, she had made mistakes, and those had brought consequences. Yet, when she stumbled in her walk of faith, God never let her fall headlong. He held her hand, guided her, and brought joy in the midst of sorrow. Now he had brought her to England to marry Rupert Cholmondeley. She didn't understand this plan of her heavenly Father's, but how could she argue?

"I recently looked into buying a mill in India." The man across from her spoke up as she flicked her silver needle through the bright fabric. "Decided against it. Rather hot on the coast, you know. All the same, I made a thorough study of fabrics—cottons, silks, muslins, the lot—and I'm quite certain you've Calicut cotton there."

Star kept her focus on her needle. The man had a strong face and mesmerizing eyes, and she didn't mind looking at him. But he seemed to enjoy baiting her, trying to draw her into an argument. Star, herself, had been labeled feisty by more than one suitor. In fact, her most recent episode of spunk and mule-headedness had lost her the catch of the county and helped land her in this predicament.

"Look, mister," she said, "I don't want to be contrary. If you tell me this calico is from India, even though I know good and well it's from Abilene, that's fine with me. I've learned my lesson where arguing is concerned. The owner of the ranch south of us courted me for almost a year, and finally I ran him off by wrangling with him over one thing or another."

"Wrangling?"

"He'd tell me Luke was one of the twelve disciples, and I'd pull the Bible right off the shelf to prove him wrong. Or he'd insist Scotland was an island off the coast of England, and I'd haul him over to the atlas to set him straight. He'd tell me a woman couldn't string bob wire, and I'd march him out to the barn and pull on my bull-hide gloves. Sure, it's an ornery job, but I've helped my daddy string bob wire since I was a colt."

"Bob wire?"

Star looked up from her stitching. Lost in her memories, she had all but forgotten she was in an English passenger coach, jolting along down a cobblestone street at the edge of London. The man across from her leaned forward on his elbows, his blue eyes intent and his attention absorbed by her words. The realization that he was actually listening caught Star off guard. Since the start of her long journey, she'd had no one but the Lord to hear when she poured out her thoughts. Why this man? And why now? Maybe the Father had felt her utter loneliness, her edge of despair, and had sent this stranger to lend a measure of comfort.

"Bob wire," she said softly. "It's used for fencing. Little sharp metal points stick out between the twisted wires and poke any critter that tries to get through. You've got your

'Scutts Clip,' your 'Lazy Plate' bob wire, and about six other kinds. My daddy's been using 'Glidden Four Line' for ten years, and we like it best. Of course, I don't suppose I'll be stringing bob wire anymore."

"Barbed wire," the man said. "In England we call it barbed wire, and I would suspect you are the only woman in the kingdom who knows how to string it. Perhaps such a skill will be of some use to you whilst you visit."

"I'm not here for a visit, mister. I've come to stay." Letting her hands relax in her lap, Star leaned back and looked out the coach window. A light snow had begun to drift out of the leaden skies. The flakes floated through the gray air like puffs of dandelion down to settle on the wreaths of holly and fir decorating the doors of the houses that lined the street. "I'm about to marry a baron from Yorkshire. His father is in partnership with my father, you see, and I'm the link that will forge the two families. My sister Bess was in the chute to marry the baron, but now she's engaged to the neighboring rancher."

"The chap you wrangled with over Bible history, geography, and barbed wire stringing?"

"That's the fellow. He decided he wanted a nice, quiet, obedient wife like Bess."

"Which left you to the Yorkshire baron."

Star nodded. The man was smiling now, his chiseled features softening from rigid angles and planes to crinkles at the corners of his eyes and the hint of a dimple in one cheek. For the first time, she noticed the breadth of his shoulders beneath the black greatcoat he wore. Strong shoulders. Shoulders like a bulwark against all trouble.

An urge swept over Star, compelling her to ask if she might lay her head on the man's shoulder and if he might put his arms around her and hold her tight and warm. But then the dam holding back the tide of emotion inside her would break and she would start to cry, and such a display would never do. Star Ellis might be a rancher's daughter, but she had attended a finishing school for a whole summer in New York City. She knew how a lady ought to behave.

"I'm traveling to Yorkshire myself," the man said. "It's not such a bad place, really. Not a great deal of barbed wire about; ancient hedgerows are used for fencing. But we've a lot of sheep and cattle. Villages are scattered here and there—jolly nice people. And of course, there are some enjoyable prospects—the Yorkshire Dales in the north, the Lake District to the northwest, and Scarborough on the coast."

"Is Yorkshire your home?"

"Was." He leaned back and let out a breath. "I've been away a long time. The prodigal son, you know."

As Star studied her fellow passenger, he began to transform from a mere object of information and slight annoyance into a human being. *Prodigal son.* What could he mean by that? Why had he left his family? And more important, why was he returning home now?

"I've always wanted to go to India," Star said. "Africa, too."

"You must be joking."

"I heard a missionary speak about India once at a tent revival. He'd been in China, and he talked about crossing the Himalayan mountains and traveling down into the steaming deltas of the Ganges. It sounded exotic and beautiful—not a thing like west Texas, which is flatter than a chuck wagon griddle. But when he mentioned the crowded villages and the people worshiping fearsome idols made of clay and stone, that's when I knew I wanted to go. I think if I could teach one woman how to sew clothes for her naked little children or tell one old man about the love and forgiveness of Jesus Christ, I'd be as happy as a little heifer with a new fence post. I just want to do something meaningful, you know, something worthwhile."

"A heifer?" The man's dark brows drew together, but the dimple in his cheek deepened. "With a new fence post?"

"Heifers like to scratch against a tree or a post. They get fly bit sometimes, and the bites are itchy." Star picked up her quilting again, embarrassed that her common way of talking had made her notions about India sound silly. For all she knew, the man seated across from her was a baron himself, or even a duke. He probably thought she was addled.

"May I inquire as to the name of the missionary who spoke to you about India?" he asked.

Star glanced up. "I don't remember. I was a little gal at the time."

"A missionary named William Carey worked in India for many years. I met some of his students. Remarkable experience."

"Why?"

He shifted on the seat. "Well, actually . . ." He ran a finger around the inside of his stiff white collar. "It was . . . ah . . ."

"I'm sorry," Star said, reaching into the traveling bag at her feet. "It says right here on page 22, 'Do not be blunt when conversing with gentlemen. Bold, straightforward questions are never ladylike.' This is my etiquette manual from the New York finishing school, and I reckon I've read that page fifteen times. Madame Bondurant told me I have a terrible habit of blurting right out what's on my mind. You know, you grow up with five brothers and three sisters, and somebody says, 'Dinnertime,' and you holler out, 'Hand over the biscuits.' You don't think about *please* and *may I* and *thank you kindly.* Somebody says, 'Remarkable experience,' and you ask, 'Why?'"

"And I shall tell you why." He gave her a nod of acceptance. "I'd been taken to church all my life. Mother always went. Father couldn't be bothered. Nonsense, he called it, and I must say I quite agreed. Incense, Latin, Gregorian chants, a great deal of formality and tradition. Lovely at

Christmastime but a bit much the rest of the year, to my way of thinking. What was it all about? I hadn't the foggiest. Far more interested in tying my brother's knickers in knots than in listening to the minister."

Star laughed. "You tied your brother's knickers in knots?"

"It's an expression rather like yours about the heifer and the fence post. I liked to annoy my brother during the service. Make him wriggle. Great fun, you know." He chuckled. "At any rate, I went off to public school and then university. When I'd had enough and struck out on my own, I might as well have been wearing a suit of armor for all the religion that had penetrated my heart. Regular rake I was—women, wine, and cards. Good fun, I thought. Spent reams of money, bought a house in London, roved off to the Orient, gadded about the Continent. Thought I'd take a look round India, the Jewel in the Crown, you know."

"Oh, my." Star couldn't help but stare. What a different life this man had experienced. And yet, there was something about him that appealed to her. Something warm and honest.

"Whilst I was in Calicut," he went on, "I grew deathly ill. I'd a raging fever, thought I was going to die, and didn't particularly relish the notion. In hospital I met a couple of chaps—students of William Carey. As I recovered I watched them work, saw the things they were willing to do, talked to them, questioned them. And that's when it happened."

"When you realized you had confused religion with faith."

"Exactly." He smiled at her. "I'm not much good at . . . well, at feelings. They're unfamiliar territory to me. But this was more than a feeling. It was as though I could hear Christ himself knocking on that suit of armor I wore. I took it off, and in he came. Right inside me. Changed everything. I can't explain it, but I became different. A new man."

"And that's why you're going home. You want your family to meet the new man."

"Indeed." He unbuttoned his greatcoat to reveal a fine suit of black worsted wool, a stiff white collar with pointed wings carefully turned to the sides, and a knotted silk tie stuck with a gold pin. "The reformed rake, so to speak. Bit of a sticky wicket, going home. My father's been in a red rage at me for years. Mother can hardly speak my name. My younger brother, no doubt, hopes I'll wander off and get eaten by a tiger so he can lay claim to the titles and the inheritance. Both sisters married while I was away. I've nieces and nephews I've never seen. Bad business."

"Consequences," Star said. She watched as the coach rolled past the last of the red brick houses and entered a vision of snowy white fields crisscrossed by black hedges. Flocks of woolly sheep clustered together for warmth, observed here and there by fat snowmen garbed in red knit mufflers and black top hats.

"Some things grab you by the throat," Star said, "and you can't escape the consequences. Last year Texas had the worst winter anybody can remember. Dead cattle lay piled up against the fences for miles around. The water holes froze. The grass was buried. Those poor creatures bawled so piteously it nearly broke my heart. The few that survived were all frostbitten and scrawny. Oh, it was a terrible spring, let me tell you. This year it's happening all over again. They're calling it the Big Die-Up."

"Dreadful."

"You can say that again. There's not a thing my daddy or any other rancher can do but pray for a warm spell and hope the investors won't pull out. On the other hand, I've learned that some consequences we bring on ourselves. Like when I ran off that rancher by being so ornery. So my Christmas present this year is going to be a wedding to the baron. Consequences."

"Consequences." The man tugged off his coat and laid it on the empty seat beside him. Then he leaned one shoulder against the coach window and with his knuckle traced a pattern on the steamy glass. "May I ask the name of your baron, madam? Perhaps I know the man."

"The name is Chol-mon-deley, or something like that." Star had practiced her new surname for weeks, but she thought she was probably botching the pronunciation. "Awkward as a bear in a bramble patch, if you ask me. Now, I'm Star Ellis. Plain and simple."

"I wouldn't call you plain, Miss Ellis, and you're certainly not simple." He thought for a moment. "I'm afraid I don't know your intended husband, though I've likely met him. Yorkshire's hardly a place where one can stay anonymous for long."

Star shrugged. It wouldn't do much good to learn about Rupert Cholmondeley anyway. Her intended husband had written her two letters since the announcement of their fathers' agreement. Both missives had been short and uninteresting. The man's primary occupation seemed to be fox hunting.

"Permit me to introduce myself, Miss Ellis," the man said. "I am the viscount Stratton, at your service. Lord Stratton, if you like."

Star felt her whole frame stiffen up like a buffalo hide in a snowstorm. This man was a *lord*? And she'd been rattling on and on like he was one of the cowhands over at the corral. Mercy!

"I'm pleased to meet you, Viscount," she said. "Wait a minute, I don't think I got that right."

Grabbing her etiquette manual, she began flipping through the pages. If only she could find that section on introductions and titles. She tucked away a curl that had strayed from her bonnet and ran her finger down the index.

"Lord Stratton," he said. "That's the formal name. My

friends call me Stratton, and you're welcome to do the same."

Swallowing hard, Star shut her book. "Don't you have a real name?"

"Grey is my given name, but you won't hear it. If you need rescuing from your baron, you'll have to ask for Lord Stratton."

"I'll call you Grey." She picked up her needle again. "And I don't think anyone can rescue me."

"Righty ho!" the coach driver called as he swung open the inn's door. "This be seven o'clock an' time to leave Nottin'am. A fine inn, good eats, an' decent beds, hey? Show yer thanks in a sovereign or two for the innkeeper, that's right. Climb aboard everybody, and we'll be off."

As Grey waited for Miss Ellis to emerge from the room in which she had spent the previous night, he peered out the window at the quaint little village with its half-timbered houses and snow-lined streets. Wreaths tied with red and green ribbons hung on the streetlights, and shoppers were filling the streets in pursuit of the ingredients for holiday feasts.

Grey had enjoyed the journey thus far, and he was dreading its end. Miss Ellis had kept up an amusing and interesting conversation all the previous afternoon as the coach wound its way north. She fascinated him with her friendly banter and amusing colloquialisms. Moreover, she was as beautiful a creature as he'd ever seen. Masses of dark curls framed a pair of sparkling green eyes, clear white skin, and a smile so dazzling it fairly radiated. Star Ellis, he'd learned, was quick to laugh and was not the least abashed when it came to defending her opinions.

Grey admired her godly spirit and her desire to help the less fortunate. But her underlying sadness disturbed him. He would like to give that baron of hers a swift kick in the backside. The least the man could have done was send a family carriage to London for the girl. Obviously, he didn't know what a treasure awaited him. Although she'd spent the evening in her room, Grey was looking forward to seeing the young American again this morning.

"No wonder Nottingham is the center of England's lace industry," a familiar voice said beside him. Grey glanced over to find the woman herself tugging on a pair of bright red gloves. "Look at the frost on all the windows, the icy tree branches, and the patterned cobblestones. The village reminds me of a fancy piece of lacework."

Grey studied the scene, trying to see it through her eyes. "I believe you're right, Miss Ellis. It does look rather lacy."

"You know, if my future didn't look as dark as midnight under a skillet, I'd be tempted to slip right into the Christmas spirit."

"That dark, is it?" Grey realized a grin was already tugging at the corners of his mouth. "Surely not. It's a fine morning—lots of snow, a comfy coach, and a dashing traveling companion."

She shot him a look that arched her dark eyebrows and set her eyes to sparkling. "Dashing? A little vain, I'd say. I hope you're not one of those roosters who thinks the sun comes up just to hear him crow."

Lifting her chin, she set out through the door. Chuckling, Grey joined Star near the coach as an elderly couple boarded. They had joined the party, the driver informed him, intending to go to Yorkshire to visit their daughter for the holidays.

This would be his first Christmas at home in many years, Grey realized. Not a particularly warm thought. A large tree always graced the ballroom at Brackenhurst Manor, but it was the servants who decorated it and laid the family gifts beneath. No doubt his parents had already issued invitations for the Christmas Eve party, a festive occasion with dancing, charades, and a charity auction. Good fun, if you didn't mind sharing your Christmas with two hundred people.

His hands shoved deep into the pockets of his greatcoat, Grey watched the snowflakes falling like autumn leaves in a strong wind. "Cold?" he asked Star.

"As the legs of an amphibian," she said, flashing that brilliant smile. "I didn't sleep worth beans last night. If I can just thaw out my toes, I might be able to take a little siesta."

"*Sí, señorita.*"

Her pink lips parted. "You've been to Mexico?"

"Spain. I've only a smattering of Spanish, I'm afraid, and not much more German or Italian. But I'm rather good at French, and I can count all the way to ten in Hindi."

"Hindi!" She laughed, a musical sound like the ringing of Christmas bells.

Grey couldn't hold in a returning chuckle. "May I help you into the carriage, Miss Ellis?"

"Star," she said, holding out her hand. "You're the only friend I have on this side of the Atlantic. You might as well call me Star."

He took her slender gloved fingers in his and slipped his free hand beneath her elbow. Miss Ellis was every bit the proper lady in her polished button boots, black velvet-trimmed coat with long, pleated peplum, and elegantly draped red dress and bustle. Her hat, trimmed in feathers and ribbons, had been purchased in New York, she had informed him the previous afternoon. As she tipped her head to step into the coach, a cascade of loose snowflakes tumbled onto his arm.

"Mercy," she said, turning toward him and brushing away the snow. "I'm sorry about that. A lady never knows what she'll find in her hats these days. When I was packing my trunks, I discovered a nest of baby mice hiding in the brim of my summer straw bonnet. They were the cutest things, so tiny and white and nestled down in among the silk ribbons.

I just left that bonnet right there, figuring if I'm going to marry a baron, he can just buy me another summer bonnet. Don't you reckon?"

Grey sucked in a breath to keep from laughing. Mice in her bonnet? What would this intriguing woman say next?

"Indeed," he managed. "By rights your baron ought to buy you a new summer bonnet for every day of the week."

"And two for Sundays!"

Her smile sent a ray of blinding sunlight straight through Grey. His heart slammed into his rib cage with all the force of a cannonball as he helped her up the steps. The warmth of the woman's light seemed to shine all around him, above him, inside him, and he frowned in confusion at its unexpected brilliance.

As Star's tiny waist disappeared into the depths of the coach, Grey took off his top hat and ran his fingers through his hair. True, he had opened his soul willingly to God. But he'd always kept himself guarded against humans, whom he'd experienced as a faithless, scheming, and generally selfish lot.

So what was this softness inside him, this gently aching warmth? He'd climbed the Alps, boated on the Nile, and hunted tigers in India. How could a woman with mice in her bonnet threaten the insurmountable walls he'd built around his heart?

"Getting in, milord?" The coachman looked up at him and gave a snaggletoothed grin. Then he leaned over and whispered, "I couldn't 'elp but notice at the inn that you and the American miss are gettin' along famously. A pretty lass she is, eh?"

Grey shrugged. He didn't intend to discuss such matters with a curious coachman. It pained him to realize that his fascination with Miss Ellis was so apparent.

"The young lady is to be married to a Yorkshire baron, my

good man," Grey said. "And I should thank you to keep your opinions to yourself."

"As you wish, milord," he said. "But I can tell you this, Lord Cholmondeley is a lucky fellow."

"Cholmondeley?" Grey grabbed the man by his sleeve. "Rupert Cholmondeley, younger son of the earl of Brackenhurst?"

"The very same, sir. Miss Ellis 'anded me the direction on this piece of paper, and I knew the family straightaway." He held out the carefully printed address. "She says they're to be married in the new year."

Grey stared at the inked letters, trying to recall the name of the Yorkshire baron Star Ellis had said she was to marry. *Chol-mon-deley*, she'd pronounced it. Of course she had. And why not? The young Texan had likely never heard an Englishman say the surname, which was rightly pronounced *Chumley*.

Brushing aside the coachman, Grey stormed into the coach and took the only empty seat—right beside the young woman herself. He jerked off his top hat, gave it a whack, and sent snowflakes in a shower over the carriage floor. Blast.

The prodigal son was on his way home to make peace with his family. And the woman who had captured his imagination, his fancy, his very heart, it seemed, was Star Ellis. Grey Cholmondeley, the viscount Stratton, had managed to trip head over heels on the radiant smile of his younger brother's intended wife.

Chapter Two

O n your way to Yorkshire, are you?" The elderly
gentleman who had joined the traveling party at the
inn addressed the viscount through an enormous
white walrus mustache. "Staying at the country house for
the holidays?"

Star waited for the man seated beside her in the coach to
answer. When the viscount said nothing, she took out her
scrap bag. "We're both traveling to Yorkshire," she replied,
laying her piecework in her lap. "The viscount Stratton is
returning home from India. I'm on my way from Texas to
marry a baron."

"Lord Stratton, are you?" The gentleman continued to
address Grey as though Star hadn't spoken. "India? Rather
hot, what? Any sign of another mutiny? Terrible business,
don't you think?"

Unwinding a length of thread, Star wondered whether the
old fellow could speak in anything but questions. And why
wasn't Grey responding? Surely a viscount knew the rules of
etiquette. Polite conversation required mutual inquiries as to
health and welfare, genteel statements about current events,

and the relation of anecdotes and humorous stories. It was all detailed in the fourth chapter of her New York City etiquette book. Star Ellis might be a country bumpkin, but she had learned about manners.

"The viscount was ill in Calicut," she said, answering for the man beside her. "He had a very high fever."

"Does Brackenhurst know you're coming, then?" The gentleman stroked his stubby fingers down the length of his mustache. "Bit of a shock for him, what?"

Brackenhurst. Star threaded her needle as she pondered the name. The earl of Brackenhurst was her intended husband's father. Although the old fellow continually failed to look her in the eye, she felt this question must be directed at her.

"The earl of Brackenhurst knows I'm coming," she said. "He wasn't expecting me at this particular time of year, but my father has written to prepare him for my arrival. I was planning to leave Texas next spring and marry in the summer, you see, but Daddy decided the wedding ought to be held right away in order to seal our family's connection with the earl. This is our second terrible winter in a row, and Daddy is counting on the earl's support. A rancher can see his spread through some mighty rough times, but not if he loses his backing. And a backer has to hang in there through all the ups and downs if he wants to turn a profit. Sometimes that takes a few years, if you know what I mean."

She deftly knotted her thread and awaited the gentleman's response. When he harrumphed and looked out the window, Star wasn't too surprised. Thus far in her long journey, almost no one but the viscount had bothered to converse with her. She didn't know if her Texas accent was too difficult to understand, if her topic choices were too boring, or if she was just plain irritating to listen to. Maybe no one she'd met knew about ranching, and maybe they didn't care to learn. All the same, if people wouldn't talk to her, she was going to have a lonelier life than she'd imagined. Maybe she ought to stick to topics anyone could discuss.

"Marriage," she said, poking her needle into a blue diamond. "I reckon running a ranch is kind of like marriage. There are good times and hard times—and a whole lot of regular old boring times. But through it all, you keep on going and try to make the best of it. Last winter when my daddy was hauling all those frozen carcasses, he just broke right down and cried. But he told me, 'Star, I ain't givin' up no matter what.' That's how marriage ought to be."

"Frozen carcasses?" The elderly lady in the coach slid a monocle from her chatelaine bag, held it to her eye, and peered at Star. "May I be so bold as to ask the subject of your discourse? Are you referring to the earl of Brackenhurst as a frozen carcass?"

"Now then, Mildred," her husband spoke up, "you've caught the wrong end of the stick on that one, haven't you? The young lady was speaking of marriage. Says her father cries over it."

"Did I not hear her mention frozen carcasses? I'm quite certain I did. Sure of it."

The woman stared at Star through her monocle. Her husband heaved a loud sigh. Star stitched to the end of her thread and began searching for her swan-neck scissors. This whole conversation was a disaster.

The viscount would be no help. Staring out the pine-trimmed window, he was completely ignoring the discussion inside the coach. Gone were his dimpled smiles and interesting observations. The moment the travelers had entered the carriage that morning, his light mood had evaporated. Star thought it was probably her fault for telling him about the mice in her summer bonnet. These days a gal never knew what would turn a man against her.

"Many of the cattle on my father's ranch in Texas froze to death last winter," she said to the elderly couple. She spoke slowly and enunciated each word as though addressing a pair of five-year-olds. "He is in partnership with the earl of Brackenhurst. I was trying to tell you that I believe a marriage is like running a ranch with a partner. Not a love marriage, but a business marriage. Which is why I'm marrying the earl of Brackenhurst's son."

"Brackenhurst's son?" the lady burst out, dropping her monocle. "I say, Lord Stratton, but that's—"

"It's Rupert," the viscount said evenly, straightening away from the window. "This young woman is to marry the earl's second son. And now, Miss Ellis, would you mind explaining this quilt in greater detail? I'm intrigued by the craftsmanship."

Star looked up into Grey's blue eyes. "You want to learn to quilt?"

"Well . . . you could demonstrate your techniques."

"Oh, Grey, don't you know you can't learn to quilt except by quilting?" Her heart flooded with warmth. "You can't learn to *do* except by *doing*. That's what my mama always told us young'uns, and I've come to believe she's right. Now you take this needle and put these two diamonds front to front."

"But I didn't mean . . . I don't really . . ."

"Hold the needle." She took his large hand and slipped her biggest thimble on his middle finger. Then she covered his hands with hers and showed him how to work the needle in and out of the fabric in tiny, even stitches.

"Daddy and Mama love to quilt together in the evenings," she said softly. "Especially in winter. Daddy worries that his friends might find out what he's doing and call him a sissy. The minute we hear the hounds barking down at the end of the road, Daddy knows a horse is coming up to the ranch house. He lights out of that chair by the quilt frame as fast as a cat with its tail afire. He heads for the kitchen to make himself a cup of java, just as innocent as you please. Well, let

22

me tell you, my daddy likes coffee strong enough to haul a wagon, and by the time the visitor leaves, Daddy's usually so high strung, he'll take up his quilting and outdo Mama by three patches to one."

She leaned back against the seat and laughed at the memory. Grey chuckled as he pierced the needle into the fabric. The silver lance went through the cloth, glanced off the thimble, and slid straight into his fingertip.

"Blast!" He jerked upright and grabbed the wounded finger. "Look, Miss Ellis, I'm not—"

"Now don't have a hissy-fit, Grey. Everybody makes mistakes at first. Learning how to sew is a tricky business." She took his hand and spread it open. His fingers were long and tanned, hardened by some unexplained work he must have been doing in India. She bent over and pressed her lips to the tiny red spot on the tip of his finger.

"Better?" she asked.

He sucked in a breath, his focus lingering on her mouth. "Not . . . not entirely."

Star smiled. "All right then. One more kiss and back to work."

As she held his hand to her lips, their eyes met, and his thumb grazed across her cheek, touching her earlobe. A ripple of surprise ran down Star's spine and settled in the base of her stomach. How many men had touched her cheek in her years of courting? And not one of them had ever sent curls of delight across her skin as this Englishman did with just the brush of his thumb.

"Much better," he said in a low voice. "Very much better."

Star swallowed. "Needles can be dangerous," she managed. "Please use your thimble."

"As you wish, madam."

Grey picked up the diamonds and the fallen needle and went back to work. As she pieced her own patches, Star covertly observed the man. She was more than a little dismayed at his inability to create straight, regular stitches. In fact, his thread leaped and danced across the fabric in long, crooked strokes that looked like the tracks of a half-drunk chicken in search of grain.

At one point he stopped to stare out the window, as if pondering some earth-shattering dilemma. When he resumed sewing, he looped the thread over to the wrong side of the patch and made three stitches that didn't know whether they were coming or going. *Good heavens,* Star thought.

Her dear mother would have jerked away that piecework and ripped out those pitiful stitches. A person ought to do things right, or not at all, Mama always said. But Star had made enough mistakes in her own life to allow the viscount to keep right on sewing to his heart's content. Later, she would iron the diamonds he'd pieced and work them into the pattern of her quilt—and no one but her mother would know the difference. Of course, her mother might never see this quilt. . . .

"Gold," she said, when the viscount's big hand reached for another blue diamond. "We're working a pattern, you see. Blue, white, gold, burgundy, green—and blue, white, gold, burgundy, green. If you put two blues together, the quilt will look all whomper-jawed."

"I beg your pardon?"

"It'll be a mess." She spread sections of the pieced fabric across her lap. "This is called Lone Star. It's a four-patch quilt pattern. I'm making it to help me remember Texas. Some women call the design Star of Bethlehem, which is a pretty name for this time of year. Later, I'll join these strips together to form patches, and then I'll join the patches into huge diamonds, like this."

She illustrated by extending the piecework onto his lap. "Then I'll sew all the large diamonds together," she continued. "Can you see how the diamonds will work outward into the points of a star? My Lone Star quilt will have eight points and nearly a thousand patches. After I've finished piecing the diamonds, I'll put a soft cotton batting between the top and a length of blue calico. And then I'll quilt it all together."

The viscount frowned as he studied the fabric. "But I understood we were *already* quilting."

"We're piecing. Quilting comes later." Star shook her head. "I sure do hope somebody will build a quilting frame for me. I don't know what I'll do if I can't work a quilt in that big manor house. Quilting helps me keep my thoughts in order; it makes sense out of the world when things are mixed up and confusing."

"Rather like the Almighty," he said, to Star's surprise. "I've learned that when nothing else makes sense, he does. He arranges events in proper order and sets our lives to right after we've put everything at sixes and sevens."

"If we let him," she murmured. She searched the man's face, praying for recognition in those blue eyes. If Grey could understand what she wanted to tell him next, Star felt, she would make her first true soul-to-soul connection in this new country.

"I've always thought of God as the master quilter," she explained softly. "He takes the little worn-out patches that we give him, the mistakes, the terrible holes we've caused with our sins, the frayed edges of our lives, and he pieces them all together into something beautiful and useful. If we give him our scraps, he can make quilts."

"I agree," he said. "Miss Ellis, have you a name for the quilt God is making of your life?"

She looked down at her lap. "Lone Star, I reckon. I'd sure like to be Star of Bethlehem—a ray of brilliance that everyone could look up to and count on, a bright light pointing the way to the Savior. But I doubt I'll ever go to India and teach anyone about Jesus, and I'm not sure I'll shine at all once I've married that baron. Lone Star, that's me."

Feeling suddenly ill at ease for revealing so much of herself, Star began gathering up the strips of diamonds. When she reached for a length of fabric on Grey's lap, he caught her hand.

"Miss Ellis," he said in a low, urgent voice.

"Star," she corrected.

"It must be Miss Ellis from this moment on. I've news I must share with you. It's about the earl of Brackenhurst. About his son. He has two sons, actually, but first I must tell you about the man you're to marry, and then I must explain—"

"Rupert's ugly, isn't he?" Star stuffed her piecework back into her bag. "I just know he is. I mean, what else can go wrong? Here I am, ten thousand miles from home, headed for a bleak old stone manor on the misty moors of England and marriage to a stranger. I've tried to prepare myself for the worst, imagining that Rupert looks like Frankenstein's monster, or Count Dracula—"

"He looks like me."

"Oh." She blinked. "Really?"

"And furthermore—"

"I thought you said you didn't know him."

"I do. I know him well. When you first spoke the surname of your intended husband, I misunderstood your pronunciation."

"That's what I've been trying to tell you, Grey." She laid her hand on his. "No one around here can understand me. It's as though I'm speaking a foreign language. If I can't talk to anyone, if I can't quilt, if I'm not allowed to string bob wire—barbed wire—well, I don't want to even think about it. These are the pieces of my life. The shreds. The tatters. I'm giving them to God, and I'm praying he can make a quilt out of me."

She struggled to hold back the tide of hot tears that stung her eyes. It would do no good to feel sorry for herself. The best thing to do was pray . . . and rest.

She leaned against the back of the seat and shut her eyes. "You'll go to India, Africa, China," she whispered. "You'll help people. You'll make a difference in the world. There's a quilt pattern called Trip Around the World. That's who you'll be. And I'll just have to trust the master quilter to make this Lone Star into something useful."

"*That* he already has done. Miss Ellis, if I may be so bold, I would term you useful, beautiful, and a far more brilliantly shining light than you are aware."

"Star of Bethlehem. No, I'm afraid not." She leaned her head against the viscount's broad, firm shoulder, his words comforting her heart. "May I rest here, Grey? I feel like I'm running down faster than a two-dollar watch. I've traveled so far, and I have to be at my best when I meet Rupert Cholmondeley."

"Chumley," the viscount said.

Star drifted in the sound of his voice as sleep wound cozily through her mind. Chumley. Chumley. Was that the pronunciation of her new surname? *Chumley.*

"Rested, Miss Ellis?" the viscount asked. "We've stopped at Doncaster for the midday meal."

"Mercy!" Star exclaimed, coming awake inside the carriage. "I forgot you were there. You just about scared the living daylights out of me."

As the elderly couple made their way out of the coach, Star realized—to her mortification—that she was snuggled against the man as though he were a cozy pillow. He had slipped his warm arm around her shoulder, and his enormous black greatcoat lay draped across her knees. Sitting upright as straight as possible, she righted her bonnet and brushed at the wrinkles in her skirt.

"I can't believe I slept away the morning," she said. "You must think I'm as lazy as a chilled lizard."

The viscount chuckled. "Not at all. My journey from India was exhausting. Had I not been occupied with such a fascinating activity this morning, I'm quite certain I should have dozed as well. But," and he made a dramatic pause, "I have been piecing."

He held up a length of calico diamonds that looked like a rattler run over by a wagon wheel. Star clapped a hand over her mouth, torn between horror and amusement. With stitches that looked like scattered hay, the jewel-colored patches marched this way and that as they dangled from the viscount's fingers. Star would have laughed out loud had she not seen the serious expression on the man's handsome face. His blue eyes were soft and his smile gentle.

"I'm afraid I don't have much to offer you, Miss Ellis," he said, "but you've made this leg of the journey my most enjoyable experience since leaving India. I thought perhaps I could help you along with your quilt. I'll admit to being more comfortable at polo and cricket, but—"

"It's wonderful," she exclaimed, receiving the gift with both hands cupped. The image of her father handing her mother his latest four-patch for the quilt they were piecing leaped into Star's mind, and her eyes clouded with tears. "I'll work your diamonds right into this pattern. And then you'll always be a part of the Lone Star quilt."

"You told me *you* were the Lone Star," he said, dropping his voice. "Shall I always be a part of you, Miss Ellis?"

She looked into his eyes, hardly able to breathe. "Oh, Grey, but I must—"

"The baron is why I must take a moment to speak with you alone. It is essential that you know the situation ahead."

"Plannin' to sit there all day are you, milord?" The coach

driver's head popped through the doorway. "I've unhitched one 'orse already and the other's restless to tuck into a nice sack of oats. I know I could do wi' a bit of hot grub meself. The eel pie at this place is tip-top, mind you. What of it, now? Why don't you and the young miss take your chat inside where it's warm and friendly-like? That's the ticket, milord."

The viscount nodded at Star. "We shall speak at the table then. After you, Miss Ellis."

"Go ahead," she said. "I've got to round up my quilt scraps and needles."

Though her scrap bag was in disarray, Star wanted a moment to mull over the viscount's comment. *Shall I always be a part of you?* His deep voice reverberated through her. They had known each other less than two days, their words had been careful, their conversation limited, and yet she knew her answer would be yes.

Not only would the man's creative stitching live on in her quilt, but his friendship and genuine concern would remain always in her heart. He had intrigued her with his tales of India, amused her with his attempts at sewing, and touched her with his understanding of her plight. His smile dazzled her, and his blue eyes thrilled her. Oh yes, Lord Stratton would always be a part of her.

But Star sobered as she tucked his pieced calico diamonds into her bag. They would spend this meal and another half day together—and she must be wary. It was one thing to marry a Yorkshire baron for business purposes. A woman could find a way to tolerate such an unemotional arrangement. It would be quite a different matter to fall in love with a Yorkshire viscount first. Then her marriage to Rupert Cholmondeley would be a torment.

She could not allow it to happen, Star thought as she reached for the leather strap beside the door. She gathered up her skirts and prepared to distance herself from the viscount. It shouldn't be hard. She'd run off plenty of suitors in the past.

As she stood to step down, the coach suddenly lurched forward, knocking her off her feet. She landed on the floor in a tangle of skirts and petticoats, the pouf of her bustle cushioning her fall. A dog barked, one of the horses neighed, and the carriage swayed from side to side. Star grabbed for the seat to keep from sliding through the open door.

"Blimey!" the driver hollered. "Me 'orse is boltin'! Wait for it, miss, don't try to get off!"

Star watched her scrap bag tumble out as the carriage rolled wildly down the street. The clatter of iron horseshoes on cobblestone echoed through the crowded streets of Doncaster. People screamed and ran for cover. Clutching the edge of the seat, Star managed to scoot backward far enough to grab one of the dangling leather straps.

Well, if this didn't beat all—a runaway horse!

At that moment the coach rammed into the corner of a half-timbered house. A wheel spun loose, wobbling on its axle and causing the carriage to bob and weave down the street. Star decided she'd had enough of being a passenger.

Gritting her teeth, she struggled to hold on as she inched toward the open door, her skirts twisted around her ankles. If she could climb onto the carriage roof, she might be able to grab the reins. *Lord,* she prayed, *help me!* Clutching the rolled canvas shade that protected the window, she leaned out through the open door.

"Miss Ellis!" Grey's voice rang out over the shrieks and screams in the street. "Get back inside the coach!"

She peered over her shoulder as she clung to the side. A dappled gray horse galloped after the runaway carriage, its rider hatless as he urged the steed alongside the swaying vehicle. For a moment, Star's senses lit up like an Independence Day bonfire. Grey was coming after her! But that would put him in danger, too.

As the coach bounced around a corner, she realized that she would have to be the one to stop the horse. If the viscount were injured . . . or killed . . .

"Stay back!" she cried. "I'm going for the reins!"

"You'll be crushed! Please stop—I'm almost there."

"The street is too narrow! You can't get around the coach. I can do this, Grey."

"Star, be reasonable!"

He edged forward until his horse's nose was almost touching her. Star debated throwing herself onto the creature's neck. But if she fell, she'd be trampled. No, there was no choice but to go up.

She set her foot on the sill of the open window and grabbed the slender iron luggage rack on the roof. Her bonnet had slid off her head and the ribbon was about to choke her. Half gagged, she groped for a foothold on the lamp that jutted out from the side of the carriage. In the collision with the house, the glass shade had shattered, leaving a jagged fragment protruding.

"Star!" Grey shouted just as she heaved herself onto the luggage rack. "There's a park ahead. Trees!"

Mercy! she thought. Fighting to hold on, Star flung one leg into the driver's box. What if she pulled the brake lever? Would that spook the horse even more? She could feel the poor critter starting to slow. What on earth had caused it to bolt like that?

"Mind your head!" Grey roared as his horse thundered past Star. "Stay down!"

Star never had been much for obeying commands—and her stubborn streak had gotten her into a great deal of trouble. On the other hand, her life was at stake here. Struggling to breathe around the bonnet ribbon, she threw herself onto the driver's seat and slid her wobbly legs down onto the footboard.

The carriage careened into the park, and the viscount

31

managed to guide his dappled gray alongside the runaway. As he reached for the bridle, Star leaned forward and grabbed the reins.

"Whoa!" she called. "Pull up there, you crazy old cayuse!"

The horse made straight for a stand of trees, and Star held her breath as she tugged on the reins. The thick leather strips burned her palms, her toes mashing down into the points of her boots. Her eyes widened as she saw the low branches.

"Star, you must jump now!" Grey shouted. "I'll catch you!"

The horse had begun to slow at last, but Star knew it would be too late. The nearest branch was only a few yards away, and the carriage rolled doggedly onward. Clinging to the edges of the driver's box, Star glanced over at the viscount racing alongside.

"Jump, Star! I won't let you fall!"

Sucking in a breath, she coiled against the footboard and then threw herself toward him. A strong hand clamped around her shoulder. An arm of steel scooped the back of her legs.

The dappled gray veered away from the trees just as the carriage slammed into the trunk of an ancient oak. Wheels flew in every direction as the body of the coach exploded like a barrel of black powder. Wood splintered in an ear-tearing screech, and the luggage rack splashed into a stone fountain. Still caught in the reins, the exhausted horse came to an abrupt stop, its foam-covered sides heaving.

"Grey!" Star clung to the man's broad shoulders, imagining herself trapped in that tangle of wood, metal, and horseflesh. "Mercy sakes! I thought I was a goner."

"Are you all right?" He turned his horse onto a side alley as people began pouring back into the streets. "Dear God . . ."

"He took care of me," she choked out. "And you. I didn't

break anything, but my hinges and bolts are sure loose. Oh, Grey!"

His arms slipped tightly around her, holding her close as she shuddered at the near disaster. "You shouldn't have tried to climb up," he murmured. "Miss Ellis, you are a rash, impulsive—"

"Mule headed, addlepated—"

His lips brushed hers for a moment, a heartbeat. "Beautiful and amazing woman," he finished. "If you hadn't climbed up, you'd have been inside the coach when it hit the tree. But when I saw you clinging to the side like a . . . like a . . ."

"Like an ol' bedbug."

Grey laughed suddenly. "Dear heaven, young lady, you have me in such a muddle that I'm . . . I'm . . ."

He pulled her closer and kissed her full and warm on the mouth. Star unfolded inside like a blossoming rose. Never in all her days of courting had a man's kiss lifted and floated her upward, unfurling her petal by petal. She clutched at his shoulders, reveling in the scent of bay rum on his skin, in the pressure of his hands against her back, in the heat of his lips on hers. Her senses danced up and over the snowy street, drifted above the chimney pots on the rooftops, soared into the downy flakes that sifted from the clouds. It was wonderful, magical . . . heaven. . . . "Star, I want you—," he began. Then he paused, his breath ragged. "Dash it, I can't . . . can't."

She swallowed hard. "The baron."

"Yes." He set her a little away from him. "It's the baron. Rupert Cholmondeley is—"

"Wicked?"

"No."

"Cruel?"

"No."

"Already married?"

33

"No, blast it. He's a fine chap. A decent, honorable human being."

"Then what's wrong with him?"

"He's my brother, that's what." The viscount looked up at the swirling snowflakes. "I'm Grey Cholmondeley, elder son of the earl of Brackenhurst. I've come all the way from India to make peace with my family, to show them that I'm a changed man, to prove that I'm upright and honest and worthy of my father's name. They're to see that I'm no longer the sort of man who would lose a fortune at cards, and drink whiskey until the wee hours. I'm not the sort of man who would . . . who would . . . ."

"Kiss his brother's fiancée?" Star grabbed his hand and squeezed it until every drop of rebellious spirit drained from her. "No, no, no," she whispered. "This can't happen. We can't let it."

CHAPTER THREE

Grey watched the familiar stone expanse of Brackenhurst Manor come into view as the carriage traveled through the iron gates and up the long, curving, graveled drive. They had managed to survive the hours since the incident with the runaway horse, but he felt less sure of his ability to manage the situation with Miss Ellis once they arrived at his family's country house.

From the moment they had returned to the inn at Doncaster, she had withdrawn into a cocoon of silence, focusing all her attention on her quilt. Bidding farewell to the elderly couple, who journeyed on toward the Yorkshire Dales, Grey and Star had continued in the same carriage eastward across the open moors. Although the intimate situation had offered opportunity for conversation, she had shown no interest in talking. She had worked on her quilt as though it and it alone had meaning in her life. Unable to entice her into even the most mundane chitchat, Grey had opened his traveling bag and taken out a heavy text devoted to the cultivation of *Camellia sinensis,* the tea shrub.

"I'm developing a tea estate in India," he said as the

rattling coach approached the manor. It would be his final opportunity to engage the young American in conversation. If they arrived in the same carriage and hadn't resolved their concerns, if they weren't even *speaking,* his family would be wary immediately. "I've bought land near Darjeeling. It's a small town in the foothills of the Himalayas."

Star looked up, spotted the manor house, and blanched. "Mercy," she mouthed.

"Tea," he said. "I'm planting tea."

Her dark eyes turned to him. "Are you going to tell your brother what happened in Doncaster?"

"No. Be assured, I've every interest in establishing a good relationship with Rupert."

"Because if I lose the chance to marry him and keep the earl's money coming to Daddy's ranch—"

"You won't. I'll not endanger your plans, Star."

"Miss Ellis. You'd better call me Miss Ellis, and you'd better keep your distance, and you'd better not . . . not . . ." The dark eyes flashed. "How long did you know about Rupert and me before you told me he was your brother?"

"I tried to tell you earlier."

"Not early enough! You were charming and funny, and . . . and you sewed my quilt. You led me around like a heifer with a ring through her nose."

"I didn't intend to lead you on. I only thought . . . I thought how delightful you were and how beautiful. I didn't intend to kiss you."

"Don't talk about that!" She began stuffing quilt patches into her piece bag. "Glory be, but this situation is a confounded mess. It's half my fault anyhow for being such a chatterbox and napping on your shoulder and all. It's just that you're the only person who seemed to understand me. I talked about the Lord being the master quilter, and you knew what I meant. I thought maybe I'd found a friend . . .

no, it was more than that. I liked you, and I was wrong—dead wrong—to let you kiss me. I shouldn't have done it."

"Star, please stop your recriminations."

"My what?"

She looked up at him, a tear hanging on the end of an eyelash, and it was all he could do not to gather her into his arms again. "Neither of us intended to . . . to enjoy the other's company quite so much. We've both apologized, and now we must do our utmost to carry on as though nothing happened. I'll be welcomed back into the family fold, and you'll . . ." He swallowed. "Well, you'll marry Rupert. And all will be as God intended."

The carriage came to a stop before the flight of stone stairs that led to the huge wooden doors of Brackenhurst Manor. Grey permitted his focus to linger on the young woman across from him for a moment longer. *Was* this what God intended? Had the Almighty contrived to toss Star Ellis headlong into Grey's arms—a rigorous test of the faith he had been so determined to uphold? If she was a test, he wasn't at all certain he could pass. If, on the other hand, she was a temptation—a luring siren sent straight from the originator of sin—he longed to curse Satan straight into the pit of eternal darkness where he belonged.

But what if his meeting with Star had been nothing but a random coincidence—sheer chance? If there were no God, no need for atonement and reconciliation, Grey could woo the young woman away from his brother. He could enjoy her charms, as he'd enjoyed so many fleeting tête-à-têtes in the past, and then gallop straight back to his adventurous wanderings without a flicker of guilt.

"Thank you," Star said, reaching out and laying her hand on his arm. "Thank you for your faith in the Lord, and for understanding why this marriage to your brother is so important to my family."

Grey managed a stiff nod. "Of course."

"Brackenhurst Manor," their coach driver called, opening the door. "Good day to ye, Miss Ellis. Pleasure havin' such a lovely lady aboard me carriage. And Lord Stratton, thanks as well. 'Appy to be of service."

Star gave Grey a last grateful look before gathering her things and stepping out of the coach. He slipped his book into his bag and followed her into the evening. He had been planning this moment for months. It was to have been a time of anticipation, reunion, and celebration. As it was, he could barely summon the enthusiasm to climb the long staircase and tug on the bellpull.

"Good evening, sir," Massey the butler said, opening the door. "May I tell my master who is—good gracious! Can it be you, Lord Stratton?"

"The very same." Delighted at the sight of the family's faithful servant, Grey clapped the old man on the back. Massey had never been one to express his feelings, always careful to pinch his lips tightly and look the other direction when the unexpected occurred. As when he was a mischievous boy, it pleased Grey no end to have caught the dear fellow momentarily off guard. "I've come from India for the holidays, Massey."

"Lord Brackenhurst will be most pleased to see you, sir," the butler said, recovering his aplomb. "Do step inside and permit me to announce you. May I say the name of the young lady, sir?"

Grey took Star's elbow and led her into the cavernous foyer with its twin curved stone staircases and marbled floor. As they strolled into a large formal parlor, he introduced his companion. "This is Miss Star Ellis. She's come from America to marry Rupert."

The butler stopped in his tracks, swiveled around on a pair of squeaky shoes, and peered at Star. "Miss Ellis? From America?"

"Good evening, Mr. Massey," she said, extending her hand.

The butler looked down at the proffered appendage, debated what to do with it, and then gingerly attempted a handshake. "Delighted, I'm sure, Miss Ellis. You have arrived earlier than expected."

"But didn't the earl get Daddy's letter?" She clutched her scrap bag. "My father wrote to say I was coming before the new year. Texas is having another Big Die-Up, you see, and Daddy thought we ought to get everything settled with the earl before spring rolled around."

"A Big Die-Up?" Massey glanced at Grey.

"A harsh winter," he explained. "The Ellis family's cattle are perishing in the cold."

"Ah." The butler tucked in his lower lip and gave a solemn nod. Then without further word, he set off in the direction of the staircase, his shiny black shoes squeaking like a badly tuned violin.

"Good chap, Massey," Grey said, showing Star to one of the long gilded settees. Embroidered in a burgundy damask stripe, it sat queenlike before a blazing fire. To one side rose a towering fir tree, as yet undecorated. Grey knew from tradition that early the following morning the servants would festoon the Christmas tree with spun-glass ornaments from the Continent, myriad miniature paper fans, silk ribbon garlands, and at least two hundred tiny candles.

"Well, I'm done-for now," Star groaned, sinking into the down-filled cushion. "If Daddy's letter didn't get here yet, that means the earl had no idea I was coming."

"I have no doubt my father will be pleased to welcome you."

Grey walked over to the fire to be as far from her as possible without seeming rude. If the young woman looked any more disconsolate, he was sure he'd be at her side in a moment. As it was, the vision of her red dress, pale skin, and luminous dark eyes sent a pang of hopelessness through him. Star Ellis was stunning, and the instant Rupert laid eyes on her, the young man would realize he'd been blessed with a rare treasure. Any hope that the arranged marriage was a mismatch would end, along with the minuscule possibility that Grey might be able to court the young woman himself.

"Your father might accept me," she said. "But what about Rupert? A fellow doesn't like to have his bride sprung on him like a rattler striking from behind a rock. It's taken me months to get used to the notion of marrying a stranger. Even though Rupert knows I'm coming, he doesn't know I'm coming *now*. Daddy was sure his letter would get here before I did. I'm hornswoggled. I doubt even Madame Bondurant would know what to do in a pickle like this."

"I shall make the introductions and everything will be—"

A loud whoop cut off his words. The parlor door burst open, and into the room raced two fluttery young ladies, ruffled petticoats flying and golden curls bobbing. A laughing man chased after them, his dark hair bouncing around his ears. One of the girls bounded up onto a footstool and then leapt into the man's arms with a squeal of delight.

"Rupey-loopy!" The girl danced away again in a swirl of silk and ribbons. "Can't catch me, Rupey-loopy! Oh!"

She pulled up short at the sight of the two visitors in the parlor. The young man came to a skidding halt on the marble floor. The second girl clapped her hands to her cheeks and flushed a brilliant crimson.

"Rupert?" Grey asked, astounded at the panting man whose hair hung over his forehead and whose shirttail hung halfway to his knees. "Rupert, what on earth are you—"

"Strat?" Raking his fingers through the thick thatch of hair, Rupert stared. "What are you doing here, Stratton? I thought you were in India or Africa or somewhere."

"I've returned."

"You're codding me." He swallowed and shook himself as

40

if to dislodge the shock. "Have you really come back? Are you in England for good?"

"Just the holidays, actually. I've a tea estate in Ind—"

"Won't father be in a fuzz over this one?" He gave a humorless laugh. "Strat, you remember the Smythes of Stonehaven, don't you? This is Polly and her sister Penny. Paulette and Penelope, I should say. Ladies, my brother, the viscount Stratton."

With tittering that would have put a pair of sparrows to shame, the two young women made wobbling curtsies. Grey did remember the Smythe girls—their father owned a profitable cotton mill in Leeds, and his daughters had been no more than children when Grey had left England. Now they were certainly old enough, pretty enough, and no doubt wealthy enough to attract the attention of any man.

"And who's this, Strat?" Rupert asked, gesturing at Star. "Don't tell me you've gone and gotten yourself married without telling Mum."

"No," Grey said as Star rose from the settee. She looked as fragile as a puff of dandelion down. "Rupert, I should like you to meet Miss Star Ellis from Texas. Miss Ellis, my brother, Lord Cholmondeley."

"Good evening, my lord," Star said, executing a curtsy far superior to those of the Misses Smythe. "My father is Joshua Ellis, owner of the Rocking T Ranch. He and the earl of Brackenhurst are business associates, and . . . and they arranged for me to come here to England and . . . and . . ."

Rupert's mouth dropped open, and his face paled to a pasty white. Grey had the distinct impression that his younger brother was going to faint dead away. At that moment Massey, the butler, squeaked into the parlor.

"The Right Honorable the earl of Brackenhurst," he said in a sonorous voice. "The Right Honorable the countess of Brackenhurst. Lord and Lady Brackenhurst, your son, the

Right Honorable the viscount Stratton and his guest, Miss Star Ellis from Texas, America."

"My lord," Grey said. "Madam."

As always, he felt a twinge of discomfort in greeting the granite rock of a man who was his father. The silver-haired earl—as handsome and imposing as ever—had taken almost no interest in his children's lives beyond a brief pat on the head each evening after their dinner. Grey could remember few moments of private contact with the man. Twice the earl had wandered into the schoolroom and ordered his son to conjugate verbs in Latin. Once at a Christmas banquet he had asked Grey to recite publicly the names of the kings and queens of England. And once he had invited the young man to join him in the library after dinner. There, father and son had sat reading for two hours without a word until the earl announced, "That will be all," and strode off to the conservatory to listen to one of his daughters on the pianoforte.

Grey's mother, on the other hand, had always been warm, loving, and as devoted to her little ones as any nanny. As a little boy, Grey had loved to climb up into her lap and listen to her read stories or watch her knit. How disappointed she had been when her elder son had chosen a life of irresponsibility and recklessness.

"Rather a shock, Stratton," the earl said. "Didn't expect you in the least."

"No, my lord." Grey squared his shoulders. This was the moment he'd been both dreading and anticipating—the time to speak honestly about himself. He lifted up a prayer for strength. "Sir, I should like to apologize for the distress I caused you and Mother, and—"

"Oh, Grey!" the elderly woman cried, throwing out her hands and crossing to embrace him. "You've come home to us! Home for Christmas! Of course, we forgive you!"

Enveloped in a cloud of heliotrope perfume, Grey hugged

his mother and gave her wrinkled velvet cheek a kiss. "Hello, Mummy."

"My sweet darling boy—how marvelous to see you!"

"Calm yourself, Hortense," the earl said. "No need to become theatrical about this."

"Rupert, Polly, Penny, did you see?" his wife gushed on. "It's Grey! He's come home!"

Rupert was busily attempting to tuck in the tails of his shirt. "Yes, Mummy. We see him."

"Isn't he handsome? Isn't he tall? You've grown three inches, darling! Oh, we've missed you terribly, haven't we, George?"

As his mother cooed and his father frowned, Grey glanced at Star. He knew she must feel awkward, waiting for her presence to be explained. But this was his moment to say what was on his mind to the entire group. There would be no feasting and joyous celebration for this prodigal son, but if he could make peace with his father, he would accomplish his mission.

"Sir," he began, "I must speak to you about the matter of my return to England. I've come with a specific purpose in mind. While I was in India, I came to the realization that I had been leading a fruitless life. I had fallen ill and was in hospital when I met—"

"I should say so," his father barked. "Fruitless indeed. Wastrel. Rake. Idler. How many thousand pounds do you suppose you lost at cards, Stratton? And did you complete your education? What of that house in Berkeley Square? We've kept it, of course. Not a bad investment, but the tales the neighbors told us. I say, Stratton, did your mother bring you up to be such a cad?"

"Oh, George, leave the poor boy in peace," the countess said. "He's come home, hasn't he? He's apologized."

"Bit late for that. And what's this?" He turned on Star. "Didn't expect you before the new year, Miss Ellis. Something of a shock, what? Rupert, have you met your bride-to-be?"

"Yes, my lord," Rupert said.

"You were to arrive in the spring, were you not, Miss Ellis?" the earl addressed Star, looking her up and down as though she were an interesting piece of furniture. "Lady Brackenhurst hasn't had time to plan a wedding, have you, Hortense? Well, never mind that bit. We'll announce the engagement at the Christmas Eve party. It's the usual affair—bonfire, charades, dancing, charity auction. The announcement should add a bit of interest to the proceedings. Massey, do speak to the staff about the change in plans."

"Of course, my lord," the butler said. "As you wish, sir."

"Hortense, were we not on our way to dinner before this interruption?"

"Yes, George. Come along, children!"

Grey watched his parents exit the room. Rupert let out a deep breath, and the Smythe sisters rushed into each other's arms. Star dropped back onto the settee and buried her face in her hands.

"Good job, Strat," Rupert said. "Now you've upset the ladies. Polly, here's my handkerchief."

"Oh, Rupey!" The elder of the two sisters grabbed the scrap of white linen and dabbed under her eyes. "It's all such a shock!"

"Quite right. Shocking deeds are my elder brother's forte." Rupert gave his shirttail a final tuck and cleared his throat. "Miss . . . Miss Ellis? Are you well?"

"I reckon I'll live," Star murmured.

"May I help you up?"

Grey watched the scene unfold before him as the young American rose from the settee to meet her intended husband. Star extended her hand. Rupert took her fingers, bowed, and pressed his lips to her knuckles. She fingered the hollow of her throat as she gave him a tentative smile. He smoothed his hand over his muttonchop whiskers and straightened his cravat. One eyebrow arched, and a twinkle appeared in his eye.

"Miss Ellis," he said, "won't you join the Misses Smythe and me for dinner?"

Star tipped her head. "Thank you kindly, sir. I do believe I shall."

As the four walked out of the parlor, Grey felt his spirits slide straight to the bottoms of his boots. So, that was that. His father would not forgive him. His mother would treat him as a child. His brother would charm Miss Ellis as he charmed every woman. And Star would marry Rupert not only to save her father's ranch but also because he was a worthy young man and would make a good husband.

As he followed his family down the long corridor toward the dining room, Grey recalled Star's words in the carriage. God was the master quilter who could take the worn-out patches—the mistakes, the terrible holes caused by human sin, the frayed edges of life—and he could piece them all together into something beautiful and useful. *If we give him our scraps, he can make quilts,* she had said.

In India, Grey had known the guidance of God's hand leading him back to England. In the carriage, he had felt the truth in Star's words of comfort and assurance. But now, in the manor that once had been his home, Grey knew nothing but the sound of hollow footsteps and the chill of looming stone walls.

"Could you hand me that angel, Mr. Massey?" Star called down from the ladder propped against the wall. "Somebody must have dropped him over there by the door."

A silver tray balanced on his fingertips, the butler paused on his route down the corridor. "Miss Ellis? Is that you in the Christmas tree?"

Star peered between the thick pine branches and gave a little wave. "I saw Betsy and Nell hauling the ornaments down from the attic this morning after breakfast, so I figured I'd pitch in and help. We've already decorated the tree in the ballroom, and this one was next. The angel is right there by that potted fern."

The two housemaids suppressed their giggles as Massey peered over the rim of his silver tray at the gilded papier-mâché angel lying on the floor. When he crouched to retrieve the ornament, his shoes gave the squeak of a frightened mouse. Bottom lip tucked firmly beneath the upper, the butler placed the angel on his tray, carried it to the tree, and lifted it within Star's reach.

"Much obliged," she said. As she looped the ornament's gold cord over the tip of a branch, Star summoned her courage to put forth the question that had kept her awake most of the night. "Did my leaving the table early last night cause much of a ruction, Mr. Massey?"

"A ruction?"

"Was the earl angry that I went to my room before dinner was over? I tried to see the meal through, but I got to feeling like a throw-out from a footsore remuda, if you know what I mean. I couldn't figure out what I was eating until Polly Smythe mentioned how good the jellied tongue was tasting, and that about threw me for a loop. I was tired, and everything I said seemed to come out wrong. When I told the story about the time I was helping Daddy brand cattle and I nearly stepped on a coiled rattlesnake, I thought the earl was going to drop his teeth right into the soup. Rupert just stared at me, and the Smythe gals started giggling like there was no tomorrow. If it hadn't been for Grey . . . for Lord Stratton telling about the cobra that crawled across his foot while he was drinking tea in India, I would have just about died of mortification."

As she spoke, Star tied a length of red satin ribbon into a

luxurious bow and arranged it on the branch beside the golden angel. The truth was, she hadn't left the dinner because of exhaustion or jellied tongue or embarrassment. She had left because of Grey. After his story about the Indian cobra, Star had followed up with a tale about a bear that wandered into the cowhands' bunkhouse. Then he had laughed and told about the time a tiger chased him straight up a tree—only Grey wasn't telling his story to the whole family. He was telling it to Star. He looked into her eyes and leaned across the table, and before she knew it, she had forgotten all about the jellied tongue and was hanging onto every fascinating word that came out of the man's mouth.

Only when Rupert chimed in with an anecdote about a recent fox hunt had Star realized that she and Grey had been the only two talking for at least half an hour. As in the carriage, they had chuckled and teased and told their most hair-raising tales, oblivious to the rest of the gathering. Worse, Star knew she'd been riveted to the viscount's sparkling blue eyes and mesmerizing mouth. Surely the others had noticed.

"The earl of Brackenhurst does not wear artificial teeth, Miss Ellis," the butler said from the floor beneath the Christmas tree. "Therefore he could not have dropped them into his soup."

Star glanced down at the butler. "I didn't mean it that way, Mr. Massey. It's kind of an expression like . . ." She tried to remember the wording Grey had used on their journey. "Like tying your britches together in a bundle."

"My breeches?" The butler looked down at the starched blue wool trousers of his livery.

"Has our charming American visitor got your knickers in a knot, Massey?" Grey said, stepping into the parlor. "Good morning, Miss Ellis."

Star nearly dropped the paper fan she was holding. Mercy, that man could make a white shirt, green vest, and black pants look fine. He drew his gold watch from his pocket, flipped open the lid, and checked the time. When he looked up at her again, his familiar smile made her heart flop around until she thought she was going to fall right off the ladder.

"You've missed breakfast, Miss Ellis," he said. "I was hoping to speak with you."

"Really?" She set the fan on a branch and wiped her damp palm on her skirt. "Betsy brought some tea and rolls to my bedroom this morning. I could barely eat anyhow."

"Are you feeling all right, Miss Ellis? You left the table rather abruptly last night."

"I'm fine." She fumbled with the fan until it slipped from her fingers and landed three branches below. "Lord Stratton, don't you have a little viscounting or something to do this morning?"

"Viscounting." He retrieved the fan and stepped onto the bottom rung of the ladder to pass it up to her. "Hmm . . . yes, I suppose I could join my father in the library. Viscounts and earls do a good bit of sitting about the library, I've discovered. Viscounting normally doesn't require much ability to brand cattle or string bob wire."

Star gave him a scowl. "*Barbed* wire. And if you intend to keep the tigers out of your tea estate in India, you'd better learn how to string it, buster."

"Tigers are carnivores, are they not? I don't suppose they'll be in hungry pursuit of my tea bushes." He grinned, taking another two rungs. "I say, is this your cherub, Miss Ellis?"

Before she could react, he was halfway up the ladder. As he handed her the papier-mâché ornament, Star clung to the swaying tree. "You'd better get down before somebody sees you," she said through clenched teeth, eyeing the two housemaids who stood by the window unrolling spools of red and green ribbon. "And don't tease me anymore, either. Or talk to me. Or look at me."

"Listen, Star, I spent most of the night pacing the corridors," he said in a low voice, "and I couldn't stop thinking. I was thinking about the two days in the carriage and about Doncaster—"

"Hush about that!" She covered his mouth with her hand. "Mercy, you're going to get us both into trouble."

He took her hand and gave her palm a light kiss. "I'm already in trouble."

For a moment he said nothing, his eyes shut and his breath labored. Star gripped the rung of the ladder until her fingers turned white. Praying for all she was worth, she could hear nothing in return but the sound of her heartbeat hammering in her ears.

"Why did God put us together in the same carriage?" Grey demanded, his eyes suddenly lit with a hot blue light. "You told me he was the master quilter. You said he had a plan. What's the plan, Star? Why has this happened?"

"Nothing's happened."

"Yes, it has. I saw it in your face last night at dinner." His voice was low but intense. "I know why you left the room. I nearly left myself. All night I paced the west wing, and all morning I waited at breakfast, praying you'd come. Praying—that's what I've been doing for hours, and I'm no closer to understanding this chaos than I was when I first saw you in the carriage. Is there a plan, Star? Does this infuriating quilt have a pattern?"

Trembling, she drew her hand from his and hung the cherub on a branch. "Every quilt has a pattern," she managed. "Even a crazy quilt has a kind of order to it. The patches fit together, and they make a whole blanket—something complete and beautiful and useful." She met his eyes again. "Yes, there's a plan, Grey, but God never promised to tell us what it is. He asked us to follow him, trust him, put the patches of our lives in his hands. Let him sew. Let him work his plan, and don't try to control things ourselves. He sent you home to England to make peace with your father. Now you need to do that."

"And you?"

"I've come to marry Rupert."

"No."

"Yes, Grey. That's all the plan I can see, and I aim to follow it."

"Strat?" Rupert's voice carried a note of surprise. "Are you in the Christmas tree?"

"I was bringing Miss Ellis a cherub," Grey said, tearing his focus from her eyes and starting down the ladder. "Our young American visitor has even had poor old Massey scampering about delivering angels on his silver tray."

Rupert gave a bark of laughter as he came into view beneath the tree. "Good show, Miss Ellis. Keep us all hopping, what?" He selected an ornament from the box. "I say, Strat, here's a Father Christmas you made of paper and paints when you were but a wee chappie. What were you, four or five?"

"Five, I think. Do you remember what the governess said?" Grey stepped down from the ladder. "She said I'd made him far too fat, and I should have followed the pattern. And I told her I was going to make Father Christmas the way I wanted him, pattern or not. So she boxed my ears."

Rupert laughed. "You always were a cheeky little brat, weren't you?"

"Still am, I should think. Never much good at following plans I haven't made myself."

Star clung to the ladder as Grey glanced up at her. Chuckling over the handmade ornament, Rupert hung Father Christmas on the tip of a branch. When he lifted his head to Star, he was still grinning.

"I say, Miss Ellis," he called. "After you've finished with your frippery here, I should be most appreciative if you'd join the family in the library for a spot of morning tea. We'll introduce you to the famed Brackenhurst scones. Mummy's all in a kerfuffle about this wedding of ours, so we might as well sit down and have it out—set the date, write the invitation list, that sort of rot."

"All right," Star said softly.

"Come on, Strat, I want to show you my new riding boots." Rupert clapped his brother on the back as the two made their way out of the room. "What do you think of those Smythe girls? Aren't they a pair of glorious birds?"

CHAPTER FOUR

S he's been here two weeks, Rupe, and you haven't had a single conversation with her." Grey walked to the fire in the parlor and set his tea book on the mantel. He was tired of reading, tired of sitting about, tired of the aimlessness in the genteel life he'd once embraced. "Our mother arranged the engagement party for Christmas Eve. Father set the wedding date for the end of January. You've done nothing but mince about with the Smythe sisters. You're dodging your duty, man."

"Cheese off, Strat." Rupert shuffled a deck of cards and began laying out a game of solitaire. "I'll do my duty by the girl. I'll give her my name, the title, and the connection between the two families—for what that's worth. Father's had a letter from Mr. Ellis in Texas telling of the deplorable winter conditions. Cattle dropping like flies, but the land is still valuable. As you know, the moment I marry, the yearly allowance left to me by Uncle William will be mine for the asking. Father has advised me to send a good bit of that money off to Texas to restock the ranch. So, thanks to my new wife, I'll have a herd of livestock and maybe a couple of heirs. That's how it's done. You can't expect me to relish this, can you? It's an arrangement, and I'm obeying our father's wishes—which is more than you can say."

"I've come home, haven't I?"

"Don't think that's all it takes to please the old man. You've got your titular responsibilities. The viscount Stratton ought to be married off to the daughter of a duke—or at the very least a marquess. After all, you'll be earl one of these days, and heaven knows the family can use the money you'd come into with a profitable marriage. I overheard Massey telling my valet the cottagers are practically starving this winter."

Grey studied the vast expanse of snowy fields outside the manor. He had no idea the cottagers in the village at the bottom of the hill were experiencing such difficulties. He was well aware that although Brackenhurst once had been a wealthy earldom, its lands were no longer turning a great profit. Mills in Leeds and York had lured many young people from the villages. The draw of city life, cash in a man's pockets, and freedom from the feudal land tenancy system had proven all but irresistible. Vast agricultural manors like Brackenhurst were paying the price for the resulting drop in productivity.

"I'm planning to do my part for the family by building a profitable tea export business," Grey said. "I've purchased significant acreage near Darjeeling—"

"India? Oh, please, Strat, it's marriage our father expects from you. You'll see what I mean at the Christmas Eve party. Mummy will introduce you to one uppish young thing after another, and, if you're wise, you'll ask the richest of them to marry you on the spot. That's all I'm doing with Miss Ellis— assuring future income. Her father owns land in America and more cattle than he can count. You want to make the earl happy? Marry well."

Grey snatched his tea book off the mantel and tucked it

under his arm. "I *shall* bring in money with my Indian estate, Rupert, and I should thank you to consider Miss Ellis as something more than a monetary asset. She's a remarkable young lady, and she's spent the past two weeks alone in the drawing room doing nothing but stitching her blasted quilt."

Rupert looked up from his cards. "I say, Stratton, what do *you* care about Miss Ellis?"

"Nothing, of course. It's just that . . . well, she's a guest here at Brackenhurst. She's to be your wife. Don't you give a twig about her?"

"I suppose she's pretty enough." He shrugged. "But honestly, Strat. The woman is odd."

"She's not odd, she's interesting. I find her amusing. And she's quite intelligent."

"Then why don't *you* marry her?" Rupert swept up his cards. "Of course, that would never pass muster with our dear father, the earl. Miss Ellis might be the richest girl in America, but the viscount Stratton will have to marry someone titled." He rose and tossed the cards in a heap on the table. "You should hear Father ranting about the Misses Smythe. Their father's not even a baronet, you know. He's nothing at all."

"He's filthy rich, I hear," Grey said.

Rupert gave a snort of disgust. "To the earl of Brackenhurst, a rich but untitled American girl is perfectly acceptable. She's *American*, he says. They haven't got titles in America. But an untitled, rich *English* girl—heaven forbid."

Grey studied the scattered cards, realizing his brother spoke the truth. Rupert would have to marry Star Ellis. And if the viscount Stratton ever hoped to make himself acceptable to his father, he ought to find the wealthiest young noblewoman in London and marry her straightaway. A tea plantation in India would not assuage the earl of Brackenhurst. An honest reputation would not do it. Nor would a conversion to a new life of piety and devotion to God. Grey needed to find someone to marry.

The face that leapt instantly into his thoughts had a pair of sparkling green eyes and a mouth that could erupt into easy amusement over a nest of mice in a summer bonnet. If he were ever to erase that face from his thoughts, Grey knew he would need to surrender the woman herself to his brother.

"Come with me, Rupert," he said firmly. "We shall go to the drawing room, and you shall make the acquaintance of Miss Ellis, your fiancée. And you shall realize that she is beautiful and witty and utterly delightful, and you shall understand why it is that you should want very much to marry her."

Rupert gave a mock howl of dismay as his brother marched him down the corridor toward the east wing of Brackenhurst Manor.

Star worked her needle through the final five stitches of her quilt, knotted her thread, and leaned back on the settee. *Done.* She had joined the green, white, blue, gold, and burgundy diamonds together, patch by patch, until they formed a magnificent eight-pointed star centered on a field of pale yellow. The glorious riot of colors spread across Star's lap, draped down the side of the settee, and rippled over the carpeted floor. She could not have been more pleased with her handiwork.

Not unless she were sitting in her Texas ranch house with the scent of mesquite smoke drifting up from the logs on the fire and the busy hubbub of her family all around her. At this very moment in Texas, candles would be burning on the mantel, and the tree would be wreathed in popcorn strings and hung with nuts and candy canes. Star's brother Jake would play his violin while Bess and the other girls sang Christmas carols. Mama would be stirring taffy on the stove, and Papa would be whistling along with the music as he whittled a train set for little Eddie. As it was, Star sat alone in one of Brackenhurst Manor's expansive drawing rooms, staring at the falling snow outside the window and wondering how she was going to survive.

God had been more than her anchor through this ordeal. Her heavenly father had been her only friend. She had relied on the comfort of silent prayer and Scripture reading as she came to realize the whole Cholmondeley family seemed destined to ignore her. The countess went about her daily activity of taking callers and sipping tea in one parlor or another. The coming wedding kept the kindly woman employed selecting flowers, menus, and garments for the trousseau. Only on rare occasion did she pause to consult the bride-to-be, who began to feel she was all but extraneous to the event. The earl paid Star no heed at all as he rode out to survey his holdings every morning and conducted business in his study in the afternoons.

Rupert treated his fiancée as some sort of curious museum piece to be ogled from a distance. The few times she attempted to speak with the man, he mumbled something unintelligible and then hurried off to hunt foxes or ride around in his carriage calling on the neighbors. Star had tried everything she could think of to make herself prettier or more interesting to him. She read her etiquette book backwards and forwards. But nothing she did earned her more than the slightest nod from her future husband.

Grey was worse. When meeting her along a corridor, the viscount would look into her eyes as if he wanted to say a hundred things. Then, saying nothing at all, he would stride past her into the nearest room. During meals she would catch him staring at her, and she couldn't suppress the heat that crept into her cheeks at the memory of their kiss in Doncaster. It was a torment to be so near the man, yet never speak together or even acknowledge the other's presence.

That very morning Grey had inadvertently walked into the parlor where she was quilting. Trying to be casual about the moment, Star pointed out to him the section of patches he had stitched while on the carriage journey from London. She had integrated his work into the pattern in such a way that only the most careful observer would note that a different hand had stitched it.

Instead of making polite observations about the quilt, Grey had clenched his jaw, muttered, "Blast," and stalked away—as if looking at a quilt were the most frustrating experience in his life.

Star ran her hand down the expanse of patched fabric. The only two people in England who enjoyed her company and appreciated her handiwork were Betsy and Nell. The housemaids had welcomed her into their humble cottage when she ventured down to the village one afternoon. Even though they lived in a far worse condition than the cowhands on her daddy's ranch, Star gladly would have moved in with them just to have someone to talk to.

"Miss Ellis?" Grey spoke from the doorway to the drawing room. "May we join you?"

Glancing up in surprise, Star discovered her future husband peering at her over his older brother's shoulder. "Lord Stratton," she said, rising. "Lord Cholmondeley, please do come in."

Grey tugged on his brother's jacket sleeve to drag him into the room. "I see you've been quilting," he said. "Miss Ellis is stitching a quilt, Rupert."

"Ah," Rupert said blankly. "A quilt."

"How is it coming along?" Grey asked.

Star slipped back onto the settee as the men settled into a pair of armchairs facing her. "I'm finished with the top," she said. "Now I need to quilt it."

"Then you'll be wanting a quilting frame."

Pleased that he remembered, Star allowed herself to look

into Grey's brilliant blue eyes. "Yes, please. I can't manage this much fabric without a frame."

"She needs a frame, Rupert."

"Ah," Rupert said. "A frame."

Giving his brother a scowl, Grey picked up the corner of the quilt. "Can you describe this frame you require, Miss Ellis? It would be of wood, I assume. And how large?"

"Big enough to hold the quilt." As Rupert gave a monumental yawn, she shook out the top and spread it across the floor. Gathering her skirts, she hunkered down beside her handiwork to demonstrate. "See, you take two pieces of one-by-two board the length of the quilt top, plus twelve inches. They make the front and back of the frame. Then you do the same thing for the side pieces. You clamp the four boards together, leaving a four-inch overhang at each corner. Then you put the frame over the backs of four wooden chairs, and everybody goes to quilting."

She paused and stared at the length of fabric. "Summers, we'd put the quilting frame on our front porch. Mama and us four girls would pull up our chairs, and we'd get to talking and laughing to beat the band. Daddy would come up onto the porch, and he'd say, 'You gals could talk the hide off a cow.' We'd just giggle and carry on like he wasn't even there. And then maybe one of the neighbors would come over, and she'd pull up a chair. Sometimes we had twelve or fifteen women quilting away. You could finish a quilt as quick as greased lightning that way, and then you'd just start in on another one."

Lost in her memories, Star gazed at the bright patches until they blurred out of focus. "Those were some good times," she said softly.

"Rupert will see that you have a frame immediately," Grey announced. "Won't you, Rupert?"

"What?" his brother said, through half-lidded eyes. "Oh yes, of course."

"Perhaps some of the house help would enjoy learning to quilt," Grey added. "Our mother adores needlework. I'll ask her to come and assist you."

Star managed a smile. "I thought I could take the quilt down to the village when I'm finished with it. Betsy and Nell have it kind of tough in that smoky little cottage. Pieces of the thatch roof are falling right down onto the floor, and the wind just rips in there—"

"Colder than frog legs?"

Delight trickled down her spine. "I reckon so. Anyhow, I figured I could give them this quilt and then maybe start on another one. A family can never have too many quilts. Betsy's got three little fillies, and one of them goes to coughing so hard she can hardly breathe. I'm afraid she has consumption."

Grey had knelt beside her and was holding one edge of the quilt. "Have they taken the child to an apothecary?"

"Betsy's husband was laid up with a broken leg this fall, and they barely made their rent. I'm sure they can't afford medicine."

Grey stroked his chin for a moment. "How soon could you finish the quilt?"

"In a day, with help. Otherwise, it'll take a little longer."

"Could you have it ready by the Christmas Eve party? Rather than give the quilt to Betsy, why not put it into the charity auction? I'll see that all the money earned from your quilt goes straight to the village for medicines and blankets."

"Would you? Oh, Grey, that would be wonderful!" She brushed back a curl that had fallen from her chignon. "Finishing this quilt ought to keep me as busy as a prairie dog after a gully washer. And I don't mind telling you, that's the way I like it."

Suddenly remembering where she was, Star glanced at Rupert. The young man had drifted off to sleep in the high-backed chair, his head lolling to one side as he snored softly.

Dear God, thank you! she prayed in silence. In five minutes with Grey, she'd forgotten all about Rupert and her upcoming marriage. Chattering like a chipmunk, she was all aglow with plans and hopes—and then she had remembered.

"You'd better go," she said quickly. "And take your brother with you. I won't—"

"Star." Grey caught her hand, drawing her back to the floor beside the quilt. "You must try to engage Rupert in conversation. Talk to him about the fox hunt or something. Let him know you as you are."

"He doesn't want to know me."

"I can't keep walking past this room and finding you alone. It's all I can do not to take you out of this wretched place and . . . and . . ."

"I've prayed myself blue in the face," she whispered. "I've done all I know to do to make Rupert interested in me, and he isn't. God made this plan, and it's going to be up to him now to work it out. I can't do this on my own."

"Did he make this plan, Star?" Grey's eyes were earnest. "How can a person know the truth?"

"Jesus Christ is the truth. If we know him, if we follow him, he'll lead us on the right path." She crumpled the fabric of her quilt. "I have to believe that! I have to keep going, walking in the direction I believe I'm supposed to take. What about you? Have you told your father about your experience at the hospital in India? Does he know you're a new man?"

"He doesn't know I'm a man at all. I'm nothing but a cipher to him, the heir to the earldom, and a grand disappointment."

"But you were led back home, Grey. You have to speak to him. That's *your* path."

"Blast this 'new man' business. It's difficult enough—"

"Nobody said it would be easy. But God is with you, Grey. He's with me."

"And I want *you*."

Star felt as though a sack of oats had slammed into her chest. "You can't."

"No, I can't." He gritted his teeth. "I've lived the old way, and I've lived the new. It was easy to choose myself over everything else. Easy to toss away my money, easy to drink until my head spun, easy to gad about the globe without a care. Easy and empty. Fruitless. Hopeless."

"And the new way?" she asked, laying her hand over his.

"Difficult. But I won't go back."

Star swallowed hard. "No."

"Then why are you in my life?" He cupped his hands around her face. "Why are you beautiful and good and amusing and perfect?"

"Please don't say those things," she said, fighting against the tide of emotion that flooded through her. "I don't know why we met. I can't see the pattern. Can't understand this quilt. Can't . . . can't . . ."

"Don't cry."

"No," she mumbled. "No."

"Rupert!" He swung around and gave his dozing brother a swift kick in the shin. "Wake up, you cabbage head."

"Oof!" Rupert grabbed his leg. "I say, Strat, what was that for?"

"Miss Ellis would enjoy a walk through the hedge maze. Are you going to sleep all afternoon, or will you take your fiancée for a stroll?"

Rupert ran his fingers through his tousled hair. "But it's snowing."

"Go on, Rupe." Grey all but hauled his brother out of the chair. "Show Miss Ellis that a snowstorm won't stop an Englishman."

Giving Rupert a final shove in Star's direction, the viscount hastily exited the drawing room. She gathered up her quilt and pushed it into her bag as Rupert massaged his shin.

"It's snowing," he repeated. "Rather a bad time for a walk, don't you think, Miss Ellis?"

Star rose and looked at the man who was to be her husband. "You could tell me about foxhunting."

"Mm. Yes, well, all right." He limped across the room to the long French doors that led out toward the evergreen hedge maze. "Fox hunt. Good sport, actually. One gathers one's dogs and mounts one's horse. A group of hunters, rather. Then with a good bit of galloping about, one hunts down a fox."

"I see." She joined him at the window. The hedge maze spread out beyond the drawing room at the back of the huge manor house in an intriguing pattern of twists and turns. "So two or three of you fellows hunt down as many foxes as you can to keep them from bothering the livestock? We do that with coyotes, when they get troublesome. I'll tell you what, I've ridden some trails that would make a mountain goat nervous. How many foxes do you reckon you've brought down in a day?"

He looked down his nose at her. "The fox hunt is a sport."

"Oh."

"If you'll excuse me, Miss Ellis, I should like to speak to my valet about some warm water for my injured leg." He gave her a smile and a slight bow. "Perhaps we shall be able to walk the maze another time."

"Perhaps," she said, watching him go.

The quilting frame magically appeared in the drawing room later that evening. As she set to work, Star tried to believe Rupert had sent it, but she knew he'd been napping as she explained the specifics of the construction. For the next three days she saw nothing of either man except at evening meals. Grey was careful never to meet her eyes.

Two days before her engagement was announced, Rupert

invited the Misses Smythe to Brackenhurst Manor to help prepare the charades for the Christmas party. Both evenings, as was their custom, the Cholmondeley family gathered in one of the drawing rooms after dinner to play the pianoforte, engage in card battles, or read aloud. Star found it a chore to watch her fiancé chattering away with the two attractive young women, while she was left unattended at the other end of the room.

"Won't you sing with me tonight, Miss Ellis?" the countess asked as the group retired to the firelit chamber on the night before Christmas Eve. "I heard you singing while working at your quilt, and you've such a lovely voice."

Star slipped her arm through that of the elderly woman. She had liked the earl's wife from the start, and she'd enjoyed her company the few times they'd chatted. She prayed that the countess would become, in time, a soul mate. "I'd love to sing with you, my lady. Thank you very much for asking."

"Do you play the pianoforte, Miss Ellis? I should like to hear you."

Star blanched at the thought of her own awkward piano banging. She could pound out "She'll be Comin' 'round the Mountain" or "Oh, Susannah" as well as the next gal, but she didn't think her talents would go over too well at Brackenhurst Manor.

"I'm not much of a pianist," she said.

"And how is your stitching coming on? Stratton has told me that you're preparing your quilt for the charity auction. How charmingly generous of you, my dear. The party is tomorrow evening, you know. Everyone is coming. Of course, George will announce your engagement to Rupert, and the two of you must lead in a dance. Oh, good heavens— do you have waltzing in America?"

Star smiled as they walked into the parlor. "Lots of waltzing, madam. And I'm quite good at it."

Comforted, the countess motioned for everyone to gather around the pianoforte. Rupert joined Polly and Penny Smythe on one settee. Grey found a chair beside his father's. Star took the stool near the instrument as the earl's wife prepared to sit.

"Bosh and horse feathers!" Hortense cried as she opened the instrument. "I've forgotten my sheet music."

"I'll fetch it, Mummy," Rupert said, standing instantly.

"No, darling, you won't have a clue where I've put it. I'll only be a moment. Miss Ellis, why don't you tell one of your amusing stories about America?"

Star could have crawled straight into a posthole as she watched the countess walk away. She bit her lip and looked around at the expectant faces. Any story she told would make her look all the more odd and different, and that was the last thing she needed. By this time tomorrow, she would be formally engaged to Rupert Cholmondeley, and the connection between the families would be sealed. She couldn't endanger that.

Focusing on Grey, she realized that he, too, was trying his best to follow the plan he felt God had set before him. He had spent the holidays exclusively with his family—no roving about in London or visiting friends. He had evidenced interest in the affairs of the earldom as he sat by the fire with his father. He even had tried to urge Rupert to build a relationship with his future wife.

But Star had recognized in his tone of voice the dismay that dogged him. Thus far Grey had made no more headway in achieving his goal than she had with her vain attempts to attract her fiancé. Maybe she could help Grey walk on the path he believed God had led him to.

"In the carriage on the way to Brackenhurst," she said, "Lord Stratton told me about a significant event that happened during his time in India. Would you be willing to share with your family what happened at the hospital in Calicut, my lord?"

Grey's eyes deepened. "Thank you, Miss Ellis," he said. "Yes, I should like to speak of that."

"Not another story of a cobra slithering about, is it, Strat?" Rupert said. The Misses Smythe burst into a duet of giggles. "We're not going to have man-eating tigers, are we?"

"On the contrary." Grey leaned forward, elbows on his knees, and addressed his family. "This story is about me. Almost a year ago I was staying on the coast of India in a town called Calicut, and I became very ill. While in hospital, I realized I was dying."

"Really, Stratton," the earl intoned, "is this the sort of topic to address in the presence of delicate ladies? And at this jovial time of year?"

"I want everyone to hear my story. I want you all to know why this time of year has become most important to me. You see, while I lay near death, a group of men visited my bed. They had been students of a missionary named William Carey. I began to talk to them about my life, the way I'd wasted it."

"Wasted *my* money," the earl put in.

"Yes, Father, I wasted your money. I lived only for myself, only for my own pleasure, only for what I thought would make me happy. And there, in Calicut, I saw the emptiness of it."

"Good show," the earl piped up. "About time, what?"

"Past time. I decided that if I survived my illness, I should turn myself around and try to behave in a worthy fashion. Perhaps then I'd find happiness and meaning in my life."

"A grand idea!" The earl motioned his wife to be seated as she returned with her sheet music. "Stratton's just telling us he had a brush with death, Hortense. He decided to turn himself about and stop acting such a cad."

Grey smiled at his father's summary of the story. "Actually, the missionaries explained to me that I could never find true happiness—and certainly never even set one toe into heaven—if I tried to be worthy in my own strength. They said I couldn't do it alone, and I knew they were right. No one can."

"Nonsense. An English gentleman, properly brought up—"

"Will never be good enough. You see, my lord, we have all done wrong. Grave wrongs, as I did, or minor wrongs—but wrongs all the same. No human is perfect. Only God can claim that honor, and because of our faults, he has every right to chuck us all out on our ears. We deserve it. But I learned a very important word in India. The word is *grace*. Grace is the undeserved gift of God's forgiveness and salvation. I can never be good enough, but if I accept God's grace—the death of his Son to pay for my wrongs—then I am welcomed into his presence as a forgiven child of the king. With his power, my life has turned around. And in his joy, I have discovered a happiness I never dreamed possible."

Grey looked into the faces of his family one by one. His mother dabbed her eyes. "Oh, darling, what a marvelous story," she whispered.

The earl scowled a moment and rubbed his mustache. "I say, Stratton," he said, "you're not thinking of entering the church? Poor as mice, most of the vicars I know."

"No, Father, of course he isn't," Rupert said and gave a yawn. "He's trying to tell you he's come round. Planning to do his duty by the family, take responsibility for the title, all that. Right, Strat?"

"In part, but—"

"There you have it, then. Come on, Mummy, do give a song now, or I'm likely to drop straight off to sleep."

"Hear! Hear!" the earl said. "Miss Ellis, will you sing?"

Star tore her eyes away from Grey's and picked up the sheet music.

CHAPTER FIVE

As the first partygoers arrived on the doorstep of
Brackenhurst Manor, Grey stepped into the evergreen hedge maze. The ten-foot-high concealing
walls of fragrant cedar had always been his chosen retreat.
He knew the maze like the back of his hand, and as a boy it
had pleased him no end to guide one of his young cronies
into the hedges and then vanish, losing him completely.
Hours later, he would march in after the poor chap and haul
him out into the open to restore his wounded spirit with hot
tea and cakes.

Today, Grey hoped he could lose himself. He needed to
think, to sort out the confusing swirl of demands that echoed
back and forth inside him. In a few short hours, Star Ellis
would be formally betrothed to Rupert Cholmondeley, a
status almost as binding as marriage. Blast!

The snow crunched beneath his boots as Grey strode
down one corridor after another. Could he afford to lose this
woman who had touched his very soul? Ridiculous to let
Rupert have her, when the young man was so oblivious to
her beauty, her wit, her intelligence. Star was a glowing light,

shining for all to see—and yet Rupert remained completely blind to her.

What if Grey simply eloped with the woman? If he declared his affection—his *love*, for that is what he knew he felt—she might willingly follow him away from Brackenhurst to build a new life far from the confines of English society. But could Grey show such blatant disregard of his avowed determination to do right? If he ran off with Star, everything he had told his family would be meaningless. He would estrange himself forever from his father and brother. His mother would be heartbroken. And his testimony of a changed life in Christ would be as hollow as the corridors of Brackenhurst Manor.

Blast, blast, blast! He slammed his fist against the cedar hedge. As a shower of snow tumbled to the ground, a startled gasp drifted through the maze.

"Who's there?" a woman cried.

Grey frowned at the unexpected intrusion. "It's Stratton."

"Oh, thank goodness! I've been racing around in this maze like a hen on a hot griddle. I'll bet I've been tracking my own footprints for nearly two hours, and I haven't found the path out yet. Are you lost, too?"

His frown transforming instantly into a grin, Grey slipped his hands into his pockets. "I say, Miss Ellis, is that you?"

"Who did you think it was, buckaroo? Listen, my toes are so cold they're about to chip off inside my boots, and I've got to get dressed for the party. Do you know the way out?"

"It would help to know where you are, first."

"A pile of snow just fell on my head. Does that tell you anything?"

Grey laughed and thrust his hand through the three-foot-thick cedar. "Can you see my fingers?"

A small hand closed around his own. "Oh, Grey, I've felt so lost. So confused. I'm scared."

"Don't be frightened. The maze has a pattern. It's very

simple, really. What you need is a good guide. . . ." Grey paused and shut his eyes. *A pattern through the maze.* Wasn't that exactly what he'd been seeking when he wandered in here? And who was the guide in whose hands he had placed his life?

Oh, God, can you help me? he prayed as he clutched Star's hand through the hedge. *Can you show me the way out of this maze?*

"Grey?" she called softly. "Are you all right?"

"I'm here. I'm going to help you." He straightened. "Stay where you are, and wait for me. I'll lead you to safety."

He drew his hand from hers and started down the familiar path. The maze was no mystery to him, nor was it frightening in the least. In fact, he often had sought the comfort of its shadows. He knew the plan.

As he turned left, then right, then right again, he spotted Star standing alone, her hands clenched tightly as she peered through the high green hedges for some sign of rescue. The hem of her dark coat carried a crust of snow, and a sugaring of flakes dusted her shoulders. Her cheeks glowed bright pink, and her green eyes shone as if with an inner light.

Star of Bethlehem, he thought.

"Grey!" Seeing him, she threw open her arms and ran down the pathway. "Oh, Grey, thank God!"

He caught her up and held her tightly. "It's all right now. I've got you."

"I didn't think I'd ever find my way out. I came in here to escape all the fuss over the Christmas fandango—Massey squeaking around in those confounded shoes, Rupert and the Smythe gals chasing each other through the drawing rooms, Betsy and Nell scurrying around like a pair of hornets in a summer bonnet. I wanted some time to myself, time to sort everything out, and then—"

"You're very cold."

"I'm half frozen."

He cupped her gloved hands inside his and warmed them with his breath. "Star, I need to talk to you—"

"Don't talk, Grey." Her green eyes clouded with sudden tears. "There's nothing to say. I've had a good two hours out here to pray, and every time I've said *amen,* I realize I've come up with the same two-word answer to all my troubles."

"And what words are those?"

"*Follow me.* Just follow the Lord. That's all I know to do, Grey. I have to trust him with my life. Every time I've chosen my own path, I've tripped right over my two big feet. Oh, the good Lord picks me up and dusts me off. He makes the best of my mistakes. But I don't want to make any more mistakes, Grey. I can't understand why God would yoke me up to an unbeliever. After listening to Rupert scoff the other night when you talked of surrendering to Christ, I was filled with doubts about the state of his soul. But it's not my place to judge—just follow. And the only way I know to do that is to complete the mission I was sent here on. I've got to honor my daddy's promise—and marry Rupert."

As tears trickled down her cheeks, Grey pulled the woman to his chest and held her as firmly as if she were a part of him. He'd done all he could to keep from loving Star, but he'd failed. He did love her, and if he chose to forge his own way in this world, he would sweep her up and carry her off in his arms.

"I could speak to my father," he began. "I could tell him—"

"He would never trust you again. If you ruined his plans for Rupert, he would disown you. Your mother was watching me quilt yesterday, and she said the earl has chosen a young woman for you. She's very well off, a London beauty. She's coming to the party tonight, and—"

"No. I won't go that far." Breathing hard, he drew her closer. "If I can't have you, I'll leave this place. To live here at

Brackenhurst with another woman while you and Rupert . . ." He clenched his jaw. "No, I'll go back to India. Right now. That's where I'm meant to be, anyway. I've known that much all along. The tea estate is the answer to the earldom's financial difficulties, and I'm the man to run it. I've done all I came to do here—I've told my family about the change in my life, and I've made peace with my father. But I won't stay here and watch the woman I love . . ."

"I love you, too," Star whispered, her words muffled by the wool fabric of his greatcoat as she pressed her face against his shoulder. "I didn't mean to love you, and I've done all I could to keep from it. But somehow you and I match . . . we fit together like a pair of patches in a quilt, seam for seam and point for point. Knowing that you love me fills my heart to the brim. And at the same time, it's killing me."

"I won't cause you pain, Star."

"Then you'd better go, and don't ever come back. Because every time I see you . . . every time I hear your voice . . ."

Grey could hardly contain the urge to lift this woman into his arms and claim her as his own. All that was in him demanded it. And yet he had already made his decision— made it in a hospital bed in India.

He took her arms, set her away from him, and looked into her eyes. "What I love most about you, Star, is the shining light of faith in your life. Don't lose that. Don't let me dim your brilliance. You *are* the Star of Bethlehem, and I want you to go on shining. Shine for my father and my mother. Shine for Rupert, blast him. Shine for Betsy and Nell and everyone in the village. And follow the Truth, who holds you in his hands."

As she wept, he turned her around. "Walk straight to the end of this corridor," he said. "Turn left, and you'll see the opening in the maze. Go forward, Star Ellis. Shine."

As she stumbled away from him, Grey turned and ran

deeper into the twists and turns of the maze. *God,* he cried as his feet beat against the snow. *God, show me the way!*

Star's toes were just beginning to thaw as she hurried into the crowded ballroom. She had jerked on an emerald gown, swept her hair into a rough tumble of curls, and jammed her damp feet into a pair of silk slippers. As she tied a ribbon in her hair, she had prayed she could survive the ordeal of this evening.

Across the room, the countess spotted her immediately. A wave of relief washed over the older woman's face as she moved toward her guest past the towering Christmas tree with its hundred tiny candles. The cavernous chamber was awash in bright silk gowns, flashing jewels, and fluttering fans. Long tables garlanded in swags of holly, pine, and ivy, groaned under the weight of silver trays filled with sweets and chilled meats. A gigantic marzipan cake studded with currants and sultanas towered over bowls of bright red punch.

"Thank goodness you're here!" the countess said. Fanning her flushed cheeks and sending out a cloud of heliotrope perfume, she took Star's hand. "You cannot imagine the kerfuffle, my dear! Do you know what my son has gone and done? He's left us! The viscount has gone back to India this very night. Wouldn't hear of waiting until the New Year. Wouldn't wait for Christmas morning. Wouldn't even stay for the party. And Grey always adored parties!"

Star gave the countess a hug, as much to bolster herself as the other woman. "I know the viscount has a lot of plans for that tea estate in Darjeeling."

"Where? Oh, you see, I never believed he was serious. I've been in such a stew about Rupert's wedding, and now Grey has gone off to India."

"Hortense, are you weeping again?" The earl held out a

silk handkerchief. "Buck up, darling, we've had a jolly good visit with the boy. He quite convinced me of the value of his tea enterprise, and I have great faith it will be good for the earldom."

"But India! It's so far away."

"Don't look at it like that, my dear." The earl gave Star a broad smile. "We'll have a tea plantation in India and a share in a cattle ranch in Texas. What could be better? The earldom on its feet again, the cottagers happy and healthy, everything as it should be. Think of the little ones running through the corridors, Hortense. Grandchildren! A marvelous notion!"

Star tugged her own handkerchief out of her sleeve in fear that she might start sobbing right then and there. The earl adjusted the tails of his frock coat and gave a loud harrumph. "Time for the announcement," he intoned. "Then we shall have the charity auction. And dinner, charades, and more dancing. Oh my, I do believe I'm having a splendid evening."

Chuckling, he escorted his wife and their guest to the low dais at one end of the ballroom. Star felt like she was climbing up to a gallows as she lifted her skirts and stepped onto the platform. Rupert gave a wave from the far end of the ballroom, left his bevy of companions, and sprinted up to the dais.

"Time for the announcement, my lord?" he asked. "Righty-ho. Let's put a good face on it, Miss Ellis."

He took her hand as Massey squeaked across the dais and signaled the orchestra for silence. Star could almost hear the hands of the clock, ticking away her freedom. Massey presented the family, and then the earl stepped forward.

"Ladies and gentlemen," he said, "a delightful evening. Welcome one and all."

Amid polite clapping, he gave a little bow and continued. "The countess and I have had the distinct pleasure of an unexpected visit from our elder son, the viscount Stratton. I regret to report that he has been compelled to return to India, where he is establishing a vast tea estate." More clapping. "Our second unexpected guest arrived a little more than a fortnight ago from Texas, in America. And now, I should be most pleased to announce that this delightful young lady, Miss Star Ellis, is engaged to marry my younger son, Rupert, Lord Cholmondeley."

Over the round of applause, a shriek of despair arose. The crowd murmured as both the Misses Smythe raced out of the ballroom, followed close behind by a stream of Rupert's friends and colleagues. Taking no notice, the earl gave his son a firm handshake and welcomed Star into the family with a peck on the cheek.

"Well done, Cholmondeley," he said. "Do accept my wishes for your continued happiness."

Surrounded instantly by a cluster of elderly ladies who peered at her through their monocles, Star felt Rupert give her hand a tug. He motioned toward the dance floor as the small orchestra began a waltz. As if in a bad dream, Star drifted out into the sea of partygoers and was caught up by her betrothed.

"Good show, Miss Ellis," Rupert said, attempting a smile. "It won't be so bad, this marriage business. I imagine you and I will learn to get along. At any rate, I'm afraid I won't be about much. I've been looking into ventures in both Leeds and London. Traveling, you know."

Star nodded, fighting the stinging tears that danced before her vision. "I suppose I'll stay here at the manor."

"Indeed. Well, I'm sure there'll be children after a bit. You won't want to go out much." He gave her a smile as the music ended. "Buck up, Miss Ellis."

Giving her a quick pat on the arm, he set off for the double doors through which his friends had exited. Star knotted her hands together and sank back against one of the velvet-flocked walls. Around her, the couples swirled and bowed, pranced and turned. She tried her best to pray, but all she could think about was Grey riding away through the falling snow toward London. As despair threatened to choke her, she turned her thoughts toward the future.

Children. Yes, they would be fulfilling. Star could find joy in children of her own. In the Cholmondeley family, too. The countess was a dear, and perhaps in time she would become a warm companion. Besides that, the village was nearby. There lived the common people who enjoyed simple things. She could help them, and maybe even become a friend.

As Star pondered her future, the countess began to announce the charity auction. Displayed across the length of the dais were gold-framed oil paintings, Chinese vases, a new saddle, and several jeweled necklaces. The first item up for bid was the new quilt.

A chorus of gasps greeted the presentation of the large, multicolored spread. To her dismay, Star realized that clusters of the women in the crowd were tittering behind their fans in subtle ridicule of her handiwork. Men stared at the quilt as though examining a painting they couldn't quite comprehend.

"This is a quilt," the countess explained. "You will find lengths of quilted fabric here in England, but they are rarely patched in such clever patterns. This one was crafted by our own dear Miss Ellis. Quilts, I am given to understand, are used in America as blankets. Though I have never made a quilt myself, I can see that the needlework in this sample is superb. I have been told that this particular quilt employs more than a thousand pieces of cotton fabric from the city of Calicut, in India."

Star felt a smile tug at her lips. *OK, you win, buckaroo,* she thought. *Calicut it is.*

"And the name of this quilt," the countess announced, "is Star of Bethlehem. Such a lovely accessory for the season, don't you think? On that note, you may begin the bidding."

Star of Bethlehem. Star shook her head as memories flooded her thoughts. *Shine, Star. Shine.*

How could she shine, when her life had all but ended? No, she realized as the crowd began to grow restless, this must not be an end but a beginning. It was not the life she would have chosen for herself, but it would be a good one all the same. Her future was in the hands of the Father, and she trusted him to fill her with his abundance.

"Come along," the countess called into the silence. "Who will cast the first bid?"

After more quiet, awkward seconds, the earl whispered to his wife, "Where is our deuced son? By all rights Cholmondeley should have a go at this. Massey, find him for me, my good man." He cleared his throat as the butler squeaked off to do his master's bidding. "Right then, ten pounds for the American quilt."

"Twenty pounds," a young man called from the back of the room.

Star peered at the bidder. He was a blond string bean of a fellow, someone she'd never seen before in her life. What would a man like that want with her quilt?

"Mr. Davies bids twenty pounds," the countess said. "That's the Christmas spirit. Who will top him?"

The room fell silent.

"Thirty," the earl shouted.

"Forty," Mr. Davies countered.

The other guests turned to peer at him. He gave everyone a broad smile. "Come on, blokes. It's for charity. Have a heart."

"Right you are," someone said. "Forty-five pounds."

"Fifty-five!" Mr. Davies cried.

Star could have kissed his skinny feet, whoever he was. The string bean kept the bids going up and up until anyone would have thought her quilt was a rare work of art. Delighted, she pictured vials of medicine for Betsy's sick daughter, stacks of warm blankets, cartloads of potatoes and bread.

"One hundred thirty-five pounds," the countess said finally. "Sold to Mr. Davies. Good show, young man! You've a fine piece of American needlework, and the cottagers will enjoy a more comfortable winter, thanks to your generosity."

As the string bean strode toward the dais, a wave of astonished gasps rippled suddenly across the crowd. What was it now? Star lifted her focus from her quilt to the double doors beside which Massey stood quaking, his face as pale as the snow outside the window.

Framed like an opulent masterpiece stood Rupert Cholmondeley, his arms wrapped around Polly Smythe as they engaged in a kiss that would have made ice sizzle. Unaware they had become the center of attention, the couple went on kissing—Polly's fingers exploring Rupert's hair as his impassioned murmuring drifted across the astonished crowd.

As swiftly as the onlookers assessed the situation, their attention swiveled to Rupert's bride-to-be. The countess grabbed Star around the shoulders as she took two steps backward. She needed to sit down. Had to have air.

"Rupert!" the earl barked. "What in heaven's name are you doing?"

The young man jumped as if he'd been jabbed with a cattle prod. His weepy-eyed paramour let out a squeal of horror. "Father . . . sir," Rupert fumbled. "I was . . . ah . . . receiving congratulations from . . . from Miss Smythe."

The crowd burst out laughing, and Star sank into a chair at the edge of the dais. Why had she been so blind? She'd known all along that her intended husband was enthralled with the Smythe girls. But she had wanted to believe he would find Star attractive, leave his other female interests, forge a bond with her like the one her own parents had. Foolish dreams! Now, publicly humiliated, she would be forced to marry a man everyone knew intended to be unfaithful.

"Cholmondeley," the earl said, his flaring nostrils rimmed in white. "Step forward, man, and explain yourself. Brackenhurst has never been home to a coward, and it won't begin now. What is the meaning of your behavior this evening?"

Rupert ran a finger around the stiff white collar of his shirt and tugged on his coattails as he stepped back into the ballroom. "I thought I might . . . I could . . ." He stopped, breathing hard. After several hard swallows, he lifted his chin. "The truth is, my lord, I love Miss Paulette Smythe."

With a burst of sobbing, the young woman herself darted forward and clutched Rupert's arm as though it were a lifeline and she were about to drown. Star groaned, burying her face in her hands. Now what? Would she lose this marriage? The hope and dream of her father? The salvation of the ranch?

"I do love Polly, sir," Rupert went on, his voice growing stronger by the moment, "and I'd hoped to earn your permission to marry her one day. But then Miss Ellis arrived, and I knew I should make good on my agreement with her father. I'll do my part in the arrangement, sir, but . . . but Polly . . . Polly is—"

"Cholmondeley!" The earl glared. "Your behavior is entirely unacceptable. You will approach the dais at once and offer Miss Ellis your sincere apologies."

The crowd swiveled around to ogle Star again. She searched for her quilt, wishing she could throw it over her head and crawl out of the room. The string bean must have gone off with it, she realized as she stood on shaky legs.

"Miss Ellis," Rupert said, Polly Smythe still firmly attached to his arm. "I apologize for my inappropriate behavior this evening, and I do hope you and I shall be able to—"

"Not on your life, buckaroo," a male voice called from the

hallway outside the ballroom. Grey Cholmondeley, the viscount Stratton, strode through the crowd and approached the dais. Under one arm he carried the multicolored quilt.

"Father, I request your permission to take my brother's place in the agreement with Mr. Joshua Ellis of the Rocking T Ranch in Texas. Miss Ellis," he said, taking Star's hand and drawing her close, "will you marry me?"

"Grey!" Star gasped.

"But she's—," the earl began.

"She's the woman I love," Grey said, his blue eyes flashing as he looked into Star's face. "Will you marry me, Miss Ellis?"

"But Rupert is . . . ," the earl stammered. "And you're on your way to India."

"I waited at the stables until the quilt had been auctioned. My old friend Davies was good enough to place my bids." He gave the string bean a thumbs-up, and the young man grinned from ear to ear. "Now that Rupert has relinquished his claim to Miss Ellis, I should like to state my intent to marry her myself. Will you have me, Star?"

"Grey, I—," she tried again.

"But then you'll have the tea *and* the cattle," the earl said.

"And I'll have the mill in Leeds," Rupert put in.

"Smythe's mill?" The earl looked at his wife. "But this isn't at all how we planned it, Hortense."

"The Almighty has greater plans than we can ever comprehend," the countess said, dabbing her cheeks. "Now, do hush, darling, and give your sons permission to marry the women they love."

"Well," the earl huffed. "All right then. I suppose so."

"Oh, Rupey!" Polly Smythe cried and tumbled backward in a dead faint. Her sister gave a scream as everyone rushed forward to attend the swooning girl.

Amid the chaos, Grey took the quilt from under his arm

and held it out to Star. "I had to have this," he said, "if I couldn't have you. I love you, Star. Will you be my wife?"

The fabric crumpled between them as Star rushed into his arms. "Yes, Grey," she said finally, "yes, I will."

"It'll mean a life in India."

"Anywhere." She clutched the wool of his coat as his hands held her close. "Anywhere with you."

"And we probably ought to check on our investments in Texas," he murmured against her hair. "Would you like to go home, Star?"

"My home is in your arms."

"Come on, then," he said, "let's take a turn around the ballroom so that I can show off the future viscountess of Stratton. And I've a sleigh all ready and waiting in the stable. Would you accompany me on a ride around the estate while the others play at charades? I promise to bring you back in time for the bonfire."

Star tapped her chin with a finger. "I don't know," she said. "It looks mighty cold out there."

"It is."

"Colder than frog legs," they said together.

Laughing, Grey lifted his future wife into his arms and kissed her lips.

"I love you," he said, "my shining Star of Bethlehem."

RECIPE

BRACKENHURST SCONES

3 cups sifted unbleached flour
2 tbsp. baking powder
½ tsp. baking soda
1 tsp. salt
2 tbsp. superfine granulated sugar
½ cup vegetable shortening
½ cup (1 stick) unsalted butter
¾ cup buttermilk
Heavy cream

Sift dry ingredients together into a large bowl. Mix in short-ening and butter until you get a moist, sandlike texture. Cover and chill for 30 minutes. Add buttermilk, gather mix-ture together with a fork, and turn out onto a lightly floured surface. Work together lightly, then roll dough into an ob-long shape about ¾-inch thick. Place on a generously greased baking sheet and cut into 1½-inch squares. Brush with heavy cream and bake at 400° for 12-15 minutes. (Do not overcook. Scones are done when they have risen and are golden brown and firm to the touch.)

Serve with clotted cream (Devonshire cream), whipped cream, or butter and jam.

A Note from the Author

My Dear Friend,

The illustration of the Lone Star (or Star of Bethlehem) quilt reveals it is one of the most difficult patterns to master. Seams must be straight, and points must meet exactly, or the quilt will pucker. Only skilled needleworkers like Star Ellis attempt this complicated pattern, which is often worked as a masterpiece example of the quilter's art.

After the Big Die-Up of the winter of 1886–87, Texas cattle ranches, like the Rocking T, slowly recovered their losses and again became profitable. Partnerships with English investors benefited both parties, though the ranchers often never met their blue-blooded counterparts, and many lords wouldn't know a heifer from a steer. English investments in Indian tea estates also brought in a good income, even when the British moved away from their role as empire builders.

This Christmas I encourage you to pour yourself a cup of hot Darjeeling tea, enjoy Brackenhurst scones or another favorite Christmas treat, and snuggle under a warm quilt as your holiday reading prepares you for the season in which we remember Christ's blessed birth.

Blessings, Catherine Palmer

About the Author

Catherine Palmer lives in Missouri with her husband, Tim, and sons, Geoffrey and Andrei. She has published nearly twenty books and has won numerous awards for her writing, including Most Exotic Historical Romance Novel from *Romantic Times* magazine. Total sales of her novels number close to one million copies.

Her recent books include *Prairie Rose, Prairie Fire, The Treasure of Timbuktu, The Treasure of Zanzibar,* and novellas in the anthologies *A Victorian Christmas Tea* and *With This Ring.* Look for *Prairie Storm and Finders Keepers* coming soon.

You can write to Catherine in care of Tyndale House Author Relations, P.O. Box 80, Wheaton, IL 60189-0080.

The Wedding Ring

Debra White Smith

For my grandmother Lorene Cole

Special thanks to

David Emprimo at the Jacksonville Public Library for
your unending willingness to assist a writer in distress.
You were a lifesaver!

Best-selling author Tracie Peterson—historian
extraordinaire—for all the last-minute details.

And an **extra special** thanks to Leah Davis Witherow
and Michael Fox at the Colorado Springs Pioneers
Museum. **You saved the day!**

I am deeply indebted to Jane Austen's *Pride and Prejudice*
for the themes woven into *The Wedding Ring*. In this
novella, I was able to employ the device that I want to
be the hallmark of my career—breathing nuances of the
classics into my novels.

Prologue

"This quilt is . . . is very special," Ma Brandon rasped.

Rose dabbed at the warm tears stinging her eyes. She sank onto the bedside of her dying grandmother. It felt as if the feather mattress were swallowing Rose just as the grief seemed to be swallowing her soul. The last few days had been the most emotionally draining that Rose had encountered in all her twenty years—for her precious grandmother was gradually dying of consumption. Dying at age fifty-five.

"Why is it special?" Rose stroked the quilt Ma Brandon gripped in her thin, deeply veined hands. Although it appeared unused, the quilt bore time's yellowing marks along the edges. Minutes ago Ma Brandon had asked Rose to retrieve the red and green and beige quilt from the bottom of the cedar trunk under the window. Before now Rose had never seen it.

"It's special because it was my very . . . my very own wedding ring." Efforts at speech left Ma Brandon gasping for every breath.

"Of course it was." Rose gently stroked the hands that nervously picked at the quilt, cloaked in the smell of cedar. "It's a beautiful Wedding-Ring quilt." She admired the tiny, uniform stitches that traced the repetitive circular pattern. A red ring. A green ring. Against a beige background.

"No . . . you don't . . . don't understand." Ma Brandon jerked her head from side to side, her ashen face crumpling into agitated lines.

"Calm down. Calm down." Rose inched the quilt from Ma Brandon's reach. Something about this memento disturbed her dying grandmother. Disturbed her deeply. Rose stood to put it back.

"Don't . . . don't take it."

Ma Brandon's pleading brown eyes drew Rose back to the bed. As she sat down, a yellowed bundle of letters fell from the folds of the quilt and landed on the worn wooden floor. Rose bent to retrieve the bundle, tied with a spindly piece of twine.

"I must . . . must tell you . . . tell you the . . . the story." Ma Brandon reached for the letters. "And ask you . . ." Her gaze drifted past Rose and out the lace-trimmed window. "Ask you to take . . . to take the quilt and these notes back."

"Back?"

"Yes." A cough, and Rose used a nearby handkerchief to blot the dark blood from her grandmother's lips. "And . . . and tell him—"

"Him?"

A slight nod. "Yes. Tell him that I never . . . never stopped loving him."

"Who?"

"Trevor . . . Trevor Riley . . . in Denver." Ma Brandon's eyes sparked with an alarming intensity. "He penned these very letters. Promise me, Rose. Promise me you'll take them and the quilt back . . . back to him . . . after . . . after my funeral." A renewed fit of coughing. More agitation. And Ma Brandon clung to Rose's hand as if it were the only thread connecting her with the living.

Rose's mind whirled with the implications of Ma Brandon's request. Denver? Ma Brandon was asking her to travel to Denver in search of a man she had never met? Rose had lived her whole life in Colorado Springs. Since her twelfth birthday she had yearned to see the world that lay beyond the perimeters of her hometown. Like a woman afire with adventure, she had devoured popular fiction and travelogues. Through her reading, she toured America with Mark Twain, England with Jane Austen, and Russia with Dostoevsky.

But now that the opportunity for travel was actually presenting itself, an unexpected blanket of doubt smothered the spark of excitement. Where would she find the funds for such a trip? The train ticket. The hotels. The meals. Two years ago her father had purchased a grocery store. Atop the store, the small family crowded into a modest apartment. There was little money available for travel.

Besides, how did Ma Brandon know this Trevor Riley still lived in Denver? Who was he, anyway? Ma Brandon declared she had never stopped loving him. Rose's saintly grandmother must have nursed a well-hidden secret for many, many years. The whole idea simultaneously shocked and fascinated Rose.

"Promise me, Rose." The eyes that seemed to pierce Rose moments before now drooped in weary pleading.

Rose placed trembling fingers against her lips. She and Ma Brandon had long ago developed a special relationship. From Rose's earliest memory, the two had shared a daily basketful of laughter, love, and God's light. Everyone said Rose favored Ma Brandon more than she favored her own mother. Silky chestnut hair. Eyes the color of dark chocolate. And an endearing, upturned nose. Along with their appearance, the two experienced a bond that rivaled the feelings Rose felt for her mother.

So regardless of her worries about money, she could not deny her grandmother's request. "I promise."

Ma Brandon's tense mouth relaxed. "Look in the cedar chest again. There's a . . ." More coughing. More blotting of blood. "A pouch of money. Take it. Use it. Use all of it. You'll need clothes for trav . . . travel as well."

Rose bit her lips. Ma Brandon had just dashed away the one obstacle that stood between Rose and the trip. But her desire for Ma Brandon to survive outweighed her need for adventure. Why was life so terribly difficult? Having her dreams of travel come true meant saying good-bye to her dearest friend.

They were dearest friends because they shared so much in common. Rose had somehow acquired the determined disposition of Lorene Brandon. After her husband's death twenty-five years before, Lorene had managed a successful restaurant and raised three boys.

Strong willed yet quiet. Highly intelligent. Stubborn beyond words. An unyielding faith in God. Rose readily recognized these traits in her grandmother because they were so prominent in herself.

The bedroom door squeaked open. Rose turned to see her plump, blonde mother, Iris, enter the attic. She moved as if she were a loving angel ready to bestow mercy on all who asked. Iris had nursed her husband's sick mother and her own parents without one complaint.

"Your father wants to see you in his office downstairs, Rose. It seems he's jumbled the bookkeeping again."

Rose bit her tongue to stay a retort. How could her father worry about bookkeeping when his own mother lay on her deathbed?

"It's his way of . . ." Iris's unsaid words seemed to dissolve into the noise of her swishing green skirt.

It's his way of dealing with it. Rose's mother had repeated those words a dozen times over the last week. Only at the end of the day, after he had totally expended himself in his business, did Zebulun Brandon grace his own mother with a few hurried moments. Rose had spent many days praying for strength to hold her tongue. How could her father be so callous? Who cared about debits and credits when a precious prayer warrior, a saint of God, was struggling for her last breaths?

Iris, bending to fluff her mother-in-law's pillows, darted an instigating glance toward her daughter.

"I'll go down to him," Rose muttered.

"Take these and . . . and read them," Ma Brandon rasped, pressing the letters into Rose's palm. "Then perhaps . . . perhaps you'll under . . . understand."

Gathering her straight, indigo work skirt, Rose stood, letters in hand. At the door, she paused to take another glimpse of her grandmother. Bathed in the faint light of the electric wall lamp, she still clutched the red and green Wedding-Ring quilt.

Rose never saw Ma Brandon alive again.

CHAPTER ONE

A nd may I say who is calling, please?"

Rose Brandon looked up into the pale gray eyes of a man she presumed to be Mr. Trevor Riley's butler. Dressed in an ebony wool suit as black as his hair, his trim frame towered over Rose's average height. He seemed a handsome metaphor of the whole imposing mansion of red brick and white pillars.

"My name is Rose—Miss Rose Brandon." Not daring to break his gaze, Rose relied on the innate composure that had enabled her to survive the condescending reproof of some of her father's most haughty customers.

Silence. And the scrutinizing butler seemed ready to ask her to leave the premises.

Finding Trevor Riley had been the easiest part of this adventure; much easier than convincing her father that she must use a portion of Ma Brandon's money for traveling to Denver.

After checking into her hotel yesterday, Rose asked the clerk if he had ever heard of Riley. With a polite chuckle, he said, "Who in Denver hasn't heard of him? He's the wealthiest man in town."

This morning Rose hired a carriage to drive her to the outskirts of Denver, where she caught the first glimpse of this domineering mansion, perched at the foot of the Rockies. Fleetingly, Rose wondered how anyone could call such a structure "home."

At last the butler stopped his rude scrutiny and posed another question. "Would you kindly expound on your reason for calling?" he asked with a slight British accent.

"No, I will not." Bristling, Rose increased her grip on the floral feed bag that held the quilt and those tender love letters from Trevor Riley. She felt as if she were holding Ma Brandon's heart in that bag. Rose wasn't about to "expound" to anyone but Mr. Riley. What a nosy, arrogant employee! "I have something of a private nature to discuss with Mr. Riley."

An amused light flashed in the butler's eyes. His tightened lips relaxed into an indulgent smile. "Of course."

Rose tried to steel herself against the late September wind that whipped around the massive porch and lifted her red cape. Nonetheless, she shivered. The icy blast held promises of an early snow. And even though Rose thirsted for adventure, she didn't have the funds or time to get snowed in. Her father would expect her to carry out her usual duties in their grocery store, especially with the Thanksgiving and Christmas seasons only weeks away. If she were trapped in Denver, working in the store would be an impossibility. Therefore, she must present Ma Brandon's letters and quilt to Mr. Riley and prepare to leave immediately.

Another shiver.

"You're cold. Why don't you come in?"

"Thank you." Rose stepped into the most magnificent foyer she had ever encountered. Decorated in the Greek tradition, it featured a pair of marble staircases that curved down each side of the circular room. Twin crystal chandeliers. Walls, pure white, intricately carved in floral relief.

Marble busts. Six doors replete with sculptured brass knobs lined the breathtaking room. Then, this mahogany table, that tasteful chair, and a scattering of brass bowls full of dried flowers.

"I see you enjoy beauty," the butler said.

"Of course," she replied as the smell of dried rose petals tantalized her senses.

"I'm sorry, but Father is out right now. He should be back within the hour. If you would care to wait for him—"

"Is Mr. Riley your father?"

"But of course, I never introduced myself. Trevor Riley Jr." A slight bow. "At your service. I was about to go for a drive in our electric buggy when you rang."

Out of habit, Rose curtsied, and Trevor gave her an admiring gaze.

Taken aback, she stifled her heart's momentary palpitation and returned his warm appraisal with a chilly one of her own. She refused, she simply refused to fawn over a man who had apparently had his every whim satisfied since birth. Ma Brandon taught Rose long ago that her worth was based on Christ's love, not on money or possessions.

"Would you care to join me in my drive?" he asked spontaneously. "The electric buggy was just delivered last week from New York, and it's quite a novelty to me. When we return, I'm sure Father will be home."

"But I have a hired carriage awaiting me."

"We can pay him and send him on his way. I'll return you to town when you finish your business with Father."

Rose hesitated. She had not anticipated this turn of events. She had seen a few of the new horseless buggies that some wealthy individuals drove. Even though they cost as much as two or three thousand dollars, many people predicted these gas, electric, or steam powered carriages would provide all future transportation. On one hand, the adventuresome Rose wanted to accept Mr. Riley's unexpected offer. On the other hand, she had never met Trevor Riley Jr. Could he be trusted?

As she pondered her dilemma, one of the brass-knobbed doors opened, and an angular, gray-haired man emerged.

"Ah, the answer to the lady's problem," Trevor said, extending a hand to the man. "My dear Oliver. He'll be our chaperone. Oliver Ghaliger, meet Miss Rose Brandon. Oliver is my dearest friend."

Oliver bowed, and his kind blue eyes sparkled unconditional friendship.

As she curtsied, Rose experienced the uncanny feeling Trevor had read her mind concerning her hesitation about riding alone with him.

Smiling assurance, Oliver, dressed in fresh wool pants and a beige flannel shirt, neared Mr. Riley. "What mischief are you planning now, my boy?" he asked with a thick British accent.

"I was just inviting the lady for a ride in the electric Spider," Mr. Riley answered, his faint British tones a reflection of the older gentleman's accent.

"Ah yes, the famous Spider from New York." Oliver's softly lined, tanned face reflected his fatherly love for Trevor.

For a moment Rose felt an overwhelming curiosity about Mr. Trevor Riley. About his life. About his family. This Oliver Ghaliger was not Trevor's father, but the two acted as close as a father and son. Trevor also shared a nuance of Oliver's accent. The two must have spent many years together.

Her musings led her to wonder if Trevor had a wife and children. She had originally assumed him to be a bachelor. Had she been mistaken? An unexpected delight danced through her heart as she realized he would most likely not have invited her for a ride if he were married.

Rose restrained her delight. Despite Mr. Riley's debonair ways, she had no desire to entangle herself with a family of such fortune. In her experience, most affluent people were arrogant, shallow, and unconcerned with spiritual matters. In short, Rose held little respect for the wealthy, in spite of Ma Brandon's wisdom.

Last year she had turned down an offer of marriage from a man with a background much like Mr. Trevor Riley's. Her father had yet to forgive her for that one. Ma Brandon, however, applauded her. Rose's mother never made a blatant comment, but Rose felt that she sided with her husband. The marriage would have extended a definite financial boost to the whole Brandon family. It would also have been a case of Rose selling herself to a man she could never love.

She firmly reminded herself that she had come to Denver to deliver some letters and a quilt, not to develop any new friendships, especially with a man whose values could in no way match hers. She opened her mouth to refuse Mr. Riley's invitation of a ride when an older version of him burst through the front door.

"That blasted Jones," he growled. "I told him Cuban cigars. And what does he order? French!"

"Father, we have a visitor," Trevor interrupted.

Mr. Riley scowled at Rose.

Despite her shock at the older man's gruffness, she once again exercised her composure and curtsied as if she had just been acknowledged with the warmest greetings.

"This is Miss Rose Brandon." Trevor produced another of those indulgent smiles.

As his eyes widened a fraction, Mr. Riley's scowl lessened.

"Miss Brandon has just arrived and requests a private word with you."

Mr. Riley removed the cigar stub from between his yellowed teeth. Dressed as a gentleman from head to foot, he wore his costly wool suit like a workhorse in silk. Unlike his refined son, Mr. Riley seemed out of place amongst his home's elegance. His gnarled hands and deeply lined, rugged face spoke of hours of outdoor labor. And the bitter twist of his mouth attested to a life of hardship.

As she held Mr. Riley's challenging gaze, Rose began to wonder if perhaps he would simply dismiss her. How had the youth who penned the love letters turned into this hardened person before her? This man seemed the antithesis of the one who wrote the letters. Those notes were full of tenderness, compassion, and even naive attempts at poetry.

"I'll see you in my office. Give me a minute," he snapped. Without another word, he took the stairs two at a time.

"You'll have to excuse Father," Trevor said. "Some days, he's a bit short."

Rose nodded. For the first time she deliberated about giving the quilt to Mr. Riley. That quilt was like a part of Ma Brandon's soul. Would Ma Brandon consent if she knew the loving youth she remembered had deteriorated into a tactless, hardened man? But Ma Brandon would never know the absolute truth, and Rose had promised her she would deliver the quilt.

"I can pull the Spider around, if you like," Oliver said. "And the lady can still enjoy the ride after her appointment."

"Of course. That's a splendid idea," Trevor said, his pale eyes sparkling with anticipation.

"N-no thank you," Rose stammered, refusing to meet his gaze. She simply wanted to hand over the quilt and remove herself from these people. The longer she stayed, the more she felt as if a heavy yoke of bondage settled around her shoulders.

Feeling Oliver's curious appraisal, Trevor seated Rose in his father's office and turned on the electric wall lamp. The bookshelves, burgundy leather, and cigar odor seemed to overshadow her. True to her name, Rose Brandon looked like spring's first rose, kissed in summer dew. She did not fit the room's somber surroundings.

At the door Trevor paused to study her profile. Chestnut hair piled high. Full lips. A cute, upturned nose. She nervously toyed with the mysterious feed bag in her lap.

And Dr. Trevor Riley Jr. found himself fascinated. Her simple clothing attested to her being below his economic standing. The classic scarlet cape and conservative, jade-colored hat were of good quality but by no means the finest. Yet despite her obvious lack of wealth, she had possessed the fortitude to refuse his offer. The effect was refreshing, to say the least. Because of his father's money, most women made a point of being overly congenial.

The last few years Trevor had wearily begun to wonder if he would find a woman who cared just for him. Even if his father weren't wealthy. Even if Trevor weren't a respected physician. Was there a woman who would love him simply for who he was? The question, so disturbing, had left Trevor a lonely man. For try as he might, he had yet to meet an unmarried woman who didn't tumble all over herself to snare him.

Until now.

Thoughtfully, Trevor closed the study's door and turned an absent smile toward Oliver, his childhood chaperon and tutor, his best friend. After Trevor's mother's untimely death during her second pregnancy, the dear British saint had virtually raised him. Trevor knew him better than he knew his own father.

Oliver, a thrifty soul, had managed to save enough money through the years to now modestly support himself in his own quarters. However, Trevor had insisted Oliver continue living in the Riley mansion after his services were no longer required. On the days Mr. Riley was particularly ruthless, Oliver seemed the only light in the household.

"I think the lady will need transportation back into town, don't you?" Trevor asked.

"But she said she didn't care for a ride," Oliver said, a questioning glint in his eyes. When Trevor didn't respond, Oliver continued, "I don't remember your ever mentioning knowing a Rose Brandon. I guess you must be keeping secrets from me. One day away from your practice and you have already become a man of mystery."

Oliver referred to Trevor's decision to leave the affluent medical partnership where he had started his career. Trevor felt God calling him to establish a free practice for the poor. When Rose knocked on the door, he had been about to drive into town to examine a potential office building.

"I'm not keeping secrets. I only just met Miss Brandon myself." Not sure he understood his own actions enough to explain them to Oliver, Trevor planned to pay the hired carriage and send it on its way. He reached for his gold money clip tucked in his suit's hidden pocket. Trevor hesitated. A voice deep inside insisted that Rose Brandon was different from any woman he had met. Her composure. The tilt of her chin. The no-nonsense glint in her deep brown eyes. Most women would be flattered for Trevor to insist he escort them. But Miss Brandon might very well be furious.

Still, Trevor felt an uncanny urgency to extend their acquaintance. Somehow, this fascinating lady carrying a mysterious feed bag had been dropped into his life out of nowhere. He simply could not let her escape him. As ridiculous as it might seem, Trevor felt as if Rose had issued a challenge of sorts—a challenge that bade Trevor to cultivate her friendship.

As Oliver continued his curious appraisal, Trevor removed the money clip, walked out the door, and sent Rose's carriage driver on his way with a handsome tip.

Chapter Two

"You're here for Lorene, aren't you?" the senior Riley demanded as he closed the office door with an ominous click.

Blinking in surprise, Rose nodded. "How did you know?"

"You look just like her. That's how," he growled. "It's been forty years since I've seen her—but don't think I've forgotten because I haven't." Rigidly, Mr. Riley sat in the leather chair behind the mahogany desk like a gnarled buzzard arrogantly perched atop a mountain.

Rose felt as if she were a truant facing the school headmaster. Still, she maintained her impassive expression, her erect posture, her steady gaze.

His pale gray eyes, the color of his son's, revealed no hint of joy. Only a hardened glare. "Are you her daughter?"

"No. I'm her granddaughter." Rose, squirming in her chair, wished she had never come. She detested the very thought of giving this man her grandmother's beloved quilt.

"Why are you here?" The old man reached into his desk's top drawer to produce a fresh cigar and a matchbox. He struck the match and held it to the end of the cigar. He smiled blandly and puffed two foul-smelling smoke rings toward Rose.

She managed to stifle all but a few coughs while she searched for words, any words, to begin Ma Brandon's message. But the means to communicate with this man escaped her. Simply put, Rose had romantically, and quite erroneously, assumed that the tenderhearted youth of the letters would be the man she would meet. The shock of reality left her speechless.

"Well, speak up," he barked.

She jumped. His sharp command released a flood of words. "Ma Brandon passed away two weeks ago," Rose rushed. "Before she died, she asked me to return this quilt to you." Fingers trembling, Rose loosened the feed bag's drawstring and laid the quilt atop the scattered papers on Riley's desk. "And also these letters." Rose produced the crumpled bundle and placed them on the quilt.

Mr. Riley's narrowed eyes opened a fraction. His face softened. For one wrinkle in time, Rose caught a glimpse of the emotion that flowed from his letters.

"And . . . and she asked me to . . ." As she hesitated, Rose wondered if her next words would increase the old man's softening. ". . . to tell you she never stopped loving you."

Immediately, a bitter mask twisted Mr. Riley's features. The momentary tenderness vanished. He threw back his head and laughed scornfully, harshly. "Surely you don't expect me to believe that one, do you?"

"Well—"

"She never loved me! I supplied all the love in that courtship. And where did it get me? Nowhere! And do you know why?"

Rose opened her mouth to speak, but he cut her off.

"Because I wasn't good enough, that's why. My father was just a poor dirt farmer. That wasn't quite enough for the daughter of a merchant."

"But—"

"She said her parents refused to let us get married, but we could have run away together. I begged her to. But she refused. Said she was afraid to cross Papa! Well, I didn't believe her then. And I still don't believe her."

Breathless from the potency of his venomous outburst, Rose felt as if she were engulfed in the infection of an unhealed wound. It seemed that Mr. Riley was vindicating his scorned love and using Rose as a replacement for her grandmother.

Menacingly, the old man puffed his cigar and scrutinized the quilt. For several minutes he seemed oblivious of Rose's presence.

When he spoke once more, the poison emanated from his whole being. "I gave her that blasted quilt the very night she rejected me. My mother made it. I couldn't afford any kind of a wedding band. So I gave her the Wedding-Ring quilt instead," he snarled, an ugly, ironic twist on his lips. "She stabbed me in the heart but took the gift anyway."

As if avenging his pain, Mr. Riley crushed the cigar butt in a brass tray. When he looked up, his pale eyes had taken on a fiendish spark.

Afraid to glance away, Rose held his unrelenting gaze.

"I vowed then and there that I would one day be so wealthy I could wipe my feet on Lorene Daley and her whole family." A smirk replaced the hatred. "I think you'll agree that I met my goal."

But you lost your soul in the process. Rose didn't speak the words, but they echoed through the corridors of her mind. Trevor Riley Sr. seemed the personification of bitterness, of hatred. Bitterness and hatred that had done more than color his outlook. They had become his driving force. His reason for life.

Bracing herself against the dismay surging through her soul, Rose recalled one letter in particular. The letter that vaguely referred to Mr. Riley's desire to become a minister. At one time this scowling man before her had been interested in spiritual matters. But Satan had ultimately claimed a victory. A heartbreaking victory.

Rose stood. "Well, I've carried out my promise," she said evenly.

He continued his stony stare. The stare of a cobra.

"Good-bye." Not waiting for a response, Rose squared her shoulders and left the room. She had kept her promise to Ma Brandon. She would now remove herself from this dreadful household with all its hate-filled shadows. Remove herself to never return.

For the third time Trevor nervously adjusted the electric buggy's black leather hood. Hopefully, the hood would keep the brunt of the wind from Rose. He toyed with his watch chain, then checked his gold pocket watch. Fifteen minutes. Miss Brandon had been talking with his father for fifteen long minutes.

Oliver, perched in the elevated driver's seat behind the passenger bench, observed Trevor with sparkling blue eyes; eyes that reminded Trevor of St. Nicholas himself. "Calm down, boy. She'll be out soon enough."

"That's what I'm afraid of." Trevor sat on the edge of the button-tucked passenger seat, then stood again.

"What's there to be afraid of?" Oliver teased.

Trevor produced a mock scowl.

Oliver chuckled.

Desperately, Trevor wanted to make a good impression on this lovely, unexpected visitor. Yet he had gone against her wishes and dismissed her carriage. In retrospect, the deed seemed rash. He would probably make anything but a good impression on her.

The mansion door burst open, and Rose rushed toward

the spot on the edge of the manicured lawn where she had left her hired carriage. The electric buggy now claimed the very same spot.

Trevor held her startled gaze. Breathlessly, he awaited her reaction. Waited, and relished the moment. Never before had he been unsure of a woman. The fortune-seeking females from his past would have purred with pleasure were he to arrange such a ride.

Rose pursed her lips. Her cheeks flushed. Her brown eyes flashed with flames of fury. Unceremoniously, she stalked toward Trevor. "What have you done?" she demanded through clenched teeth.

Another chuckle from Oliver. Trevor had never wanted to punch his closest friend. Until now.

"I—"

"I told you I didn't need a ride back to town."

"I just thought—"

"What did you think? That-that just because you're wealthy you could arrange my life in the way you see fit?" The way she gripped her square purse's black handle made Trevor wonder if she wished the thing were his neck.

"Now don't be too hard on the boy," Oliver began indulgently.

Rose directed her fury to poor Oliver. "Boy? He is not a boy! He is a grown man who should learn to respect the wishes of others." She turned to Trevor. "I refuse to ride anywhere with you." Throwing decorum to the wind, Miss Brandon stomped her foot. "I demand that you go into town and tell my carriage driver to return."

"That's ridiculous!" Trevor countered as his own ire began to rise. How dare this little spitfire tell him what to do! "I'm available and will be most happy to escort you into town," he said, attempting to control his irritated tone.

Another chuckle from Oliver. Another scowl from Trevor. Whose side was Oliver on anyway?

"I'll walk before I ride with you!" Head held high, Rose turned for the road.

"You can't walk! It's nearly a mile, and this wind will slice right through you."

As if on cue, a puff of frigid air mercilessly whipped her scarlet cape and deep green skirt. Despite her haughty posture, Rose shivered, then mutely continued up the narrow, graveled road.

Trevor could never remember meeting a more obstinate woman. The effect was bedazzling. He wanted to shake some sense into her, but at the same time he was fascinated. Absolutely fascinated.

The same abstract force that had urged Trevor to dismiss Rose's carriage now urged him once more—*do not let Rose Brandon escape you.* In several quick strides, Trevor narrowed the space between them and did something he had never dreamed of doing. He scooped her up in his arms and turned back toward the carriage.

"Put me down!" Rose gasped. "How dare you!" She lashed at him with her petite purse as she squirmed against his grip.

Clamping his jaws, Trevor trudged toward the electric buggy. She weighed a good twenty pounds more than he had predicted. The unexpected weight, added to her resistance, left Trevor hoping he would make it to the carriage without dropping her. But at last, amid her heated outbursts, livid sputterings, and dislodged hair combs, he deposited Rose on the buggy's passenger seat.

"Now," Trevor growled as he plopped beside her and adjusted his gray fedora. "I will not let you walk to town. It's entirely too cold."

From behind, Oliver snickered. Was laughter all Oliver could produce?

Mutely, Rose crossed her arms and stonily stared straight ahead. As if to punctuate her predicament, her jade-colored hat, adorned with burgundy feathers, toppled into her lap. A frustrated huff. She grabbed the hat, removed one of the sharp, enameled hat pens, crammed the hat back on her disheveled hair, and attempted to reanchor it in her locks. But the pin missed its mark, and the hat shifted forward.

"It's not—," Trevor began.

"Don't speak to me," she snapped, her defiant eyes daring him to continue.

Oliver began the journey, and the electric carriage rolled forward with the sound of rubber tires crunching against gravel. That movement sent Rose's hat tumbling to the floorboard.

Assuming Rose's corset would never allow her to bend enough to retrieve the hat, Trevor reached for it.

Surprisingly, she agilely beat him to his goal, but at the expense of her precarious locks. Already in disarray, her silky, chestnut hair cascaded onto her shoulders. She furiously swept the fragrant cloud out of her face, settled the hat into her lap, and scooted as far from Trevor as the confining seat would permit. Miss Brandon then turned her face toward the roadside, mere feet from their opened seat.

Trevor looked to the opposite side of the road. So that was that. His questions about how she would react were answered. And thoroughly. What a bitter dose of poetic justice. The one woman who had intrigued Trevor Riley wanted no part of him. As her hair's lavender scent enveloped him, a pall of gloom settled about his soul. And Trevor grappled with the various means of repairing the harm he had inflicted on his image.

An unexpected sniffle broke his reverie.

He darted a startled gaze back to Rose. She courageously tried to hide her tears while repeatedly blotting her cheeks with a dainty pink handkerchief.

Trevor considered patting her back and stroking her shining hair. He wisely resisted that impulse. A touch would likely result in Rose knocking his hand away and jumping from the rolling carriage.

At last Denver's clean streets came into view. Because of the nationwide "City Beautiful Movement," Denver city officials had begun creating attractive parks and cracking down on crime. The results left Trevor with a new pride in his city.

Oliver cleared his throat. "Where are you staying, Miss Brandon?" His voice floated down from the driver's seat behind them.

"At the Spaulding House," she uttered through diminishing sniffles.

Trevor suddenly panicked. Once Rose entered her hotel, he might never again see her. She would disappear as quickly as she had appeared, and he had no idea where she lived. Trevor must not let her escape him.

He sat in silent misery. His mind flitted from one desperate plan to another. His palms, clammy. His stomach, churning. His forehead, perspiring. At the end of his wits, Trevor resorted to prayer. *Lord, I should have started out consulting you. But nonetheless, I didn't, and now I've done a tremendous job of royally botching things. Please show me what to do from here.*

Oliver halted the electric buggy outside the inn, a modest, although quality, establishment not as refined as some of the prestigious hotels dotting the city. Trevor removed his tall frame from the cramped quarters, took Rose's hand, and assisted her descent. Her mouth set in a stubborn line, she avoided his gaze. Reluctantly, Trevor released her hand. Shoulders erect, she turned toward the frosted glass doors.

CHAPTER THREE

Rose resisted the urge to run toward the door. The sooner she removed herself from that infuriating man and his laughing driver, the better! Trevor Riley Jr. was well named. He was just like Trevor Riley Sr. Even though he was more debonair than his father, Trevor apparently cared little for the feelings of others. Rose wished Ma Brandon had never asked her to deliver that quilt. True, Rose had seen Denver, but the Rileys had shown her a great deal more ugliness than the fascination of the city could overcome.

When Rose touched the inn's brass doorknob, she reveled in knowing that she would never have to see Trevor again. But Rose was wrong. The second she heard his footsteps behind her, she wanted to cringe. Now what did he intend? Was he going to plop her back into that electric buggy of his?

"I'm terribly sorry." A light touch on her shoulder.

She paused, head still bent, debating whether to shake off his hand or scream with frustration.

"I should never have dismissed your carriage. It was completely uncalled for. I simply—"

For the first time since she had declared that she would walk to Denver, Rose met his gaze with a challenging one of her own. "And what about tossing me into the buggy? Did that bring you any shame?"

"Yes, it brought me a great deal of shame," he said solemnly, his every feature pleading for understanding. "I humbly beg your forgiveness."

Her stinging eyes rounded in surprise.

As if her reaction encouraged him, Trevor rushed, "Would you be so kind as to allow me the honor of taking you to dinner this evening? It would be my way of repairing the damage I've caused to . . . to your . . ." Like a flustered youth requesting his first courtship, Trevor floundered for words.

Despite her injured pride, Rose experienced an alarming awareness of his conservatively handsome features. The dark brows and hair. The firm, narrow lips. The straight, prominent nose. And those pale eyes that beseeched her with childlike uncertainty. Unexpectedly, her heart quivered as it had at their formal introduction in the mansion's doorway.

Then she remembered Trevor's wealth. She remembered his father's motive in amassing that wealth. She remembered how she detested the attitudes, the values of the wealthy.

Rose left the Riley mansion with no desire to return, no desire to associate with any of its habitants. Despite her heart's betraying interest in Trevor, she would not accept his offer.

"Thank you, but no," she said firmly and turned back toward the inn's door.

"Is it because of Father?"

Arrested by his astuteness, Rose swiveled back toward him. "Not completely, no."

"Tell me what he said to you." He reached for her arm.

She stepped away. "I—" New tears stung her eyes. How

did she explain to this man that she had left a remnant of a saint's soul with a person who seemed to possess the heart of the devil himself?

"He deeply wounded you, didn't he?"

"He—" Rose stopped abruptly. The intensity of their conversation began to attract the indiscreet glances of those passing by. She had no desire to continue. Rose simply wanted to find refuge in her room. The more scrutiny they received from strangers, the more distracted, the more nervous she became. Besides, the icy wind blasts were tormenting her skirt and mercilessly tossing her hair into her eyes.

Trevor glanced toward the electric carriage. "I see Oliver has wandered off. Won't you please join me in the Spider?"

She opened her mouth to protest.

"Just for a few more moments. It will protect us from the wind, and I feel I simply must know what Father has said to you. He is . . . well . . . he is not always the gentleman." Gently, Trevor took her arm and propelled her back toward the electric carriage.

For a reason beyond her understanding, Rose didn't resist him.

As she resumed the spot she had recently vacated, Rose wondered if she had lost her mind. Where had the fiery coals of her anger gone? With great determination, she tried to scrape them back together and rekindle the flames of her fury. But the coals were cold and lifeless. Only interest in Trevor remained—the same interest that had posed itself during the first moments of their acquaintance.

"Now tell me what Father has done."

Rose bit her lips. Then the story spilled out. It spilled out, right along with a new supply of tears. Her beloved Ma Brandon was dead. And a hardened ogre ungratefully held the Christmas quilt that had meant so much to her.

"I'm sorry," Trevor muttered when Rose finished. "I'm terribly, terribly sorry."

With a shaking sigh, Rose determined to stop her tears. "It's not a situation of your making. You shouldn't apologize." She scrubbed at her cheeks with the pink kerchief.

"But it reflects badly on our family and me. And . . . I guess I didn't add a positive dimension to the whole ordeal, did I?" A lopsided smile twisted her heart again.

Despite herself, Rose returned the smile.

A new glimmer of hope flickered across Trevor's face. "I would still be deeply flattered if you would grace me with your presence at dinner."

"I—" Rose once more found herself drawn to this tall, slender man. Some mysterious power seemed to perpetually tug her toward him. But that was preposterous. Regardless of her attraction to Trevor, they could never share the same values. He was from the class Rose had long scorned. That scorn had never wavered. Only intensified.

"Would six o'clock be appropriate?" he asked.

"I don't think so. I—"

"Then seven perhaps?"

"No. I—" She peered at the petite black purse whose handle once again received the punishment of her tense grip. "I'm sorry, Mr. Riley, but I never court men who don't share my faith in Christ. I'm afraid it would be terribly unfair to you for me to accept your offer. Because you see—"

"But I do share your faith."

His unexpected words riveted Rose's attention. "You do?" she blurted, searching for any sign of dishonesty in his expression. She found none.

"Yes. Oliver introduced me to Christ when I was but seven. Oliver and I almost never miss worship on Sundays. It's the highlight of our week."

"It is?" Rose steeled herself against letting her mouth gape in shock.

Trevor looked toward the dusty street teeming with carriages and pedestrians. "I wish I could say the same about

Father," he muttered, a slight tinge of distress lacing his words. "He isn't young anymore, and—" With a renewed smile, Trevor turned back to her. "Enough of my worries. Now, we were deciding on the hour we would dine. Would six be OK?"

"Uh . . . yes," Rose heard herself saying. "Six is fine."

Trevor watched with great admiration as Rose finished the last bite of her baked salmon and took a final sip of her mint tea. She bestowed a cautious smile upon him, and Trevor returned it. He had chosen his favorite eating establishment as their spot to dine. Abby's Tea Room. A quality restaurant without a pompous air. The cozy dining room, replete with green velvet drapes, eighteenth century antiques, candle-light, and an accomplished harpist, set the exact tone Trevor desired. Inviting, yet private. Friendly, yet discreet.

From the start of the evening, the waiters had been as meticulously attentive as always. Trevor had desperately wished they would be a bit more nonchalant because the attentiveness that might impress most women would per-haps stifle Rose.

So far, she seemed anything but stifled, and their conver-sation had been light and entertaining. Trevor had learned quickly that Miss Brandon possessed an element of wit which he found extremely refreshing. And even though Trevor had seen a spark of interest in her eyes, he still felt that she withheld herself from him. Now that the meal was over, would their light, flowing conversation turn to awkward, obligatory remarks? As Trevor grappled for something, any-thing to say, the graying waiter, dressed in a tailored black suit, came to remove the now empty plates of their main course.

"And would you and the lady enjoy a dessert, Dr. Riley?" the waiter asked in his most respecting voice.

Rose's eyes rounded in surprise.

Trevor suppressed a groan. He had not yet told Rose he was a physician, and so far the restaurant employees had miraculously avoided using his proper title. Until now. Trevor had wanted to save the news of his profession until he knew Rose was truly interested in him. Just him. Without a title. Already Trevor sensed with great relief that she didn't care one flip about his wealth. But would his being a man of respectable profession color her opinion? That remained to be seen.

"Would you care for dessert, Miss Brandon?" Trevor repeated as the solemn waiter cleared their dishes amid the clink of white china and crystal.

A mischievous smile touched her peachy lips, and Trevor knew her answer before she voiced it. "I would love dessert."

"Might I suggest our newest dessert—the pumpkin roll," the erect waiter said.

"I've had it," Trevor supplied. "A pumpkin bread topped with nuts, wrapped around a cream cheese filling and topped with whipped cream. It's delicious."

"Sounds marvelous."

"Would you care for one slice or two?" Trevor teased.

A soft giggle. "Make it three."

"It's so refreshing to see a woman enjoy her food."

She flushed.

"Oh, but I didn't mean that as any sort of an insult. I am often disturbed at my female patients who deprive themselves for the sake of fashion. And then those dreadful corsets! Whoever invented those things must have hated women. I believe they have cost the lives of two of my patients."

"Dr. Riley, please!" Her flush increased.

"Forgive me, Miss Brandon. I sometimes forget myself. I

would never intentionally bring anything suggestive into our conversation."

Her eyes downcast, Rose discreetly dabbed the corners of her mouth with her white, linen napkin.

Earlier that day her scarlet cape had hidden most of her, and Trevor had presumed she wore a corset like every other woman. But the moment she had greeted him that evening, Trevor immediately noticed Rose's normal-sized waist. Dressed in a simple, russet-colored skirt and jacket, which complemented the red highlights in her hair, she moved too freely to be bound by a corset. He recalled her agilely bending to retrieve her hat from the floorboard during their ride into town. Apparently, Miss Rose Brandon was more than attractive, more than a delightful conversationalist. She was also sensible.

"So, you are a doctor?" she inquired as the waiter served her a slice of pumpkin roll topped with a fluffy mound of whipped cream.

"Yes." He smiled slightly. "I studied medicine in England, actually."

"That explains your accent. I assumed it was Mr. Ghaliger's influence."

"Partly. Of course, my studying in England was because of Oliver. He went with me. We stayed with his sister. They were wonderful years."

Her deep brown eyes sparked with curiosity. "I've always wanted to travel."

"That doesn't surprise me in the least," he said, his voice warm with admiration.

She averted her gaze. "And . . . where is your office?" Rose took a generous bite of her dessert.

"I'm in the process of finding a new one, actually. That's where I was going today when I opened the door and saw you. I recently left a partnership to strike out on my own." Trevor began eating his slice of pumpkin roll. Should he tell her he wanted to rent an office in the most destitute part of Denver? Should he tell her God had called him to minister to the poor for free? He hesitated.

No.

Trevor wouldn't expound. Rose might think he was bragging about himself. And he desperately wanted to repair the negative impression he and his father had rendered.

Her eyes sparked with respect. "I feel I owe you an apology."

"Really?"

"Yes. It seems I made an erroneous assumption about you."

Trevor warmed with pleasure. "Really?" he repeated.

"I naturally presumed that—that you—" She gazed in consternation at the fragrant, white candle that was producing a puddle of melting wax around the brass candlestick's base. The candle's flickering shadows accented the confusion playing on her features. And she looked as if she would like to bite off the end of her tongue.

"That I was rich and idle?" Trevor supplied with what he hoped was an encouraging smile.

"Well—"

"Oliver would never have permitted that."

"You seem very close to him." Rose grabbed the new subject.

"I am. He raised me, you know. Father—well, after Mother died when I was five, Father withdrew. I must admit I know Oliver better than I ever knew my father."

"That's terribly sad."

He produced another encouraging smile. "Well, it would have been without Oliver. But still, there have been some difficult times." Would anyone but Oliver ever understand just how difficult his life had sometimes been? As a motherless child of an unfeeling father. As a wealthy teenager and young adult. Most of his past acquaintances, both male and female, were interested in his fortune, not Trevor himself. For years now, he had prayed for a wife who would love him just for himself.

Would Miss Rose Brandon prove to be that woman?

Rose stared into eyes that were a pale sea of churning emotion. Something within the deepest recesses of her heart was drawn to Trevor Riley as she had never been drawn to any man. The depths of his character. His slight British accent. His dark hair, as sleek as a raven's wings. This magnetism she felt was at once invigorating and laced with fear. The fear took control as her mind began a series of what-ifs.

What if Trevor asked to call on her in Colorado Springs?

What if they fell in love?

What if he proposed and she accepted?

What if Trevor ensconced her in that foreboding mansion with his horrid father?

What if Trevor's new practice kept him away a lot?

Rose would be trapped in the detestable world of the wealthy with a father-in-law she abhorred. She almost gagged on the last bite of the pumpkin roll gliding down her throat.

Upon accepting Trevor's dinner invitation that afternoon, she had experienced alternate fits of anticipation and dread. The dread returned. It returned, to replace that uncanny delight she found in Trevor's presence.

Why was Rose even here? Had she taken leave of all her senses? Trevor Riley represented everything she despised. Regardless of the rapport they enjoyed, regardless of their shared faith, Trevor was still a part of a societal hierarchy Rose scorned.

She must escape. And quickly.

"Would you care for more mint tea?" Trevor inquired, lifting the silver pot the waiter had left with them.

"No. No, thank you." A stiff smile. "I'm terribly tired, actually. Would you be so kind as to—"

His limpid eyes implored her not to end the evening.

Rose's breath caught. Her heart gently pounded. Her fingers trembled. And from the depths of her soul a voice begged her to remain in Trevor's presence.

Then the reverie was broken by another—the scowling face of Trevor's father, the imposing mansion, that costly electric carriage. Rose pressed her lips in determination. She must not let this man blind her to his origins.

"Would you be so kind as to escort me back to the inn?" she repeated. "I have a long train ride to Colorado Springs tomorrow. I need all the rest I can get."

"Of course. I wasn't thinking." He moved swiftly to assist her with her chair. "I've probably tired you with all my talking."

"No, no, not in the least. I've enjoyed myself immensely," Rose heard herself saying, despite her negative emotions. But it was the truth. And something about Trevor Riley made the truth emerge from her like daisies from the warm spring earth.

She must remove herself from this man's presence and establish herself firmly in reality. Rose would be going back home tomorrow. Back to the store and to the approaching Christmas season. She was a simple store clerk who wanted nothing but a simple cottage on a simple farm. The respected Dr. Trevor Riley did not fit into that picture.

They walked back to the nearby inn. Neither said a word. And what should have been companionable silence vibrated with tangible tension. Rose felt as if she would explode. Trevor's arm, taut and stiff under her hand, attested to his own tightly drawn emotions.

A myriad of questions spun through Rose's mind. Was Trevor hoping she would allow him to call on her regularly? Would he ask permission? And what would Rose tell him?

They crossed the rutted street alight with gas lanterns. The horses. The occasional carriage. The smell of evergreens on the Rockies. The call of a distant, lonely owl. The kiss of a full moon. Then, they entered the inn. The modest foyer. The drowsy clerk. The waiting stairway.

But every sight, sound, smell blurred when Trevor removed Rose's fingers from his arm and slowly pressed his lips to her gloved hand. As the kiss lingered, his ardent gaze never left her face. At once Rose felt as if she were the melting wax that had pooled at the base of the candle on their table. All warm and pliable and spent.

"May I have the privilege of calling on you tomorrow morning before you leave for Colorado Springs?"

No! No! No! a voice within her urged.

"Of course," she heard herself whisper.

Trevor produced a relieved smile.

Rose returned it.

CHAPTER FOUR

THE NEXT DAY
7:45 A.M.

The overcast skies and icy air threatened snow. Rose, awaiting the boarding call, nervously paced beside train number five, The San Francisco Express. In one hand she held her burgundy carpetbag, in the other, her petite square purse. She wore the same green dress, the same felt hat, the same scarlet cape she had worn on her trip to Denver. But she was by no means in the same frame of mind as when she had arrived early yesterday afternoon.

Yesterday she had been naively anticipating the impact that red and green Wedding-Ring quilt would have on Ma Brandon's first love. This morning Rose was running from that very man's son. Trevor had requested permission to call on Rose for breakfast at eight-thirty. By then, Rose hoped to be on her return journey to Colorado Springs.

A part of her shriveled at the thought of disappointing Trevor. But a more rational side demanded that Rose flee his presence. When she was with him, her heart seemed determined to control her decisions. Last night Rose had fully intended to refuse Trevor's request to call this morning, but she had lacked the fortitude to reject him. Rose, ever decisive, had never experienced such conflict. Waking early this morning, however, she had realized what she must do.

Only one solution remained.

Avoid Dr. Trevor Riley at all costs.

Return to Colorado Springs on an earlier train.

Pray, pray, pray that Trevor would never contact her.

Then forget him forever.

"All aboard!" the conductor called while smiling porters opened the doors to the passenger cars.

As the familiar train smells of coal and smoke and the sound of steam teased her senses, Rose boarded a car the color of wheat and chose a wooden seat beside the window. Sightlessly, she stared out at the busy Denver and Rio Grande railroad station and reflected upon Ma Brandon's asking her to travel to Denver. Rose relived the clasp of her grandmother's hands, the intensity of her eyes, the unrequited love from a heart once broken. Ma Brandon would never know how the years had drastically changed Mr. Riley. Rose was glad. The truth would have shattered her memories. Innocent. Unscathed. Sweet.

Perhaps Mr. Riley had once been a bit like his son. If so, no wonder Ma Brandon had never stopped loving him. The Riley men didn't seem to be easily forgotten.

Could Rose really forget Dr. Trevor Riley?

7:55 A.M.

Trevor bolted from the Spaulding House, jumped into his handsome, black buggy, snapped the whip on the white stallion's haunches, and raced toward the train station. He had chosen the horse and buggy this morning because he sensed Rose might be more comfortable with traditional transportation. Trevor arrived early to await her descent from her room. He blamed his excessive promptness on nervous anticipation. During the night, Trevor took advantage of his nervous insomnia to beseech God for guidance in courting Rose.

Perhaps his early arrival this morning was by God's design. The clerk had politely informed Trevor that Rose had left to catch the eight o'clock train for Colorado Springs. Had he not been early, Trevor would have missed her altogether. Now, if he hurried, he might at least be able to secure her address.

Please, Lord, if she is the woman for me, please let me catch her.

Once again he cracked the whip over the horse's back and veered to miss a carriage coming from the opposite direction.

Rose's leaving both disappointed and invigorated Trevor. Never had a woman walked away from the possibility of his courtship. Absolutely never. For the first time, Trevor was pursuing a woman. Literally. His mounting desire to know Rose better seemed to rival the size of the westward mountain peaks.

As he rounded the last turn, the brick train station came into clear view. And behind it, the eight o'clock train. Within seconds, Trevor secured his horse, raced through the station, and toward the train.

"Sir . . . you need a ticket to board," a tense mail voice called.

Trevor ignored him. At each car he halted and scanned the numerous passengers. Rose was on one of these cars. Could he find her?

The train whistle blew.

His pulse leapt.

The steam hissed.

The shining steel wheels started their laborious turning.

"Miss Brandon! Miss Brandon!" Trevor called, running to keep up with the train. Only if she were at a window seat on this side of the train would Trevor see her.

O Lord, if I can't talk with her, let me see her.

If he could at least make eye contact with Rose, perhaps she would begin to understand just how much she fascinated him.

The train continued its slow crawl. Trevor sped up. His legs ached with the strain.

"Miss Brandon!" he called again, as if she could somehow hear him.

Suddenly he caught sight of a familiar profile sitting near the window of a wheat-colored car. A profile with hair, the color of chestnuts, piled high under a jade-colored hat.

Trevor raced forward, his lungs feeling as if they would explode with every breath of the frigid air. At last he trotted parallel to her window. As she glanced out the window and looked down, her dark eyes widened in shock.

"I must see you again, Miss Brandon! I'll find you in Colorado Springs!" Trevor yelled above the thumping of the wheels against the tracks.

She stood.

The train picked up speed.

And she was gone.

Trevor halted and stared after the retreating train. Was his heart still with him? Or was it speeding toward Colorado Springs? At once Trevor felt empty and joyous and forlorn. His heart was bound for Colorado Springs. If he were ever to see it again, he would have to go get it. Shoulders slumped forward, he gasped and pondered the bittersweet moment.

For weeks Trevor had prayed for God's guidance in quitting his medical partnership and opening a free clinic for the poor. Once he had decided to leave his partnership, Trevor had received a good dose of flack from his two partners as well as from his own father. As always, Oliver backed Trevor's decision. Two days ago Trevor had left his medical office for the last time. Now he was free. Free to pursue his new practice in Denver, or so he had thought.

Until Rose.

As he turned to leave, Trevor pondered God's timing. Last week his professional commitments would not have allowed him to take a spontaneous trip to Colorado Springs. Today he could. Perhaps the Lord had brought Rose into his life at just the right moment. Just when Trevor's life was already in transition.

SAME DAY
12:30 P.M.

"Father—" Trevor knocked lightly on the office door.

No answer. Another knock. Still, no answer.

Dreading what he most likely would find, Trevor turned the sculptured brass knob and peered around the door. Sure enough, his father lay sprawled on the burgundy leather sofa, staring into the dying fire, a half empty bottle of whiskey in hand.

Trevor, pursing his lips, deposited his oversized traveling case outside the door and approached his father, who was shrouded in the smells of alcohol and cigars. "I'll be spending a few days in Colorado Springs. I wanted to let you know I'll be gone."

"What for?" Riley slurred, glaring up at his son with bloodshot eyes. "Chasing L-Lorene's skirts?"

"Who?"

"Lorene! Lorene D-Daley!"

Trevor remembered the story Rose told of her grandmother. "No, Father. Lorene is dead," Trevor said, his voice much calmer than his emotions. Seeing his father like this always infuriated Trevor. He had repeatedly warned Riley that this excessive drinking could be fatal. "I'm going to visit her granddaughter."

"That family is—is nothing but a bunch of l-lying snobs!" Riley hurled the whisky bottle into the fire's glowing embers. The crash sent coals bursting into flames as they fed on the alcohol. Riley stood and leered at his only son. "And I won't—won't have you r-ruining our name with—with theirs!"

Silently Trevor stared at his father, pondering who the man really was. Riley had never allowed Trevor close enough to know him. Trevor wasn't even sure how he truly felt about his father. Was it love? Or just pity? An ocean of sadness washed over Trevor.

This man before him must have once loved Lorene Daley Brandon. Loved her deeply. But his love had fermented into a venomous mixture of bitterness and hatred.

Trevor wondered how his own mother fit into the whole picture. According to Oliver, she had been from a family of great fortune. And she was beautiful. Trevor didn't remember much, but he did remember the beauty. By the time Riley married her, he had already amassed most of his wealth. He seemed to have the touch of Midas when buying and selling property. Riley took that talent to the New York Stock Exchange and made his fortune. Had he also "bought" his young wife? And had she been forced to live in Lorene's shadow until her death in her second pregnancy?

"As I was saying, I'm going to be in Colorado Springs for a few days." Trevor reached to assist his father back to the couch.

Riley knocked his hand away and staggered toward the massive desk. "I tell you—stay—stay away from those people." He pivoted to face Trevor.

Silence.

As an adult, Trevor had gone against his father's wishes several times. Riley protested Trevor's studying medicine in England. Through the years, Riley tried to arrange a couple of unsuitable marriages for Trevor. And, of course, Riley thought Trevor insane for wanting to establish a medical practice for the poor.

Now Trevor would once more choose his own dreams. "But I must go, Father," he said firmly.

"You must! You must!" Riley roared. Arms flailing, he rushed toward his son.

Trevor caught him as he tripped over his own feet.

Once Riley regained his balance, he rejected Trevor's assistance and lunged toward the chair behind the desk. Collapsing into it, he pulled out a drawer and produced the bottle of whiskey that he sipped whenever he didn't want to walk across the room to his bar. Crudely, Riley bit the cork, pulled it out with a muffled pop, and spit it onto the blue Persian rug. After a generous guzzle, he set the bottle on the desk with a decisive thud.

"If you g-go to Colorado Springs after that—that Brandon woman, I'll—I'll dis-disinherit you," he slurred. Then Riley's head nodded, his eyes closed, and he slumped over the desk.

An astonished blink. This was a first. Trevor Riley Sr. had never threatened his son with disinheritance. Did he know what he was saying, or was the whiskey talking? Staring at his father's sleeping form, Trevor deliberated his options— disinheritance with Rose or wealth without her. He recalled the last twenty-four hours: Rose at his door, Rose in the electric carriage, Rose during dinner, Rose as he kissed her hand, Rose at the train window. And Trevor knew there was no choice. If his father meant what he said, then so be it. Trevor could support himself. And easily. He had done exactly that since he began his medical practice anyway. No amount of money was worth his freedom, was worth sacrificing his friendship with Rose.

If Trevor was to follow Rose today, he must leave soon. The number nine Canyon City Passenger Train departed for Colorado Springs at 1:15. He had little time to spare. Trevor must find Oliver. Oliver would see to the situation. Would settle the older man in bed. Would wire Trevor of his condition.

As he turned for the door, Trevor noticed his father's favorite Irish Setter dozing near the sofa. Languidly the dog rolled onto his back and turned his stomach toward the dying fire. The presence of the dog was nothing unusual, but what he lay upon was. A Wedding-Ring quilt. Trevor had never seen the quilt Rose had delivered the day before. At dinner she had told him it was crafted in the colors of Christmas. This was the piece that had been the token of love between his father and Rose's grandmother. And his father was using it as a dog mat!

Gritting his teeth, Trevor rushed forward, grabbed the quilt's edge, and unceremoniously dumped the unsuspecting dog from it. With a surprised yelp, the dog lowered its tail and skulked across the room. Trevor gave the quilt several rough shakes, folded it, and tucked it under his arm. If love determined ownership, then this cloth memento belonged to Rose, not his father.

Chapter Five

October marched into Colorado Springs with a three-inch dusting of snow that had been hovering over the mountains for two days. Shivering against the cold, Rose clicked on the electric wall lamps around the grocery store. Her father was downstairs stoking the coal furnace. Rose's job was to build a fire in the small fireplace, which added a touch of home to the grocery store. She picked up the poker and stirred the coals left over from the previous evening. Rose placed a generous supply of fragrant pine knots on the coals, then the sticks of wood. In minutes fresh flames licked at the wood to produce a balsamy odor. Rose moved to the spacious store's large front window, which said Brandons' Grocery Store in red.

As usual, she and her parents were early risers. Her mother was preparing breakfast in the tiny kitchen upstairs, and her father would soon be up from the basement to sweep the snow from the store's walkway.

Hopefully the new snow would invigorate the local citizenry, and the store would see a profitable day. Rose was always amused at how much higher sales were after such a change in weather. Ma Brandon used to quip, "These customers are like a bunch of frisky puppies. They think they need to go out and play in the snow." Rose smiled with the memory of her spunky grandmother. She also blotted a tear.

What would Ma Brandon think of Rose's encounter with Trevor? She would probably chuckle, especially at Trevor's picking Rose up and depositing her in the electric carriage. Rose felt anything but humorous.

Instead, she experienced her own dose of restlessness. Not from the change in weather. Her restlessness had started when she met Dr. Riley. Rose peered through the dawn at the three-story, red brick buildings lining Cascade Street. Would she ever see Trevor again? She had left the inn yesterday morning, planning to expunge him from her thoughts. That had been easier said than done. During the whole two-and-a-half hour train ride, during her evening at home, during her restless night, Rose had thought of Trevor and Trevor only.

His depth of character.

His sparkling, pale eyes.

His charming smile.

His chasing the train like a wild adolescent.

His vow to follow her to Colorado Springs.

The last memories left Rose simultaneously thrilled and ashamed. She had rudely walked away from her promise to breakfast with Trevor. Still he had run after her. And she had barely heard him say, "I'll find you in Colorado Springs." Rose had stood in the train and watched his form until it disappeared from view. Could he suspect that Rose regretted her hasty departure?

Who was Dr. Trevor Riley, anyway? What stuff was he really made of? He seemed the antithesis of most of the wealthy men Rose had known. But despite all that, Trevor was still wealthy. Rose wasn't sure she could ever overcome her aversion for his class enough to build a relationship with him. She simply wasn't prepared to join the hierarchical ranks of pretentious society. Not for any man. Turning from the window, Rose wondered if he really would come to Colorado Springs to find her. And, if he did, how could she ever explain the truth to him?

She took in a lungful of air and slowly exhaled. She must begin the day. Out of habit, she straightened some merchandise—cans of syrup, bags of dried beans, citrus fruit shipped from California.

As she drifted back up the stairs, another image troubled her. Ma Brandon's worn Bible lay unopened on Rose's nightstand. For the past few weeks, Rose had missed her morning appointment with God. She had told Trevor she only courted men who shared her faith in Christ. But exactly how strong was her faith? Guilt, like a surgeon's scalpel, pierced her soul.

At the top of the stairs, Rose walked across the creaking wooden floor toward her bedroom and the waiting Bible. Once her palm encountered the cold, glass knob, she halted. Something deep in the recesses of her heart resisted the thought of speaking with God. At once she felt troubled and anxious and wanted to hide.

As if she were running from her own thoughts, Rose released the glass knob and rushed for the kitchen. Her mother needed help with breakfast.

Rose would think about God later.

Her prediction of the change in weather stimulating business was well grounded. The brilliant sunshine turned the fresh snow into a frosting of diamonds. By midmorning the Brandons had already seen a generous number of customers. When a lull occurred at eleven, Rose and her parents began immediately restocking and straightening shelves.

"You would think it was the week before Christmas," Zebulun Brandon said, a joyous lilt to his voice. He stood behind the counter, filling the large glass canisters with fresh coffee beans and tea leaves.

"Perhaps we should put out some of our Christmas merchandise left over from last year," Rose suggested as she straightened the mess a toddler had made of the brooms. She referred to the inexpensive tree ornaments, candles, bows, and bells that Zebulun always stocked.

"What a good idea!" Iris Brandon stopped in the middle of arranging the canned goods to nod her approval.

"But it's just now October," Zebulun protested. "None of the other grocery stores will be doing such. Our customers will think we're crazy."

"So, let them think it!" Rose walked toward her father. "At least they'll be thinking about our store," she said with a shrug. "Besides, Mr. Calcutta always opens his Christmas Store by the first of November. Who knows? We might beat him to a few sales."

A sparkle of mirth played in Zebulun's brown eyes. "Oh, why not?"

A round of clapping resounded from the canned goods.

Rose's family possessed a certain zeal for Christmas. It was the one time of year when her parents put aside their worries and enjoyed themselves. Really enjoyed themselves. Some years Christmas was the only time Rose and her father shared any rapport whatsoever. Zebulun Brandon seemed forever too preoccupied with his debits and credits the rest of the year.

So Rose's desire to put out the leftover Christmas merchandise stemmed not only from the possibility of selling the items but also from her need to feel a camaraderie with her parents. Ma Brandon and Rose had shared that camaraderie the year round, and Rose desperately missed her grandmother. Perhaps an early display of the Christmas merchandise would cheer Rose and sweeten the relationship with her parents.

As she headed toward the storage room, the bell on the door jingled merrily. Immediately, Rose turned around and headed toward the customer, hidden from view by a display of canned vegetables. But as soon as she saw the plump woman with rouged cheeks, she wanted to groan.

Mrs. Mary F. Rothlord. The wife of Edward T. Rothlord II. The mother of Edward T. Rothlord III. The mistress of Rothlord Manor. The woman who would have been Rose's mother-in-law had Rose accepted Edward's proposal last summer. She wore her costly fur coat and matching hat like a queen wearing the crown jewels.

Rose stifled two primitive reactions. First, to run. And second, to blurt, "What are you doing here?" All of Colorado Springs knew that Mrs. Rothlord never, absolutely never, did her own shopping. That was one of the tasks she assigned to her servants.

Soon the socialite made it vividly clear why she was shopping today and why she had chosen Brandons' Grocery Store.

"Rose, dear, there you are," Mrs. Rothlord began in her nasal tones. "I desperately need some coffee. We ran out this morning. I was wondering if you would be so kind as to grind three one pound bags for me and deliver them to the manor? You know how I detest my servants taking the time to grind it at home."

Clamping her teeth, Rose marched toward the glass coffee canister, which her father had just refilled. Where was he anyway? She scanned the store and caught a last glimpse of his white shirt as he ducked into his office. He probably didn't want to encounter Madame Rothlord any more than Rose did. But their reasons were totally different. Rose wanted to avoid the woman for the same reason she wanted to avoid most of the wealthy. Mrs. Rothlord's snobbery nauseated her. Zebulun Brandon, on the other hand, had been utterly humiliated when Rose rejected Edward's proposal.

"We aren't busy at the moment, Mrs. Rothlord," Rose said in an attempt to sound cheerful. "I'll be perfectly happy to grind the coffee while you wait."

"Oh, but I don't have time, dear," the old lady oozed, a malicious spark in her round, black eyes—eyes of a serpent.

"It will only take a few minutes. Really." Rose, turning toward the glass jar, calculated the number of destitute children Mrs. Rothlord could feed and clothe if she didn't purchase so many luxury items. The fur coat alone might provide a year's care for ten children. Rose pictured the coal deliverers of Rothlord Coal Industries and their tattered children she saw every Saturday. Last year Rose had talked her parents into allowing her to take the week's worth of leftover fruit and produce to the poor. The Brandons would have discarded it anyway. Why not give it to somebody who desperately needed it? As Rose contemplated those children's thin frames and smudged faces, her fury burned all the brighter at the selfishness Mrs. Rothlord represented.

Under no circumstances was Rose going to deliver anything to Rothlord Manor. If Madame Rothlord insisted on a delivery, then Rose would tell her to take her business to Angle's Grocery on Bijou Street. They would be happy to deliver the coffee.

Her lips pursed, Rose began measuring the coffee beans. When the bell on the door rang again, she glimpsed her mother moving toward the front. Maybe if enough customers crowded in, Mrs. Rothlord would simply leave.

"But dear," the old lady said, growing more condescending by the second. "You do not understand. We are having a reception tonight for my son's fiancée, Wanda. Wanda Pate." She hesitated and continued in a measured voice, "Do you know her?"

"Of course." *And God help her.* Rose refused to do anything but smile. "Her father owns the bank, doesn't he?"

"Yes. And I must say how eternally glad our family is that dear Edward has waited until now to get married."

Rose paused in the middle of weighing the first pound of fragrant coffee. So. Mary's scheme was clear. Her order for coffee was but a thin cover for a more malicious motive. She had come to play her trump card. How little this woman understood Rose. Rose couldn't care less what Edward F. Rothlord III did or whom he chose to marry. Rose had spent two months trying to convince Edward himself of that very truth. Finally, when she soundly turned down his proposal, he came to the realization that there was a woman alive who would actually reject his wealth and "charm."

"We would love to have you at the reception tonight, Rose. As an old friend of Edward's you would be more than welcome."

"I'm sure I would be," Rose said, her jaw set firmly.

"Perhaps you could come early and bring the coffee then. Yes! What a splendid idea. That way, you could visit with Wanda." The matron removed her black leather gloves, strategically placing her bejeweled fingers on the wooden countertop. As Rose examined one particularly large ruby, she wondered if the Rothlords ever felt guilty for all the money they wasted on such useless possessions while so many children went without the necessities of life.

"But perhaps," the socialite continued, "in my eagerness to include you, I haven't given you sufficient time to find an appropriate dress." She pointedly eyed Rose's brown homespun work skirt and plain beige blouse.

"I greatly appreciate your offer, Mrs. Rothlord," Rose said in an overly polite tone. "But I'm afraid—"

"Miss Brandon has promised to have a meal with me, and I was hoping for tonight," a familiar voice interrupted.

Turning wide eyes toward that voice, Rose stared into the face of Dr. Trevor Riley.

The same erect frame.

The same raven-black hair.

The same charming smile.

CHAPTER SIX

The next second seemed an eternity. Trevor wasn't sure who was more astounded. The fair Iris Brandon, standing wide-eyed at his side. The haughty Mrs. Rothlord, her mouth gaping. Or Rose, whose cheeks were flushing a particularly charming shade of scarlet.

"You didn't think I was going to forget your promise, did you, Miss Brandon?"

"I—"

Trevor addressed the plump, fur-trimmed woman. "Allow me to introduce myself. Dr. Trevor Riley, at your service. My father owns Riley Investments in Denver. You may have heard of us?" A slight bow.

"Uh . . . yes . . . I believe my husband has done business with your . . . your father," she stammered.

"How delightful, then, that we share a mutual acquaintance. Miss Brandon's family and mine have known each other since before the Civil War."

"Oh, really?"

"Yes." After slipping into the store, Trevor had briefly informed Rose's mother that he was there to call on her daughter. Then he had politely stood back and awaited Rose's completion of the sale. However, Trevor had heard enough of Mrs. Rothlord's disgusting comments to raise his ire and prompt his interruption. He seldom used his proper title in a social setting and never, absolutely never, referred to his father's business. But this situation called for something different. Rose deserved better treatment. Trevor wasn't about to let this woman leave before she realized a thing or two. "And I believe I heard Miss Brandon refer to you as Mrs. Rothlord. Am I correct?"

"Yes," she said, scrutinizing Trevor as if he had just told her he lived on the moon.

"Well, as a friend of Miss Brandon's it is a great pleasure to meet you. I'm terribly sorry that I have interfered with your plans for this evening with Miss Brandon. Please accept my humble apologies. But, as I've already mentioned, Miss Brandon did promise to dine with me."

"That's perfectly fine," Madame Rothlord said, her eyes narrowing.

"If you would like," Trevor continued, "I would be delighted to deliver your coffee myself. I'm sure Miss Brandon would willingly give me the directions to your home." He looked toward Rose, who didn't appear as pleased with him as he had hoped.

"That's not necessary," Mrs. Rothlord clipped. "I'll send a servant after it."

Before Trevor could politely insist on delivering the coffee, she stalked out the door and slammed it behind her. The bell's puny tinkling contrasted with the door's resounding bang.

"Well! I never!" Iris Brandon exclaimed through a chuckle.

Trevor produced what he hoped was his most endearing smile and directed it toward Rose. "Now that we've cleared the . . . um . . . air, what time would you like to meet me this evening?"

"I never said I would dine with you tonight," she returned peevishly, her eyes flashing fire.

"No, but you did say you would dine with me yesterday morning," he said with a hopeful smile. Rose probably had no idea how unsure he felt with her, and Trevor was determined not to let her see his uncertainty.

She was angry. Clearly angry.

Her anger definitely was not part of his plan. Trevor had never suspected that his handling of Mrs. Rothlord would reap this reaction. He had expected Rose to be eternally grateful for his intervention. But here she stood ready to have his head.

How invigorating!

Finally, Trevor had met a woman who possessed the character to actually oppose him. "Since you were . . . prevented from our meeting yesterday morning, I assumed you would be willing to fulfill your promise this evening."

"You are more than welcome to dine with us tonight," Mrs. Brandon interjected, her kind smile encouraging Trevor.

"Mother," Rose said evenly, her lips stiff. "I would like to speak with Dr. Riley upstairs. Do you think you and Father can handle the customers while I'm gone?"

"But of course," Mrs. Brandon said, her hazel eyes glimmering with approval and curiosity.

Rose turned to Trevor. "If you will please follow me, I would appreciate a word with you, Dr. Riley."

Trevor produced a slight bow. "Consider my time yours." His heart flipped like a schoolboy's. *What a fascinating woman!* He followed her up the creaking stairs and entered the apartment's shadowed hallway. As soon as she closed the door behind them, Rose glared at him.

"Exactly what did you think you were doing back there?" she whispered loudly.

"What do you mean?"

"You know exactly what I mean! I never asked you to hunt me down, throw your family name around, and drop innuendos on my behalf."

"But I was just trying to—"

"You were trying to impress Mrs. Rothlord with your wealth. That's what you were trying to do. And you were trying to convince her of my worth because of my association with you."

"But she was behaving in an unforgivable manner. I was just—"

"I've got news for you, Dr. Trevor Riley!" She jabbed her index finger into the middle of his chest. "I'm of worth because I am a human being and because God made me. It has nothing—absolutely nothing—to do with money or position or the lack of it, for that matter!"

"I—"

"And I don't care what the Rothlords in our world think or say or do." Her eyes filled with tears of fury. "It has absolutely no bearing on me whether she believes me to be of worth or not! Her standard of what is worthy is based on nothing but a lie." Another jab with her index finger. "And you should be ashamed of yourself for buying into her values."

Trevor blinked. He had known Rose Brandon for a grand total of forty-eight hours. Already she was turning his world topsy-turvy. Because of Oliver's careful tutelage, Trevor had believed himself completely removed from his father's values.

Had he been fooling himself?

Why had he so readily played Mrs. Rothlord's game? It wasn't like him. But then neither was chasing after a train. The reason for his encounter with Mrs. Rothlord immediately became poignantly clear.

Rose Brandon.

His need to defend her, to protect her, had dashed away all

logic. He should have known that Rose would never approve of his actions with Mrs. Rothlord. Every other woman in Colorado might. But not Rose.

As she awaited his response, Trevor drank in the flush of her cheeks, the sparkle of her eyes, the cute turn of her nose. His thoughts blurred, and he momentarily forgot what they were discussing. All he could contemplate was the incredible woman before him. Her lavender scent . . .

"Well!" she demanded, stomping her foot. "Are you going to answer me?"

"Uh . . . what were you saying?"

"I was saying—," she began through gritted teeth, "that I didn't appreciate your handling of Mrs. Rothlord." Her voice rose in agitation and echoed down the narrow hall.

"And I was thinking how much I would like to hold you." Trevor dared stroke Rose's cheek and reveled in anticipation of her response. Would she jerk from him or welcome his affection?

As if his very touch cast a spell on her, Rose took a shuddering breath and half closed her eyes.

"Rose?" Trevor breathed, barely realizing he had overthrown decorum in the familiar use of her name.

"Trevor, I . . ." She swallowed. "I . . ."

He pulled her into his arms and drank in the lavender smell of her hair, piled atop her head. Trevor had never been so complete. He felt as if his arms were made for this particular purpose at this particular time. To hold Rose Brandon. To hope that she would care for him.

"Would you please join me for dinner?" he whispered into her ear. "I traveled nearly seventy miles and searched you out just for the privilege."

"Yes," she muttered against his handsome black overcoat.

Did regret lace her simple answer? Trevor prayed he had imagined it. Prayed that Rose would enjoy the evening as much as he planned to.

With this tender moment, Trevor's ardent courtship began. For the next two months he wooed Rose. Much to the delight of her family. Much to the delight of Trevor. Yet he often had moments of doubt, wondering whether Rose was truly growing to love him as he was growing to love her. Even though a certain admiration glowed in her eyes when she was near, Trevor still detected a shadow. A faint shadow that left him more than a bit uneasy.

During these weeks of courtship, Trevor took up residence in a nearby hotel suite and maintained a regular correspondence with Oliver. His old friend supplied a running report on the senior Riley's health and his continued bouts of drunkenness. Even though Trevor had written to his father, he had never once received a reply. Occasionally Trevor wondered if his father would follow through with the threat to disinherit him. Just in case, Trevor had tucked away the money he had saved from his earnings and drew on his trust fund these last two months.

He seriously sought God regarding his future. More and more he felt that he should settle in Colorado Springs permanently. He felt so strongly about it that he had even given verbal agreement on leasing an office with adjacent living quarters. Even though he still hesitated to share with Rose his dream of serving the poor, she had shown him a great medical need among the less fortunate in Colorado Springs. If Riley didn't disinherit him and Rose accepted Trevor's proposal, they could minister to those families together. What a joy he felt at the thought of having Rose by his side.

Last week he had received Zebulun Brandon's cheerful permission to propose. Soon he would share his dream of service with Rose and ask her to be his wife. If she accepted, he would surprise her with her grandmother's Wedding Ring quilt. As they used the quilt in their home, it would be a constant reminder of how their love began.

With all these thoughts occupying his mind, Trevor answered the knock on his hotel door late one December afternoon to behold Oliver's smiling, radiant face.

"Trevor, my boy!" Oliver grabbed Trevor's arms, then embraced him.

Delighted to see his graying friend, Trevor returned the hug and ushered Oliver into his hotel suite's sitting room. Trevor was to dine with Rose's family at six. Now Oliver could join him. "What an absolutely wonderful surprise. I wasn't expecting you. Did I miss a letter telling me you were coming?"

Oliver, his blue eyes sparkling, settled his thin frame on the floral settee. "No indeed. This is as much a surprise to me as it is to you. After I awoke this morning, your father asked me to hand deliver a letter to you."

"Oh?" Trevor felt a mixture of dread and relief. At last his father had written. "And how does this day find Father?" He sat in the wing chair that matched the settee.

A cloud entered Oliver's eyes, and he shook his head. "I must say Mr. Riley seems to be doing tolerably well physically. But—" Oliver worried the chain on his pocket watch.

"I see." Trevor didn't need to hear more. As he had done a thousand times before, Trevor once again wondered what it would take to bring his father to his knees.

"Well . . ." Oliver rummaged through his tan carpetbag. "Here's his letter."

"Thanks." Trevor accepted the sealed beige envelope, his hands trembling in anticipation.

"Do I happen to smell fresh tea?"

"Indeed you do. I just ordered a pot of mint tea not ten minutes ago. Help yourself to a cup while I read the letter." Trevor motioned to the silver-plated tea service sitting on the cherry drop-leaf table near the window.

"Delightful . . . delightful," Oliver muttered, walking toward the tea.

Within seconds Trevor opened the brief, scrawled note and began devouring its contents:

Trevor,

I have exercised enough patience with you. If you do not return home within the week, I will be forced to action. I will not permit my son to ruin our family name and fortune by associating with any kin of Lorene Daley. You will return home within the week, or I will disinherit you.

Trevor Riley Sr.

So Riley had finally spoken. Trevor could not deny that he was shaken. All his life he had desired his father's approval. Despite the senior Riley's coldness. Despite his selfishness. Trevor had still needed his blessing. Oliver had filled the void in Trevor's life as much as a surrogate father could. Nonetheless, deep inside Trevor, a small boy cried because he would never know his father's approval. This letter was the final stroke in a lifetime of rejection. Whether Riley would carry out his threat remained to be seen. But whether he did or didn't figured little into Trevor's decision.

Trevor would not return to Denver.

He would not leave Rose.

He would not enslave himself to his father's money.

O Lord, Trevor breathed. *Give me the strength to survive this tearing in my relationship with Father. And continue to direct me, Lord. Show me your path. Help me to rely on you.*

Suddenly Trevor experienced a deep peace, an ocean of love. And he knew that whatever his earthly father's decision, he would always have his heavenly Father. He would have Oliver. And, if Rose accepted his proposal that evening, he would have her.

Chapter Seven

While awaiting Trevor's arrival for dinner, Rose slipped down to the store. Preferring the gentle light of her candle, she walked toward the eight-foot Christmas tree, which filled the air with the evergreen smells of the holiday. After Thanksgiving she and her parents had decorated the store and apartment with all the usual Christmas trimmings. Garland. Wreaths. Red bows. Mistletoe. Christmas cards from their many friends. Then, the Christmas trees. One upstairs. One downstairs in the store. They had decked the store tree in a collection of expensive ornaments that Zebulun had ordered from Denver. Somehow, that lover of Christmas decor had struck a deal with the well-known artist who crafted the ornaments. Zebulun would pay for only what he sold. The rest he could return.

During the last week, Rose had lovingly admired each of the handpainted ornaments—stars, squares, ovals, circles. In varying colors of silk, all were plump with cotton stuffing and decorated with gold-toned fringe and tassels. Hand painted with scenes from the very first Christmas, these ornaments pulled at Rose as no other expensive item ever had. Rose would have loved to have several of them, not because of their material value, but because of their spiritual implications. They each seemed to capture the very soul of the true meaning of Christmas. Ironically Rose couldn't afford *one* of them. Even at the artist's cost. With a wishful sigh, she deposited her candle on the nearby counter and removed her favorite ornament from the tree—a red star painted with a manger scene.

Soon her mind drifted to a more troubling decision, and the ornament she held blurred. Earlier that day, Rose's father hinted that Trevor had asked permission to propose. Deep in her heart, Rose had known all along that this whole courtship would build to Trevor's requesting her hand in marriage. That was the reason she had run from him in Denver. Rose did not want to become part of the life he represented. The very thought of having to attend society functions with women like Mrs. Rothlord nauseated her.

Yet she anticipated Trevor's every word, his every smile, his touch. What a wretched ordeal. Was she in love with him? Rose was unsure. Or at least she thought she was unsure. Perhaps she just didn't want to know the truth of the matter.

Many times in the last few hours she had tried to pray about Trevor's pending proposal. But, as with all of her prayers recently, Rose didn't feel that God had heard her. Again she experienced that recurring need to hide from God.

A sigh. She focused on the star-shaped ornament once more. If only she had an angel to direct her as Mary and Joseph had.

"Pretty, isn't it?" Trevor uttered from behind her.

Rose jumped. "You scared me!" She pivoted to face the man who had brightened her life in a way no man ever had. He smiled, and her pulse quickened.

"Sorry. With all the noise I made coming down the stairs, I didn't think I was sneaking up on you."

"I was distracted."

"Oliver and I took the outside stairs up to the apartment. If I had known you were in the store, I would have knocked on the door."

"Mr. Ghaliger is here?"

"Yes. He arrived just this afternoon. He'll be joining us for dinner. Do you mind?"

"No. Not in the least." Uncomfortable with Trevor so close, she averted her gaze toward the star-shaped ornament.

"A penny for your thoughts," he teased.

"Actually, I was admiring these ornaments," she said, still avoiding his gaze. "Have you seen them? We got them a few days ago."

"I don't believe I have." He examined the tree, loaded with the various ornaments. "Exquisite."

"Yes." She dangled the star from her index finger. "This one is my favorite."

"Will you put it on your tree upstairs then?"

She chuckled. "I doubt it. These things cost the earth." Rose replaced the ornament, tucked her hand through the crook of Trevor's arm, and began walking toward the stairs. Being alone with Trevor in the shadowed store left Rose more than a little uneasy. She was afraid, terribly afraid, he was looking for the best opportunity to propose. Rose did not want to give him that opportunity. Not now. Not tonight. She didn't know her heart enough to give him an answer.

"Are you going to leave the candle?" he queried, looking over his shoulder.

"The candle. I almost forgot. Thank you." She went to retrieve the candle only to have him follow her.

"Rose . . . there's something I've been praying about and I

feel I must discuss with you." His voice shook with uncertainty.

The time had come.

Trevor was about to propose.

She hadn't been able to put him off.

Her stomach fluttering, Rose gazed at the candle's burning wick and the tiny moth that danced around the flame. She felt like that moth. And Trevor was the flame. He both lured her and repelled her. She lived for the moments they shared. Yet Rose despised the world from which he came. If that moth flew too close to the fire, it would meet its demise. Would Rose likewise shrivel and die if she entered Trevor's world?

She felt him watching, waiting for some response.

"Yes, what is it?" she rasped.

Trevor lifted her chin with the tips of his trembling fingers. Rose had no choice but to look into his eyes.

"I love you, Rose." He stroked her cheek.

A shudder, all delicious and warm, flowed down her spine and left Rose weak from his touch.

"I don't think that's a surprise, is it?" he teased.

A wobbly smile.

"I . . ." He swallowed. "Rose . . . I . . ."

Impulsively, Rose placed her fingers over his lips. To halt the proposal. To sooth Trevor's nerves. But her touch only heightened the tension between them. Trevor kissed her fingers. Then her palm. Her wrist.

Many times Rose had thought Trevor would kiss her. Many times she would have willingly responded. But never had she anticipated the explosion of emotion she felt now as his lips brushed hers in a gentle kiss. Trevor's arms tightened as he pulled her closer.

At last he cupped her face in his hands and whispered against her lips, "Ah, Rose. None of this has gone as I anticipated." Despite his denial, a spark of glee twinkled in his eyes. "I didn't plan to kiss you until after you accepted my proposal." His voice had taken on a nuance of assurance, as if Trevor assumed her answer would be yes.

An alarm clanged within Rose. Despite her strong attraction to him, she still had doubts. Plenty of doubts. Would he understand? She inched back.

"There's so much I want to share with you that I haven't already shared. I have a wonderful plan concerning—"

"Trevor," Rose interrupted, desperate that he should understand exactly where she stood. "There are also things *I* have refrained from sharing with *you*." She pulled away and went back to her observation of that fated moth, still flirting with the candle.

Rose felt cold without Trevor's arms around her. But she must be honest with Trevor.

"Oh?" he said cautiously.

"Yes. I—" She cleared her throat. "Father hinted today that you might be proposing."

"He did, did he?"

Nodding, she kept her focus on the moth. "I think he wanted to make sure I understood his opinion on the matter."

"Which is?"

"Well, he never exactly said it, but I felt like he might bury me alive if I didn't accept."

"At least I have your family's approval."

She chuckled nervously. "Before I say what I have to say, I want you to know that I have the utmost respect . . . the . . . the highest regard for you—"

"Does that in any way relate to love?"

Rose's cheeks grew uncomfortably warm. She had yet to sort through her emotions. How could she tell him she loved him? Rose studied the toes of his shiny black leather boots. She grew flustered and anxious and unsure of exactly what to do.

"Perhaps we should just repeat the kiss." He stepped toward her.

She stumbled backward. "No, no, I don't think that would . . . That is, I don't believe we should . . . I mean I can't seem to think straight when . . ." She gripped the sides of her dark green skirt.

His longing gaze trailed to her lips. "I know. Neither can I."

She straightened her shoulders and looked him in the eye. "Trevor," Rose said firmly. "I don't think this is the time to . . . to behave in such a manner."

He smiled again, and Rose was reminded of the first moments of their acquaintance and that exasperating, indulging grin of his.

She resisted the temptation to stamp her foot in annoyance. "There's something about . . . about myself which I have yet to reveal to you. Something you might find quite unsettling."

"Oh?" He raised his dark brows in genuine curiosity.

"Yes." She hesitated, wondering exactly how to tell a well-to-do gentleman to whom she had grown uncomfortably attached just how much she detested people of great fortune. "Do you realize that I don't really care much for most of the wealthy?" she asked, feeling a coward for softening the true intensity of her feelings.

"Yes. You have made that fairly obvious."

"Obvious?"

"Of course. I suspected that from the first of our acquaintance. You confirmed it the morning you dragged me upstairs after I rescued you from Mrs. Rothlord."

"I in no way dragged you upstairs."

"But of course you did. I would have gladly discussed our problem here in the store, but—"

She gave in to the need to stamp her foot. "You are distracting me from the point."

"And the point is that I find you highly fascinating for a

myriad of reasons. Only one of which is your refusal to cater to the wealthy."

Her irritation dissolved into confusion. A confusion heightened by his warm appraisal, bathed by the candle-light. Rose swallowed against a throat as dry as sandpaper. "Well, I just . . . I-I find it terribly difficult to . . . That is, I—"

"Are you trying to tell me my wealth is the only obstacle you find in accepting my proposal?"

"Oh, Trevor." She turned her back to him and stared at the Christmas tree, decorated in those beautiful ornaments. Never had Rose felt so torn. Part of her desperately wanted to throw herself into his arms, declare her love, and plan the wedding. Yet another part of her simply could not overcome the fact that she despised what Trevor was. Or perhaps, what he represented. Marrying him would mean going against her own values.

"Have you prayed about this, Rose?"

She whirled to face him. "About what?" she snapped.

"About your attitude toward the wealthy."

"Why do you have to say it like that?"

"I didn't say it any particular way. I just wanted to know if you had consulted God on this."

Rose glared at him. Something about his keen eyes made her extremely uncomfortable. She felt as if he saw more of her than she ever wanted to reveal. "That's a painfully per-sonal question. I—"

"Then let me pose another question," he said. "If I weren't wealthy, would you marry me?"

She couldn't look away, but she knew the answer. He knew it too.

"So," he said with a satisfied smile, "you do love me. You do want to marry me. If you can just get it through your head that my being wealthy doesn't make one difference in who I am."

"You are making some rather startling assumptions, Dr. Riley."

"I am assuming nothing. You informed me all too clearly only minutes ago of your true feelings."

"If you are speaking of our kiss—"

"That's exactly what I'm speaking of." He walked toward her.

She stepped back.

"And I am determined to repeat it." He paused, looking deep into her eyes. "That is, unless you don't want me to."

She gulped. "Trevor . . ."

Then his lips brushed hers once more.

Eyes narrowed, he pulled away. "When will you give me your answer?"

"Uh . . ." The world was still tilting, and Rose couldn't comprehend his meaning.

"Would Christmas Day be too soon?" He stroked her cheek. "Could you tell me by Christmas whether you will accept my proposal? That's two full weeks."

"Do I have a choice?" she chided, clinging to his lapel.

His face clouded with uncertainty.

Her heart twisted in regret. "Oh, Trevor," she said through threatening tears. "Why do you have to be so wealthy?" Rose rested her forehead against his chest. A shuddering breath.

"By Christmas?" he whispered, ignoring her outburst.

"Yes, by Christmas. But . . . but you must grant me the freedom of making my decision alone."

"So I should keep my distance then. Is that it?"

"Do you mind so terribly?" She looked up into a face that was greatly pained at the thought. "It's just that . . . that when I'm with you, I can't seem to think. My common sense goes all askew, and—"

"That's tremendously good news," he teased.

Although he teased her, Trevor was quaking inside. This must be the most poignant form of poetic justice. His whole life, Trevor had shied from women who wanted him because of his fortune. Now he had fallen in love with one who *didn't* want him because of his fortune.

Should he tell her his father had threatened to disinherit him? As he poised his lips to tell her the news, Trevor stifled it. No. He wouldn't tell her. Riley had not yet officially disinherited him. And Trevor wanted Rose to accept him regardless of his financial standing. Whether he was wealthy or penniless, Rose must love him just for him or it wasn't true love. If her love was true, it would overcome this prejudice she held against the wealthy.

Even though he had planned to tell her of his desire to start a free medical practice for the poor, Trevor likewise refrained from telling Rose that. She might feel guilty for turning down the proposal of a wealthy man who wanted to serve others. And, out of that guilt, Rose might reverse her decision. Trevor did not want anything but love to drive her acceptance. Besides, he could establish the free practice only if he weren't disinherited.

As he silently released Rose and tucked her hand into the crook of his arm, Trevor prayed with a fervor he had never before experienced. *O Lord, please make her love me just for me.*

"I'll call on you Christmas morning then." With a last, aching smile, he escorted her upstairs to enjoy dinner with Oliver and her family; a dinner he had erroneously hoped would be an engagement celebration.

CHAPTER EIGHT

With a conservative dip of his brush in the bucket of white paint, Trevor began painting the examination room in his recently leased office. Last week he had left his rooms at the Alta Vista Hotel to rent the office on the third floor of a downtown building. The last few days had proved hectic. Oliver and Trevor had settled into the furnished living quarters adjacent to the office. Three days ago Oliver had left for Denver to escort Trevor's medical equipment on the train. Oliver also planned to deliver Trevor's tasteful, though firm, reply letter to Riley Sr. Trevor expected Oliver back sometime today. His arrival couldn't be soon enough.

"Did you hear from Rose while I was away?" Oliver asked amid the squeaking of door hinges.

"Oliver! You're back!" Trevor carefully arranged the paintbrush and paint, wiped his hands on a smudged cloth, then rushed across the empty room to clasp the hand of his friend.

"Yes, yes, I made it soundly." Oliver placed firm hands on Trevor's shoulders. "Now tell me about Rose. Any news?"

"Not a word." Trevor shook his head and tried to hide the dull ache in his heart. Daily, Trevor petitioned God for Rose.

Daily, he placed the whole situation in his Lord's hands. Daily, God supplied a new assurance that all would be according to his will. Trevor would accept whatever that entailed. Even so, his heart still longed for Rose.

"I told her I would be calling on Christmas morning." Trevor was aware Oliver already knew this, but saying it again somehow eased his anxiety.

"That's only a week." Oliver's eyes sparkled.

"I just hope she won't forget me altogether."

"She won't, boy, she won't."

"You know, there's something I've been meaning to ask you to do." Trevor grabbed Oliver's arm to steer him from the exam room and toward his next-door apartment. "Come into the apartment. I left my money clip in my bedroom. And if you would be so kind, I would appreciate your going to Brandon's store and purchasing a Christmas ornament I found Rose admiring the evening I proposed. I would like to give it to her as a gift. If you would, please tell her father or mother to wrap it and give it to her. I'll also send along a note to put with it." Trevor talked until they entered the apartment.

"You want me to go now?"

"Well, yes." He turned and, for the first time, closely examined his friend. "Oh, but you're tired from your journey. How thoughtless of me. I just finished a cup of tea, and there's plenty left. After a spot of tea then, perhaps you would feel like—"

"Of course." Oliver chuckled and gripped Trevor's shoulder. "I won't have one moment of peace until I do."

Trevor removed Oliver's overcoat and settled him in the tiny apartment's sitting room. Sunlight streamed through the many apartment windows, accentuating the furniture's shabby condition. The green settee and two matching chairs were functional, despite the wear. Trevor hoped to replace them, but that depended on his father's decision.

One of the chairs was particularly threadbare, and Trevor

had draped the red and green Wedding-Ring quilt across it. So far, that quilt proved to be Trevor's only attempt at Christmas decorating. He planned to give the quilt to Rose for Christmas, whether she accepted his proposal or not. Trevor knew that as Lorene Brandon had cherished it, so Rose would likewise cherish that heirloom of love.

He tossed another log into the stone fireplace, stirred the fragrant fire, dusted his hands, and turned to Oliver. "Now, for the tea."

"First, the letter," Oliver said, his mouth set grimly. "I think it best for me to serve my own tea while you read what your father has sent." He removed a cream-colored envelope from the inside pocket of his olive-colored jacket.

Trevor relived the moment only a week ago when he had received the letter that threatened his disinheritance. He had responded with only three sentences: "I cannot acquiesce to your demands. Please do what you feel you must. You are in my prayers."

Not bothering to sit down, Trevor ripped open the envelope and scanned the message:

> Trevor,
>
> Because you have chosen to betray me, I have no choice but to disinherit you. I will redirect my money where it is appreciated. As of the date of this letter, your trust fund and position in my will no longer exist. Do not ever bring that Brandon woman near this house.
>
> Trevor Riley Sr.

Sinking into the nearest chair, Trevor dropped the letter onto his lap and covered his face with his hands. He ached from head to foot as a trio of emotions surged through him. The first, uncertainty. The second, freedom. The third, regret.

Uncertainty, because Trevor had never been without his

father's money. And even though he had supported himself the last few years, Trevor had still experienced a certain comfort in knowing he could fall back on his trust fund.

Freedom, because he no longer had to please his father. For the first time in his life, Trevor was his own man. Truly his own man. He recalled all the years others had identified him as the son of Trevor Riley Sr. Even when he had introduced himself to Mrs. Rothlord, Trevor had himself tangled his identity with his father's. Well, now he was Dr. Trevor Riley. Period. And he would make his own life, even without that trust fund. He relaxed against the chair.

The uncertainty vanished.

However, an element of regret remained. Regret, because his father had deteriorated into a sullen, misanthropic, slovenly man. During the last week of Rose's consideration, Trevor had wondered if he was experiencing some of the emotions that his father had experienced when Rose's grandmother rejected him. Forlorn and lonely and half a man. For the first time he began to understand how his father had turned into the ogre that he was. If Rose rejected Trevor, only God's healing power would keep him from his father's fate. With renewed fervor he prayed that the senior Riley would allow God to work that healing in him.

"Are you OK?" Oliver asked, quietly, reverently, as if he were attending a funeral.

Trevor looked up. Oliver had never moved to make his tea. His understanding expression attested to his knowledge of the letter's contents. "Yes. I'm fine. I'm going to be fine." Trevor smiled. A relaxed smile. A smile of emancipation.

Oliver returned the smile. "I do believe you are."

Standing, Trevor dropped the letter and envelope onto the nondescript cherry table between them. "Now for your tea."

"Ah, the tea. How could I have forgotten?"

Lunch. Normally an hour when Rose could relax on her bed after a light meal. Her father usually closed the store from twelve to one o'clock, and the three of them ate, then napped. But napping was not an option for this day. Rose lay on her narrow bed, staring at the ceiling of pine boards, polished and gleaming in the afternoon sunlight. Even though her focus remained on the ceiling, her thoughts roamed to her simple oak nightstand where Ma Brandon's Bible lay.

An unopened Bible. A Bible once loved. Once cherished. Once read. But not by Rose. Not during the past two months.

She thought of Trevor.

Of his proposal.

Of her pending decision.

Several times during the last few days, she had repressed the impulse to spontaneously accept his offer of marriage. One part of Rose wanted nothing more than to spend the rest of her life with Trevor. Another part kept asking if she could indeed overcome her aversion to his wealth. Rose had missed Trevor terribly this last week, and she wondered if she could actually bring herself to reject his proposal. Yet, there was still that intangible something that forever barred her from actually accepting him.

Could Ma Brandon's Bible somehow direct her? Once again Rose felt that overwhelming need to hide from God. Finally tired of the struggle, she dared ask herself the avoided question.

Why do I need to hide?

The answer that entered her thoughts shook her to the bottom of her being. Why had Adam and Eve needed to hide?

She sat up and swung her feet to the floor. "Because they sinned." Rose gripped her indigo work skirt. "But I haven't sinned."

She remembered something Trevor had said: *"Have you prayed about the attitude you have toward the wealthy?"*

She remembered something Ma Brandon had said: *"We are all equally worthy before God. Poor man. Rich man. Slave or free. God loves us all the same. As Christians we should mirror that kind of love."*

She remembered the way she felt toward Mary Rothlord. And toward all the Mary Rothlords of the world.

"But it's because the Rothlords are so . . . so . . . selfish and haughty and prejudiced against the poor," Rose muttered, reaching for the Bible. As her fingers encountered the Word of God, the truth struck her. "And I have been prejudiced against those who are prejudiced against the poor."

That was why Rose had felt the need to hide. She had considered herself better than the wealthy. She had become a participant in the very sin she despised. And that sin itself had stopped her from accepting Trevor's proposal.

"Oh, Father—" Clutching the Bible to her chest, Rose felt as if a veil had been ripped from her eyes. And she saw. She saw for the first time just how wrong she had been. Rose dropped to her knees as a sob escaped her. For half an hour she could form no words. Only tears. The tears of the repentant. While the Holy Spirit reached deep into her being and purged her heart. Rose let the tears flow as if they were the very sin itself, fleeing her soul.

"I am so sorry," she finally prayed. "Without your grace, I would be like Mary Rothlord."

A new torrent of tears flooded her cheeks. She thought of Trevor, of that dear, sweet man. Rose had almost rejected him because of his wealth. He was nothing like Mary Rothlord, yet Rose's prejudice had stopped her from seeing the real Trevor Riley.

Rose's sin was not only against the wealthy. This sin was against Rose herself. She loved Trevor. Rose could no longer deny it. For the first time, she allowed herself to acknowl-

edge her love, all shining and new and glorious. Her prejudice had almost smothered the longings of her own heart.

How could I have been so foolish?

As if she were a doe panting for streams of water, Rose
opened Ma Brandon's Bible and began devouring the
Psalms. So long. It had been so long since she had allowed
these words of wisdom to wash over her soul, to inspire, to
uplift.

A soft knock at the door startled her from her spiritual
pursuits. "Rose?" Iris Brandon called.

"Yes, Mother?" Rose dashed away the remaining tears.

Iris, smiling in delight, opened the door. "You've just received a Christmas present." She extended a gift, wrapped
in red with a green satin bow. "It's from Dr. Riley."

"Trevor? Is he here?" Rose scrambled to her feet.

"No. He sent Mr. Ghaliger. That delightful man Dr. Riley
brought to dine with us last week. Isn't he a dear?"

"Yes." Disappointed that Trevor wasn't in the store, Rose
took the gift and absently fingered the bow.

"Well, aren't you going to open it?" Iris urged. "I simply
cannot wait to see your face."

"Of course." Rose untied the bow and allowed it to slide
to the floor. She recognized the gift wrap as their own, and
that intrigued her all the more. What could Trevor have
given her? Within seconds, she held her favorite tree ornament. The exquisite red silk star, painted with the manger
scene. A note in the box read, "Just so you won't forget me.
Trevor."

"How could I ever forget you?" Rose whispered through
threatening tears.

She read the remaining message that he had written in
smaller letters at the bottom. "I am no longer at the hotel. I
have leased an office with apartment. My address is 417
Pike's Peak Avenue."

Pike's Peak Avenue ran perpendicular to Cascade Street,

the address of Brandons' Grocery. The two intersected in the center of town. Trevor was only a stone's throw away. Rose smiled.

Iris embraced her daughter. "I am so glad for you, dear."

Rose returned the hug. "What do you mean, Mother?"

"Your father and I were so worried since Dr. Riley quit calling this last week, that . . . that . . . And he had asked your father's permission to propose, and we were both wondering why—"

"I should have explained," Rose said, peering into her mother's kind hazel eyes. "But I have been so confused, I—"

"It's quite all right, dear. Your father wanted me to pry for details, but—" a sigh—"for once in my life, I stood up to him. I have felt so guilty for our trying to pressure you into marrying Edward Rothlord—"

"Mother, it isn't necessary for you to—"

"Oh, but it is necessary. It is very necessary." Iris held up her hand. "I must apologize. For me and your father. He's a proud man and may never ask your forgiveness, but I know he is just as delighted as I am with the way things have turned out. Now I can see that you made the best decision. Had you accepted Edward, you would have never been able to marry Dr. Riley."

"But why do you and Father like Trevor? Is it just because of his wealth?"

"No," Iris said firmly. "Not for me. I can't speak for your father, but you know I've never been quite so bent toward—" She cleared her throat. "I think Dr. Riley is a fine gentleman, with or without his wealth. And I think he will make you an excellent husband."

"So do I," Rose said with a smile, glad that at least her mother was more interested in character than in wealth. Rose's father had inherited a preoccupation with money, position, and prestige that had long been distasteful to Rose. Although she respected him as her father, his materialistic bent greatly disturbed her. Instead of adopting her father's attitude toward the poor, Rose found herself rejecting the wealthy.

"Well, I've got to get back down to the store. Your father has run an errand, and no one is down there."

"What time is it?" Rose asked.

"One thirty."

"I didn't realize I had stayed up here so long."

"Did you oversleep?"

"No. I was . . ." Rose hesitated. "I was talking to God."

With a smile, Iris lovingly squeezed her daughter's arm. "Never stop that, Rose. It's what keeps you sweet." She turned for the door.

"Mother, is the store terribly busy right now?"

"No. We've only had Mr. Ghaliger."

"Do you mind if I—" She squared her shoulders. "I would like to go visit Dr. Riley. I think the time has come for me to accept his proposal."

"Of course, dear!" Iris bobbed her head in ready permission. "Even if we were absolutely swimming in customers, I wouldn't dare stop you from that!"

CHAPTER NINE

Trevor paced his modest apartment. To his bedroom. To the sitting room. The kitchen. The dining room. And back to the bedroom. He paused by the wide bedroom window to examine the frozen street, teeming with horses and buggies and people. His gaze roamed westward to the snow-covered mountains. Another band of dark clouds hovered over the peaks and threatened yet more snow.

He should have already gone to the train station and picked up his medical equipment, but Trevor could think of nothing but Oliver's mission. Would Oliver see Rose? How would she react to Trevor's gift?

More pacing. More anxiety. More praying.

He stopped to wash his hands with the lavender soap on the side of the kitchen sink. Thankfully his apartment and office were among those that had running water and electricity. The scent of the lavender soap reminded him of Rose. Could he ever get away from her?

As if leaving the apartment would erase her from his thoughts, Trevor walked toward the adjacent office. He had wasted enough time. At least he could continue painting the examination room. Trevor planned for everything to be fresh in his office by the first of the year. He had already begun advertising his services in the newspaper and hoped for a successful practice.

One day a week Trevor planned to work in the poor communities. Tending illnesses. Providing vaccinations. Delivering babies. All for free. Hopefully, Rose would be a part of that.

As he entered his office, the front door opened with the squeak of hinges. Reminding himself to oil those hinges, Trevor rushed into the spacious waiting room to greet Oliver.

"Oliver! You're back. At last. What did Rose—" Trevor halted. For an unexpected guest accompanied Oliver.

Zebulun Brandon.

"Dr. Riley." Zebulun bowed slightly.

"Mr. Brandon. What a delight! How does the day find you?"

"Exceedingly well."

The two clasped hands.

"Mr. Ghaliger arranged for your gift to my daughter, as you requested."

"Yes. And how is she faring?" Trevor anticipated any news from his beloved.

"She is doing extremely well. Extremely well. Although she has seemed a bit lonely this past week." Zebulun, his dark brown eyes sparkling mischievously, leaned forward as if he were confiding the deepest of family secrets.

Trevor experienced the uneasy feeling that Mr. Brandon wished him to explain his absence. Had Rose not told him?

"Would you care to share a quick spot of tea with us?" Oliver asked quickly. More than once Oliver had used his charmingly British "quick spot of tea" to deliver Trevor from an awkward situation.

"Yes. I would be delighted. Absolutely delighted." The

smell of paint trailing them, Rose's wiry father followed Trevor through the office, making the appropriate comments, extending the appropriate congratulations, verbalizing the appropriate praise.

His uneasiness growing, Trevor insisted on preparing the tea. Before Oliver could step into the kitchen, Trevor settled him and Zebulun on the worn settee and entered the all-white kitchen. He simply wasn't ready to make small talk with Mr. Brandon. Why was he here anyway? Had Oliver invited him?

As if in response to Trevor's thought, Oliver entered the tiny kitchen. "I thought it might be more proper for me to make the tea. Why don't you go and entertain your future father-in-law?"

"Why is he here?" Trevor whispered as he sprinkled a generous supply of tea leaves into the blue porcelain pot.

"I believe the chap has come out of respect for you and your intentions toward his daughter."

"Well, he makes me nervous." Trevor turned toward the sink and filled the teapot with water.

"Of course he does. That's natural."

"I'm not even sure that Rose will accept my proposal. And he doesn't seem to know why I haven't courted her this week. What am I to tell him?" He deposited the teapot on the gas stove.

"Tell him the truth."

"But what if Rose doesn't want him to know? Wouldn't she have told him already if she wanted him to know?"

With a sober expression, Oliver laid a consoling hand on Trevor's shoulder. "You're acting like a schoolboy." His lips twitched. His blue eyes danced. "I must say I've never seen you in such a state."

"The stove needs to be turned on," Trevor clipped, annoyed with Oliver for making sport of his genuine nervousness.

"I'll take care of it."

And Trevor walked back into the sitting room. But the instant he realized what Zebulun Brandon was doing, he stopped.

Stunned.

He had never been so stunned.

The letter.

Zebulun was reading Riley's letter to Trevor. The letter that Trevor had left on the simple cherry table. The letter that confirmed Trevor's disinheritance. The letter that prohibited Trevor from ever bringing Rose to Riley Mansion.

Mr. Brandon looked up. At once Trevor wanted to yank the letter from Zebulun and request his departure. But something restrained him. Perhaps Mr. Brandon's guilty expression. Perhaps Trevor's devotion to propriety.

"I see you have discovered my latest news," Trevor said, his strained tone barely hiding his anger.

"Yes. I-I . . . um . . ." Zebulun, floundering for words, tossed the letter back to the table as if it were a hot coal. "I didn't realize I was prying until—"

"You certainly *were* prying, sir," Trevor said in a forced, even tone. Deliberately, he retrieved the letter, folded it, and slipped it back into the envelope.

Zebulun, his color heightened, stood. "Please allow me to offer my sincerest apologies. I never planned for our kinship to start off on such a note."

"So you still want me for your son-in-law?" Trevor asked, schooling his features into a bland mask.

"But of course. You must love my daughter tremendously to sacrifice your inheritance for her." Even though the words sounded good, his tone betrayed a deep disappointment.

Trevor relived all the times he had been adored by women and their families because of his wealth. Although Rose seemed free of that materialistic bent, her father apparently was as eaten up with it as the next man. In despair, Trevor wondered if anyone besides Oliver would ever approve of him just because he was Trevor Riley. Period.

He walked to the stone fireplace. "I would appreciate your not telling Rose." Turning his back on Zebulun, Trevor stared into the snapping fire.

The closing door attested to Mr. Brandon's quick departure, and Trevor knew in his soul that Zebulun would share the news with Rose. That Rose would be delighted. That she would accept his proposal on Christmas Day.

But Rose and her family had a shock in store. For even if she did accept Trevor's proposal, he could never marry her. Not now. Not knowing the terms on which she would accept him. Every other woman had wanted Trevor because he was wealthy. Rose wanted him only if he wasn't wealthy. The situations were opposite. The motives were identical.

Conditional love.

It wasn't enough for Trevor.

He propped his elbow on the rustic mantel and rested his forehead against his palm. The smell of the lavender soap, still clinging to his hand, seemed to mock him. "Oh, Rose . . . Rose . . . ," he whispered as he sank into an ocean of despair. "I never thought it would end like this."

After opening the Christmas ornament, Rose quickly changed into the outfit she had worn in Denver when dining with Trevor. The russet suit. Nervously, she peered into the dresser mirror, fussed with her hair, and rearranged her copper-colored hat, replete with black feathers. Satisfied at last with her appearance, Rose put on her black cloth gloves and grabbed her scarlet cape. Instead of her petite purse, she carried the painted star in its gift box. Rose would walk. The brisk air and exercise would refresh her mind.

While descending the stairs into the store, Rose relived Trevor's kiss. Would he take her in his arms when she accepted his proposal? She relished the delicious delight and rushed all the more.

Her mother, smiling excitedly, awaited her at the foot of the stairs. Impulsively, Rose embraced her, feeling closer to her mother than she ever had. Neither spoke. But Rose knew they would soon enter a deeper level in their relationship. They would both be married women. They would have much more in common. They would share a new bond. Rose hoped it would be the kind of bond she had shared with Ma Brandon.

As she approached the store's garland-laden door, it opened. Zebulun Brandon entered, his face a mask of grave concern. "Rose," he said, "where are you going?"

"Father, I—"

"She is going to visit Dr. Riley," Iris said, moving to Rose's side.

"Oh?" Zebulun said.

"Yes. I am going to accept his proposal. He proposed last week, and I asked him to give me time to make up my mind. I have made my decision."

"So that explains his absence." Zebulun removed his black homburg and studied Rose. "Iris, are there any customers now?" He scanned the store.

"No. We've had only a few since you left. It seems the morning rush has slowed."

"Good. There's something we need to discuss, Rose." He looked uncertainly toward his wife.

Zebulun's tone chilled Rose. He seemed ready to relate disturbing news. She didn't want to hear anything that would dampen her joy.

"I have just been to visit Dr. Riley."

He paused.

Rose bit her lips.

"Your mother knows this. I left with Mr. Ghaliger after he purchased your Christmas ornament."

She nodded.

"I went simply to pay my respects to the man I hoped would be my son-in-law and thank him for his kindnesses to you. But I discovered some terribly disappointing news." The fine lines around his mouth and eyes deepened with his troubled expression. "And I might as well tell you and be done with it."

Rose's mind whirled with what her father was saying. Was there another love that Trevor had hidden from her? She gripped the gift box, her hands damp, her heart gently pounding. "OK," she rasped at last.

"Dr. Riley, it seems, has been disinherited."

Iris gasped.

Rose drew her brows. "Is that all?" she blurted with relief.

"All?" Zebulun stared in disbelief. "I would assume this would cause you to reconsider—"

"Father, whether or not Dr. Riley has a fortune has nothing to do with my accepting his proposal."

"But you must consider the whole family, Rose," Zebulun continued.

An old pool of anger bubbled up within Rose; the same anger she had felt as a child when her father acted disappointed with her choice of less-affluent friends. She resisted the impulse to express her frustration in words she would regret.

"Zebulun," Iris said, "Rose and I have already discussed this matter. And I'll tell you what I told her. I think Dr. Riley will make her a fine husband, whether he's wealthy or not. I'm glad she turned down Edward Rothlord's proposal. I'd rather Rose have love than money."

Zebulun stared at his wife as if she had just sprouted pink wings out her ears. Finally he silently clamped his teeth and walked toward the counter, removing his bulky overcoat as he went. "Suit yourself," he muttered begrudgingly. "But don't come to me begging for money when your dear Dr. Riley runs out of patients."

"We'll help you any time you need it," Iris whispered, winking at her daughter.

"Thanks, Mother," Rose whispered back.

"Don't you worry about your father. He'll come around."

"And I don't appreciate you two whispering about me," Zebulun barked.

Stifling a mischievous giggle, Rose rushed out the door as a group of customers whisked their way in. "Merry Christmas!" they called.

"Merry Christmas," Rose responded, knowing this would be the merriest Christmas of them all.

CHAPTER TEN

Within minutes Rose had maneuvered through the bustling streets and found Trevor's new office. Everywhere she turned there were familiar smiling faces. Shop windows wearing their Christmas best. Restaurants bulging with cheer. Christmas wreaths. Red bows. Children merrily shopping with their parents. Sleighs zipping here and there at alarming rates. The smell of evergreens. The feel of fresh snow powdering her cheeks. And every sight, sound, smell, seemed to echo the calls of "Merry Christmas." Inside, Rose felt as if she would bubble over with joy.

What a blessed season.

What a blessing to be alive.

What a blessed man God had given her.

She quickly found the address and noticed the shingle hanging on the side of the three story, red brick building. "Dr. Trevor Riley," it read. "Third Floor, Suite D." She entered the building and trotted up the narrow flight of stairs. Once she found Suite D, Rose started to tap lightly on the door's glass window but decided to try the knob instead. The door opened with the slight squeak of hinges, and the smell of fresh paint greeted her. Rose peered around what must be a waiting room. All white and clean, the spacious room was sparsely furnished with a few wooden chairs.

"Hello—Trevor?" she called, clutching the gift box to her.

Footsteps. Coming from another room. Then the door on the far wall opened. Trevor halted in the doorway.

Rose smiled, joy welling within her. She had missed him more than she ever knew. Rose rushed forward.

Hands on hips, Trevor gazed at her stonily. No welcoming smile. No attempt to meet her midway.

She halted mere feet from him. "Trevor?" she said hesitantly.

"Let me guess," he said sarcastically, crossing his arms across a shirt stained with paint. "You have come to accept my proposal."

Rose's stomach knotted. Something was wrong. Dreadfully wrong. Could Trevor have changed his mind about wanting to marry her? "Well . . . yes . . . I . . . that's exactly why I came," she said tremulously.

"It won't work, Rose," he spat out, his sad eyes portraying a disillusioned man.

"Wha-what do you mean? What are you t-talking about?" she stammered.

"Answer just one question for me. Has your father told you of my disinheritance?" He sneered as if he already knew the answer.

She hated having to confirm his suspicions, but she could not lie. "Yes, but that has nothing to do with—"

"So. Now that I'm no longer wealthy, you decide to marry me. Is that it? You wouldn't have me when I was the son of Trevor Riley Sr., investment maven. But now that I'm penniless—"

"No. No!" Rose insisted, her mind whirling in despair.

"You don't understand. I didn't know about your disinheritance when I—"

"You are the one who doesn't understand!" he yelled.

She jumped.

"My whole adult life I have been chased by women because of my father's wealth. Do you have any idea how many times I could have gotten married?"

"I—"

"Then I met you. Rose Brandon. The one woman who doesn't give a flip about my money." A harsh laugh. "As a matter of fact, Miss Brandon has another problem. She doesn't like me *because* of my money."

"Trevor, I never said—"

"And the minute she discovers I have no money—" he clapped his hands together—"boom! She decides to accept my proposal." He stepped toward Rose and looked intently into her eyes. "Well, I do not want to marry any woman who cannot and will not accept me based on who I am. You must love me regardless of my wealth, or you do not love me."

"B-but I decided to accept your proposal before I learned of your disinheritance. Today . . . today, I was resting after lunch. I began to pray. And God . . . God showed me how wrong I had been to-to harbor such feelings toward—"

"You are lying," he said, looking away. "I do not believe you."

A sickening reality settled in the pit of Rose's stomach. No matter what she said or did, she would never convince Trevor that she had decided to marry him *before* she learned of his disinheritance. Tears stung her eyes. A sob forced itself past her compressed lips.

"How touching," he mocked, looking at her once again.

She stumbled backward. Silently, Rose peered into the pale gray eyes that had once mirrored love, acceptance, indulgence. Now those eyes overflowed with anger, betrayal, pain. Enough pain to last a lifetime.

Another sob. A flood of tears. Rose cast the boxed Christmas ornament at his feet and ran. She raced blindly from the office and into the snow, which was falling from the sky like a million tiny pieces of sorrow, ready to pierce her soul.

Trevor picked up the Christmas ornament and slung it into the nearest trash basket. Furiously, he pounded his fist against the wall then stalked toward his apartment. He had never been so angry in his entire life. Rose had not even possessed the decency to wait a few days before approaching him. She had done nothing but trample his love with her immediate response to Zebulun's news.

He had been painting the exam room when she came in. Trevor had been so amazed at Rose's brazenness that he had been tempted to refuse to talk with her. Now he wanted nothing more than to remove himself from this office. He needed a time of solitude. A time to nurse his livid emotions. Trevor would retrieve his overcoat, hat, and gloves, then pour his rage into the mountainous air.

As he approached the apartment, he glanced up to see an incredulous Oliver standing inside the open door.

"How long have you been there?" Trevor snapped, angry that Oliver might have overheard his outburst with Rose.

"I heard everything, if that's what you want to know," Oliver replied, a disapproving note in his voice.

"That is what I wanted to know. And I resent your eavesdropping."

"Eavesdropping! I couldn't help but hear. You were yelling like a shot bear."

"I had every right to yell."

Silence.

And Trevor brushed past Oliver. Within minutes he had

retrieved his overcoat and carpetbag. He turned to Oliver who, remaining ominously quiet, warmed himself near the rock fireplace. "I won't be back tonight," Trevor snapped before leaving. "I'll be taking a hotel room."

"And what about your medical equipment? You never got it from the train station," Oliver said simply.

A groan. Trevor had completely forgotten the medical equipment. "I'll hire a wagon and pay to have it delivered."

"Be careful with your money. You aren't as wealthy as you—"

"I know that," Trevor barked, feeling betrayed. Oliver sided with Rose. He didn't have to say it. Trevor saw it in his every expression, heard it in his every word. Feeling like a miserable wretch, Trevor opened the door.

"Why didn't you believe her?" Oliver asked. "I think she was telling the truth."

Trevor halted and slowly turned to Oliver. "And I think she was lying." The two shared a challenging gaze, and Trevor realized a grievous truth.

Oliver would never fully understand the scars Trevor bore. Even though he had been with Trevor most of his life, he had not experienced those wounds. Oliver had seen them. He had witnessed their infliction. But he couldn't understand why Trevor desperately needed Rose's love confirmed with no doubt attached.

If Trevor accepted Rose now, he would always have doubts about whether she would have married him had he not been disinherited. Those doubts would gnaw at him and grow into a malignancy that would eat the life out of their marriage, leaving it nothing but an empty shell.

No.

Trevor could not marry anyone on those terms. He would go his whole life unmarried before doing that.

"I'll see you in the morning," he muttered and began closing the door.

"I'll warrant you should ask God about what he thinks of you," a soft British voice called.

Try as he might, Trevor couldn't ignore the stinging words.

THE NEXT MORNING

Rose looked up when the store's bell rang. All morning she had looked up when the bell rang. Expecting Trevor. Hoping he would appear in the doorway. Wishing he would take her in his arms and tell her he was sorry.

But instead of Trevor, Oliver Ghaliger entered, all proper in his tweed, wool suit and matching brown fedora. He looked past Iris near the front, and his kind blue gaze roved the store, as if he were searching for a particular someone. Rose figured she was that someone. She stepped from behind the counter, where she had been arranging the red and green and blue wooden Christmas crates that customers often filled with food and gave as gifts.

"Hello," she said simply.

"Hello." A kind smile. As Oliver approached Rose, her mother resumed her job of sorting fruit into red Christmas baskets that would go to the coal deliverers' children. "May I have a moment of your time?" Oliver requested.

"Of course." She was eager for any news of Trevor. "We could go upstairs. Would you care for some tea?"

His eyes twinkled. "Need you ask?"

"Mother," she called. "May I have a moment with Mr. Ghaliger?"

Iris smiled and nodded her approval. She glanced at Zebulun, who was waiting on a pair of chattering matrons. "Your father and I can handle it. Go ahead."

Within minutes Rose settled Oliver into their quaint yet cozy white-and-yellow kitchen. Feeling as if the air were laden with unanswered questions, Rose poured their steaming tea into beige mugs and sat across from him at the worn kitchen table.

Oliver cleared his throat. "I heard you and Trevor talking yesterday afternoon."

"Oh?"

"Please forgive my listening, but it was a wee bit hard not to. I was just entering his office from the apartment when you arrived. And well . . . Trevor was yelling, so . . ." He trailed off, his expression speaking a comfort he had yet to verbalize.

As that haunting memory flooded her thoughts, Rose's swollen eyes stung. Yesterday, she had run all the way back to the store. Due to their increased Christmas trade, Rose had been forced to suppress her emotions. Other than a brief, intense cry as she shared details of the incident with her parents, Rose had saved her tears for the privacy of her room at night. Therefore, she had slept little.

"I'm sorry." Oliver squeezed her hand in fatherly comfort.

Compressing her trembling lips, Rose nodded mutely and took a generous swallow of the sweet tea.

"I just came to tell you that I've known Trevor since he was five, and I've never seen him behave so. I've tried to reason with him, but he refuses to listen. He went off and spent the night in a hotel and came back this morning, all stony faced and angry." Oliver shook his head. "I'm greatly worried. He has never reminded me of his father so much as he does now."

"Oh no," Rose gasped.

"It's the truth." He sipped his tea.

"And it's all my fault."

"Your fault?"

"Yes," Rose wailed, covering her face. "I was so—so wrong about something. I have harbored a horribly nasty attitude toward all wealthy people. Then, when I met Trevor, I lumped him in with all the other wealthy people I'd known.

I couldn't seem to get Trevor the man separated from Trevor the wealthy man."

"Yes. Yes, I know all that. He told me. But you are in no way responsible for his actions any more than he is for yours."

"All my life," Rose continued, as if Oliver hadn't spoken, "I've watched wealthy people misuse the poor, and it has caused me to despise them." Desperately, she gripped his arm. "Oh, Oliver, my resentment has cost me the man I love!"

"There, there, now," Oliver crooned. "Don't be so distraught. You two young people beat all I've ever seen. One of you won't talk to me, and the other one is blaming herself for the whole ordeal."

"But it is my fault. If I hadn't—"

"Rose, you aren't the only person alive who has been prejudiced."

"But that doesn't excuse me—"

He held up his hand. "No. It doesn't excuse anything. But it is a basic human misjudgment."

She sniffled. "What do you mean?"

"I mean that the problem with the wealthy not helping the poor doesn't lie in the ownership of money or possessions. The problem lies here." He tapped his heart. "There's something within the heart of man that causes us to think we are somehow superior to others. Sometimes it's the poor toward the rich. Or the white toward the black. Or one church denomination toward another. It has nothing to do with whether or not people possess money. It has to do with the fact that they have not had a life-changing encounter with a holy God. Just think about it, Rose. How many of the poor people you know are capable of hoarding money and not giving?"

Rose stared at him.

"How many poor people are cruel to their own children just as the wealthy are cruel to the poor?"

What Oliver was saying made perfect sense. Rose remembered her own realization that she had been prejudiced against people who were prejudiced against the poor. She had been a participant in the very sin she despised. Without Christ, many of the poor partook of the sins that wounded them. Selfishness. Cruelty. Hatred. And returning prejudice for prejudice.

"I'm not saying any of it is right," Oliver continued. "I too grieve for the poor people I see, especially the children. They're the ones who suffer."

Rose nodded gravely.

"But there are some wealthy people who use their money for the right purposes. Trevor, for instance. You know yourself that before he was disinherited, he had planned his practice to be a free service solely for the poor."

"He did?"

"Well, yes." Oliver stared at her in astonishment. "You didn't know?"

"No. He never told me."

Oliver snorted. "I can't believe it."

But Rose remembered the night of Trevor's proposal. She remembered his saying that there were things he had yet to share with her—plans he had made. She also remembered interrupting him at that point.

"I think he tried to tell me," she said forlornly. "But I was so preoccupied with my own worries that I didn't give him a chance to explain. Oh, Mr. Ghaliger . . ." She gripped his hands as her eyes stung once more. "Do you think he'll ever forgive me?"

"I was more worried about whether you could ever forgive him. He was horrid to you. Despicably horrid."

"Yes, I know. But-but I've been horrid too."

With a weary sigh, Oliver stood. "Well, you've answered the question that was tormenting me."

"I have?"

"Yes. I was worried that a lady of your quality might never speak to Trevor again after the way he has acted."

"But I love him."

"I can see that."

"And how is he?" Rose stood, twisting her fingers until they ached.

"Ornery as a buzzard. But other than that, he is faring well. Quite well."

"Do you think he might call on me?" she rasped, not daring to hope for a positive answer.

"I can't tell." A shadow of worry darkened Oliver's expression. "That's the other half of my concern. You, of course. And then, him." He turned for the doorway. "But I will keep praying."

"So will I," Rose said as they left the apartment. "So will I."

CHAPTER ELEVEN

CHRISTMAS DAY
5:00 A.M.

Dressed in a red velvet robe, Trevor silently prepared his breakfast. Eggs. Bacon. A leftover biscuit. Coffee. One of the many things Oliver had taught him through the years was how to cook. To be self-sufficient. Looking back, Trevor wondered if his father had ever comprehended exactly the scope of what Oliver had taught him. Hired to be a chaperon and academic tutor, Oliver Ghaliger had served as much more. He had shaped everything about Trevor, including his view of the world. Without Oliver, Trevor could have easily grown into the image of his father.

He gathered the full plate and coffee cup and moved to the sitting room. Settling on the indigo rug in front of the fireplace, Trevor watched the flames dance among the logs.

As he thoughtfully chewed the salty bacon, Trevor reflected over the last week. A tense week. A week of heartache. Of sadness. His mind wandered to Oliver once more. Trevor had closed him out the last week. For the first time in his life, he had erected unseen barriers between himself and the man who had been father, confidant, friend.

But Oliver had betrayed Trevor when he sided with Rose.

183

The two hadn't discussed the situation again. They had talked of precious little during the last week. Trevor had continued in his efforts to arrange his office while Oliver silently helped. During that time Trevor had resisted all feelings of guilt and stubbornly clung to his opinion that he was not in the least bit wrong. He was the one who had been wronged.

Still, Oliver's words haunted Trevor. "Why didn't you believe her? I think she was telling the truth."

Had Rose been truthful?

Trevor rested against the worn chair behind him. The chair with the Wedding-Ring quilt. The quilt that had introduced Trevor to Rose. On impulse, he placed his breakfast plate on the hearth and pulled the quilt from the chair. As he stroked the tiny stitches and the texture of the fabric, Trevor scrutinized the repeating red rings and green rings. He pondered his father giving the quilt to Rose's grandmother.

Rose had told Trevor that Riley had never believed Lorene told him the truth about her parents prohibiting their marriage. Riley had chosen to believe that Lorene never truly loved him. Furthermore, he had never forgiven her. The whole ordeal had sprouted a bitterness in Riley that had destroyed him spiritually and emotionally.

Last night Oliver had peered at Trevor over their evening meal and said, "You remind me of your father more than you ever have." That was all he said. Nothing in their stilted conversation had prompted Oliver's remark. Trevor had compressed his lips in silence and dashed the comment from his mind.

Now Oliver's words tormented him. Was he really behaving like his father? The parallels were too great to be ignored any longer. Riley had chosen not to believe Lorene. He had chosen a harsh path. A path of unforgiveness.

Likewise, Trevor had chosen not to believe Rose. He had dealt harshly with her. He had offered no forgiveness.

Another of Oliver's comments barged into Trevor's thoughts. *"I'll warrant you should ask God what he thinks of you."* How similar these words were to his own words to Rose the night of his proposal: *"Have you prayed about your attitude toward the wealthy?"*

But Trevor had refused to pray since he sent Rose away. He was too busy mentally lambasting Rose and women in general. He remembered thinking he had placed the whole situation in God's hands and would accept God's will, regardless of Rose's decision.

Where had Trevor strayed from that determination?

Fingering the quilt, he gazed into the flames and began to pray for the first time in a week. *Oh, Father, show me. Show me. . . .* He remembered thinking that Oliver could never understand the injuries Trevor had received because of his father's wealth, because of people "loving" him just for his money. His response to Rose had been spawned from those wounds. Wounds that had never healed.

He crushed the quilt until his hands ached. Often Trevor had seen God heal a physical wound when his own expertise was spent. In those cases Trevor always glorified his Lord. But there were other types of wounds. Wounds that no one could see. These wounds ached just as deeply as any physical injury.

Injuries of the emotions.

Trevor recognized that his injuries were not only from people who valued him because of money but also from his own father. Perhaps the reason the injuries from supposed friends penetrated so deeply was because Riley himself had initiated the first wounds. Trevor had never felt his father's approval. His whole life, he had thirsted for even one word of praise, one acknowledgment of love. The disinheritance was the final evidence of the unfathomable gulf between him and his father.

Unexpectedly, Trevor began to weep. Surprised at his own

reaction, he tried to stay the tears, only to feel them bursting forth like water from an artesian well. He buried his face in the quilt and let the tears flow freely. Tears of grief. Of mourning. Of healing.

As his sobs increased, he felt a hand grip his shoulder. Oliver, Trevor's rock, was once again offering his support. Despite their disagreement, Oliver still exuded unconditional love.

At long last the tears ebbed. Trevor experienced an overwhelming sense of peace, freedom, joy. And he knew the healing had begun.

Still, Oliver silently gripped his shoulder.

"I owe you an apology." Trevor turned to his friend. They shared a brief, powerful embrace.

"All is well with me." Oliver's moist eyes sparkled. "But—"

"I must see Rose."

"Exactly."

"Do you think she'll have me now?"

"I think the lady loves you more than you know."

Abruptly, Trevor stood and folded the quilt. The Christmas ornament still lay in the trash basket in his office. For some reason, he hadn't been able to set it out for the garbage collectors. Now he knew why.

Dawn's first sunlight diminished the room's shadows as church bells began their joyous celebration of Christmas morning. Rose sat on the side of her bed, wondering if she would survive this day, the very day Trevor should be calling for her answer. Earlier in the week she had fruitlessly hoped Trevor would call. As the week progressed, her hopes had been dashed.

Forlornly, Rose began dressing for church. Once again she donned the russet-colored suit, purchased with Ma Brandon's money. She possessed few high quality suits, and this one she had already worn on many occasions.

This morning her family would attend the Christmas worship service their small congregation always enjoyed. They would pray together. Share communion. Sing worshipfully. And enjoy their pastor's brief sermon.

In past years the service had been the highlight of Rose's Christmas Day. But she doubted if anything could brighten this Christmas. Her lips quivering, she suppressed the tears that had threatened all week. Rose would not cry. She would put on a brave front for her mother and father. She would not spoil their Christmas. Later, Rose and Iris planned to take Christmas baskets full of fruit and candy to the coal deliverers' children. Perhaps Rose would then experience some Christmas cheer.

Already the smell of fresh sausage and coffee wafted down the hallway. Iris, always the early bird, greeted her daughter and husband every morning with a smile and a warm breakfast. Often Rose tried to relieve her mother of this duty, but Iris always refused, saying she enjoyed the task. So as she had done her whole life, Rose finished dressing, opened her bedroom door, and headed toward the kitchen to help.

But someone was pounding on the door in the cozy parlor. Could it be the postman? Mr. Mellinger usually delivered the last of the Christmas cards on Christmas morning. She walked into the parlor, gaily decorated in the trappings of Christmas. Trying to avoid the Christmas tree's prickly limbs, Rose peeked out the window that opened onto the outside stairway. Personal callers normally used this entrance rather than the store's. A lanky, red-headed lad stood on the landing and balanced a large package wrapped in green. Her pastor's son, Charlie Wade.

Another knock.

Rose opened the door. "Hello, Charlie," she said, surprised to find him there. "What brings you calling so early?"

"This, Miss Rose." He handed her the package. "My folks and I are on our way to church, but Dr. Riley stopped us and asked if I would deliver this package to you." Charlie pointed across the snow-lined road.

Trevor, dressed in his black overcoat and gray fedora, stood beneath a gas streetlamp. He gazed up at her. Cloaked in morning shadows, he seemed forlorn, uncertain.

Rose's heart gently pounded as she absently thanked Charlie. Before the boy had reached the bottom of the stairs, she had untied the green bow and ripped open the package. Her eyes blurring, Rose lovingly picked up the hand-painted Christmas ornament, then stroked Ma Brandon's Wedding-Ring quilt. How had Trevor ever retrieved the quilt from Mr. Riley?

Then she noticed an attached note, written in Trevor's distinctive scrawl. "I'm sorry. Will you forgive me? Will you marry me?"

"Yes," she whispered. "Yes. Yes. Yes."

Not bothering to close the parlor door, Rose clasped the quilt to her chest and raced down the stairs. "Yes!" she yelled, rushing toward Trevor.

He met Rose in the middle of the empty road and wrapped his arms around her. "Oh, Rose . . . Rose," he murmured against her ear. "I've been foolish. Can you ever forgive me?"

"I'm the one who should ask for forgiveness."

"No, I should have listened to you. But instead, I jumped to conclusions. All the wrong conclusions." Cupping her chin in his hands, he stroked her cheeks with his thumbs.

Rose gazed into his reddened eyes.

"I've been praying this morning," he said. "I've seen that I have some wounds from the past that made me react so despicably last week."

"I was leaving to accept your proposal that day when father told me—"

"Shh." Their lips brushed in a promising kiss. "Don't. I need no explanation. I know you love me. That's all that matters."

"I do love you." She rested her head against his chest.

"And I love you."

A frigid breeze danced around them, and Rose shivered.

"Here." Trevor took the quilt, wrapped it around her shoulders, then steered her toward the stairs.

Caressing the silk ornament's painted surface, Rose gladly snuggled into the quilt and leaned against Trevor. "How did you get the quilt back?"

"I took it from Father's study and brought it with me when I moved here." He hesitated. "Father was letting his dog sleep on it. I simply couldn't—"

"Why would he do such a thing?"

"He's a very hardened person, Rose."

Her immediate reaction was one of judgment on the man who would soon be her father-in-law. Then she remembered what God had shown her. She remembered that it was only by God's grace that she didn't share in the attitudes of Mr. Riley and all the Mr. Rileys of the world.

"I'm going to send him a telegram, telling him I forgive him for disinheriting me, even though he hasn't asked for forgiveness."

Rose halted, stroked Trevor's face, and caressed him with an adoring gaze. "You are a wonderful man, Dr. Trevor Riley."

"Not on my own," he replied. "Not on my own."

RECIPE

PUMPKIN ROLL

This resembles a jelly roll, and the powdered sugar coating makes it very attractive.

Roll	Filling
3 eggs	1 cup sifted powdered sugar
1 cup sugar	8 oz. softened cream cheese
⅔ cup pumpkin purée	4 tbsp. softened butter
1 tsp. lemon juice	½ tsp. vanilla
¾ cup flour	
1 tsp. baking powder	
2 tsp. cinnamon	
1 tsp. ginger	
½ tsp. nutmeg	
½ tsp. salt	
1 cup chopped nuts	

Beat eggs on high speed. Blend in sugar, pumpkin purée, and lemon juice. Stir in dry ingredients. Spread on a cookie sheet lined with waxed paper. Top with nuts and bake at 375° for 15 minutes.

Heavily dust a clean dish towel with powdered sugar. When the roll is done, turn it out onto the towel, peel off the waxed paper, and roll it and the towel up together like a cinnamon roll. Allow to cool that way for 1½ hours.

Blend the filling ingredients together until smooth. Unroll the towel and roll, spread filling evenly over flat surface, then reroll without the towel.

A Note from the Author

To My Readers,

The "Wedding Ring" quilt (or "Double Wedding Ring") plays a role in some of my earliest memories. My late grandmother, Onie White, was a quilter extraordinaire. As a child, I remember snuggling under one of her "Wedding Ring" quilts on a cold winter's evening. The "Wedding Ring" has a long line of romantic ancestors. Its earliest predecessors were "Cupid's Arrow" and "Bridal Stairway." Quilters complicate these designs to create "The Eternal Triangle," which culminated in the "Wedding Ring." This quilt pattern appeared in the latter part of the mid-nineteenth century and was one of the most popular designs in the 1920s.

After writing "The Wedding Ring," I was struck with the spiritual implications quilts lend. Often our own lives are like carefully crafted quilts. God, of course, is the master designer. He lovingly pieces together the scraps of our heartache and bright colors of our joy, all against a background of his peace. Sometimes, after life's hardest blows, we do not recognize the beauty of the pattern for many years. But the beauty is still the thread that holds the whole masterpiece together. And even in life's most sorrowful moments, he carries us in his arms and teaches us from his infinite wisdom.

As you celebrate Christ's birth, allow his love to wrap around you like a comforting quilt and warm your spirit to new dimensions. Sit at his feet. Look on his face. Invite him to permeate every stitch of your soul.

Merry Christmas!
Debra White Smith

ABOUT THE AUTHOR

Debra White Smith lives in east Texas with her husband, Daniel, and son, Brett. She has authored numerous articles and books, including *Castaways,* part of the CBA best-selling romance anthol-
ogy *Only You* (Barbour). Her novel, *The Neigh-bor,* was voted by Heartsong Presents readers in the 1997 top-ten favorite contemporary ro-mances. And Debra was voted in the 1997 top-ten favorite new Heartsong authors. In the last year, Debra has seen 119,000 copies of her books in print.

Visit Debra on the World Wide Web at http://www.getset.com/debrawhitesmith, or write to her at P.O. Box 1482, Jacksonville, TX 75766.

Log Cabin Patch

GINNY AIKEN

PROLOGUE

A house is built by wisdom and becomes strong through
good sense. Through knowledge its rooms are filled with all
sorts of precious riches and valuables.{xepi}
PROVERBS 24:3-4, NLT

NEW HOPE, WASHINGTON
FALL 1897

As he paced the crowded office of the New Hope Lumber Company, Cal Stevenson raked his fingers through his hair. "Klondike fever," he muttered in disgust.

"Quite an illness, son," replied Sam August, his partner, from the worn leather chair behind the paper-laden desk.

Cal turned on his heel and came back to where he had started. "One that's sucking the lifeblood from our business. One that could ruin what we spent years building."

Sam stood and rounded the desk. "I know, I know. But it won't do to rehash what's happened. We need a plan to stop the bloodletting." He shrugged, then shook his pewter-haired head. "Can't say as I have one."

"I'm no closer to an answer, even though I've near worn my knees down from praying."

"So have I, son. So have I."

The men fell silent. Cal thought back over the past nine years. They had been good ones, filled with backbreaking work, true, but satisfying, as they watched the fruits of their labor grow.

He met Sam when, as a green nineteen-year-old, he had traded the familiarity of home for adventure out west. The older man had taken one look at the starry-eyed youth and tucked him under his wing. Sam then shared everything with his new friend: his few belongings and his powerful love for Christ, leading Cal back to the faith he'd been taught as a child. As the pair spent two years working at what odd jobs they found on ranches and lumbering enterprises throughout Washington State, a dream took hold. They would someday have a logging company of their own.

When that day finally came, both men had doubled their determination to succeed. They had been doing just that—succeeding—until last spring. As word of the discovery of gold in the Yukon spread, men of all ages traded their common sense for gold lust. New Hope, the tiny town Sam and Cal had built around their business, became very nearly a ghost town. Even loggers and millworkers had gone to seek their fortunes in Alaska.

"We know our problem," Cal murmured, again turning the matter over in his mind, "and we know what we need to solve it. It's men we need, good workers who won't fly off at the fool notion of gold. The question is, how do we go about bringing them here?"

Sam scrubbed his salt-and-pepper beard as he always did when in deep concentration. "Seems to me we have to let them know what all we got going for us. You know, regular work with fair wages. A clean place to live. A nice, quiet town. . . ."

Cal grimaced. "Put that way, I'm not sure it sounds so attractive. What would it take to draw men here? What would appeal as much as the chance to get rich?"

Sam scrubbed harder but said nothing.

Cal paced more rapidly.

After long, silent moments the older man drawled, "We-e-ell, son, what is it *you* want in a town? What would it take to make our New Hope the perfect place to live?"

The sudden memory of a farmhouse in Iowa darted into Cal's mind. A homey kitchen, fragrant with fresh bread and roasted meat. Curtains in the windows. Feminine smiles and comfort. Sunday morning rides to church for a rousing sermon, followed by fellowship.

Life at the Stevenson farm had been happy. Until the moment Sam asked his question, Cal hadn't realized how much he missed the flavor of those days from his youth. Now, the desire to reclaim it stunned him with its strength.

But New Hope lacked the main ingredient.

Women.

Ladies were in short supply throughout Washington State. Cal didn't remember meeting many females who would trade life in a nice town for a rough lumber settlement with little to offer but lonely men.

"Seems to me," he said as he pondered their predicament, "we have to make New Hope a town, a *real* town."

"How do you plan to do that, son?"

"With women. They can make *any* place a home. And men always flock to where there are women."

Sam scrubbed ever harder, making Cal marvel at the beard's endurance. "How do you mean to get women here?" the older man finally asked. "Don't know many who want to cut trees."

"Of course you don't. We need loggers and millworkers for that. I'm thinking, though, that we want a schoolmarm, a new cook for the Dinner Bell—"

"*Amen!*" chimed Sam, grimacing. "If I have to eat another of Mabel Sauerbehr's meals, I might take off for the Klondike myself."

Cal gave his mentor a mock glare. "You wouldn't dare! Besides, you know I'd chase you right back, you old scoundrel." Then he chuckled. "But I know what you mean. I've suffered my share of dyspepsia, too."

A grimace twisted the copious silver whiskers. "You're the one who promised Fritz Sauerbehr you would watch over his Mabel as he lay on his deathbed."

Cal blushed. "What would you have had me do? Turn her out on her ear? Where would a widow her age go? Besides, seems to me she's got her beribboned cap set on you."

Sam's forehead—about the only part on his face not sporting hair—glowed red, and he scowled. "Yeah, well, would be nice to have someone wash my clothes and stitch them missin' buttons back on." Then a crooked grin curved his mustache. "Pastries. I sure miss those. We need us a bakery."

With a mischievous wink, Cal said, "What? Don't you want Mabel doing for you?"

A hint of horror filled Sam's blue eyes.

Cal eased up on his teasing. In the spirit of planning, he asked, "What about a store clerk? I hate having to open the mercantile after I've spent the day sweating at the mill."

"A good sawbones would be nice."

"Aw, Sam, you're letting your imagination go too far. No doctor would come to a town this small. Maybe we could get a nurse, but you know what I'd especially like?"

"Tell me, son."

Cal glanced at his worn Bible atop the mountain of paper on the desk. "I'd like to have our own preacher in New Hope. We could build us a church, you know, and call a young man to fill that pulpit. Then we wouldn't have to travel for hours to hear a real sermon no more than a handful of times a year."

Sam donned a speculative look. "You know, you might have something there. A preacher would make our town seem more respectable. Women really like respectability and all. 'Sides, a man of the cloth might encourage family men to move here. The kind who have a passel of kids to feed and need steady work."

Cal nodded, his enthusiasm for the project growing. "Most of all, I want to worship of a Sunday with others. To sing God's praises and hear his Word taught. I want fellowship with fellow believers."

Sam huffed. "What am I, boy? I won't be having you call me a heathen—"

"Of course not," Cal hastened to say. "But it's just the two of us now, and neither one of us can carry a tune worth beans."

Mollified, Sam nodded. "You got that right."

"Well, then, we're agreed. We need to draw new blood to our town, and I know just how I'm going to do it."

Sam gave him a suspicious look. "What kind of crazy scheme are you cooking there?"

Cal smiled. "No scheme. I'm going to place an advertisement in every newspaper within five hundred miles. You'll see. So many folks will come that we'll soon be turning them away."

"Not a one, son. 'New Hope' will offer just that—Christian hospitality and the hope of heaven to those who hunger."

CHAPTER ONE

Melissa Barnhart stepped from the offices of the New Hope Lumber Company feeling tons lighter than she had felt going in. "I did it! Really and truly. I, Melissa Ann Barnhart, got me a job and a home. Now all I have to do is build me a family."

That last sobered her immediately. She had given her brother, Craig, permission to go exploring while she spoke to Mr. Samuel August, owner of the logging operation, about the cooking job he had advertised in the *Seattle Intelligencer*. The boy had been itching to get out of the wagon and stretch his legs. She had seen no harm in his looking over the small town she hoped would soon be their new address.

At twelve, Craig lacked bulk, but what he lacked in size and maturity, he made up in arrogance. Melissa wasn't sure how to cope with his attitude. Much less discern what had caused it.

Nearly a dozen years had passed since she last saw her brother. After Mama died giving birth to him on the Oregon Trail, Papa pushed himself and their oxen even harder to reach the Willamette Valley. Once there, he put all his energy to helping his older brother in exchange for a home for his children. He'd worked so hard. . . .

Melissa would never forget that last night. Papa came inside after milking the cows looking drawn, so weary he refused supper and collapsed onto a chair. With sadness on his dear face, he watched her rock a finally napping Craig, then said, "Melissa, even if you're only nine, you're the heart of our family now that Mama's gone. If anything happens to me, you make sure the two of you stay together, keep Craig with you always, take special care of him. He's only a baby."

The tears in his eyes had made Melissa think of the tiny graves in the family plot back in Ohio. Mama had lost part of her heart each time she'd buried a lifeless child. No wonder Papa wanted Melissa to watch over Craig. Mama had given her life to have him.

"I promise, Papa," she said. "I'll take good care of him."

He died in his sleep that night. Days later, despite her objections and Craig's piteous cries, they were sent to different sets of relatives. No one wanted to shoulder the burden posed by two little ones.

Mama's aunt and uncle, Erna and Bert Clemson, took Melissa. Soon after joining them, she began her apprenticeship in their kitchen. If she learned anything over those next twelve years it was to cook very well indeed.

That was why, upon spotting the advertisement in the Seattle paper the day she turned twenty-one, she knew exactly what she would do next. As a full-fledged adult, she could make her own decisions. Her first one was to retrieve her brother from where he had spent all those years so she could finally keep her promise to Papa.

But carrying out her plan hadn't been as simple as devising it. Melissa shuddered, remembering that day last week.

She found Fred Clemson, Erna and Bert's oldest son, unwilling to part with the boy. He needed him on the farm, he'd said. No matter what argument she presented, Fred wouldn't relent. Then she noticed that while the middle-aged farmer's small black eyes glittered with a troubling light, Craig stared doggedly at his scuffed brown boots, refusing to look at the man who had raised him. The strained atmosphere in the parlor so affected Melissa that a sense of urgency overtook her. She knew she had to get her brother away, no matter what it took.

Later that night, ignoring every bit of caution, every ounce of self-preservation, Melissa went to the barn loft where she'd learned Craig slept and asked him to come away with her. To her relief, he grabbed his change of clothes and fairly flew down the rickety ladder.

Hoping Fred wouldn't send the law after them, Melissa then drove Gertrude, her aged mare, as hard as she could to get away from the Willamette Valley. She'd had no concrete reason on which to base her feelings, but every instinct had told her she *had* to get her brother away from Fred Clemson.

To play it safe, she swore Craig to secrecy. No one must find out what she'd done. She wouldn't put it past Fred to send the sheriff after her to get Craig back. Even now, despite her precarious position, she felt she'd done the right thing.

Another shudder racked her. Then she shook her head. No. She wouldn't let herself think of trouble today. She had just achieved one of her grandest goals. She was an independent, employed woman. And she had a house.

If she could find it.

"Oh, silly," she muttered. "How could you forget to ask directions?"

"You said, miss?"

At the sound of the masculine baritone, Melissa looked up. And up. *Way* up.

The man wore a red flannel shirt to ward off the nip in the October air. Navy suspenders descended over a broad chest, and faded denim trousers clad his long legs. As Melissa glanced upward again, she noticed his green eyes. Clear and bright, they reflected curiosity and interest. A shock of black hair fell on his brow.

"Excuse me, miss, but are you all right?"

Melissa's cheeks grew warm. Oh, dear. The lumberman had spoken to her, and she had been too busy staring at him to answer. Well, he was such a fine-looking man, surely her momentary lapse was excusable.

"Er . . . yes, I am," she said. "Just a mite lost. I'm new in town, you see."

A smile tipped the man's mouth. "Who exactly are you?"

"The new cook at the Dinner Bell," she answered, satisfaction flowing through her.

His right eyebrow rose. "You are, are you? Who decided?"

"Why, Mr. August, of course." Melissa waved her much-creased bit of newsprint before his eyes. "I came in answer to this. He hired me a few minutes ago."

"He did, did he?" The lumberman's eyes narrowed, and he subjected her to a closer scrutiny.

Melissa felt uncomfortable for a moment. Who was her inquisitor anyway? The owner of the New Hope Lumber Company himself had found her experience sufficient to offer her the position. This man had no right to question the decision. Did he?

"Yes," she said, lifting her chin. "I'm a fine cook. You'll see. Make sure you come for supper two days from now. I figure it will take me that long to set things to rights."

"You can be sure I'll come sample your meals. After all, your employment is temporary until you prove yourself."

"Mr. August said no such thing!" Melissa exclaimed, dismay pooling in her middle.

The tall logger chuckled. "He's desperate, that's why. I think he would hire just about *anyone* if it meant no more of Mabel's rock-hard biscuits and stringy chicken."

Melissa allowed herself to relax. "I'm confident you will find my meals satisfactory—even if I can't imagine why you're taking on such airs about this. Mr. August is the boss. He hired me."

At that, the man's laughter rang out deep and rich. Melissa was captivated by the sound. It sent a ripple of pleasure through her, reminding her that it had been a while since she had felt that good about anything.

Still, she couldn't see why he was laughing at her. "Pray tell, let me in on the joke, sir."

"Gladly. Allow me to introduce myself. I'm Calvin Stevenson, Sam August's partner and owner of the New Hope Lumber Mill. Your employer, as much as my canny cohort himself."

Melissa felt her cheeks heat again. Her eyes widened and dread filled her. Had she ruined her chances? "I didn't know. I-I didn't mean to offend—"

"Neither did I," said Mr. Stevenson, cutting off her apology. "Shall we start over then?" He extended his hand. "I'm pleased to make your acquaintance, Miss . . . ?"

"Barnhart. Melissa Barnhart."

"Pleasure indeed, Miss Barnhart. And you say we can sample your cooking two days from now?"

Melissa quickly ran down the mental list of things she needed to do. "I think that should give me just enough time."

"I'll be looking forward to it then. In fact, every bachelor in New Hope will, I reckon."

Melissa donned a mischievous grin. "On account of Mabel's biscuits and chicken, no doubt."

Again Mr. Stevenson laughed, and Melissa felt herself charmed. What a pleasant sound—contagious, too. She found herself chuckling, then laughing outright, just for the joy of it.

A sense of rightness filled her then. Suddenly she knew she had done the right thing coming to New Hope. *Hope.* Something she had fought to cling to for years.

"Well, Miss Barnhart, please let me know if there's any

way I can help. You'll find me at the mill or at the men's dormitory on Main Street. I'd be happy to be of assistance to someone who promises to improve our lives so richly."

With his words, Mr. Stevenson winked one of those bright green eyes. A shimmer of . . . something sped through Melissa. My goodness! What a charmer. A novel experience, indeed. It surprised her how well she liked it.

But she wasn't sure it was the sort of thing she should encourage. He was, after all, her employer. She grew serious. "Thank you for your kind offer, but I have a strapping brother who is up to any task."

The black eyebrows rose again. "Brother? How old? Is he interested in steady work?"

"Craig is only twelve, and he needs schooling more than work. But as you can see, I'll have plenty of help getting settled."

Mr. Stevenson gave her a nod. "Very well. Just remember, there's help if you need it and a job at the mill for Craig when he's ready."

Melissa frowned. "I've heard mills are risky places. I don't want my brother in danger." Not now that she was fully responsible for Craig. She couldn't let anything happen to him; she couldn't fail to keep her promise to Papa this time.

"I'll make sure he's safe when he works for me, ma'am. I take care of my workers. Always have and always will."

Melissa liked the ring of conviction in his voice. "That's good to know," she said, remembering the mean glint in Fred's eyes and Craig's refusal to look at the man.

Before the bad feelings took hold again, her companion continued. "Seeing how you have so much to do," he said, "and since it's in my poor stomach's best interest that you do it quickly, I'll be letting you go. It's been a pleasure making your acquaintance, Miss Barnhart."

Melissa nodded and made herself smile. "I'm glad to be in New Hope, Mr. Stevenson. You have no idea how much."

Turning toward the wagon, Melissa remembered she had no idea where to go. "Er . . . there *is* something you could do for me."

"That is . . . ?"

"You could give me directions to my ho—the cabin Mr. August said we would use."

With a nod, Mr. Stevenson came to the wagon. "Let me give you a hand." He did, then followed her with a leap onto the bench at her side. "I'll drive you there and show you our town as we go."

In the minutes it took to cross the settlement, Melissa found herself charmed, not just by her companion, but by the town that filled his voice with pride. Obviously, he had worked hard to establish his business. The clean street and well-maintained buildings showed dedication and prosperity.

She had come to the right place.

"Here we are," Mr. Stevenson said, pulling old Gertrude to a stop before a neat, rectangular log structure.

Melissa drew in a sharp breath. In moments she would enter her new home.

Home.

Something she had lost when the Barnhart family drove their prairie schooner away from the farm in Ohio twelve years ago. Something she longed for as she mourned the death of her mother on the way out west, and that of her father soon after reaching their destination. Something she'd vowed to find again, to build for herself and her brother.

And here it was.

Plain it was, but sturdy, too. The cabin's log walls were pieced and notched in a way that made them look solid enough to withstand whatever came their way. White chinking filled the cracks between the wood, and clean plate glass covered the two small windows on either side of the door. A brick chimney rose up the right side of the structure. Joy filled Melissa's heart.

How unbelievably appropriate! The Barnhart family would make their home in a log cabin in Washington State. As Papa had planned their move west, Mama had begun piecing a quilt in the Log Cabin pattern. She'd worked on the coverlet every evening, and she'd told Melissa all about the new home the family would build when they arrived at their destination. The gold, rust, and brown blanket had come to represent all the good things awaiting the Barnharts. Although Mama died before finishing the piece or reaching their destination, Melissa was sure the perfect little log home would have delighted her mother.

"You're sure you don't want to go to the Dinner Bell first?" Mr. Stevenson asked, longing in his voice.

"I'm sure," Melissa answered, her heart pounding, her cheeks chilled by the nip in the late fall air. The cabin would provide shelter from the fast-approaching winter season. Suddenly, her excitement threatened her decorum. "Let's go inside. Please."

"I'm sorry, ma'am," he said, his voice contrite. "I was thinking of my tortured taste buds rather than your exhaustion. Of course, you want to rest before heading to work."

Making a vague sound, Melissa scrambled over the side of the wagon. She approached the cabin, drinking in every detail. Next spring she would hang flower boxes beneath the windows and plant rosebushes to flank the door.

And curtains! Curtains would look inviting behind the shiny glass. A curl of smoke rising from the chimney would always welcome her brother at the end of the day.

Ah yes. The Barnhart family had a home again.

As a thrill wriggled through her, a long-forgotten memory returned. She caught her breath.

Christmas.

The Barnharts would be together again this Christmas.

Melissa would do whatever it took to recreate the merriment and wonder her mother had always cooked up for the holidays back in Ohio. Christmas would offer her the perfect opportunity to make up to Craig all he had missed because she hadn't kept her promise to Papa. And she would do it in this solid, cozy, rough log cabin in the town of New Hope in Washington State.

Oh yes, indeed. Melissa Barnhart was finally home.

Craig scuffed his cracked brown boots against the packed dirt of New Hope's Main Street. He wasn't sure how he felt about living here with his sister. They were strangers, after all.

Then a strident female voice caught his attention.

"You shoulda seen her, Ida Mae. Brazen as any hussy you could *ever* imagine."

"Ooooh! Tell me, do, Mabel. You know how I always want to know the latest."

Craig glanced in the direction of the women. A fat old lady with scarlet hair nodded at her equally aged though skinny companion. "She sashayed up to Sam August and batted her eyes at 'im. 'I'm Melissa Barnhart. Your new cook,' she said. That old coot just smiled and toppled at her mincing little feet."

Craig narrowed his eyes. He didn't like those comments about his sister one bit.

"I tell you, Mabel," offered the skinny one, "sometimes a body has to wonder about men's common sense."

"Especially when a floozy simpers at 'em," added Mabel, hanging laundry on the line.

Anger grew inside him. He didn't know Melissa well, but nothing about her called for such ugly words. Besides, she was kin. A Barnhart like him.

The skinny one—Ida Mae—bent down and grabbed

something from the basket between the two biddies. She shook out an enormous green item, then stuck it with a pin on the line. "So what came of all this?" she asked.

Mabel glowered at her friend. "What do you think? *She's* taking over the Dinner Bell."

Ida Mae clucked in sympathy as she spread what looked like a bedsheet on the line. "What are you going to do now?"

"Do?" asked Mabel. "Why, I'm going to do what any smart woman would. I'm gonna run the little hussy out of town."

Craig's rage reached the boiling point. "I can't let 'er get away with it," he muttered. Fear of what the two gossips might do to his sister and indignation at their insults bubbled up inside him. "Not on your life."

Then a sly grin widened his mouth. He knew just how he'd teach the loose-lipped women a lesson and protect his sister's honor at the same time.

Chapter Two

As Melissa unloaded the box of Mama's treasures from the wagon, she blew a strand of hair off her forehead and wondered where Craig had gone. True, she had given him permission to explore the town, but New Hope wasn't precisely a sprawling capital.

"Where in the world could he be?" she muttered while carrying the box inside the cabin.

Huffing from the exertion, she became aware of a hubbub outside and down the street. From the doorway, she glanced in the direction of the sound and noticed a group of men gathered at the corner where Pine Street—her new home's address—met Main Street. Male laughter and conversation drifted her way.

Curious, she climbed back into the wagon, hoping for a better look at the commotion. All she saw was some green fabric flapping from the roof of a house and the congregated loggers.

"What could possibly be so interesting?" she asked Gertrude, who swished her tail but did not respond.

When she saw a tall, gray-haired lady come out of a house

across from the men, Melissa decided to indulge her curiosity. She slipped off the buckboard and strolled down Pine Street in as indifferent a manner as she could don.

Then the rail-thin woman emitted a wail.

The men laughed louder.

A large woman with unlikely red hair charged out from another house on Pine. Moments later her bellows joined the squeals of the other.

"Whoo-eee!" whistled one logger. "Will ya lookit them things? They're pert near big enough to sail a ship all the way to Pea-king!"

A round of laughter followed.

"Seems to me," said a man with thinning hair, "Mabel's been eatin' too much of her own cooking. I wonder how she and all that green stuff stay on that bicycle of hers."

Melissa sped up her pace, dying to learn the cause of the stir. As she approached, she identified the emerald fabric fluttering in the breeze and blushed in mortification.

Oh, dear! How embarrassing. Someone had hung a pair of voluminous bicycle bloomers on display. If Melissa wasn't much mistaken, they belonged to the heavyset redhead who continued to clamor over the garment.

"Give those back to me," the woman yelled, reaching for the green cotton. "You uncivilized savages! I tell you, a woman's got a right to respect."

With a dramatic wave, she smacked her hand across her bountiful chest and swooned. Three flannel-shirted men rushed to catch her, and Melissa watched them strain as they tried to keep their burden from hitting the road.

Although the scene abounded with humor, Melissa felt sorry for the lady. She would hate to have her undergarments displayed like that before a group of rowdy men. Who could have done something so mean-spirited?

The crowd then parted, and Cal Stevenson strode up to the porch. He grabbed the offending garment, wadded it up, and hastened to the collapsed woman. "Here you are, Mabel," he said in a kind voice. "It's all right now. Go on home while I deal with this bunch."

Suddenly the men grew silent. Mabel straightened, hugging her bloomers. The thin woman clasped her friend's chubby elbow, and together the two made their way to Mabel's home.

Mr. Stevenson turned toward the men. "Well, now, I want to know which one of you stooped so low as to humiliate Mrs. Sauerbehr. If no one confesses, I'll be forced to dock everyone's pay for taking part in this disgrace."

None of the men spoke up. Mr. Stevenson narrowed his green eyes to scour each male face before him. Apparently, what he saw there satisfied him. With a nod and a frown he said, "I can't say as I think any of you is lying to me."

The gathered men shook their heads.

"I tell ya, boss," said a lanky blond man, "I didn't do it. I don't reckon none of the rest did it, neither. We all just quit working and came back together. Don't know who coulda done it."

General agreement resounded in the street.

Mr. Stevenson shrugged, the frown still on his forehead. "Fine. I'll leave things as they stand. But this isn't over. I'll find out who the culprit is, and he will have to take responsibility for shaming Mabel. He'll have to reckon with me."

The men broke up into pairs and headed for Main Street. Melissa snuggled her woolen shawl tighter against the late autumn chill and returned home.

Home. She smiled. A haven for the Barnharts, where they could get to know each other, where they could stand on their own, a family once again. No trouble would come their way here.

As she unpacked their belongings, Melissa began to hum. "Turkey in the Straw" was an excellent tune to keep one moving as one worked. Contentment filled her, something she hadn't experienced in many years.

At the sound of steps on the front stoop, she called, "It's about time you returned, Craig. I can certainly use your help. . . ."

Her words died off when she turned and saw Cal Stevenson at Craig's left, a fistful of shirt filling the man's right hand. "I regret making his acquaintance under these circumstances, Miss Barnhart, but I'm returning your troublemaking brother. He caused a scene not too long ago."

"Oh, dear," she murmured, fearing she knew what Mr. Stevenson would say next.

But she didn't. "Tell your sister what you did. Confession is good for the soul."

Craig jutted his chin up and stuck out his bony chest.

When the boy didn't speak, her employer tugged him forward by the shirt. "Come on, now. You're guilty, and you have to talk. I'm not leaving until you do."

Craig shuffled his feet, then glared at Melissa. His fair cheeks blazed with anger. "I took something from where I found it and moved it somewhere else."

At her brother's carefully worded statement, Melissa fought a smile. Not that she condoned his actions, but Craig's so-called confession showed cleverness—perhaps too much. "And?"

More footwork. "And . . . some people thought it was funny, only some others didn't, and *he*—" Craig jabbed his thumb in Mr. Stevenson's direction—"said I'd humiliated someone, but she deserved it—"

"Enough!" Melissa cried. "I saw the spectacle myself and did not find it particularly funny. I agree with Mr. Stevenson. You owe the lady an apology, and you will be punished besides."

"Can't make me," Craig growled.

Mr. Stevenson turned the boy until he was facing him.

"No, but I can make you see the error of your ways. Would you like someone to embarrass you the way you embarrassed Mabel?"

Craig stared at Mr. Stevenson's shirt in stony silence.

Melissa's hackles twitched at the man's authoritative tone.

"You know," Mr. Stevenson said, "the Good Book says we're to do unto others as we would have them do unto us. Would you like someone to treat your sister the way you treated Mrs. Sauerbehr?"

Craig's cheeks flared red. "She's a sour old bear, all right. And she treated Melissa to some pretty nasty gossip first."

Melissa was taken aback. Mr. Stevenson looked as stunned as she felt.

"What do you mean?" he asked, releasing his captive.

With an obvious effort to regain his dignity, Craig stuffed his dangling shirttail back inside his trousers. "I heard her say nasty things about Melissa. The old biddy called her dirty, ugly names, and she doesn't even know her! I couldn't let her get away with it. I had to defend my sister's honor."

Mr. Stevenson studied the boy. "Hmm . . . ," he said. "Justice?"

"Yeah."

After awkward moments of silence, Melissa's new employer continued. "Justice belongs to the Lord, Craig. Because we're his creation, he calls us to obey his commandments, and one of those says we're to love our neighbors as we love ourselves. God takes care of everything else."

Craig shot him a skeptical look. "Who is this God person?"

Mr. Stevenson's eyebrows shot up to his hairline. "You don't know who . . . God is?"

Craig shrugged.

Mr. Stevenson gave Melissa a strange stare. Her hackles sprang to immediate and full attention.

Who did he think he was, coming in like that, scolding her

brother as if she couldn't handle him herself? She was, after all, an independent woman. She opened her mouth to object to Mr. Stevenson's highhanded manner, but he began speaking again.

"Seems to me you need instruction as much as correction, young man. I'll start by saying that you're now responsible for helping Mrs. Sauerbehr around her place. You'll do any work she needs done." When Craig glared, Mr. Stevenson shook his finger at the boy. "Without grumbling."

Although Melissa wanted to refuse him the right to exact punishment on her brother, Mr. Stevenson was in charge of the town and his demand made sense. "Sounds fair enough to me," she said with reluctance.

"We're agreed, then," he continued. "But if, in spite of helping Mrs. Sauerbehr, I find you still have too much free time, you will start working for me at the mill. Idle hands are the devil's playground, you understand."

Craig grunted unintelligibly.

Although relieved that the punishment would be no harsher, Melissa made up her mind right then to keep her brother under tighter control. She didn't want to risk another opportunity where Mr. Stevenson could so easily impose his authority on her again. She stiffly thanked her employer, then added, "I'll handle my brother from here on in."

"Ah," he said, a smile playing on his well-shaped lips, "but there's more. I'll expect him in my office come nine on Sunday morning. We have our worship time then, Sam and I. Craig can come and meet God. You're welcome yourself."

Although she was glad the escapade had come to no worse end, Melissa felt distinctly uncomfortable with her boss's last demand. She balked at trusting a stranger, especially one who could so easily hurt her and hers. Even if he was impressively attractive, eminently fair, and scrupulously reasonable, Mr. Stevenson could take away her job and her home. Still, since she didn't want to jeopardize the position she so needed to make her dreams for her family come true, she nodded with ever greater reluctance.

"Remember, Miss Barnhart," he went on to say, "if you need me, and I suspect you might, I'm happy to help."

Squaring her shoulders, Melissa responded. "As I said, I can most certainly handle my brother. Thank you very much."

Mr. Stevenson left utter silence in his wake. Melissa's bravado went with him. She studied Craig for a moment, then closed her eyes. What had she taken on when she retrieved him from Fred's farm? She scarcely knew him. How was she going to ensure he became a decent, upright young man? How would she ever manage all alone?

In the days that followed their ignominious arrival in New Hope, Melissa had plenty of time to ponder her situation as she worked at the Dinner Bell. Deep in her heart she knew she had made the right decisions. The Barnharts belonged together. Her position as cook would keep them from having to rely on anyone else. Thanks to that job, she could finally make right what others stronger than a nine-year-old girl had made wrong; she was finally going to keep her promise to Papa.

As she and Craig had traveled north from the Willamette Valley, she had hoped she'd left her troubles behind, but now it seemed she had undertaken a brand-new set.

Raising a young man suddenly seemed a daunting prospect. As she remembered Mr. Stevenson's handling of Craig, Melissa experienced an uneasy gratitude for his intervention. He had been firm with her brother, making it clear that he would not stand for bad behavior. At the same time, he had kept his composure, not once losing his temper. Oh, how she wished she'd had his strength, his assurance, that she could have handled the situation as competently, demonstrating that she could manage on her own.

How different Mr. Stevenson was from Great-uncle Bert. At the least offense—real or imagined—her mother's uncle would fly into a frenzy, his face reddening and his voice thundering. Everyone, neighbors included, always ran for cover at the first sound of Bert's rage. Soon after the yelling started, he used his hammy hand on whomever was closest. Melissa learned to dodge the attack from a very early date. She also came to admire those who displayed control over their emotions.

Like Calvin Stevenson.

To thank him for his fair treatment of her brother—and to display her talents as a cook—she had baked him a buttermilk pie the first day she made supper at the Dinner Bell. He'd helped himself to not just seconds but thirds, forcing Sam August to wheedle a slice from the leftovers.

The two still talked about the treat.

They weren't the only ones. Her cooking had made the loggers of New Hope mighty happy. They lavished her with compliments, and Melissa found herself the uncomfortable belle of the ball—so to speak. At odd hours of the day, as she tried to attend to the business of cooking and running the dining hall for the town's unmarried men, she often had to cope with unwanted attention from the bachelors.

She had never been on the receiving end of so much help.

"Miss Melissa," one would say, hat in hand, a sheepish smile on his weathered face, "is there anything I could be doing for you today? I'd be beholden if you'd let me be your willing servant."

Flattered by the attention but fully aware that the men wanted more than to help for the sake of helping, she gently turned down the offers. Besides, she could handle the kitchen on her own. If she needed help, she had a brother to call on. But as soon as she sent one would-be suitor on his way, another filled her doorway.

As she opened the oven to check on her bread, she again heard the harrumphing that announced the arrival of another "helper."

"Afternoon, Miss Melissa."

Rapping her knuckles on a risen loaf, Melissa spared a glance for the caller. Marcus Whitlow's portly bulk filled the doorway. Since the bread needed more baking, she closed the oven, turned, and smiled at the blushing man. "Hello, Mr. Whitlow. How may I help you?"

"No, ma'am, I didn't come to ask fer yer help a'tall. I came to help *you*. I've peeled my share of 'taters over the years, and if you would do me the honor, I'd like to peel some more fer you."

As the millworker shifted his weight from foot to foot, the floorboards beneath him gave a protesting creak. "Thank you for your kind offer, Mr. Whitlow, but as you can see, I'm about done for tonight. You should enjoy your time off, you know. Perhaps read a good book."

Despite her efforts, the man grew flustered. His ears turned as red as his cheeks. "Aw, pshaw, miss! I never did hold much fer book larnin' an' all. Can't read more'n my name and some ciphers. But if you're sure you don't need my help, I'll go get myself cleaned up fer your wonnerful supper."

"You do that, then."

Relief washed over her as the door closed. Melissa had no desire to be courted. She had only recently achieved independence. Marriage didn't feature in her plans. Making a home for herself and Craig—making up for the lost years—mattered more than becoming somebody's missus. Besides, she had found steady work that paid good wages and entitled her to a fine home.

The log cabin had proven as snug and solid as she had

initially thought it would be. She had spent the past few evenings after cleaning up supper setting out her treasures, those precious items Mama had packed in Ohio all those years ago. Melissa finally had a home where she could display them.

With supper nearly ready to serve and the bread needing more time in the oven, she went to the corner of the kitchen, where a large rocker held court. From a plump carpetbag at its side, she extracted her beloved mother's Log Cabin quilt and resumed stitching where she had left off the night before. She was determined to finish it by Christmas and put it to use in the Barnharts' very own log cabin home. Satisfaction simmered inside her, even if it never quite canceled the guilt she felt at having failed to keep her promise to Papa.

That failure had led to her current troubles. What exactly had happened between Fred and Craig during those lost years? Melissa didn't know, but she had her suspicions. She was determined to extract an answer from the boy, but in order to do that, she had to win his trust. She hoped that by making a peaceful, happy home for him, sharing her joy at the rapidly approaching holiday, showing him how important it was for them to grow close, she could ease the way for that conversation. She just *had* to do everything she could to make things right for Craig.

To her dismay, she again heard footsteps at the kitchen door. "Really, Mr. Whitlow," she said in a firm yet friendly tone, "I don't need—"

"Was he bothering you?" asked Mr. Stevenson.

The unexpected voice startled Melissa, and she stabbed herself with the needle. "Ouch!"

"Are you all right?"

She grew flustered, then shook her hand to ease the pain, too self-conscious to stick the thumb in her mouth. "Oh yes. It's just a little jab. I'm fine."

"Don't move," he warned, then strode to the sink and

grabbed a clean kitchen cloth from the hook where it hung. "Here, let's see that stab." He wiped away the drop of blood that had beaded, then took the heavy blanket from her lap. "You don't want to stain this beautiful quilt. Let me help you."

His immediate concern and kindness warmed Melissa's heart, and she again felt drawn to the man. But as soon as she felt her resolve weaken, she reminded herself of his position in her life. He paid her wages, owned the house where she lived. She couldn't afford to let down her guard.

She stood. "Thank you for the assistance, but I could have seen to my thumb myself." A frown lined his brow at her words. Perhaps she'd been too harsh, but she had to keep a distance between them. Still, simple courtesy wouldn't hurt. "I do appreciate your compliment on my mother's quilt."

Mr. Stevenson folded the blanket, his long fingers caressing the strips of brown, rust, and gold fabric that formed the squares. "Your mother's?"

"She began piecing it in Ohio as my father prepared for our move west. Every evening she stitched away while telling stories about life in Washington. Her relatives had come this way earlier."

A solemn look appeared on Mr. Stevenson's face. "Since you're still working on it, I can assume she didn't—"

"Mama died when Craig was born on the Oregon Trail. She never got to see the Willamette Valley."

"I'm sorry."

"So am I."

Mr. Stevenson fingered the tiny stitching along a piece of gold calico. "She left you something beautiful."

Nodding, she felt a tug of sadness for the years she hadn't been able to share with the mother she loved. "The memories are even more so."

The back door burst open, and Craig clattered inside. "I

sure hope you're serving supper soon, Sissy. I'm hungrier'n a—"

He fell abruptly silent, and Melissa looked to see what had halted the flow of words. Craig's chocolate-brown eyes glared at Mr. Stevenson. A mixture of defiance and fear played over his thin features. "What's *he* doing here?"

Melissa gasped at his churlishness. "Craig Barnhart! Mind your manners. Please apologize to Mr. Stevenson."

Craig grimaced, mumbled something that might have been "Sorry," and stomped to the sink. He pumped a glassful of water, then noisily chugged it down.

Melissa felt mortified, wishing she could turn the boy over her knee. With a glance at her employer, she found him studying her brother, sympathy and kindness in his green eyes. Amazing. Craig had been as rude as she had ever heard him, yet Mr. Stevenson had responded with more kindness. How did he do it?

Then it occurred to her that her brother did have a point. "Although Craig's manner was all wrong, he asked a good question. Was there something you needed, Mr. Stevenson?"

"Oh yes, I nearly forgot. We have excellent news. New Hope has found a pastor for the church we're building. Mrs. Sauerbehr wants to hold a social to welcome him after his first service. Sam and I would like you to organize the food. You won't need to do all the work, as the ladies of the town want to contribute to the celebration, but someone should oversee things."

A vague, pleasant memory of Sunday mornings and organ music came to Melissa. "I haven't been to church since we left Ohio. Will he arrive in time for Christmas?"

"Yes. New Hope will celebrate that holy day properly this year," he answered with satisfaction.

"Then let's make it a Christmas party. I'd be happy to help—"

"Hey, Sissy, quit talkin'. Somethin's burning!"

Spinning, Melissa saw smoke belching out of every orifice in the stove. "Oh no! My bread!" What would Mr. Stevenson think of her now?

She ran to the black metal monster, grabbing another cloth from the hook, and opened the hot iron door with a clang. Black billowed around her, making her cough.

Swatting the cloud from her eyes, Melissa reached into the oven, hoping she could salvage some of the bread. To her dismay, she withdrew eight rectangles of coal.

"Oh, dear, what will I do now?" she moaned, wringing her hands. "The men like to soak up their gravy, and I made venison stew. I wanted to do a good job, and here I've burnt the bread—"

Strong hands landed on her shoulders, and Melissa felt herself being turned. Embarrassed, she stared at Mr. Stevenson's sawdust-covered boots.

"Miss Barnhart," he said in his deep voice. "It's only bread. The stew will be plenty for tonight. Please don't fret like this."

Melissa fought welling tears. Would Mr. Stevenson finally lose his temper? Would he lash out as Uncle Bert always had? Hoping to avert such an outburst, she said, "Yes, but I wanted to do a good job, and I'm afraid this doesn't reflect well on me."

"You're doing fine, as I'm sure you'll continue to do. This is just a small hitch. Do you have any breakfast biscuits left?"

"Not a one," she said, relieved by his apparent lack of anger. "But I could whip up some more." As she made her suggestion, she heard men troop into the dining room. "Oh no. It's too late."

Turning, she said to Craig, "Please pass me the bowls. While you take them out, I'll slice the first batch of bread."

"The *first* batch of bread?" Mr. Stevenson asked, an eyebrow raised, a lopsided grin on his lips. "You had already baked bread, and you're this upset?"

"Well, the last time they ate all eight loaves straight away and asked for more. I want to keep up with your men's appetites."

With a chuckle, Melissa's employer said, "The men will love whatever you serve. It's a great deal better than what we had before you came to our rescue."

The last he said in Craig's direction, then winked. To Melissa's pleased surprise, her brother's face lost its surly expression. He even smiled. Briefly, but he did smile.

"Thank you for your kind words, Mr. Stevenson. Rest assured I'll do better in the future. And for the Christmas party."

"I won't worry a minute, Miss Barnhart."

As he left the kitchen, Melissa let herself relax. "We're fortunate I found this job. Mr. Stevenson seems to be a good man."

Craig's expression hardened. He snorted. "If you say so."

"He's been fair with us. Your punishment was light, and he even laughed about the bread. It could have been far worse."

The boy gave her a strange look, one full of bitterness. It startled her. Twelve was too young for such emotion.

"Craig, honey, what's wrong?"

He left the kitchen without a word. Later, she took note of his grim silence despite Mr. Stevenson's efforts to draw him into conversation. Misgivings again filled her middle. Something was wrong with her brother. Something worse than resentment toward the man who had made him accountable for his actions.

Again Melissa became painfully aware that she and Craig were virtual strangers. What had happened to him during those lost years to cause the torment in his eyes?

CHAPTER THREE

In the weeks that followed, Cal was happy to see his dream for New Hope beginning to take shape. A fair number of families responded to his advertisement, and the sound of children playing became commonplace as he walked the streets.

A bevy of single ladies had also flown into town. Clean laundry had become the weekly norm, and loose buttons and ripped shirts soon found swift remedy. A twinkle appeared in many a masculine eye as loggers and millworkers took to sprucing up.

Work on the church building proceeded at a brisk pace. Even the pews were coming along nicely. Residents eagerly awaited the arrival of an upright piano and a brass bell, not to mention Pastor Andrew Mosely from Pennsylvania.

Dyspepsia mercifully became a thing of the past.

Cal thanked his heavenly Father for leading Melissa Barnhart to their small town. The young woman had shown herself to be a fine cook, and she ran the Dinner Bell most efficiently. She was also a pleasure to look at, but that had caused a flap.

Not only was Marcus Whitlow smitten with Miss Barnhart, but Stewie Grimm was as well. The two had become a hazard rather than a help at the mill, and Cal's patience was running low.

He couldn't wholly blame them. Miss Barnhart easily turned a man's head. Cal often found himself thinking of her. Even though he shouldn't.

Despite her many endearing attributes, Melissa didn't know Cal's Lord and Savior. As a Christian, he knew that he needed to avoid any attraction between himself and an unbeliever. While he longed to settle down with a mate and—if the Lord so blessed them—start a family, Cal preferred to remain single rather than marry a woman who didn't share his faith.

Still, he couldn't help noticing Melissa at suppertime. Her dark-honey eyes and sunny smile never failed to brighten his evenings, and her meals were nothing short of scrumptious.

Despite the attention from the men, Melissa seemed unaffected. She treated everyone the same, bestowing smiles and animated chatter on one and all.

Yet Cal longed to see a special light brighten those golden eyes when she turned them on him, and he couldn't deny wishing for a private smile. Even though he knew better. His hankering became a frequent topic of prayer, as he wanted more than anything to do his Lord's will.

Then there was her continued rejection of his assistance. He couldn't understand why she fought so hard against him. He only wanted to help her, get to know her better. Besides, her hands *were* full with Craig, and Cal, having once been a boy, could give her the benefit of his experience. He admitted to feeling a sting of pain each time she said in that tight, determined voice, "I can handle it."

"I know what your Word says," he murmured this day, kneeling by his bed, the worn Bible open before him, "but I can't stop my feelings for Melissa. I want to spend time with her, to make her laugh and smile, to speak with her for hours on end."

Then Cal acknowledged his secret wish—secret only to him, as surely God had known the silent desire of his heart all along—to lead Melissa to a saving knowledge of Jesus to ease the way for his budding emotions. He feared that he had been using the Barnharts' need for salvation to his advantage. Had he been sharing his faith with them on Sunday mornings for merely selfish reasons?

He preferred to think he wanted to lead them to Christ for their eternal benefit or to fulfill his Lord's command, but he had to be honest. He wanted to court Melissa, but before he could do so he wanted her to know his God.

Confessing his sin, Cal flipped through the pages and stopped at a much-read passage. The words of the psalmist had always served him well. *Search me, O God, and know my heart: try me, and know my thoughts: And see if there be any wicked way in me, and lead me in the way everlasting.*

"Your will, Father. Your way, not mine." As he prayed, Cal felt peace return. He had given the matter to the Lord. He would trust God to search his heart for any possible wickedness. As always, his heavenly Father would lead him down the right path.

Come Sunday morning, Melissa fought the usual battle to get her brother to the informal worship time at the New Hope Lumber Company office. She had come to look at the hour spent there as a highlight of her week. Not only was it a pleasure to listen to Mr. Stevenson's deep voice, to watch his green eyes sparkle with interest, to study his incisive gestures as he emphasized a particular point, but it was also especially satisfying to learn what the Bible had to say.

Melissa had lacked opportunities for spiritual growth in

the last twelve years, and now she hungered to learn all she could. On Sunday mornings she soaked up everything Mr. August and Mr. Stevenson had to offer, not yet certain she had anything to contribute to the conversation.

It troubled her that her sibling didn't seem to need the kind of nurture she had come to crave. Craig argued and balked and glowered, acceding to attend only on the threat of further punishment by Mr. Stevenson.

When they finally left the log cabin on Pine Street and headed for the office, the Barnharts inevitably bore soured dispositions. This Sunday was not unlike preceding ones.

"Can't see why you're makin' me go," Craig shot at Melissa as he dragged his feet along the dirt road. "All this yackety-yackety stuff is boring."

"It's part of your *instruction*," she replied, reminding him of her boss's words. "Besides, it will do you good. I daresay decent, upright men like Mr. August and Mr. Stevenson can teach you plenty. They both say they learned everything they know from Scripture."

Craig shrugged and muttered under his breath. To Melissa, it sounded as if he'd said, "What do *they* know about anything?" but she didn't challenge the boy.

At the office she greeted the men, both of whom invited her to drop the formality of her address.

"Even if I'm old enough to be your papa," said Mr. August, patting her hand, "I'd be right pleased if you called me Sam."

Mr. Stevenson grinned. "If you call him Sam, then you'd better call me Cal. I refuse to have you make me sound older than Methuselah there."

"Watch who you call old, boy!"

"Just calling things as I see them."

Melissa couldn't stop a chuckle. "I wouldn't want you men to fight over such a minor detail. You're Sam and Cal from now on."

As he took her shawl and hung it from a wooden peg on the wall, Cal said, "And you're Melissa. It's a beautiful name."

A snort at the open doorway informed the adults that Craig had finally arrived. At the boy's scowl, Melissa's cheeks warmed. He then graced the men with that same glare. Something had to be done about his attitude, but Melissa didn't know what. She only knew she had to do it before Cal jumped in to rescue her yet again. She couldn't rely on her employer to solve her problems. She had to handle things herself.

Before she could dwell on the matter, Cal called the group to prayer. Then Sam stood, and after much clearing of his throat, he handed each Barnhart a brown paper-covered parcel. "I was saving these for Christmas, but the Father led me to give them to you today. I figger he knows better 'n I do the right time."

When Melissa removed the wrapping from her gift, her breath caught in her throat. A brand-new, leather-bound Bible lay in her hands, gilt letters sparkling in a ray of sunshine from the window at her side. "How lovely!" she said with a sigh of pleasure. "But it's far too valuable. I can't accept such a pricey—"

"Nonsense!" Sam exclaimed. "Consider it part of your wages. And I'm right pleased you like it."

Melissa ran her hand over the fine burgundy cover, relishing its soft, supple feel. "I've never owned anything this beautiful."

"You have your mother's blanket," Cal said.

"You're right," she answered with a smile. "Our Log Cabin quilt *is* beautiful, and I treasure it. As I will this special gift."

Sam blushed and coughed. "Let's be gettin' on with it, else we'll be wasting this fine day the Lord has given us. What text did you choose for today, boy?"

Cal raised an eyebrow. "At twenty-eight I'm no longer a boy, Sam. Think you can remember that?"

"You're still wet behind 'em ears to me, but if you insist, I'll try and remember your druthers. Go on, read the Father's words for us."

Cal opened his Bible, then helped Melissa find her place in her brand-new one. She in turn found the spot for her brother, ignoring Craig's mutinous expression.

Cal began to read. "In his second letter to the Christians in Corinth, Paul says, 'Therefore if any man be in Christ, he is a new creature: old things are passed away; behold, all things are become new. And all things are of God. . . .'"

As the reading continued, Melissa found her attention riveted to the first passage Cal had read. The teaching seemed particularly befitting to her situation. She had come to New Hope seeking a fresh start with her brother, to rebuild the family that had been torn apart. But if she understood the Scripture properly, it was in Christ that she would find that fresh start, not in a new location. God was the one who would provide the chance to build a new family, one rooted in his promises.

She could truly leave the pain of separation behind, the ugly memories of Uncle Bert's rages, the sense of being ill-used for someone else's gain. She could be washed clean of the urge that had led her to kidnap her brother. If she understood the Bible's promise correctly, God would make her life brand new. And maybe, just maybe, God could take away the sting of guilt she had carried for so many years.

Melissa's heart began to pound in anticipation. Yes, she wanted to be a new creature in Christ, but she didn't quite know how. She would have to ask Cal what she had to do to achieve that, how she could come to be "in Christ." Perhaps she would have the opportunity after he finished discussing the verses, before she left for the Dinner Bell to warm up the noon meal she'd cooked the day before.

A short time later Sam and Cal again bowed their heads in prayer, and Melissa followed suit. As soon as the amen was said, Craig leapt up from his chair. "I'm going. I'll be back for lunch."

Melissa had no time to object. Shaking her head, she stood. "I must apologize for him. I'm not sure why his manners are so lacking, but it's something I must correct."

Cal looked puzzled. "What do you mean, you're not sure why? Surely you've watched him grow up."

"That's just it," Melissa said, sadness and guilt returning, bringing with them bitterness as well. "We were separated twelve years ago, just after Papa died. I only saw him again the week before we came to New Hope. We're practically strangers."

"Hmm . . . that would explain some things."

"Such as his frequent disobedience."

"Your being a sister rather than a brother might have something to do with it, too."

"Perhaps."

His green eyes glowed earnestly. "I did offer to help you with him once before. My offer still stands."

Melissa firmed up her spine. "I'll thank you again, but I can handle everything."

At her response, the now-familiar frown bloomed on Cal's forehead. Sam cleared his throat. "I'll be on my way now," he said, cutting off Cal's intended comment. "I've been wanting to ride up to the new section of trees the men'll be cutting into tomorrow. Won't be back before supper."

Relieved by the distraction, Melissa smiled at the older man. "It's a lovely day for a ride. Cool and dry." When he nodded and donned his hat, she added, "Thank you for the Bibles. They're just what we needed."

"'S what I thought," he responded with a satisfied nod, then opened the door. "I'll see you at supper."

"I'll save you a big wedge of pie."

When the door closed, Cal took a step toward Melissa. She again noticed his height and solid build. Added to his decent, caring ways, she suspected that most folks who knew him depended on Cal Stevenson, no matter what their circumstances.

For a moment Melissa found herself wishing she dared count on someone besides herself, but the years at Uncle Bert's had taught her she was the only one she could trust. Everyone else was too busy seeing to their own matters and would betray you at the first chance. Although a still-hopeful part of her insisted Cal wouldn't do such a thing, the other, sadly experienced part of her warned her against weakening her resolve.

Cal's voice broke into her thoughts. "I meant to speak to you about the welcome supper for Pastor Mosely."

Melissa smiled. "I put away a dozen Christmas fruitcakes yesterday. To age them, you know. I made them according to Mama's favorite recipe. Ida Mae plans to play Christmas carols on the new piano, and I have lovely ideas for the decorations. I love the holidays, and I'm glad they're so close now!"

"Well, yes, we did discuss that, but I didn't mean to talk about the preparations. I wanted your permission to escort you—"

"Cal!" Sam yelled from outside. "Come quick! The privy's on fire."

Donning his coat, Cal ran outside. Throwing her shawl around her shoulders, Melissa followed the men. She found Sam tossing a pail to Cal, then pumping water into a bucket by the trough at the logging company's stable. She hurried to their side. "How can I help?"

"Pump!" Cal said on his way to the outhouse. "We'll keep the buckets coming."

As she worked the iron handle, she saw a flame lick out

from the tiny window high on the privy wall. Then, to her horror, she heard a cry. "Oh no! Someone's in there!"

"Can't be," huffed Sam as he held his pail under the pump's spigot.

"But there is," she insisted. "I heard them call for help."

Still pumping, she turned toward the outhouse. Suddenly, the door burst open. Smoke spewed out and two bodies emerged, stumbling, slapping vigorously at sparks that smoldered on each other's garments.

Dropping his bucket, Cal ran to help. "Roll on the ground!" he ordered. "To put out the flames."

As the two tried to follow instructions, Melissa recognized the victims.

"That was a dumb thing to do," groused Richie, a tow-head she'd seen talking to Craig a few times.

"You didn't think so at first," Craig retorted.

"Yeah, but then *you* went and dropped the match!"

"*You* made me laugh!"

"What happened?" Melissa cried, joining Cal.

Wriggling like a night crawler, Richie offered, "The privy caught fire."

"I know *that*," Melissa answered, batting at an ember on his jacket. "How did it start?"

"Don't matter now, missy," Sam said. "The boys look like only their clothes got scorched. We need to put out the blaze afore the barn and the office and the mill catch fire, too. You boys best lend a hand. We'll sort out the whys and where-fores later."

Melissa resumed pumping, her mind teeming with questions. How had the outhouse caught fire? Why had both Richie and Craig been inside when it did? Were they as unharmed as they seemed at first glance?

Soon Sam cried, "We're winnin', boys! It's dying now."

When Melissa felt confident they had virtually doused the flames, she pressed Craig into manning the pump and went to find Cal. "I'm going to the Dinner Bell. Everyone can use a cup of coffee and a bite to eat."

Gratitude and admiration spread over his face. "That's a splendid idea. I know we agreed you would let us fend for ourselves until noon on Sundays, but this is very welcome. We'll be there in a bit."

Melissa hurried, buoyed by his approval, concerned by how quickly it had come to mean so much.

At the dining hall she filled coffeepots and mixed flapjacks while warning herself against her foolish attraction to the successful man who could so easily bring her dreams crashing down around her. She couldn't afford to put her trust in anyone, no matter how good-hearted, generous, or appealing he was.

She had broken the law. A man like Cal Stevenson would never permit a criminal to live in his town. She had to protect herself and her brother. She had to keep her actions secret. She couldn't get close to Cal. No matter how much she might want to.

Soon the sizzle of batter and the aroma of coffee filled the empty building. She didn't have long to wait for the others. Working swiftly, she delivered platters piled high with fragrant cakes and mugs of bolstering brew.

Thinking about Craig's latest escapade, she washed the pans she had used to prepare the spur-of-the-moment feast. As she sudsed a bowl in the enamel sink, she heard footsteps approach. "Cal sent me and Richie to help," said Craig. "What can we do?"

Melissa shot a smile over her shoulder that faded the minute she glimpsed her brother's grim expression. She had to find out what lay behind his dreadful disposition before she could help him change it. And he had to change. Again, the suspicion that Fred had something to do with Craig's problems flitted through her mind, but this certainly wasn't the time to ask. "You can collect the dirty dishes and stack them on the kitchen table. Richie can dry, then put things away where I tell him."

Before long they had washed and stored the crockery. Melissa finished wiping the table, and when the boys tried to slip out the back door, she called them to a halt. "I suggest you take a seat. We have things to discuss."

Craig glared, and Richie looked contrite.

When the two sat, Melissa raked them with a solemn stare. "Suppose you tell me what you were doing in the privy?"

Richie seemed to shrink in contrast to the lively tuft of hair standing upright on his crown. Craig jabbed his chin higher, his expression pugnacious. Neither spoke.

"I'm waiting," she said after the kitchen clock ticked the passing of a long minute.

"As am I," inserted Cal from the doorway.

Melissa, Craig, and Richie spun their heads in his direction. Richie sighed in what sounded to Melissa as defeat. Craig gave one of his patent snorts. She groaned inwardly. "Mr. Stevenson," she said firmly, "I can handle my brother and his friend. Craig's discipline and choice of companions is my business."

"True," Cal answered, the frown again on his forehead. "But a fire on my property is my business, too."

Blushing furiously, Melissa caught her bottom lip between her teeth. She gave Cal a curt nod.

For a moment he clamped down his lips, making a white line appear at their rim. Then he nodded tightly back. "Fire is mighty dangerous in a mill town," he said. "There's an abundance of cut wood everywhere, especially near the office. We could have had a tragedy on our hands today. It's only by the grace of God we didn't. Now I expect you boys to tell me what happened."

Richie sighed in resignation. "We were . . . reading, and . . . a match fell on the book. It burst into flames and Craig dropped it on the pile of . . ." His cheeks turned scarlet beneath the wealth of freckles. "You know . . . *papers.* Then everything else went up."

Melissa narrowed her gaze. "You went into the outhouse to read? Why would you—"

"What were you reading?" Cal asked.

Richie opened his mouth to respond, then with a yelp, turned on his pal. "Why'd you go and kick me?"

"You dummy!" Craig snarled. "You don't hafta tell 'em *everything.*"

"What's the use?" Richie countered. "They know we were in the privy, and they know we started the fire."

The familiar, mutinous rigidity took over Craig's face as he faced forward in silence.

"What were you reading?" Cal asked again.

Richie flushed deeper. "Wasn't as bad as you might think. Craig snitched a dime novel about a gunslinger from some uncle or cousin he useta live with. He said it was more excitin' than the Bible you made him read all morning."

Cal's eyebrows rose. "So, it's exciting reading you're after?"

"Yeah!" Craig shot back. "Not a bunch of rules and don'ts that mean a whole lot of nothin'!"

Melissa gasped at the venom in the boy's voice and the sentiment he expressed. "That's a terrible thing to say, Craig! Everything we've learned from the Bible has been powerful and worthwhile. Why, it's God's own Word."

Cal smiled at her, then faced the boys again. "Tell you what. If I can show you that Scripture has stories more thrilling than any dime novel, will you stop sneaking to the privy to do your reading?"

Richie nodded and said, "I'm real sorry about the outhouse, sir. We didn't mean to start a fire."

"Of course you didn't, and I expect you to make amends."

Richie rolled his eyes dramatically. "Oh, all right."

"Craig?" Cal asked.

"What?"

"Will you give me the chance to show you the Bible is as exciting as your other reading?"

"Will you give me the chance to say no?"

Melissa held her breath as Cal considered her brother's surly response.

"You can say no," he finally said, "but I hope you will let God and me prove ourselves to you."

Craig studied the tall man before him. A challenge burned in his gaze. "You do that. Prove yourself."

Cal nodded. "Gladly. Now that you have your own Bible, I suggest you start reading about Joshua. If you don't have a Bible, Richie, I can lend you one. I'll expect you both in my office on Wednesday evening after supper to discuss what you've read. Now, you'd best head back to the privy and help Sam clean up. There's plenty of work to do."

Head defiantly high, Craig opened the door. Richie, a serious look on his face, paused before Cal. "I'm glad you're letting me make this up to you. Even if it takes my whole life long."

Clearly fighting a grin, Cal said, "It won't take that long. I promise. Now go tell Sam what we've discussed."

As the boys trooped out, Melissa heard Richie say, "I wonder how bad that burned-out privy's gonna stink. Think a clothespin on the nose'll help?"

She smiled momentarily, but once the door closed, silence filled the kitchen. In the quiet, numerous emotions tumbled through her—embarrassment, gratitude, inadequacy.

"I don't know what to say," she murmured when the silence grew awkward. "I'm glad Craig has made a friend, but I'm not sure Richie is a good choice. My brother doesn't need help to find trouble. And you. You've been more than kind, especially since this is the second time Craig's gotten into mischief."

"Craig and Richie are boys," Cal said with a grin. "I was

one myself, and I know just how much trouble they can make. But I also know they need to learn, and I'm happy to help."

Half of her wanted to tell him she didn't need his help. Her other half wanted to know how he kept his temper under control, how he handled difficult situations with so much confidence, such clear assurance. Her curiosity and admiration got the better of her. "You're not even angry at them?"

"What good would anger do? It wouldn't have soothed Mabel's ruffled feathers, it won't get the privy back, and it sure won't teach Craig or Richie anything of value."

"They've cost you plenty. You have to build a new outhouse."

"There's enough lumber around a logging operation. It won't put us out much to rebuild, and the boys are strong enough to handle the construction. They'll learn from the experience." His green eyes studied her, and Melissa wondered if he could see right through to her confused thoughts.

"How do you do it?" she asked before caution could stop her words. "How do you keep from yelling and sending us away? We've been nothing but trouble."

"It never occurred to me to send you away. And the best way I know to handle problems is to turn them over to my heavenly Father. Then all I have to do is my human best."

"How do you do that?"

A smile curved Cal's lips. "I hoped you would ask. As his child, I can go to God in prayer and trust him with everything that happens to me. He has promised to make all things work together for good for those who love him, those who are called according to his purpose. I know he has called me."

"How does one know when one is called?"

"God creates a hunger for himself in your heart."

Melissa felt a surge of excitement. "You mean, like what I

feel when it's almost time for Sunday worship? That need for those new things I'm about to learn?"

"There's more, of course, but it sounds as if he's calling you."

Melissa took a deep breath, remembering her thoughts earlier that morning. "Could you tell me how I can come to be 'in Christ,' like the verse you were reading this morning said?"

"Nothing would make me happier," Cal said with warmth in his eyes. Then holding a hand toward Melissa, he smiled. "Let's kneel."

Melissa stared at those extended fingers, the longing to grasp them burning inside her. As her hand unfurled, she caught herself and fisted it tight. Cal appeared sincere, genuinely caring, but her fierce need for independence rose to the forefront and tempered her yearning. She couldn't hold hands with her employer, her landlord. Cal's position gave him too much power over her. Such an intimacy would surely leave her too vulnerable to him.

He was practically a stranger, too. She couldn't trust him.

Then her hungering heart reminded her that he had offered to lead her to Christ.

She raised her gaze from the strong, square hand still outstretched, and studied Cal's face. She remembered his assurance, his calm and serenity, his closeness to God. Her need for the fresh start she'd learned about in the morning's verses grew greater.

Averting her gaze, Melissa pressed her lips tight, then knelt, firmly lacing her hands at her waist. She would let Cal lead her in prayer, but nothing would make her take that extended hand. She dared only trust God and herself.

Then risking a glance at Cal's face, Melissa caught her breath. For a brief moment, she thought she saw pain flit across his features. Oh, dear. Had her refusal to take his hand hurt his feelings?

He clenched his jaw and knelt at her side. "First you must confess that you are a sinner," he said, his words measured, controlled. "Jesus, who was sinless, took our place on the cross and suffered our punishment. When you accept his sacrifice, the Father cancels out your sins. Invite God's Son into your heart, into your life. Claim him as your Lord and Savior. The Holy Spirit will do his saving work, and you will be God's child forever. A new creature in Christ."

Drinking in every word he said, Melissa felt her eyes well with humble tears. "A new creature in Christ . . ."

CHAPTER FOUR

W hat a lovely custard pie!" Melissa exclaimed, taking the proffered dish from Mrs. McCreary, New Hope's new seamstress.

"Ach, lassie, 'tisn't much, but we wanted to help the town celebrate."

"I understand. I feel the same way. You're settling in well, then?"

"Indeedy so. And you?"

The joy Melissa had come to know since the Sunday the privy burned down returned in full force. God was so good. "This is home, Mrs. McCreary, really and truly home for the Barnharts."

"Call me Moriah, do. And 'tis home for our wee clan, too."

Melissa gave the older woman an impulsive hug. "Thank you so much, and I hope you enjoy yourself today."

Turning, she saw Ida Mae Harper lugging a massive kettle toward the table. "Here," she said, rushing to the rail-thin lady. "Let me help. It looks heavy . . . oh, but it smells wonderful! I do love cider."

Mrs. Harper looked down her nose at Melissa but didn't reject her offer of help. "See that you don't overset it."

As had become her new habit, Melissa prayed for patience. Ida Mae was a friend of Mabel Sauerbehr, who had stated that she would like to see Melissa ousted from the Dinner Bell, if not from town. It was a matter of professional jealousy. Mabel wanted her position back as cook, even though Cal and Sam continued to pay her wages—as a widow's portion, they said.

Melissa had never found it worthwhile to respond in like fashion to unpleasant folk, and since coming to know Christ, she had learned that he wanted his children to treat their enemies with love. "I would never do that, Mrs. Harper," she said with a smile. "I wouldn't want to deprive anyone of your tasty cider."

Ida Mae gaped at the gentle response. Her eyes widened, then she blinked. "Well. Thank you. I guess. Seems sensible." In a nervous, birdlike fashion, she searched the group that had gathered at the Dinner Bell. "Ah . . . I see someone I must speak to."

With that, the woman rushed off, but not before casting another quizzical look at Melissa. Gladness filled her as she remembered the verse she had read just that morning. *A soft answer turneth away wrath: but grievous words stir up anger.* "Thank you, Jesus," she whispered.

"Talking to yourself, are you, now?" asked Sam August as he carried firewood to the cast-iron stove in the corner of the room.

"Not at all. I was talking to my Lord."

"Can't go wrong doin' that," he answered, grinning proudly.

"So I've learned, thanks to you."

"And Calvin, I'd say."

Melissa felt her cheeks warm. Turning her gaze toward the table, she unnecessarily straightened two evergreen-and-red-ribbon decorations. "Yes, Cal has been most diligent in helping me learn from the lovely Bible you gave me."

"Pure pleasure, missy, to see you growin' in the Spirit."

Pleased with the new topic, she patted the older man's cheek. "You make a fine father. Why haven't you married?"

"Indeed, Sam August," trumpeted Mabel Sauerbehr from in front of the food table. She made a show of placing an elaborate, frosted cake among the other sweets, then checking to make sure no flakes of exotic and expensive coconut had drifted from their proper places. "Why is it you haven't settled yourself to wedded bliss? It surely isn't due to the lack of interest from a lady."

Melissa watched the portly woman preen and pose for Sam's benefit. All Mabel accomplished, however, was to send the man scurrying back outdoors. Then she turned on Melissa, a mean look in her round brown eyes. "As I'm sure you've made clear to the poor man. Rest assured, Miss Barnhart, Mr. August has too much sense to let flighty baggage like you addle his mind."

"Why, Mrs. Sauerbehr! I've done no such thing. Mr. August is nearly old enough to be my father. Besides, I have no intention of marrying any time soon. I'm too busy running the Dinner Bell and raising my brother to spare a thought to marriage."

Again those small eyes glared. "See that you remember your words next time you speak with Mr. August."

Steaming away from the table like a ponderous battleship, Mabel called for Ida Mae. Melissa watched the two women put their heads together and braced herself for the scowls that soon came her way. The jealousy Mabel had revealed stunned her. Melissa had never considered Sam a potential suitor; she had never considered *any* man that way. If she did, the younger partner at the New Hope Lumber Company would be the one to capture her interest, since he already filled her thoughts more often than he should.

A particularly attractive man, Cal Stevenson had been generous with his time and knowledge. He had spent the past few Wednesdays revealing the fascinating tales of the Bible to her brother. Although Craig hadn't made any positive statements to date, he no longer fought vehemently against Sunday worship. This morning, as the Barnharts had prepared to attend Pastor Mosely's first service, he had not once refused to go.

Melissa thought back on the time spent in the church still redolent of sharp wood polish and mellow beeswax. As Reverend Mosely intoned the closing prayer, she had stolen a glance at the man at her side. The past few weeks had been the most exciting of her life. Since Cal led her to Christ, she'd found a new sense of purpose, a new meaning to her days. Their friendship had grown as she sought him with questions about her deepening faith. Questions he seemed eager to answer.

He frequently invited her to join him in prayer, but she usually refused, fearing the intimacy such openness would bring. Unwilling to let anyone that close, she felt prayer was between her and God. Still, it warmed her heart—against her better judgment—to know Cal cared enough to pray for her. Especially when it came to dealing with Craig, since the boy continued to tumble in and out of scrapes, usually in Richie's company.

To her relief, today's service had concluded in peace, no complaint coming from the Barnhart male. As Ida Mae banged out the melody of the closing hymn on the new upright piano, Melissa turned to the book Cal held between them with a sigh of pleasure. She smiled shyly up at him, recognizing the light of admiration in his bright green gaze. She joined her voice to his, singing, "All hail the power of Jesus' name! Let angels prostrate fall. . . ."

Now, remembering those warm feelings of rightness, Melissa wondered where her escort had gone. Everyone expected at the celebration had arrived, and she would soon announce the meal.

"Are we ready, Miss Barnhart?" asked the boyish-featured Pastor Mosely, startling her.

"Oh! I . . . yes, I believe we are. Would you like me to ring for attention?"

"Yes. It's time for the blessing."

Melissa clanged her cowbell, and soon the sound of benches scraping across the floor joined that of multiple conversations. As she watched, a gentle grasp at her elbow caught her by surprise. "Oh!"

Cal had returned. "I apologize for startling you," he said, "and for abandoning you in the first place."

"No apology needed. I've been busy, as I imagine you have, too."

"That I have. We just rolled the piano down from the church so Ida Mae can entertain us with her carols. I didn't know how much work it would take to make my dreams for New Hope come true. Especially since the town's growing faster than I ever imagined it would."

"You must be proud. Your efforts have certainly paid off."

A twinkle appeared in his green eyes. "Yes, I'm pleased with the town, but it's your presence here that I'm celebrating."

Melissa's cheeks warmed at his compliment, and she relished the ripple of excitement that ran up her spine. Cal was one of the best things she'd found in New Hope, and as she heard the interest in his voice, saw the admiration in his eyes, she wished she dared let it grow to something more.

Then she remembered who he was, who she was, what she'd promised, what she'd done . . . and what she'd failed to do. She couldn't let herself dream of romance or any such wonder. She had no time to waste on a flirtation, no matter how thrilling, especially not with her boss. She had to think of Craig, of the many wrongs she had to right. To diffuse the charged moment, she said, "On account of Mabel's chicken and biscuits, right?"

Cal laughed that wonderful laugh of his and winked. "Among other things." Then, taking her elbow again, he led her to a table near the kitchen door. "Shall we sit?"

"Of course."

Melissa and Cal bowed their heads with the rest of the diners. Pastor Mosely cleared his throat before voicing his prayer.

"Blessed are you, Lord, God of all," he said in his resonant voice. "Through your mercy we enjoy the bounty of the earth and receive your gifts of home and work and fellowship. We ask your blessing on our meal and offer thanks for the joy with which we will partake of it. Make us mindful of the needs of others, that we may show our thanks in the manner of our living. May our hearts be filled with love and praise for you. We ask this in Jesus' holy name, amen."

As soon as the responding amens rang out, heaping platters flew from hand to hand. Golden-skinned chickens, slabs of roast venison, mountains of potatoes drenched in yellow butter, piles of carrot coins polished with honey, tangy pickles and savory relishes, all yielded their distinctive aromas, setting many a middle to grumbling. Minutes later, dishes overflowed and mouths munched on the feast Melissa had coordinated.

Her own fork a scant breath from her lips, she heard what she had dreaded all day.

"Who do you think you are?" Craig demanded in his most aggressive tone.

Dropping the mouthful of food, Melissa looked for the boy but didn't find him at Richie's side, where he should have been.

"Mabel Sauerbehr, that's who. And *I'm* tellin' *you* to stop."

She realized the voices came from the kitchen and that thankfully no one else seemed to have heard.

"I suppose you're gonna tell me all about the Ten Commandments," Craig taunted. "Well, don't. Mr. Stevenson took care of that already, an' I'm sick of being preached at."

"You wouldn't get preached at if you stopped your stupid behavior."

"Don't call me stupid!"

"I didn't, I called your actions stupid because they are."

"What do *you* know about anything?"

"I know you're committing a crime."

Melissa stood.

"So?"

"So the sheriff'll catch you, lock you up for good."

She went toward the kitchen, hoping nobody noticed her departure.

"If he catches me." Running footsteps rang out.

"Wait!" Mabel yelled. "You crazy thief—"

Melissa burst into the room as the back door slammed shut. Shaking away her shock, she ran after Craig and Mabel. What on earth had her brother done now? If one could believe Mrs. Sauerbehr, then Craig's actions had gone beyond his usual mischief. A crime, she'd said, then called him a thief.

"Wait for me," Cal said, reaching for the doorknob. "It sounds as if you'll need help."

"Thank you, but he's my brother," she answered over her shoulder, mortified that he'd heard the whole debacle. "I can handle the situation. He's my respo—"

What she saw twenty yards away put an end to her words. Craig wobbled down the road on Mabel's beloved bicycle, fighting furiously to keep the contraption upright, hampered by something he clutched in his left hand. Behind him, the green-bloomered, heavyset redhead struggled to keep up.

"Come back here—you ruffian! That's—*my bicycle* you're—stealin'." With single-minded determination, she charged the boy, looking more than ever like a battleship, the steam that powered her every step waving after her in the cold December air. "You're no better'n that—floozy of a— sister of yours. But I'll show—the both—of you! You can't steal—from Mabel Sauerbehr and—get away with it."

Ignoring his pursuer, Craig pedaled faster, leaving a trail of coins on the frozen mud surface of the road. Shame brought flames of heat into Melissa's cheeks at the evidence of his theft, and the fluffy snowflakes fluttering onto her skin did nothing to abate the sting. "Craig Barnhart! You stop right there!" she cried. "Running away won't change what you've done."

At the sound of her voice, the bicycle lurched sideways, and the pastor's collection plate flew out of her brother's hand. Melissa groaned, then ran after the boy.

Taking advantage of Craig's momentary distraction, Mabel upped her pace, reached his side, and grabbed a fistful of white shirt. "Gotcha!"

"No you don't," he countered, pedaling with all his might.

The struggle ended before it really started as Craig jerked away and the sound of tearing cloth filled the air. From where she stood, Melissa saw Mabel's eyes widen in horror.

Then Melissa gasped in shock.

Cal intoned, "Dear God!"

Craig froze.

His naked back displayed a mottled mass of scarred tissue, some silvered with age, some still bearing a hint of healing redness, a graphic testimony of repeated brutality.

"How—?" Melissa's throat knotted before she could utter the rest of her question. Tears stung her eyes. She reached a hand to the boy, whose earlier defiant expression gave way to one of fear.

He cringed.

Her tears fell, hot against her now-chilled cheeks. She finally understood his moods, the dark turbulence she had seen in him since the day she took him from Fred Clemson's farm. His ravaged flesh spoke of suffering too great for one so young. Betrayal of the worst kind.

Clearly Fred had inherited his father's bent toward violence. Great-uncle Bert's rages had been legendary, but Melissa had always managed to stay out of his way. The thought of that kind of power unleashed on a child turned her stomach. Staring in misery at her brother's ruined back, she wondered how young Craig had been the first time he met abuse firsthand. How had he survived? He must have bled profusely. Had anyone tended to him?

She would have, had she known his need. Again guilt seared her, the knowledge that if she had kept her promise to Papa, none of this would have happened.

Forcing her gaze from the savagery etched on Craig's flesh, Melissa blinked away her scalding tears and sought his eyes. She found warring emotions there. Defiance. Shame. Rage.

Directed her way.

At that moment she became aware of movement to her rear. Glancing over her shoulder, she realized the rest of the diners had come out to satisfy their collective curiosity.

Then she heard Cal's voice. "Let's go back inside, folks. Let Melissa see to her brother. Come, Mabel, I need your help."

Unable to speak, she sent him a grateful look. A person as wounded in body and spirit as Craig could not handle public scrutiny, especially not when he stood stripped of all defenses, of even the meager cover provided by a cotton shirt. She herself didn't know how to deal with what she had just learned, much less cope with the inevitable stares, the questions, the pity onlookers would send their way.

But that didn't matter right now. Only Craig mattered. He needed tenderness, love, forgiveness, and, yes, he still needed correction. The stolen coins catching the weak, wintry daylight proved it.

Now she understood why he fought rules and authority with such determination. In his troubled mind, they equaled pain and suffering. It was no wonder he rebelled against her efforts at discipline, no wonder he regarded Cal with such contempt.

On shaky legs, Melissa approached the boy, tears still washing her face. To her dismay, he held out his hands, shielding himself as if from a blow. "No! Don't—"

"I love you," she said in a breaking voice.

Chocolate eyes peered between his protecting palms, mistrust burning in their depths. Melissa took one of those hands between both of hers, brought it to her lips. "I'm so sorry, Craig." The lump in her throat grew, but she swallowed against it. "You have no idea how sorry I am. I didn't know. If I had, I would have—"

"What?" he asked, his old belligerence reappearing. "What do you think you could have done? Fought him off? Beat him back?" Bitter laughter rent the quiet afternoon, the laughter of a man who had seen too much, not that of a boy. "Nothing. You could have done nothing."

The knowledge that he was most likely correct hit her with another pang of anguish. She had thought she had suffered at Uncle Bert's hand. What a fool she had been! Compared to what Craig had gone through, she didn't even know the meaning of the word.

"What are you gonna do now?" he asked, defiance tipping his chin upward.

Bewildered, she took a step toward Pine Street, tugging on his hand. "I'm going to take you home."

He didn't budge. "I mean, about that." With his free hand, he gestured toward the strewn money.

"Oh. I'd forgotten about the collection. Well, I'm going to pick it up and return it, of course. And you're going to help. Then I'll take you home."

"*Then* what?"

"Tell me what you want me to do, what you need me to do."

Suspicion again filled his eyes. "I suppose that's when you'll administer the 'discipline' you feel I need. Fine. You can't do any worse than Fred did."

Melissa's stomach churned again as she caught the meaning of his biting comment. "You think *I'm* going to hit you?"

He shrugged, a hard set to his still-downy jaw.

"Craig! How could you? I would never, ever hurt anyone, much less you. You're my brother. I love you. I only want what is best for you."

He scoffed. "That's what Fred always said. He was doing what was best for me—what I needed."

The enormity of his tragedy struck her again. "Oh, dear. I can see we have much talking to do. The first thing I'll say is this: I won't hit you or make you suffer in any way. Yes, you committed a crime, a sin against God, and there will be consequences to your actions. But no one will ever hurt you as you've been hurt before. I'll make sure of that."

Although his expression said he didn't believe she could carry out her promise, she saw a new spark glimmer to life in his gaze. Could it possibly be . . . hope?

Lord Jesus, she prayed silently, *I don't know how to heal him, but I know you do. Use me to show him your love, to teach him that not everyone is as evil as Fred. Help me keep this new promise.*

After they had gathered all the money they could find, they headed home in silence. Melissa's mind continued to form question after question, image after hideous image. From the closed expression on Craig's face, she knew better than to voice a single word.

At home, she sent him to his room, telling him she would bring him something to eat.

As he opened the bedroom door, he said, "I'm not hungry."

"I know. Still, you need a bite or two. Then a time of

reflection wouldn't hurt. Perhaps even a nap—and, no, I don't think you're a child at all. I just think there's likely a lot on your mind, and you'll soon be exhausted from too much thinking."

A snort came from the room. She thought she heard him say, "Who wants to think?" but she didn't ask him to repeat himself. He had done as she'd said without argument, and for the moment, that would do.

Twenty minutes later, after the pot of tea had brewed and last night's stew had warmed, she approached his bed with care. It seemed the emotion of the day had drained Craig, for he slept like the babe she had refused to call him.

Setting the bowl and cup on the dresser, she went to pull the covers higher and saw the tear tracks down his cheeks. Again, her heart quaked at the thought of what had happened to her baby brother.

An idea came to her, and before she could stop herself, she took Mama's Log Cabin quilt from her carpetbag, removed the needle, and tucked the unfinished piece around her broken brother.

"Dear God," Melissa sobbed quietly, "I'm only glad Mama's not here to see this. How I wish she and Papa hadn't died, then Craig wouldn't have had to suffer. Forgive me, Lord, for failing Papa. I should have tried harder, done something to keep Craig with me. I can't change the past, but I can make up for what I failed to do. I can make his life from now on what it should have been. And *nothing* will keep me from doing that."

Craig was really still a boy. In sleep, the sharp angles of adolescence had softened, and his lips curved gently, slightly parted. Tousled dark blond hair contrasted against the pillow, against the fair skin of his forehead. He was a handsome boy and would someday be a very attractive man, one she fervently prayed would not carry with him all he had suffered in a vengeful, destructive streak.

Still, Craig had survived. Melissa took comfort in the strength that had carried her brother through the horrors he had borne. They were sure to face rough patches in the days to come, but she decided right then to teach her brother about love, the gift God gave to those who came to him, to all who had been wounded. If anyone's heart needed healing, it was surely Craig Barnhart's.

She again turned to her heavenly Father, pouring out her pain, her sadness, her dreams, her wishes. She promised to finish Mama's quilt to honor her memory, to restore the Barnhart family for Papa's sake, to make sure Craig healed, and to make up for her own earlier failure.

She would do it all, since life in New Hope offered her a new beginning, and she was now a new creature in Christ. She would establish a new family, one built on God's love.

Although she had felt twinges of guilt in the days since, and she still had to make sure her actions remained secret, she no longer regretted stealing her brother from Fred's home. She feared that if she hadn't, the boy would sooner or later have died.

She thanked God for Cal Stevenson and the advertisement he had placed in the *Intelligencer*. That decent, godly man had led her to Christ. Now, through Cal's faithful sharing of God's message, she could hold out hope for Craig.

As he stored the last dish Mabel had dried, Cal looked out the kitchen window wondering if Melissa would return to the Dinner Bell. It was nearly time to start supper, and he didn't relish asking Mabel to do so.

Not that he would blame Melissa if she stayed home with Craig. What the boy's torn shirt had revealed had stolen his appetite. Fury with the perpetrator still simmered inside him, and Cal found himself again questioning God about such profound evil.

No answer came beyond the one he had always known. He lived in a fallen world, one where evil occurred only too frequently as a result of man's rebellion against his Creator. Craig Barnhart's injuries proved it.

With grim determination, Cal prayed for the tortured soul who had vented his hatred on this child. Hating the sin, he tried not to hate the sinner, but wasn't certain he succeeded.

The door opened, interrupting his prayer. Melissa slipped inside. "I can take over now," she said, that tight, resolute quality again in her voice. "Thank you for your help."

Mabel sniffed, then glared at her but merely said, "Good day," and left.

Cal studied the pretty face that had come to mean so much to him. The crease between her arched eyebrows and the lack of color in her cheeks revealed her pain. Anger toward the person who had hurt her brother and, as a result, her, too, hit him once again. He fought to tamp it down. "How can I help?" he asked, even though he knew she'd refuse him.

"You can't. I don't think anyone can." She sounded defeated, beaten, and his heart ached for her.

"God can," he said. "He can do anything."

"I know that up here," she responded, tapping her temple, "but I don't feel it here." She placed her palm over her heart.

"What do you want him to do?"

Melissa's golden-brown eyes met Cal's. "I want him to make everything the way it was before Mama and Papa died. I want Craig's anger gone . . . no, I don't want there to be a reason for his anger, none for my guilt. But even God can't do that. What happened happened, and we can't go back."

"True, we can't go back, but God can and does heal."

Shaking her head, she propped her hip against the table, clearly seeking strength, support. "I don't know if Craig can even accept God's healing love. I understand now why he fights authority so fiercely, even God's. All he has ever known is that power hurts. He can't trust."

"Yes, he's been hurt, and his view of life is badly damaged, but God can heal even that. You have to trust in the Father's might and pray for your brother."

"There must be more that I can do, and I *will* do it. I'm responsible for what happened."

Thinking over her words, Cal hung the kitchen towel he'd used on a peg by the sink and came to her side. He longed to hold her in his arms, cradle her against his shoulder, but he knew she wouldn't allow that. She clung too stoically to her independence. "I don't understand why you feel such guilt," he said. "You did nothing to cause Craig's suffering."

"That's where you're wrong. I broke a promise to my father. I didn't keep Craig with me as he asked me to do."

Cal's confusion grew. "I don't understand. You told me relatives took you in, that none wanted both of you. What could you have done to keep Craig with you under those circumstances?"

She shrugged. "I don't know. I just know I was responsible for Craig, and I failed. If I had been with him, I would *never* have let anyone hurt him. I should have kept my promise, but I didn't, and I'm responsible for what happened to my brother."

He could see where a strong, independent woman like Melissa would think that way, but she wasn't right. Not at all. "That makes no sense. Your relatives separated you two children. You said you were—what, nine?"

When she nodded, he went on. "How could you have fought a group of adults? You didn't have a choice, and you couldn't have known things would turn out this badly."

"Maybe not back then," she conceded, "but I should gave gone after him as soon as I was old enough. I didn't. I was too scared of Uncle Bert. I was a coward, and because of that my brother suffered."

Give me the right words, Lord, Cal prayed. "Don't take on the guilt of those who earned it. You did nothing wrong. Look at me." Grasping Melissa's shoulders and ignoring the stiffening of her back, he waited until those honeyed eyes met his. "You did what you could when you could. You went back as an adult, and you're making a home for him now. There's no reason for your guilt."

"But I broke my promise. God can't honor that—"

"Stop! God doesn't see it that way, and he doesn't want you to suffer with false guilt. He only asks you to obey his Word. It calls you to love those around you as you love yourself, and I know you love Craig."

A spark of . . . something caught in the depths of her eyes. "Do you think that might be true?"

Praise God, he could answer with certainty. "I *know* that's true. Whoever beat Craig is the guilty one. Besides, if you do sin, forgiveness is yours when you sincerely repent. God gave you that gift when you accepted his Son as your Savior. He died on that cross as your atonement. All you have to do is ask forgiveness."

To his surprise, when he spoke of her sin, she blanched. Averting her gaze, she murmured weakly, "I . . . I guess."

The uncertainty in her voice and the haunted look in her eyes bothered him, nearly broke his heart. Her faith was untried, too new to carry her through all her troubles. He wished he could give her his assurance in God's grace, but that was something she needed to find for herself.

There was, however, something else he had to say, something she wouldn't want to hear, something he didn't want to remember. But it was something his Lord required of him. After a bracing breath, he began, "There is one more thing you must do, and it's tough. But as difficult as it is, God will be with you every step of the way."

Wariness filled Melissa's features. "And that is . . . ?"

"You have to forgive the person who did this—"

"No! Never!"

He understood her vehemence. Every fiber of his all-too-human self felt the same. But he knew what God asked of his children, even if it cost them greatly, even if obedience hurt. "We must, or God says he will withhold forgiveness from us. Hate and anger will eat you up inside. Unforgiveness is the sin that destroys the bitter victim but does nothing to the attacker."

Melissa closed her eyes. A tear squeezed past her lashes. "I know what the Bible says, but I just can't forgive Fred."

"Fred?"

"Fred Clemson. Uncle Bert and Aunt Erna's oldest son. He's the one who did this to Craig."

"Fred, then. We must forgive him, no matter how hard it is. I'm struggling with this myself, and Craig's not even my brother."

Doubt took over Melissa's face. "It's too hard, this being a Christian. God can't expect me to forgive Fred. Not really."

"I'm afraid he does. All we can do is ask the Father to work in our spirit, to change our feelings when we can't change them ourselves."

"I'll try, Cal. I can't promise I'll succeed, but I'll try."

"Give it to the Father, Melissa. Scripture says we can do all things through Christ who strengthens us. Remember that; hold onto that promise."

Slowly she straightened, a hint of determination returning to her gaze. "After supper I'll seek his promises in his Word, and I'll try to lean on his strength." Then she shook her head. "No, I *will* trust him, since I can't do it on my own."

Cal sighed with a measure of relief. Her defeat had gone, replaced by the resolve he'd come to expect. He was glad he'd had the courage to speak God's truth. Now, if he could only practice what he'd oh-so-eloquently preached. . . .

CHAPTER FIVE

Monday morning Cal awoke with Melissa on his mind. He wondered how the Barnharts fared after the overwhelming events of the day before. Each time he closed his eyes, he could still see bits and pieces of what he knew he would never forget.

Craig's scars . . . Melissa's horror . . . her acceptance of his comfort . . . her admiration . . . perhaps even her budding trust.

That last caused him to quicken his efforts to dress and reach the Dinner Bell sooner rather than later, if for nothing more than to catch a glimpse of the woman he was coming to love.

Her tenderness toward Craig, her sense of responsibility, her diligence in her work, her hunger for closeness with God. There was much to admire and respect about Melissa Barnhart—and to love, as well.

Was she the one the Lord meant for him? Had he led her to New Hope to fill the void in Cal's life?

Then he remembered her determined independence, her repeated refusal to accept his help. Those rejections hurt. He

261

didn't deserve such treatment; he only wanted to help, to comfort her. He fought to keep his temper under control, to keep his injured pride at bay, but his efforts didn't always succeed, and he wondered how he could feel so much for a woman who obviously didn't want to share his feelings.

Was there some way to reach her? To prove to her he was worthy of her care? Her trust? Maybe even her love?

She'd trusted him enough to lead her to Christ, but then, she'd been hungry for God's love. She'd easily accepted God's authority, never fearing for her blasted self-reliance. Would she ever see Cal didn't want to take away her independence but merely wanted to share his life, his love? Could Melissa ever come to love him?

There was only one way to know. He would turn the matter over to his heavenly Father, get to know Melissa better, and trust God to reveal the answer in his time.

By half-past eleven, Cal conceded defeat. He'd tried waiting on the Lord, but his thoughts sped to Melissa with dogged persistence. He had no alternative but to go to her, spend pleasant moments in conversation, perhaps pray with her for Craig's healing. It didn't matter what he did, he just had to see her again.

Hurrying to avoid the crush of lumbermen who would arrive at the Dinner Bell by noon, he loped up the three steps to the porch of the building. Without knocking, he entered and headed straight for the kitchen. From the doorway, he spied Melissa. She stood near the enamel sink beneath a window, a sheet of paper in her hands. Her trembling hands.

He shot a look at her face, and the raw emotion there hit him square in the chest. Fear and rage mingled in her delicate features; a white line rimmed her pinched lips. The page held her expressive eyes riveted, wide and haunted.

"What's wrong?" he asked, concern filling him.

Melissa started, darting a glance in his direction, then crumpled the paper and stuffed it in the pocket of her navy serge skirt. "N-Nothing," she stammered, voice rough, gaze on the floor.

Remembering her reaction when he'd mentioned her supposed sin the night before, Cal narrowed his eyes. "I don't think so. You're shaking like those custards you made the other day, you're white as that sheet you just stuffed into your pocket, and something's clearly frightened you. Please tell me. I can't help if I don't know what's troubling you."

She shuddered, stiffened her spine, and shook her head. "Nothing's wrong. And you have already done more for our family than I can ever repay."

"You don't need to repay a thing," he said, irritation simmering. "I don't do things with gain in mind."

She smiled weakly. "I know, Cal. I didn't mean my words the way you took them. I meant that there's nothing you can do because there is nothing *really* wrong. If there was, I'm old enough and capable enough to meet my responsibilities. I can't spend the rest of my life depending on someone else to come to my rescue anytime anything needs doing."

She was at it again. The ground he thought he'd gained the night before had been reclaimed. Discouragement hit. "Self-reliance is admirable, but stubborn independence can lead to more trouble than one started out with." As her chin shot skyward, he came to her side and took her cold hand. "You would tell me if something was seriously wrong, wouldn't you?"

She refused to meet his gaze. "Of . . . of course. *If* there was something wrong, and *if* I couldn't handle it myself. Which I can. Not that there's anything wrong, you understand."

Cal fought the urge to press her. Clearly something *was* wrong, and just as clearly, Melissa refused to share her troubles with him. Short of forcing her to confess whatever secret she was keeping, he had no alternative but to go along with her evasion.

For the moment.

The depth of his anger, his pain at yet another snub, showed him how much he had come to care for the lovely young cook at the Dinner Bell. In the deepest recesses of his heart, Cal recognized he would do whatever the Lord empowered him to do to spare Melissa Barnhart trouble, suffering, misfortune. He would gladly give his life to protect her and hers.

As the Scripture said, "Greater love hath no man than this."

Stunned by his sudden understanding, Cal stared at the woman who had come to mean perhaps too much to him. The woman who didn't trust him enough to share her troubles.

His pain grew deeper, enough to spark his own considerable determination to full force. He would win her over, prove himself to her, show her he meant her nothing but good.

If it was the Lord's will.

He sighed. He still had to seek his Father's will. Did God intend for Cal to marry Melissa? That was what *he* wanted to do. To spend the rest of his life caring for her, loving her, raising a family with her. But only if it was God's will.

"Cal?" Melissa asked, a quizzical look on her face.

He flushed. "I'm sorry, I missed what you said. I was . . . thinking about . . . something else."

Oh no! He sounded more foolish than he had ever sounded before. But then again, he had never been in love before.

And he didn't know how she felt about him.

Only one way to find out. Melissa needed to get to know him better, and for that to happen, they had to spend a good deal of time together. That struck him as an excellent course of action. He smiled. He would stick to her like honey did to her breakfast biscuits from now on. He would make sure they got to know each other well enough to make the second most important decision of their lives.

A questioning look still on her face, she asked, "Is there something I can do for you? After all, you're early for dinner."

She could do plenty for him. Like trust him. Love him. Say yes when he proposed, but this wasn't the time to push. "Ah . . . er . . . I came to ask how your brother was today."

A hint of sadness stole onto her face. "I'm afraid I don't know. Craig was . . . more closed than ever. I wonder if he hates me for seeing what he obviously didn't want seen."

"I don't think he hates you, but I'm sure he hates that everyone knows what happened to him. It's clear he feels ashamed, even though he has no reason to."

"Fred's the one who should twist and turn night after night from shame. And Uncle Bert and Aunt Erna. After all, they raised that beast. How anyone could do what he did. . . ."

At her words, dread crept into Cal's gut. "I'm sorry, Melissa, but I have to ask . . . did that Bert do to you what Fred did to Craig?"

Horror filled Melissa's eyes. "Oh no! Uncle Bert's temper got the best of him often enough, and he swatted out in his rages, but he never, ever took to beating me. If he had, I wouldn't be here today. I would surely have died."

Cal nodded. "I'm afraid you're right. I'm so glad the Lord kept you away from Fred."

"But why didn't he protect Craig?"

"How do you know he didn't? I believe God must have been watching over him. Not many would have survived what Craig did, and his strong constitution is a heavenly gift. A weaker boy wouldn't have made it."

"But why didn't God keep Fred from doing what he did?"

"I don't know, but I suspect it's because Fred rejected God first. God gives us the freedom to choose him or not. Fred's choices were the wrong ones, and there are always consequences to our choices. These were particularly grim."

She nodded slowly. "I understand that Fred is not following God's will, but I still don't know why God, in all his power and mercy, didn't prevent Craig's abuse."

Cal took a deep breath. "We can't know the reasons for everything God does or doesn't do. Life remains a mystery even to his children. All he asks is that we continue to trust him, even in the face of tragedies like this."

She nodded again, slowly. "I guess. I still don't know, and never will, why my parents died when they were so close to reaching their dream. If they hadn't died, then Craig would never have gone to Fred. We would never have been separated. Mama would have finished her quilt, Papa would have built our new home, started his ranch. Christmases would have continued as they'd always been in Ohio."

"Christmas?" he asked.

"Yes. Mama loved the holiday season. She made gifts for us all, and cooked and baked her specialties. She filled the house with evergreen branches and made decorations from scraps of fabric. She even knitted snowflakes and stars to hang on the tree Papa always cut down for her. She played the piano so we could sing carols and hymns. It was wonderful."

The nostalgia in Melissa's voice tugged at Cal's heart. "There's no reason you can't do the same now that Craig's with you. You even have your own home. The Advent season is a wonderful time to acknowledge the gifts God gives his children. I would be happy to cut down a tree for you."

To his delight, her cheeks warmed, and a twinkle appeared in her eyes. "Thank you for your offer. I've been making gifts in my spare moments, and I've nearly finished Mama's very appropriate Log Cabin quilt. It's my dream to properly celebrate the blessed event in the Barnharts' new home."

"That's a wonderful idea. You can tell Craig about holidays with your parents, give him the memories he doesn't have. And you can help him make new ones, the ones God will give you, now that you're a family once again."

"That's exactly what I've been working for since I arrived in New Hope. I want to do everything I can to make up for failing to keep my promise to Papa. I must make that up to Craig."

Melissa's words disturbed Cal. Apparently his earlier eloquence hadn't had the effect he'd hoped for. "You didn't fail Craig, the Clemsons did. And there's nothing for you to make up. Only God can redeem what's been lost. And he did it by giving up his only Son for us."

"You mean . . . Christmas, since it's Christ's birth, is all about restoring what's been lost?"

"Exactly! God redeemed his lost children through Christ."

A thoughtful look spread over her delicate features. Then she said, "Yes, I believe Christ took on human form for my sake, then died for my sins." She again paused, stared blindly at the far wall. "Do you think that Christmas, being the time of his birth and all, is a time for healing? For redeeming a broken soul?"

"It certainly shows how much God cares and how much he will do for us."

A soft smile curved her lips. "I always liked the holiday. Now that I really understand, I love it even more. I'm so happy it's just around the corner. Perhaps if I can show Craig what it all means, God can begin his healing work." She straightened her spine and gave a firm nod. "I pray God will help me show Craig that Christ's birth is a chance for healing, for restoring what we lost, the promise of a new beginning. A new life in him."

It seemed as if the weight of the world had fallen from her

shoulders, or at least that she'd given most of it to the one who could best carry it. Hope had returned to Melissa's heart.

Cal smiled, relieved. "So when would you like me to bring you that tree we discussed?"

"Oh, any time I'm not working."

The clatter of footsteps at the dining hall entrance told Cal their privacy had ended, but nothing could dim his pleasure. He had made progress. Melissa hadn't refused his help—at least, not with her Christmas preparations. And she had shared some of her deepest feelings. It wasn't all he wanted, but it was a start. Sooner or later he'd find out about the letter.

With a smile, he said, "I'd better head on out there and let you serve. Those hungry lumbermen will turn mean if they suspect I've delayed their meal. Especially now that you're running the Dinner Bell. They love your cooking, and I lo—" He caught himself before he said too much, before he voiced what was in his heart. "I'm very glad you're here."

Again her cheeks tinted a deeper rose, and she gave him her wonderful smile. "Thank you, Cal. I'm very glad God brought us to New Hope. Our lives are so much better now than they were for a very long time."

And they'll only keep getting better, he promised silently. *With God's help, I'll see to it that they do.* The first thing he'd do was find out why that letter had scared her so.

Melissa found herself holding her breath during much of the noon meal. Each time she turned around, she noticed Cal's gaze on her. The attention might have been flattering, but she didn't think he was admiring her. He wore a strange, intense expression that made her think of Mrs. Terwilliger's letter more often than she would otherwise have done.

Cal's appearance in the kitchen had caught her off guard.

Not only had she received frightening news, but his offer of help disturbed her. She didn't want to involve him in any more of the Barnhart family's troubles.

Mrs. Terwilliger, Uncle Bert's elderly neighbor, had taken Melissa under her wing from the day she went to live with her relatives. When Melissa confided her fondest wish to reunite with her brother, Mrs. Terwilliger had encouraged her and helped her make plans. She'd promised to stay in touch the day Melissa left to get Craig, and this morning Melissa's heart had warmed at the sight of the familiar script.

Her pleasure had vanished when she began to read. It seemed Fred Clemson had been to visit his parents. He had not taken well her absconding with Craig after he refused to let the boy go. He felt the child belonged to him; he wanted what was his.

Mrs. Terwilliger had heard the younger Clemson vow to take the boy back to his farm. "Nothing," the elderly woman wrote, "will likely stop Fred. And I'm afearing what he will do to get Craig. You be careful, now. It's a good thing what you're doing for your brother, but Fred is trouble. Always was a cruel one growing up. I don't want anything to happen to you. Watch yourself, Melissa. That man means what he says."

Melissa didn't doubt Fred's determination, nor did she question his capacity for evil. She had seen all anyone needed to prove him the foulest of humans.

That was why she couldn't let Cal become any more enmeshed in their situation. A man like Cal Stevenson didn't deserve to be dragged into such ugliness. She doubted he had ever been forced to deal with anyone as awful as the Clemsons. She couldn't bear to think what Fred might do to Cal if he tried to help.

At that moment Melissa realized how much she cared for Cal—godly, hardworking, honest, and . . . she was coming to love him.

269

But she had to stand on her own. Didn't she?

She had been a helpless child when she went to live with Uncle Bert, depending on him and Aunt Erna for everything, a fact they'd used to coerce her cooperation. She wound up being treated as an indentured servant instead of a family member. Finally, her twenty-first birthday had arrived. Upon becoming an adult, she had gladly taken responsibility for herself. Since she had also assumed the care and raising of her brother, it was up to her to keep them safe.

Besides, she would hate to see disgust in Cal's eyes, which would surely happen if he ever met Fred or Bert. He would probably view her in the same light afterward. They were, much to her shame, related by blood.

Cal deserved better than an orphan with a nasty streak in her family and an unruly brother to raise. He would soon find a woman who would gladly become Mrs. Stevenson, what with all the folks coming to New Hope in response to his advertisement.

It would break her heart to see him walk down the aisle with his bride, but it was for the best. His best.

She prayed that the Lord would help him find that woman fast, for she couldn't stand to entertain even the slightest hope much longer. She would trust in her heavenly Father's assistance and comfort as she went through the trying times ahead.

In the days that followed, Cal was true to his word. He brought her a massive evergreen, its branches still dusted with the latest light snow, and bundles of branches to decorate her home. Enough to decorate two or three homes, at that.

They spent hours threading ribbons through dried pinecones she had collected, then hanging them on the tree. He watched her crochet snowflakes and stars, starch them, dry them, and scatter them among the branches. Then he helped her attach the candles, dozens of them, and insisted on lighting them whenever she wanted—he feared she might burn herself without his assistance.

As they worked, they talked about everything and anything, making it impossible to keep her resolution to maintain a distance between them. A troubling development, since her feelings for Cal shouldn't deepen. He was an honest man. She kept a dishonest act secret. She shouldn't set herself up for the heartbreak that would come the day he married someone else.

A very fortunate, mightily blessed someone else.

But Melissa continued to look forward to his arrival at the end of her day, when he walked her home and spent an hour or two chatting and helping with her Christmas preparations.

As she worked on Mama's beautiful Log Cabin quilt, she often remembered how Craig had cuddled into it the night of the Christmas social. Cal often ran his fingers over the tiny seams, admiring the handiwork that had gone into making the colorful squares. "What a wonderful gift your mother left you," he said one evening. "And how perfect that you now live in a log cabin of your own. You do wonderful work," he'd added, making Melissa blush at his praise.

Each time he paid her a compliment, she made light of her efforts, emphasizing her mother's artistry, but Cal would not be deterred. He seemed bound to persuade her of her many talents, abilities, gifts. One evening, to change the subject, she shared with him her latest spiritual effort. "Remember when I told you I would pray for Craig's healing?" she asked.

"Of course."

"Well, since Christmas is the time of new birth and I'm determined to finish the quilt by then, I've begun to match stitches to prayers. Each time I start a log, I pray for Craig's healing. And even though I don't want to, I've begun to pray that God will help me forgive Fred every time I quilt a chimney piece."

Cal's lips twisted ruefully. "I confess I haven't been that diligent. May I join you?"

"Of course."

They'd prayed their way through a number of quilt blocks, but that hadn't stopped his compliments. He continued to rave about her cooking skills, her patience and gentleness toward her brother, her diligence in her every endeavor.

Knowing he saw her that way brought Melissa a warm glow deep inside, making her dread more than ever the moment he would learn her secret—that she had kidnapped her brother, that Fred was on their trail.

She considered pulling up roots and running, but such cowardice didn't set well with her. What kind of upbringing would she give Craig if she subjected him to a fugitive's life? And for what? Fred Clemson?

She had to take a stand. Deep in her heart she believed God had led them to New Hope for a purpose. The Barnharts belonged here. She wouldn't leave unless the Lord made it perfectly clear he wanted them elsewhere, and he hadn't yet done that.

So Melissa fell in love with Cal a little more each day.

With a glance at the kitchen clock, she realized it was half-past seven. If he followed the pattern he had set in recent days, Cal would arrive any minute now to escort her home. Despite her better judgment, her heart picked up its beat. She couldn't help but look forward to seeing him again.

Giving the kitchen table a last swipe with her towel, Melissa heard heavy footsteps in the dining hall. "Are you about done for the night?" Cal asked a moment later.

She hung the towel from the peg by the sink and smiled.

"Just done. If you'll give me a moment, I'll collect my things."

"Take your time. I'm in no hurry. How about you?"

After donning her wool coat, Melissa gathered her carpetbag. "Not at all. I can't work on Craig's gifts tonight. He brought home a difficult assignment and will be at the table for a time yet. The new schoolmarm is most demanding."

"What will you do?"

Patting the bag, she answered, "I planned to work on Mama's quilt. I'm almost finished. She and Papa would be so happy to see us celebrate Christmas in our own home." She extinguished the lamps as Cal held the back door open for her.

"Would you mind if I kept you company for a while?"

"Never," she answered with a genuine smile. "Besides, you can help Craig with the complicated sums. I can't figure out such troublesome problems, but I'm sure you can."

"I've always had a way with numbers . . . and puzzles."

Something in the way he said that last word made Melissa glance in his direction. She found him studying her face, seeking perhaps the answer to one of those puzzles. She feared she knew precisely which one he was pondering. Flustered, she tried to change the topic, but he wouldn't be put off.

"About that letter you received a few days ago," he began. "I haven't forgotten the fear in your face. You *do* know you can trust me enough to tell me about it, don't you?"

Melissa sighed. "You're the most decent and honorable person I've ever known, but the letter doesn't concern you. It's nothing for you to worry about. I can handle it."

His jaw tightened, and his brow furrowed. "I'm sure you can," he said in a controlled voice, "but I like to think you can discuss your troubles with me. Sometimes two can come up with solutions better than one. I'm always happy to help any way you need."

"That's just it. I don't need help. There is nothing to do."

"Then there's no reason you can't tell me what the letter said."

With another glance his way, Melissa realized he wasn't going to drop the subject. Perhaps if she told him the whole shameful tale, he would of his own accord put a distance between them. "It's not very pleasant, you realize."

"Of course. I saw it in your face that day. And your question dodging since then has only strengthened my opinion."

Squaring her shoulders, Melissa came to a halt. The full moon provided enough light to see Cal's features washed in silver, his dark hair gleaming with health. Such a handsome man, beautiful in more than just his physical appearance. Too wonderful for her.

With a deep breath of wintry air and a prayer for courage, she began. "The letter came from Great-Uncle Bert's neighbor."

Cal's eyes narrowed, his jaw squared in a rigid line. "I assume the neighbor had something to say about your relatives."

Melissa looked down at the dirt road. A light snow dusted the frozen mud ridges. If one didn't take care, one could easily stumble. As she would if she didn't say the right things. "Fred's looking for us. He wants Craig back."

"It took him this long to decide that? Why didn't he object when you went for the boy?"

Melissa's cheeks blazed despite the falling snow. "He did. He wouldn't let Craig leave."

"Then how . . . ?"

"I told you it wasn't a pleasant tale. You see, I had to . . . sneak him away in the night. I kidnapped my brother."

"And Fred wants him back." It wasn't a question.

"Yes."

"To misuse him again, I suppose."

"One would think."

"You don't intend to let him have the boy, do you?"

"Of course not!"

"Then what do you plan to do?"

"I'm not sure what I'll do. I just know I'll do something."

"Your loyalty and love are admirable," he said in a tight voice that belied his words. She could almost touch his anger. "But you need more of a plan than that. I'm glad you haven't run away."

She couldn't meet his gaze. "The thought did occur to me, but I realized that wasn't the solution. I've prayed long and hard, and I'm trusting the Lord."

He took a step closer, and something in Melissa urged her to lean on him. She pushed the longing aside; she had to be strong.

"Perhaps I can be your solution," he said. "I meant to wait before asking, but . . . you don't have to face trouble on your own. I've grown very fond of you and would be honored if you became my wife."

Melissa gasped. She hadn't expected that. While a part of her soared with elation, another crashed with despair. Cal thought her too weak to handle her problems. Again, he felt he had to come to her rescue. He saw her as a helpless woman. He deserved better in a wife.

Fighting back tears, she shook her head. "I'm afraid that isn't the solution. I can't run to you every time the slightest thing goes wrong, and that's what marrying you to avoid facing Fred would be. Your proposal is very kind, but . . . my parents taught me that marriage should only be entered into for the right reasons. There must be love, respect, and true, deep friendship. That's what I want if I ever marry. Not a dear, kind man who feels he must rescue me from my failures."

"I don't feel that way at all! I love—"

"Don't say it! Please." She swallowed down the lump in her throat. "I didn't mean to offend. I just think your sense of decency has grown out of proportion lately. I can handle our problems. You needn't saddle yourself with them—or us."

The spark of temper burned brighter in his eyes. "I wouldn't be saddling myself with anything. You're the woman I want—even if, to my eternal regret and irritation, you're the most stubborn woman I know—and I'll persuade you of that if it's the last thing I do."

Melissa's eyes opened wide. She had never heard such vehemence in Cal Stevenson's voice. If she dared, she might allow herself to believe he truly cared for her, that he had proposed for the right reason.

Common sense put a halt to her fancy. She turned and resumed walking. Over her shoulder she called, "No need to see me home. It would be best if you didn't come calling for a while. And thank you for all your help."

She heard him mutter something about hard heads and mules, but since she doubted it put her in an attractive light, she didn't stop. Her heart felt heavy, sore. She had done the right thing, but it didn't feel good. She again prayed for God's help, for him to give her the strength and wisdom to deal with Fred so she wouldn't have to ask anyone—especially not Cal—for assistance.

She couldn't bear to be rescued again by the man who might have been hers.

CHAPTER SIX

Five days before Christmas, Melissa's nerves had reached the fiddle-string point. Anything and everything startled her, and she spent more time glancing over her shoulder than working. So she took to asking Craig to help her clean up after supper at the Dinner Bell.

Tonight was no different from the past few nights. Every creak of the floorboards and cry of the wind tightened her middle in fear of Fred. She felt certain his arrival was at hand.

"Are you ready to leave *now?*" asked Craig as she hung up her kitchen towel.

Dreading the walk home in the dark, Melissa nodded. "I think so." She took her coat from its place by the door, and Craig went for her carpetbag. "Wait!" she cried. "You can't take that. I have—things in there you shouldn't see." *Mrs. Terwilliger's letter, for one.*

"What things?" he asked, his curiosity suddenly awakened.

Melissa wished she could take back her words. "Why . . . oh, the gifts I'm making for Christmas. You wouldn't want to spoil my surprise, now would you?"

"What's so special about Christmas, anyway? It's just a day like any other day."

Dismay struck Melissa, but she bit back a rash response. She opened the door, waved for Craig to precede her, then took her time locking up. "You're right, of course," she finally said, as they walked toward home. "The day is like any other day, but what we honor is special indeed."

"It's just a story, Sissy."

"No, it's history. God loved people so much that even though they'd sinned against him, he sent his Son, Jesus, to restore the broken bond. That is what we celebrate."

"You believe all that?"

Melissa smiled. "Yes, Craig. I believe. God is powerful and loving and wise. When you come to him you wonder how you could have not known him before. You see his handiwork, his goodness, in everything around you, and you never want to stray from his side again."

"Why are you so bent on all this preparation and decoration, then? If all you mean to do is recognize God's gift, you don't need to make a fuss."

At the cabin, Melissa hung her coat on its hook near the hearth, then faced her brother. "Of course I don't need to make a fuss. I don't think I have. I just remember the wonderful times we had back in Ohio. Mama used to do these same things. She tied ribbons on holly and pine boughs, and the house looked and smelled . . . well, of Christmas. She spent hours making gifts for us all. Then on Christmas Day we opened the presents and had a big dinner. I want to celebrate Christmas like that in our new home. To thank God for the many gifts he gives us, to celebrate the new life we receive through his Son—"

"Don'tcha tell a purty tale," mocked Fred Clemson as he threw open the door, slamming it against the wall. "But you ain't as saintly as you make out. You *stole* that boy after I toldja you couldn't have him. He's coming back with me."

So it had come to pass. Although Melissa's knees weakened and her stomach churned with fear, she called on the Lord for strength and chose to reason with Fred. "My brother and I belong together. I tried to explain, but you wouldn't listen. You just wanted to have your selfish way."

Fred's piggish eyes narrowed, and his nostrils flared. "I need him on the farm. Craig's coming with me."

As he reached for Craig's arm, the boy ducked, darting behind him. Fred spun around and, to Melissa's dismay, backed her brother into a corner. "Don't you give me no trouble, boy, or I'll have to discipline you again."

Craig compressed his lips and darted his gaze around the room, clearly seeking escape. Fred continued his approach, blocking him in.

Hoping to distract the man, Melissa said, "Why don't we sit at the table? We can discuss this calmly, then decide what to do."

"Ain't got time for chitchat. I'm going back to the farm with the boy now." He took Craig's slender arm in his meaty hand, and Melissa saw her brother flinch. Then he pulled himself to his full height and crushed his heel into Fred's instep.

"*Ow!*" bellowed Fred. "See? This is why I need to take him back, little girl. He's a wild one. I'll take care of him right good." He swung at Craig's head. Trying to avoid the blow, the boy hit the wall with a sickening thud and slid to the ground, unconscious.

Horror froze Melissa in place. What could she do against this man? How would she get them out of this mess?

Shaking off her fear, she ran to Craig's side. "Look what you've done, Fred! He can't even walk now. How do you expect to take him with you, much less make him work?"

"I didn't hurt him bad. You'll see." He reached down and, grasping Craig's shirt lapels, gave him a shake. The boy opened his eyes, blinking dazedly.

Melissa lunged for Fred's arm. "Leave him alone! You've done enough already."

He caught both her hands in one of his. "What? You gonna take me on, girlie? I've smashed flies bigger'n you!"

"Melissa, don't," croaked Craig.

"Yeah, Melissa, don't fight me," taunted Fred, dragging her away from Craig. "You shouldn'ta taken the boy. He's coming with me."

"No, he's not!" she argued, fighting to free herself.

Craig tried to stand but collapsed in a heap again. "Good," said Fred. "He'll be easy to take like that while you sit pretty right here in this chair."

Melissa wriggled wildly, to no avail. Fred was large and beefy and determined. He dragged her to the chair, pushed her onto the seat, and, pulling twine from a pocket, tied her down. "Craig!" she cried. "Run!" Then turning her face heavenward, she prayed aloud, "Lord Jesus, our lives are in your hands. I can't save us but you can. Help us."

Fred aimed a faded red bandanna at her lips. Melissa bobbed her head to the left, but he caught her by the hair. "Fool woman. You're all the same, always gabbing, never shutting up." The handkerchief filled her mouth, and Melissa gagged, repulsed by the stale smell of the fabric and the bile of fear in her throat.

As she watched, Craig stood, swayed a moment or two, then went toward the door.

"You ain't going nowhere, boy!" thundered Fred. He clapped a hand on Craig's shoulder, then shook him again. Like a broken toy, the boy wilted in the large man's hands.

"That's better," muttered Fred, reaching for the doorknob.

As it opened from the outside, the door caught his hand, smashing his knuckles. Howling like a wounded dog, Fred dropped Craig and cradled his injured hand.

Cal stepped into the room, a steely glint in his gaze. "Fred Clemson, right?"

"Yeah. What's it to ya?"

"I just needed to know I had the right man." Turning, he called out, "Come on in, Sheriff Bolton. He's here."

Fred's small eyes darted between Melissa, still tied to the chair, Craig, limp on the floor, and Cal, a formidable presence by the door. "What's the sheriff here for?" he asked, a whiny note entering his voice.

"To arrest you, of course," answered Cal, crossing the room to where Melissa sat. In seconds, he had stripped the foul cloth from her mouth and began working at the knots.

"I ain't done nothing."

Cal's eyebrows rose. "You've tied Miss Barnhart to a chair, and I saw you drop her brother. He's flat out on the ground now. It seems to me you have a few counts against you."

"Nah," countered Fred, shrugging. "That's my boy there, and he was giving me what-for. I had to discipline him. For his own good, you know."

A pudgy, balding fellow with his hat in his hand then entered the room, panting from exertion. "I got seven kids of my own, and I never disciplined none to where he couldn't get up. Looks more to me like a matter of assault. And that lady doesn't look quite right trussed up like a roaster."

Fred's beady eyes lit up. He pointed to Melissa. "She's the one you're after, sheriff. She's the criminal. She stole my boy. At night. After I told her she couldn't take him. Arrest *her*."

Melissa's heart stopped. Would the sheriff believe Fred? Would her dreams come to such a miserable end?

The lawman studied her face. Then he stared at Fred, whose forehead sprouted beads of sweat. He glanced at Cal, then came to Craig's side. After checking the boy's wrist for a pulse, he smoothed the hair back from his forehead. Finally, he turned to Fred again. "What do you want with the boy?"

Fred blinked. Fast. Two, three times. "Why, he's mine. I took him in when he was orphaned at birth. I've raised him since. I missed him when she took him away." For effect, he sniffed audibly. "I . . . I love this boy."

Melissa gasped, and she heard Cal suck in a breath. Sparks of temper heated the green of his eyes. "You love this boy, Mr. Clemson?"

"'Course I do."

"You've cared for him, seen to his needs, and *loved* him all these years?"

"That's right."

"And you don't want any harm to befall him, do you? You do everything a father does to provide him with a good life?"

"Ye—e—es . . ."

Cal swooped and lifted Craig's shirttail. The mass of scars gleamed in the light from the lamp above their heads. "Then you don't know anything about these, do you?"

"Ah, man," moaned the sheriff.

Fear crossed Fred's stolid face. "N-no. They . . . ah . . . were there when I took him in."

Melissa inhaled sharply. "He had no scars on him when Papa died! He was only three months old! Fred Clemson, you're a liar and a beast! You beat Craig over and over. If I hadn't taken him away that day, who knows if he would be alive today. You'll *never* take my brother away from me again!"

Craig stirred and opened his eyes. "You mean that, Sissy?"

She ran to his side. "Of course I do!" Kneeling, she took his hand. "That's why I came for you in the first place. We're a family, we belong together, and we finally have our very own home. *No one*—certainly not Fred Clemson—is going to change that. I know this is God's will for us. He brought us to New Hope, and this is where he means us to be."

A sudden blur of motion at the corner of her eye caught Melissa's attention. "Watch out!" she cried as Fred made a dash for the open door.

Despite his girth, Sheriff Bolton was ready with handcuffs.

Moments later he dragged Fred from the room, assuring Melissa the man would never bother them again. "In fact, Miss Barnhart, the only time you'll ever see him again is when we try him. He'll spend a long time locked up."

As the lawman and his prey left, Cal said, "Will you be all right?"

"Of course," she answered, helping Craig stand.

"I have to go with them," Cal explained. "After you told me about Clemson, I suspected he would come calling. I alerted the sheriff, and we got ready. Since you insisted you could handle *everything*, I didn't want to take over, but I wasn't going to let him hurt you or Craig again. No matter how all-fired independent you wanted to be." Running a hand through his mussed black hair, he added, "Since Fred trespassed on company property to attack you, there are papers I have to sign. I'll be back as soon as I can."

"You needn't worry. I can take care of us—"

"I know you can," he countered, his patience clearly gone, "but I said I would be back, and I will. I want to see how you're both doing. Then you and I have to talk."

Melissa lowered her gaze. "If you insist."

He crooked a finger under her chin and made her look straight at him. What she saw in his eyes made her heart beat faster. "I insist," he said, his voice deep and sure. "You won't put me off with weak arguments this time."

Melissa's jaw dropped. He had never spoken to her like that. And he had never gazed at her with such emotion, such intensity in his expressive eyes. Could it possibly be . . . ?

No. She couldn't let herself speculate. Who knew what Cal wanted to talk to her about? Perhaps he wanted to discuss the problems caused by Fred's appearance. There would have been no trouble in New Hope if she hadn't brought her family here.

Perhaps he was going to ask them to move on. Her stomach flipped as disappointment landed there. "Good-bye, Cal."

He shook his head and gave what sounded like an exasperated sigh. "I won't be long." He left the room, closing the door gently in his wake.

Melissa turned to Craig. "How is that bump on the head?"

"Which one?" he asked, a crooked grin tipping his mouth. Then he waved carelessly. "I'm fine, Sissy. Better than fine. Did you see that?"

His question caught her off guard. "I saw plenty. I saw Fred take a swing at you, then shake you like a rag. I saw him fight me and tie me and gag me—"

"Not that. I meant how fast God answered your prayer."

Melissa suddenly couldn't draw a breath. With great effort, she said, "My . . . *prayer* . . . ?"

"Yeah! You told Jesus you couldn't save us and asked him to help. Two minutes later Cal showed up. God sure worked fast!"

Melissa stared at her younger brother in awe. "You know—you're absolutely right. God did help us, didn't he? He sent Cal and the sheriff just when we needed them most. I wasn't weak or dependent or—"

"Know what, Sissy? I think there may be something to all that praying and Bible reading of yours and Cal's. I don't know exactly what, but maybe there *is* something to it, after all."

Chuckling, Melissa took hold of his elbow and directed him toward his room. "Why don't you go on to bed and ponder the mysteries of our Almighty there? While you're doing that, maybe you'll get some sleep, as well. It will do you good."

Still wearing that bemused expression, he allowed himself to be led. "Yeah, maybe I will do that."

Giving him privacy, Melissa closed the bedroom door. Joy filled her heart, and tears of wonder and happiness welled in her eyes. She crossed the main room of the cabin and sat in her armchair, taking up her needle and quilt. The tears flowed down her cheeks unchecked.

"Thank you, Jesus! Oh, thank you, Lord, for your love and care. You helped and protected us. I've been stubborn and foolish and proud. It's one thing to be a useless sort, and quite another to accept help that is freely given. Especially when you send that help in answer to prayer. Forgive me, Father, for my sinful pride. Help me, too, Lord, to forgive Fred. That isn't easy, but with your help, I now know I can."

As she continued to stitch and pray, Melissa felt peace seep through her, a peace she had never experienced before.

She smiled. "Yet another gift, Lord. Another one I don't deserve. You've given me back my family, provided me with a living, given us a good, solid home, and now you've kept us from harm. What more could a woman want?"

From the deepest corner of her memory, a dear voice whispered, *"I've grown very fond of you and would be honored if you became my wife."*

Could it be? Did God truly mean to give her all the desires of her heart?

Melissa placed her trust in her ever faithful God, and gathered his peace around her as she settled in to wait for Cal's return.

By the time Cal finished telling Sheriff Bolton everything he knew about Craig's abuse and signing everything necessary to leave Fred to man's and God's justice, two hours had gone by. It was late, perhaps too late to go calling, but he didn't care. He would never catch a wink of sleep until he checked on Melissa.

Besides, a few things needed saying, and he refused to wait any longer to say them.

When he arrived at her snug cabin, Melissa's newest

Christmas decoration caught his eye. She had made him hammer an arrangement of red-cheeked apples and pine boughs over the doorframe. It looked festive and welcoming, and he smiled.

He loved her. Melissa, the consummate homemaker, a true nest builder. She had turned the little cabin into a haven, a place where he could find rest after a busy day at the mill.

She had covered the worn kitchen table with a bright tablecloth, garbed the windows in checkered curtains, spread a braided rug before the hearth, and through her Christmas decorations, scented the air with pine. She had made a home.

The home he hoped to make his own soon.

But first he had to persuade a stubborn lady that God meant the two of them to spend the rest of their lives as man and wife.

He knocked on the door, suspecting that his summons would wake her. When it opened, his suspicion proved correct.

"Oh!" she cried, her voice husky from sleep.

Although he knew she would not be happy that he had caught her looking like this, he thought her the most beautiful woman on earth. Her blonde hair had slipped from its pins and tumbled in tangles over her shoulders. Her dress had been reduced to a mass of wrinkles, and her right cheek bore a crease from whatever she had leaned against in slumber.

With a smile, he asked, "May I come in for a moment? I know it's late, but we really need to talk."

"Of course," she responded, stepping back with a yawn. "How is Craig?"

"Fast asleep."

"And you?"

"Not any longer."

He chuckled. "And it's purely my fault."

She blushed. "I'm sorry. I'm not being very hospitable. Won't you have a seat on the sofa?"

With a nod, Cal did as asked. He motioned for her to join him, and when she went toward the armchair, he shook his head. "Sit with me, please."

A shy expression spread over her features, but she took the seat at his side. Cal viewed her agreement as encouragement. He clasped her hand in his.

"I don't know where you got the idea that anyone would think you irresponsible or less than capable, dependent, or weak. I sure don't. I want to help you because I . . . care for you. I want to do everything I can to make things better for you, to share everything with you, my thoughts, my strengths, my life. I asked you to marry me once before, and you turned me down. Please don't say no again. Let me court you. Get to know me better. Think about the wonderful life the Lord could give us. Then answer me."

A smile curved her lips. "How long do you want to wait for that answer?"

"How long do you need?"

"Oh . . . a moment or two."

"What?"

"I know what my answer will be now or ten years from now."

He started to speak, but she put her hand out to halt his words.

"I have to ask your forgiveness," she said, all sign of teasing gone. "I realized tonight how I let my pride interfere with the blessings the Lord was giving me. I was trying to work everything out through my own efforts. I didn't know how to accept his gift for what it truly was." She swallowed hard, then went on. "I didn't dare count on you because I had never been able to count on anyone. I felt I had to do everything myself in order to be a responsible adult. And I was wrong to kidnap Craig, then keep that information from you. I should have helped you prepare for Fred. Can you forgive me?"

"Of course, I forgive you." A rueful twist tipped his lips. "And I must confess I didn't behave as I should have. Instead of waiting on the Lord's leading, I kept rushing in to prove my worth. My pride couldn't accept your independence. I'm sorry, Melissa. Can you forgive my overbearing attitude?"

"Of course!"

"I'm just glad I finally did wait on God and let him use me when you most needed me."

"So am I," she said, her gaze warm on his face.

"Can we discuss this another time?" he asked. "I would like the answer to my proposal sooner rather than later."

"How soon?"

"Now."

"Then . . . yes."

"When?"

"When what?"

"When will you marry me?"

"When do you want me to marry you?"

"The sooner the better. How about Christmas Eve?"

"Oh, Cal!" she cried, her eyes sparkling with happiness. "How perfect. We can celebrate our first Christmas in New Hope with a wedding!"

"It will also be our first Christmas as man and wife."

"The first of many."

"Of course." Unwilling to wait another moment, he placed a tender kiss on her lips. "I love you, Melissa."

"I love you, too."

At precisely two o'clock on Christmas Day, Melissa went to the bedroom she had shared for the first time the night before with her new husband and removed her gravy-splashed apron and blouse. The meal was ready, the platters and bowls full and on the table. Her menfolk waited for her to join them.

She shook out her wedding gown, the cream wool dress trimmed in hand-tatted lace Mrs. McCreary had sewn in a rush. Melissa wanted to wear it again, since Cal had told her many times during the wedding party how beautiful it made her look.

What a party it had been. Everyone in New Hope turned out for the event. Melissa was touched by her neighbors' good wishes.

Ida Mae Harper had surprised her. First, by insisting on playing the piano during the ceremony, then with the gift of a pair of embroidered pillowcases. "I was wrong about you," she said, her cheeks scarlet.

"I'm glad you changed your mind," Melissa answered.

"If you like, I can give your brother music lessons."

Melissa had fought back the laughter that threatened at the notion of Craig sitting for such tutoring. "Thank you for the offer, but Cal and Sam keep him busy after school."

Nodding with satisfaction, Ida Mae strolled toward Mabel Sauerbehr. The heavyset redhead had yet to wish Melissa well, but she had shown up with another of her magnificent coconut cakes. And she hadn't once insulted the Barnharts.

When Ida Mae reached Mabel's side, the two matrons put their heads together and whispered avidly. Then Mabel scoured the room with her eagle gaze. Moments later her voice trumpeted over the hubbub of the guests. "There you are, Sam August! I've been looking everywhere for you."

The hunted look on Sam's face proved too much for Melissa. She burst out laughing when he turned tail and ran from the room. At that point, she wondered where her brother had gone. She looked through the crowd and found him head to head with Richie. Frowning, she caught his gaze, and he flushed. The two hurried to stand at Cal's side, manufactured innocence beaming from their mischievous faces. Later, as she and her new husband cut the wedding cake, firecrackers went off outside. She had known who set them off without needing to look.

Now, as she finished buttoning her dress, she caught sight of the brown, rust, and gold quilt over the bed, where she and Cal would sleep for the rest of their lives. With a loving pat, she smoothed one of the Log Cabin squares. "We made it, Mama," she whispered. "The Barnharts made it out west, and we're finally in our new home. We're starting that wonderful new life you and Papa talked about, only God has made it so much better than I think even you imagined. Certainly much better than I did. I just wish you and Papa were here today."

"I'm hungry, Sissy!" called Craig.

Melissa's heart warmed at the cheerful note in his voice. Her brother had come so far in the last few days. Although he hadn't yet given his life to Jesus, she was certain it was only a matter of time before he did. After all, he had been the first to recognize how mightily their righteous God had prevailed. In the days since, Craig's surly responses had disappeared, and although he and Richie still cooked up plenty of trouble, he no longer fought her and Cal on every point of direction they offered.

"Coming," she said, and closed the bedroom door.

At the table, she studied the two waiting there. Her men.

"Are you ready to serve, love?"

Melissa's heart sped at Cal's tender question. She met his gaze and thrilled at the emotion there. "Will you say the blessing?"

"Of course." He held out a chair for her. Craig took his seat, and Cal followed suit. Clasping her hand in his, he gave it a gentle, private squeeze. Melissa had never known such happiness.

"Heavenly Father," Cal began, "we thank you for all you give us, for the meal prepared by loving hands, for the home you provide for us. I'm truly thankful for the love you've brought Melissa and me at this time when we celebrate your greatest gift."

Melissa looked first at her husband, then at Craig. "Thank you, Father," she said, "for patching together a family out of three separate lives. Amen."

RECIPE

CHRISTMAS FRUIT CAKE

3 cups cake flour
2 tsp. baking powder
½ tsp. salt
1½ tsp. cinnamon
1 tsp. cloves
¼ tsp. nutmeg
¼ tsp. mace

1 cup shortening
1½ cups brown sugar
3 eggs

½ cup grape juice
1 cup apricot jam

2 cups raisins, finely chopped
1 cup figs, finely chopped
2 cups dates, finely chopped
2 cups walnuts, coarsely chopped
2 tbsp. candied lemon peel, coarsely chopped
1 cup candied cherries, coarsely chopped
½ cup pineapple, coarsely chopped
2 tbsp. candied orange peel, coarsely chopped
¼ cup candied citron, coarsely chopped

In a medium-sized bowl, sift together flour, baking powder, salt, and spices. In a large mixing bowl, cream shortening and brown sugar together; add eggs and beat well. Add flour mixture, alternating with grape juice and apricot jam. Then add chopped fruits and nuts. Mix thoroughly. Pour into a large tube pan lined with waxed paper and lightly greased. Bake at 275° for 1 hour. Increase oven temperature to 300° and bake for another 1¾ to 2 hours. If top browns too quickly, cover loosely with aluminum foil. Cool, remove from pan, and place cake in an airtight container to age for two to four weeks.

A Note from the Author

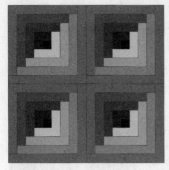

Dear Reader:

The "Log Cabin" quilt pattern is one of the most familiar and enduring ones—certainly one of my favorites since I began quilting seventeen years ago. In my opinion, its popularity comes from its representation of a universal longing for hearth and home. With its rows of "logs" surrounding the central "chimney" piece, this block certainly embodied everything Melissa wanted for her brother and herself—what she found in the cabin in New Hope.

"Klondike Fever" broke out and spread like wildfire the moment George Washington Carmack announced his find of gold in the Yukon. Men swarmed northward in search of treasure, leaving behind stable jobs and families. The logging camps in Washington State were hit hard by this exodus, and logging entrepreneurs often advertised the benefits they offered in the hope of building up the small towns they had established.

I sincerely hope this Christmas is a time of joy in your home as you celebrate the birth of our Lord. Have a slice of fruitcake, count your blessings, and take a break from the busyness to enjoy a story—or four!

In his love,
Ginny Aiken

ABOUT THE AUTHOR

A former newspaper reporter, Ginny Aiken lives in south-central Pennsylvania with her husband and four sons. She discovered books early on and wrote her first novel at age fifteen. (She burned it when she turned a "mature" sixteen!) That first effort was followed, several years later, with the winning entry in the Mid-America Romance Authors' Fiction from the Heartland contest for unpublished authors.

Ginny has certificates in French literature and culture from the University of Nancy, France, and a B.A. in Spanish and French literature from Allegheny College in Pennsylvania. Her first novel was published in 1993, and since then she has published six additional novels and two novellas. Her novellas appear in the anthologies *With This Ring* and *A Victorian Christmas Quilt*.

When she isn't busy with the duties of a soccer mom, she can be found reading, writing, enjoying classical music, and preparing for her next Bible study.

You can write to Ginny in care of Tyndale House Author Relations, P.O. Box 80, Wheaton, IL 60189-0080, or E-mail her at GinnyAiken@aol.com.

Crosses and Losses

Peggy Stoks

For all the Mary Roses I have known

CHAPTER ONE

Mama? How long till Daddy comes home? Four minutes?"

Joyce Colburn knelt to stroke her daughter's cheek, delighting in its downy smoothness. Two neat braids contained the child's fine, nutmeg-colored tresses, each decorated with a violet bow to match the ivory-and-violet dress she wore. "I don't know how many minutes it will be until Daddy comes home, Audrey," she replied to the three-and-a-half-year-old, who so badly wanted to be four that she used the beloved number in her speech as often as possible. "But he sent word that he would be home for dinner tonight."

Muffling a sigh, Joyce wondered if there had been any change in her husband since she'd last seen him. He had been away on business for more than a month. Given their situation at home, she suspected that he deliberately chose the traveling assignments that so often kept him away weeks at a time. Even when he was in town, he kept long hours at his office in the city.

"Mama? I like you. Do you like me?" Audrey melted against her, and Joyce enfolded the petite child in her arms, carrying her to the plush armchair nestled near the library's bay of windows. "Of course I like you . . . and I love you, too." Settling into the chair with her daughter on her lap, she breathed deeply of the essence of little girl, her lips seeking the downy-soft cheek. "Nanny certainly has you looking smart this afternoon. Did you pick out this dress for Daddy?"

"Yes." Audrey nodded and was silent a long moment. "Mama, does Daddy like me?" she finally said in her piping voice, turning to look into her mother's eyes.

"Why, yes, of course your daddy likes you—and loves you, too. I'm sure he can hardly wait to be home and give you a great big kiss." The declaration rang false in her own ears, but she felt Audrey relax against her. "Does Nanny know you're down here, pumpkin?"

"No. Kathryn was waking up from her nap, and I just runned down to see if Daddy was home yet."

"I see. And what are Lynelle and Bobby doing?" Despite the approach of Christmas, the older children, ages eleven and nine, had become more somber with each day that passed. Did the loss of their baby sister two Christmases past still grieve them so deeply? Or were they more aware than she suspected about the gulf between their mother and father? This sigh that escaped couldn't be disguised.

Audrey wriggled off her lap. "I'd better go back upstairs. Nell and Bobby are back from skating, and I don't want Nanny to be cross with me." She started to run off and caught herself, slowing to a walk. At the doorway she turned, extending her index finger with importance. "Mama? Remember to tell me when Daddy comes home."

"Of course, Audrey."

"Maybe it will be in four minutes." A pair of index fingers now pointed toward her. "Or four hours."

"Yes, sweetheart, no doubt it will be somewhere between four minutes and four hours."

Satisfied, the youngster blew her a kiss and retreated. With a third sigh, Joyce settled back into the chair, alone with her worries and thoughts. *Mama, does Daddy like me?* Did even little Audrey sense the troubles that strained the fabric of her family? Things had gotten to the point where Joyce wasn't sure Samuel even liked—or loved—*her* anymore. And certainly, there would be no kisses shared between them. Perhaps a formal brush of his lips against her cheek. No closeness, no embrace.

Glancing around the library, she took in her home's lovely furnishings and the elaborate holiday decorations she'd painstakingly placed. So many material blessings. Across the room, a small blue spruce bore an elegant profusion of ornaments, bows and candles. Swags of fragrant pine graced the mantel. And wafting through the house were the aromas of many good foods being prepared in honor of Samuel's homecoming. For days she'd thrown herself into adorning their home in St. Paul's fashionable Irvine Park neighborhood, as if by creating a perfect environment she could create the illusion of a perfect family.

But an impeccably adorned home could not bring life to a marriage that was all but dead. Who was she fooling? The household staff was aware of the ever-widening chasm between her and her husband. The children, with whatever level of understanding, also knew things weren't right. Once their overgrown but grand playmate, their father was now a distant stranger. And he barely acknowledged little Kathryn, soon to be two.

Something inside Samuel had withered when Kathryn's twin sister, Mary Rose, had succumbed shortly after her birth. At first Joyce was secure in thinking time would heal her husband's wounded heart, but almost two years had passed with nothing and no one being able to breach its woody cords and ligaments.

She stood and walked to the window, staring at the snowy

neighborhood. Dusk approached. As she watched a sleigh and team of horses pass down the street, she allowed herself to hope that this homecoming would be different. That a miracle had been worked in her husband's absence. She had prayed without ceasing for him to accept the Lord's comfort, but he seemed to have walked as far away from his faith as he had from his family. Never could she have traveled through such a valley of despair if not for the daily mercies of her Savior.

With a bittersweet stab, she allowed her thoughts to dwell on Mary Rose. Both Joyce and her physician had suspected that Joyce carried twins when she'd gotten large well ahead of her time, new mother's marks multiplying on top of the old. She and Samuel were delighted with this turn of events, chuckling and speculating at what bountiful fruit her womb might contain. But nearly two months before the end of her confinement, her waters had burst and labor was upon her like a galloping horse.

Mary Rose had arrived before Dr. Pfeiffer. The silver-haired gentleman scarcely had time to remove his jacket and roll up his sleeves before Kathryn joined her sister. Babies died, she knew, but she'd always had such easy births and healthy children that she secretly believed she would forever be preserved from such calamity. Her anxiety at delivering prematurely accelerated to gut-wrenching fear when Dr. Pfeiffer sat down and told her how slim were the girls' chances of survival.

He was correct on Mary Rose's account. Born plump and as red as a tomato, she took her last breaths only a few hours after her birth. But scrawny, pale Kathryn clung tenaciously to life, refusing to give up the battle. Even so many months later, tears burned behind Joyce's lids, and she released a deep, shuddering sigh as she recalled the raw emotions of that endless night. One baby dead, the other near death. Waiting. Wondering.

Samuel had tried to be strong for her, but the intensity of that time had proven to be too much for him. He'd always warned her that he didn't do well with death. Even before Mary Rose was gone, he'd fled the room with a choked apology. Two years later he was still running—from her, from their family, and from little Kathryn. It broke her heart to know that he had only the barest acquaintance with their surviving youngest daughter.

The survivor. That's how Joyce thought of tousle-headed Kathryn Cecilia. Quiet determination was readily visible in her character, tempered by a winning smile and expressive hazel eyes. Just like Samuel's eyes . . . used to be.

Letting the curtain fall back into place, she glanced at the needlework she'd set aside upon Audrey's escape from Nanny's watchful eye. The crewel still life was a promising piece, but she absolutely could not sit down and place one more stitch. As Samuel's arrival drew ever closer, the more unnerved she became.

The plush Oriental carpet absorbed the sound of her footsteps as she walked from the library to the hallway, her silk skirt swishing gently. Soft laughter and the clink of china drifted from beyond the closed doorway of the dining room, telling her that Carol and Ida were setting the table for this evening's meal. The two young domestics were good-natured and hardworking, and Joyce knew she was fortunate to have such wonderful household help. Ida lived in, while Carol came three days a week. Gertrude, their live-in cook, had been with them for the past seven years.

The house was as clean and shining as she'd ever seen it, as if the servants also thought that by putting things in order amidst the wonder and hope of the Christmas season, she and Samuel might somehow be set to rights.

If only it could be so.

Climbing the carpeted curved staircase, she continued down the second-story hallway to the staircase that rose to the third story. This was the children's area and also where Nanny, Ida, and Gertrude slept. From above, the reassuring voice of Margaret Murray could be heard, no doubt treating the children to one of her wonderful stories. As often as not, Nanny's tales came from her childhood in Scotland or wealth of imagination rather than the pages of a book. Many times had Joyce paused, listening outside the nursery door, enthralled.

Instead of going upstairs, however, she turned and walked toward her and Samuel's bedchamber. Why had she visited the room so many times today, making certain everything looked as warm and inviting as possible? Each time she'd also checked her appearance in the tall mirror near her wardrobe, satisfied that the blue silk suited her rounded figure and pale complexion, yet unsatisfied at some intangible thing about it all. Her hand closed on the knob, the well-oiled hinges of the door making not a sound as it swung open. She was at a loss to control her restlessness this afternoon, at a loss to—

She was brought up short at the sight of her husband. With his back to her, he unpacked his luggage, having not yet noticed her presence. With love and longing, her gaze drank in the details of his appearance. His hair, the color of lakeshore sand, appeared to have just been trimmed. Did he still have his mustache? His hat and suit coat had been tossed across the end of the bed, and the way the fabric of his shirt strained across his shoulders as he worked did not escape her notice.

An ache—almost like a physical pain—began in her chest as she thought about what their marriage had become: a cohabitation of strangers. How she longed to feel his arms around her again, to press her face against the warmth of his neck . . . to whisper the deepest feelings of her heart into his ear during the dark of the night. Prayer and patience had been her sustenance these two years past, but she didn't know how much longer she could go on this way. While he was home, he spent more nights in his sitting room than he did in here. She was losing him; they were all losing him.

"Welcome home, Samuel," she spoke with a tentative smile, not wanting to startle him or be caught staring. Why had he come in so quietly? Did he have a surprise for her? Her heart throbbed against her ribs as he turned, and she hoped with all her might that in his gaze she would find peace and joy.

But the hazel eyes of the stranger blinked once, twice, taking in her presence; his head inclined politely at her greeting. "Hello, Joyce. You're looking well." With that, he returned to his unpacking, as if dismissing her.

A mixture of potent feelings surged inside her, anger not the least among them. What had happened to Samuel, her husband? The man she thought she knew so well? Did he think he could keep his grief in check forever? And didn't he know that by doing so, he'd abandoned her to her bereavement? She opened her mouth to speak, but before she could utter a word, a flurry of footsteps sounded behind her.

"I heared Daddy! Daddy! Daddy!"

A chorus of whoops and shouts and footfalls carried into the room as Audrey pushed past Joyce's skirt and ran to her father. "I heared you come in, Daddy!" she cried, wheeling on her older brother and sister. "I told you I heared him. He sneaked in as quiet as a mouse up the back stairs, but you didn't believe me."

Lynelle and Bobby stood just outside the doorway, tentative about entering, their faces eager nonetheless.

"Why should we believe you?" Bobby spoke with the superiority of a much-older brother. "You're only three."

"Merciful heavens, children! Such manners!" came Nanny's unmistakable voice. "And Master Robert. Is that any way to speak to your sister?" Slowed by her arthritic knee as well as by Kathryn's halting descent, she did not reach the second story landing until well after the older children, her admonitions competing with the toddler's insistent cries of "Da-dee! Da-dee!"

Joyce swung her gaze from Samuel to Nanny and the children, then back to where Audrey stood before Samuel, her breath catching in her throat as the seconds drew out. Samuel had not outright rejected the children before, but he looked as though he wanted to repack his items and be gone. She saw his gaze flick past her to Kathryn, now borne in Nanny's sturdy arms. Now quiet, their youngest child's wide hazel gaze was fixed on her father.

Unaccustomed to receiving her father's attention, Kathryn snuggled deeper into Nanny's bosom. Her thumb disappeared into her mouth, but she continued to hold Samuel's gaze until Audrey tugged several times on his trouser leg.

"Daddy, are you happy?" the three-year-old asked. "You don't look happy. Are you sick? I was sick one day when you were gone, and my tummy hurted. Is your tummy hurting? Nanny can give you a dose of castor oil and make you—"

"Audrey, darling," Joyce interrupted in the nick of time. "Your poor daddy has barely gotten in the door. Think of how fatigued he must be from his travels. Let's all give him some time to collect himself; then we can have a nice visit."

"Indeed, lass," Nanny seconded in a no-nonsense tone that thirty years' experience had perfected. "Come along."

With grudging obedience, Audrey walked toward the door. "I'm going to be four, Daddy," she persisted over her shoulder. "In Febillary. But Kathryn has the next birthday. Do you remember? She's going to be two. And so is Mary Rose, up in heaven. But I'm bigger. Four is bigger than—"

"That's enough, Audrey." Samuel spoke for the first time since the children had assembled, his expression having gone rigid at the mention of Mary Rose. "Go with Nanny, all of you." His voice was stern yet flat, his hazel gaze lacking the indulgent light with which it once shone.

Joyce stood in the doorway after Nanny and the children's hasty departure, her protectiveness toward her children sparking maternal, righteous anger at this father who would spurn their affections. Yet at the same time she was troubled by the subtle signs of suffering she read in his appearance. Faint, dark hollows encircled his eyes, and his cheekbones seemed to indicate a new leanness.

"Samuel," she said, at a loss to know the right feelings, the right words for this moment. *Patience, Joyce,* she told herself, taking a breath. Trying to remove any stain of censure from her voice, she went on. "The children have been so looking forward to your return." Extending her arm, she walked toward the bed in an attempt to engage him as gently as possible. "Please don't be angry at Audrey for mentioning Mary Rose. With Kathryn's birthday coming up, it's only natural that she would remember her, too." She fingered the corner of the leather bag on the bed. "We all remember her."

A long, controlled sigh sounded from the man next to her. "I'll be downstairs in half an hour." Keeping his back toward her, he walked to his wardrobe.

Tears blurred Joyce's vision as she walked from the bedchamber and pulled the door shut tight. Taking a long moment to compose herself, she prayed, *Dear Lord, I hurt so deeply at times that I don't think I can bear it. Why does he continue to reject us? If you can do such things as part a sea and place a babe in a virgin's womb, won't you please do a miracle in Samuel's heart? In this season of hope, I ask for your grace and healing for this family.*

With one last dab at her eyes with her delicate handkerchief, she set off down the stairs to the library for her Bible. Surely the Lord would provide some passage or verse that spoke to the pain and desolation that washed through her like an icy current.

Chapter Two

The moment Samuel heard the door click quietly closed, the air left his lungs in a long, slow breath. Shoulders sagging, he leaned against the wardrobe for support. Waves of weariness coursed through his body, the urge to crumple to his knees nearly overwhelming.

How much longer could he continue battling the weakness that threatened to level him? It was a mistake to have come home for the holidays; maintaining a stalwart frame of mind was all but impossible around Joyce and the children.

He had nearly succeeded in not thinking of the night of the twins' birth until Audrey had brought up Mary Rose. In a trice, memories of that terrifying night had rushed forth from the neat compartments in which he'd stored them. Joyce, moaning and writhing with pain. Mary Rose, sliding into his shaking hands. Dr. Pfeiffer's arrival; his grave expression. The cradle near the foot of the bed. His miniature newborn daughters gasping for breath. And Joyce again, pale and weak, shivering despite a mound of covers, crying an endless stream of tears.

How powerless he'd felt. How helpless. How out of control. There wasn't anything he could do for Joyce or the babies except pray, and his ineffectual pleadings certainly hadn't been enough to alter the course of Mary Rose's short life.

Laid out in the parlor after her death, she'd looked like a beautiful little doll. A child-size patchwork quilt of cranberry and green and white, made by his elderly aunt Millie in the southern part of the state, swaddled her still form. A second quilt of another design had arrived at their home some weeks later, also fashioned by Millie's arthritic hands, once she heard their tragic news.

Stepping away from the wardrobe, he pinched the bridge of his nose between his thumb and forefinger in an effort to halt the sudden sting of tears. *Concentrate, Samuel. Don't think about it. You can't do anything to change the past, but you know how to prevent such a tragedy from happening again. Be strong and go on from here.*

He knew his rejection of Joyce caused her pain. It caused him pain, too. Today she had looked so beautiful standing in the doorway that his resolve had nearly crumbled. In her arms he knew he would find sweet solace from the burdens he carried. He remembered how her fingers would stroke his hair and rub the knots from the back of his neck. . . .

For so long now he'd discouraged any contact between them that she no longer ventured to make such gestures. But she had to understand it was for her own good. Never again would there be a chance of a baby—or losing one—because if he lived to be a hundred, he would never forget Mary Rose's eyes.

He remembered leaning over the cradle to look at the girls while speaking to Dr. Pfeiffer, Mary Rose's gaze fixing upon him the instant she'd heard his voice. There had been something unearthly about her eyes, the color of her irises so dark as to appear bottomless. Yet, there was trust to be read there, as well. Like a slow-spreading stain, panic had begun in his vitals, radiating outward to his limbs. What could he do for this wee, gasping child who stared at him, silently pleaded with him, looked to him for something he couldn't give? And Joyce, sobbing for God to spare her babies?

Panic overcoming him, he'd bolted from the room, learning a few hours later that Mary Rose had died. For nearly two years he'd carried the shame of his weakness, having failed both his wife and daughter in their time of need. Never again would he be weak, he'd vowed, for his family deserved better. They deserved a man they could respect.

Taking his hand away from his face, he walked to the mirror and willed himself to collect his wits. Good. He'd managed to forestall any emasculating tears. A washcloth to his face and a stiff brush through his hair ought to put his appearance in order. Steeling himself to endure time with his family, he turned away from the mirror, not liking the grim man he saw reflected in the glass.

"I dinna ken whar that mon's brains are at!" Nanny muttered, her Sutherland brogue intensifying with her aroused sense of justice. "An' Audrey, dearie, I'm thinkin' you're absolutely correct aboot a healthy dose of castor oil bein' just the thing to poot 'im to rights. Indeed!"

Back upstairs in the third-floor nursery, Lynelle and Bobby watched their gray-haired caretaker settle into her cushioned rocking chair near the stove. Neither Audrey nor Kathryn wasted any time clambering into her lap, snuggling in and awaiting a story.

"An' why stop a' castor oil?" she continued in an undertone, rocking her two young charges, "when jalap or calomel would do the job e'er so mooch better?"

"Nanny?" Lynelle queried with a meaningful glance at her brother. "Do you mind if Bobby and I write some letters while you tell the girls a story? We'll just be at the table by the window."

"Certainly not, young miss," came a most proper reply, the inflection of the older woman's speech changing remarkably. "'Twould be most beneficial for you to keep up your penmanship while on your holiday recess."

"Thank you, Nanny." Tugging Bobby's arm in an urgent, disguised manner, Lynelle pulled him over to the table on the opposite side of the large open room, several feet from where the others sat.

"Ouch! Let go of my arm! What do you think you're doing?" Bobby knew enough to keep his voice low, but his irritation was plain to hear.

"Nanny just gave me the most wonderful idea," she whispered in reply, elation coursing through her. Forcing her actions to be unhurried, she walked to the shelf and took down paper, pens, and ink. With a smile and a nod at Nanny, who had launched into the Tale of the Laird of Logie, she returned to the table, where Bobby waited.

"Well, what is it? What's your idea?" he asked before she had fully taken her seat.

"Castor oil."

"Castor oil? What are you talking about?"

"Giving Daddy castor oil, silly. A great big dose." Waiting for him to grasp her logic, she uncorked the ink bottle and dipped her pen. It was a marvelous scheme, really. So romantic.

"You're calling me silly?" His expression was both incredulous and scornful. "At least I haven't taken leave of my senses. Why on earth would you want to give Daddy a big dose of castor oil?"

"So he would need Mother to take care of him . . . ," she drew out, raising her eyebrows meaningfully.

"Ohhh." The sandy-haired boy was quiet a moment,

thinking. He scratched his nose with puzzlement. "You mean to poison him, then."

"Poison! Castor oil's not poison."

"If you say so." Bobby's hazel gaze spoke his disbelief. "And just how do you think Daddy's going to drink a big dose of castor oil without knowing it?" A shudder racked his thin shoulders. "I can taste it in anything."

"You have a point." Doodling against the plain white paper, Lynelle leaned closer to her brother. "But did you hear Nanny mention jalap and calomel? Those are even stronger than castor oil, and I know where Gertrude keeps a bottle of calomel." Excitement growing, the petite, dark-haired girl made an effort to keep her voice down. "We can put it in his pudding. You know how he always likes a dish of pudding in the evening. He'll be so sick that he'll think of Mother as an angel of mercy attending to him, and he'll fall in love with her all over again."

"She *is* awfully good to us when we're sick, isn't she? Do you really think it'll work?"

She nodded, a ripple of pain undulating across her heart. "We've got to do something, Bobby, and soon. Things between them are getting worse all the time. I'm afraid . . . I'm so afraid . . ." Her throat grew thick, and she wasn't able to continue.

"Aw, Nell, don't cry." Bobby's expression was sober as he awkwardly patted her arm. "Tonight we'll doctor the pudding and see what happens."

An impressive ham, scored neatly in a pattern of diamonds, sat on a platter at the head of the table near Samuel's right hand. Studded with cloves and glazed with brown sugar and honey, the roast put forth a sumptuous fragrance, mingling with other tantalizing aromas of Gertrude's finest work.

Joyce watched her husband as he focused his attention on carving the meat. After offering the briefest of thanksgiving prayers, he had not spoken another word. Glancing across the table at her eldest children, she gave them an encouraging smile. She had hoped to prevent this homecoming dinner from becoming a stilted affair by asking Lynelle and Bobby to be present for the entire meal rather than having the children join them only for dessert, as was customary when Samuel was home. Many nights while he was away, she and the children dined together informally in the kitchen.

She could see how much this opportunity meant to them, noticing the pains they'd taken with their appearance. Lynelle, on the brink of adolescence, already fussed with her hair and clothing a great deal. Her dress of yellow velvet set off her dark hair and eyes in a striking way, presenting a glimpse of the lovely young woman she would become. Next year she would move down from her partitioned area of the nursery into her own room on the second story.

Bobby, who most days couldn't care less about the state of his dress, had selected his finest clothing for the occasion. His sandy hair lay in place, and telltale dampness near his temples gave evidence of a recent face washing. In itself, that was remarkable. His countenance was solemn while he waited for his meal, and it struck Joyce how much more he resembled Samuel with each passing year.

The meat was sliced and plates were passed without a word. It broke her heart to know that these good, dear children were so hungry—not for food, but for their father's attention. He was feeding them, indeed providing for them in a generous manner, but not nourishing them in the ways they needed most. *O Lord, these children need their daddy back,* she prayed silently. *The grinning, rough-and-tumble man with whom they used to play for countless hours on the nursery floor.* Audrey was too young to remember her father during her first year of her life, and little Kathryn had never known Samuel in such a way.

"How was skating this afternoon?" she asked, hoping Samuel might be drawn into the conversation with the children. "It looked like a nice day to be outdoors."

"Peter Christiansen got a bloody nose when we played crack the whip," Bobby offered, eyes brightening.

Lynelle glanced at her brother with disapproval. "Lawrence Sayles and Paul Robinson and some of the big boys got the whip going way too fast, and poor Peter was on the end. I think they let him go just to be mean."

"Oh, my. Is he badly injured?"

"He's fine, Mother," Bobby reassured, spearing a bite of ham and glancing toward his father. "By the time I walked him home he wasn't bleeding no more."

"*Any*more," Lynelle corrected while sampling the spiced gooseberries. "But his coat was a mess."

Bobby nodded eagerly. "It was. The blood poured out of his nose just like someone turned on the faucet—"

"I hardly think this is a subject for the dinner table." Samuel's voice was curt, and he did not look up from his meal.

"Oh . . . sorry." The animation left his son's face. Lowering his gaze, he stirred his whipped potatoes with his fork.

After a long, uncomfortable silence, Lynelle and Joyce started to speak at the same time. "Pardon me, Mother. Please go ahead." Though only eleven years of age, Lynelle's manners were impeccable. Margaret Murray was a kind and loving caregiver, yet her standards for the children's behavior were high.

Joyce managed a warm smile despite her disappointment at how the meal was progressing. "I was going to say that we should enjoy Gertrude's holiday cookies in the library this evening. We can light a nice fire and have Margaret bring down Audrey and Kathryn."

"Do the little ones have to come?" Bobby sighed and made a face. "Audrey talks so much that she makes my ears want to fall asleep, and Kathryn just gets into everything."

"Hmmm." Joyce laid her forefinger against the side of her cheek. It was awkward conversing with the children with Samuel's troubled presence at the head of the table, but she was determined to give it her best. "I seem to remember an adorable little boy who never tired of asking questions *and* who used to get into everything—"

"Aw, Mother, please don't tell any 'adorable little boy' stories tonight. I'm sorry I said that about the girls. I'll be patient with them, I promise."

Samuel cleared his throat. "Did Gertrude make me any pudding? That's the one thing I've missed, being away. You can't get a decent bowl of creamy chocolate pudding anywhere."

Pudding? He cared only about his pudding? Joyce watched a look pass between the children while hurt and anger conflicted within her. Had it struck the children, too, that what their father seemed to miss the most while traveling was his nightly bowl of Gertrude's pudding? What about his wife? His children? Not trusting herself to speak, she took a small bite of ham and counted to ten while she chewed and swallowed.

"Yes, Samuel, Gertrude made you your chocolate pudding." Again she noted a meaningful glance pass between Lynelle and Bobby before both children became suddenly very busy with their dinners.

"I hope you find it as satisfying as you remember."

CHAPTER THREE

"H urry up, Nell! Ida's going to be back for the tray any minute."

Bobby's voice was low and urgent, making her nervous hands tremble all the more. Having pilfered from a high shelf in the pantry a small bottle labeled "Calomel," Lynelle tried to figure how much of a teaspoon the recommended dosage of one-tenth to twenty grains might be. A quarter? Half? Oh, why weren't the conversions coming to mind? She reread the small print on the label, willing more information to be there than was.

A plate bearing an assortment of Gertrude's cookies waited atop a tray on the wooden table in the center of the kitchen. Gingerbread men, pfeffernuesse, lemon snaps, and nutmeg logs were arranged in a concentric pattern on the round dish. And next to the cookie plate was the lovely glass bowl holding their father's beloved chocolate pudding.

A few pans remained soaking, but most of the dishes had already been washed, dried and put away by Ida and Carol. The stout cook had retired to her room an hour before, having earned a well-deserved respite from her duties.

Carol, too, had hung up her apron and let herself out the side door. Lynelle and Bobby had been waiting on the back staircase for Ida to take the tea into the library, knowing they would have only a few minutes during which to accomplish their task.

Now, huddled over the pudding bowl, the air between them was electrified. Neither one of them was tempted by the delicious-smelling cookies on display. Bobby looked as though he might begin wringing his hands as Lynelle tapped a small measure of white powder onto the spoon. *Hydrargyri Chloridum Mite. Dosage: One-tenth grain to twenty grains.* One-tenth to twenty grains! Why such a wide range?

"That little bit isn't going to do anything," Bobby insisted. "Fill up the spoon, just to be sure."

"Aren't you the one who was concerned about us poisoning him?" she whispered in return, feeling her heart pound against her ribs. Nanny had implied the potency of this medication—and a grain was a small measurement. "Half a teaspoon should be plenty," she countered, tapping out a little more. Quickly, she stirred the powder into the still-warm, thickened milk and cornstarch mixture and did her best to smooth the surface of the pudding.

No sooner had she tucked the bottle into her pocket and whirled back from laying the spoon into the sink when the door swung open, admitting Ida. The short, slender young housemaid regarded them with amused tolerance. "Snitching cookies, are you? Seems a little silly when I'm about to serve them to you in the library."

"We haven't taken any cookies, Ida," Bobby responded with wide-eyed innocence. "See? None are missing. We just came to see if we could help you carry anything."

"Mm-hmm," she responded with suspicion, eyeing the plate. "Well, if you took any, you did a fine job of straightening the others. Off with you now, and no one's the wiser."

Up the steep, narrow servant's staircase they ran, peering

into the hallway when they reached the second story. Empty. Their footfalls were nearly noiseless on the thick carpet as they rounded the corner and ran to the opposite end of the hall. Breathing hard, they were nearly to the top of the third-story staircase when the nursery door opened.

"Come away, wee yins," Margaret spoke to the little girls. "'Tis a wonderful treat to have cookies in the library wi' yer father and mother—" She broke off when she spied her two older charges coming up the stairs. "An' jist whar have the two of you been?" she queried, the gentle quality of her voice assuming its familiar no-nonsense tone.

"Oh . . . Bobby had a spot of gravy on his shirt. I helped him get it out," Lynelle replied while her brother nodded his head. Being winded from her exertion and the excitement of their conspiracy gave her words a breathless quality. One untruth uttered, she hoped she'd be forgiven for a second. "We were hurrying back so we could all go downstairs together."

"Aye, then. Come on, all of you. Maybe the grand meal has been just the thing to set this home to rights again."

"Daddy? Do you want to see Miss Hillary? She's my doll, and she's four years old. Did you remember that I'm going to be four on my next birthday?"

"Yes, Audrey, I remember that you're nearly four," Samuel replied in a tolerant tone before finishing the last few bites of his pudding. He had made the most of his treat, consuming the chocolate concoction slowly over the past half hour. Folding the newspaper he'd been reading, he set the dish and spoon on the small table next to his chair. "Bring Miss Hillary over, will you? I'd like to have a look at her."

The breath caught in Joyce's throat, and she nearly pricked her finger at her husband's agreeable tone. Securing the needle in an unworked section of her crewel piece, she watched with misting eyes as Audrey carried her dolly to-ward Samuel. What a good idea this had been, having the family gather together in the library for cookies and tea. Perhaps things were going to work out this Christmas, after all.

"Daddy, can Kathryn come by you, too?" Without waiting for his reply, she pulled her younger sister down from the chair where she sat nibbling a rich nutmeg log. Together, they approached their father. "We like you, Daddy, and we miss-ed you," she went on, the inflection of her suffixes often forming their own distinct syllable. "Me an' Kathryn, we'll be good girls, I promise. We won't talk about anything—Kathryn!" she interrupted herself. "Don't suck your thumb. Remember? You'll get butt teeth."

"*Buck* teeth. Like the deer." Bobby corrected from across the room, his patience with his garrulous little sister never very great. The entire time they'd been in the library, he and Lynelle had been huddled together whispering at the small table set farthest away from where the rest of the family sat, their private conversation interspersed with several glances at their father. Owing to their miserable dinner experience, Joyce did not correct their poor display of manners but instead allowed them to be off by themselves.

Modern gas lighting shone from frosted-glass wall sconces, and a merry fire burned in the grate, its gentle glow adding to the rich texture of the library's wine-colored fleur-de-lis wall coverings. The Christmas tree and holiday deco-rations set off the room to perfection. In years past, countless cozy family evenings and lazy Sunday afternoons had been spent in this room; dare she hope this gathering place would see many more such happy times?

Samuel made a great show of admiring Miss Hillary's hair and clothing while Kathryn looked on with wide eyes, thumb firmly planted in her mouth. He had not yet ad-dressed her or the older children, but Joyce's spirits soared as she watched him interact with Audrey. Could something so simple as a bowl of favorite pudding have warmed his heart so?

Watching the light strike the planes and angles of his face as he spoke to Audrey, she allowed herself to realize the full measure of how much she'd missed his companionship, his tenderness, his smile. His friendship. Sometimes she thought the loss of her husband, though he still lived and breathed, hurt even more than losing Mary Rose.

"Are ye bairns ready for your good-night story? Wee Robin Redbreast, the finest singer in all of Scotland, has set off to see the king and queen on their golden thrones. Will he make it, I wonder?"

"An' the bad, bad cat tries to eat him!" Audrey cried with delight.

"Hush, wee yin. We canna tell the tale till faces are washed and teeth are brushed. Now bid your father good night and along ye come."

Nanny's entrance couldn't have been better timed. Taking advantage of the distraction of the children filing past, Joyce dabbed her eyes with her handkerchief. "I'll be up for kisses shortly," she managed to call out.

A long moment of silence passed.

"We're invited to a holiday ball at the Forepaugh's this Wednesday evening," she remarked, referring to their neighbors on the other side of the park. A successful entrepreneur, dark-mustached Joseph Forepaugh had established the largest wholesale dry goods house in the Midwest. "And just two days after that is Christmas Eve already," she added, hesitant to mention Kathryn's birthday, which fell between those two dates on the twenty-third.

"I can't believe how the children have grown." Samuel's gaze was upon her, an inscrutable expression on his handsome face. A log snapped in the fire, followed by the sound of setting wood. "They're fine children, Joyce. You're doing a wonderful job with them."

"Why . . . thank you, Samuel. They are getting big, aren't they?" Her pleasure at his compliment, however, was momentary. Taking up her needle, she began working a flurry of stitches.

Why the sudden discomfort in speaking a few sentences of conversation with her husband? What was the matter with her? Wasn't this the new beginning she had been hoping for? Once again the troublesome moisture gathered in the corners of her eyes. "I'd best go up and kiss the children good-night," she managed to say, rising from her chair. As much as she'd longed for such an opportunity, it was proving to be too difficult for her emotions to handle.

"And Joyce?" Samuel added, reaching for the paper at his side, his hazel gaze lingering on her. "Kiss them again for me."

Nodding, she exited the library without daring another glance at this man who caused such disturbance inside her.

"You said Daddy had to go to work 'smorning, Mama," Audrey spoke between bites of oatmeal. "But he's not gone. I heared him upstairs, talking."

Talking? That was one word for it, Joyce thought, still smarting from her husband's ill-tempered words. "Your daddy is feeling unwell this morning, Audrey," she replied, "so you and Kathryn must do your best to play quietly today."

"What's the matter with Daddy?" Lynelle asked, eyes wide. Both she and Bobby had stopped eating, their spoons coming to rest in their bowls.

Hastening to put their fears to rest, she explained, "He woke with some griping pains in his belly earlier this morning. He's not feverish, so I'm sure it's nothing serious. Please don't worry, my darlings."

"Oh . . . but doesn't he need you to take care of him?" Glancing at Bobby, Lynelle continued to look alarmed despite the reassurance she'd given. "I mean, when we get sick, Mama, you care so kindly for us."

"I would love nothing more than to attend to your father," she replied truthfully, "but he prefers to be alone in his misery. Now eat before your breakfast gets cold."

A wry, sad smile curved her lips as she recalled waking to dull light filtering into the bedroom. As troubled and confused as she'd been last evening, sleep had been a long time in coming. When she'd returned to the library after tucking in the children, Samuel had wished her a more amicable good-night than he had in months, yet had made no move to put down his paper. Alone, she'd climbed the stairs one more time.

What an odd mix of sentiments he had displayed since his return home. Irritability. Gruffness. Wanting to be left alone, yet displaying the first glimpses of softening any of them had seen in many, many months. She knew that hidden behind all these things were unplumbed depths of grief and sadness. Why he was unable to move forward, to let his family help him, she did not understand.

Her first waking thought this morning had been to wonder whether or not he had come to bed. Since the birth of the twins, he spent more than half his nights on the sofa in his study. Leaning up on one elbow, she'd checked the bedcovers next to her and seen that his side of the bed was mussed.

He'd been there.

Oh, Lord, was there a reason to hope the tide was turning, even a small bit? As she began to mull things over in her mind, the door to the water closet adjoining their room had opened, and Samuel had shuffled toward the bed, holding his abdomen.

"Are you ill, Samuel?" she'd asked, alarmed by his disheveled appearance.

With a groan, he'd sunk onto the bed and curled tightly on his side, facing away from her.

"Samuel?" she'd tried again, laying her hand on his shoulder. Through his nightclothes, his skin was damp but not hot.

"Are *you* sick?" he'd snapped, albeit weakly.

"No, I feel . . . fine."

"The children?"

"I haven't heard a thing from upstairs. I'm sure Nanny would have woken me if they were ailing."

"Well, I wonder what I could have eaten to give me such a bellyache? If no one else is sick, I have to wonder about that pudding. Maybe Gertrude used spoiled milk . . . or she poisoned me with bad eggs. She hasn't been very friendly toward me for quite some time now."

And no wonder, she'd thought. He and Gertrude used to have such fun kidding one another, but nearly two years had passed since he'd given any of their help more than a brusque hello. "Samuel, you know Gert would never do such a thing," she had spoken with gentle reproach. "She uses only the freshest ingredients to prepare our foods. Any spoiled milk or eggs would have been sent straight out the door."

"Aahh." He'd half sighed, half moaned as his belly rumbled loudly. "My middle is twisted up in knots." Groaning again, he'd rolled his head toward her, wearing a vexed expression on his pale features. His hair, usually so neat, was as tousled as she might find Bobby's on any given day. How she'd longed to smooth her fingers through the sandy-brown strands and lay her palm against the lean plane of his cheek, a motion her hands used to make as naturally as her lungs drew breath.

"Can I bring you something?" she'd asked, her heart turning over at his distress. "Mush? Tea and toast?"

"Nothing," he'd snapped. "I want nothing but to be left alone. No mush, no tea and toast, no doting wives, no company, no *nothing*."

"Mama?" Audrey broke in on Joyce's thoughts, pulling her mind back to breakfast at the kitchen table. "Are you happy? I eated four more bites of my oatmeal, and it's all gone. See? I'm being a good girl, amn't I?"

"Eat!" Kathryn exclaimed with shining hazel eyes, wearing as much oatmeal on her face and bib as she had in her stomach. Pearly-white baby teeth gleamed in a messy but beatific smile. "Wuv you, Mama."

Quiet joy flooded her soul as she gazed around the table at her four children. How a heart so heavy could simultaneously know such gladness was a mystery she would never comprehend. Much the same was the bittersweet stab she experienced whenever she thought of Mary Rose, gone from this earth but alive with Christ in the heavenlies. *Suffer little children, and forbid them not, to come unto me; for of such is the kingdom of heaven.* No matter how her heart might ache for her daughter, Jesus' words in the Gospel of Matthew never failed to bring her comfort and courage.

And so should she have the same faith as she suffered in this situation with Samuel. Together, before the Lord, they had made this marriage covenant for better or worse. This morning she would meditate upon verses extolling God's mercy and his mighty power.

And upon the virtue of hope.

325

CHAPTER FOUR

Food poisoning. He was sure of it. The only other time Samuel had felt this miserable was when he'd eaten tainted chicken salad as a youth. The intestinal griping continued throughout the morning and early afternoon, leaving him weak as a pup. When he could, he dozed, having fitful dreams of being sick . . . only to awaken in the darkened bedchamber, sick.

Beyond the walls and door of his sickroom, he heard the ongoing routines of his household. Ida and Carol's hushed voices carried to him as they went about their tasks, and from above were sounds of his children's movements and laughter. From time to time he heard Joyce speak, but he hadn't seen her since he'd sent her away earlier in the morning.

Remorse for his uncivil words scuttled his already low spirits. He hadn't meant to be so short-tempered; he knew she had only wanted to help. The loving warmth of her hand upon his shoulder had also unsettled him, bringing with it the full realization of his emptiness and longing for human touch.

He didn't deserve such a wife, such faithful children. If only things could have been different—if only Mary Rose had survived, then his cowardly weakness would have never been brought to light and his family forced to suffer a double loss. They had not only lost a precious and innocent child, they had lost a husband and father worthy of their respect. What dishonor he'd brought upon this household.

It was best he was leaving again so soon after the holidays. Architects from his firm were in demand not only in St. Paul but also in many other cities. Joyce obviously had things well in hand at home, and the children were healthy and strong and full of life. He knew the Good Book had been her source of strength and comfort since the twins' birth. He'd been a believer once, and he supposed he still was, but the verses and teachings he recalled didn't speak to the burdens he carried.

A strong cramp gripped him, drawing his belly so tight that he was forced to pull his knees upward. He'd thought the worst of this sickness over, but maybe he was wrong. Finally, the spasm released its clutch, leaving him depleted and ready to fall into more disturbed slumber.

How much time passed until he awakened, he did not know, but the sounds from the nursery above had stilled. Murky, overcast light stole in around the drawn drapes, signaling twilight's early approach. His belly had quieted, he noticed, and for the first time since he'd been stricken ill, he thought a bit of tea and toast had appeal.

Rolling carefully from his side to his back, his shoulder blade came to rest upon a hard, cold object. What on earth? With some difficulty, he pushed himself to a semisitting position. Grogginess clouded his mind as his hand reached back and closed over the offending item.

The textures of springy hair and soft fabric confused him until he pulled Miss Hillary before him, her lovely hat and clothing in disarray from his inadvertent ill treatment of her.

How had . . . Audrey. A curl of warmth began in his chest at the thought of his willful daughter tucked into her bed for her afternoon nap, plotting to sneak away and pay him a visit.

Quiet as a whisper, she must have stolen in while he slept, leaving her beloved doll to keep him company. Resting back against the pillow, he gazed at his daughter's porcelain treasure until his eyes blurred. It wasn't good to get too sentimental, he told himself, carefully laying the doll on Joyce's pillow beside him. Closing his lids, he longed for the oblivion of dreamless slumber to carry him away from the mess he had made of his life.

"It didn't work, Lynelle," Bobby said in an accusing tone, bringing up the subject they'd avoided all day. His breath formed white clouds in the late afternoon air as they neared home, skates slung over their shoulders. "All he did was stay in his room all day, and Mama didn't even go up there again after breakfast."

"Well, you never know . . . she could have tended to him while we were gone this afternoon."

"Do you really believe that?"

"No," she said, sighing with discouragement, wishing things had gone differently. "No, I don't."

Quietly, they entered the side door of the house and removed their boots. Gertrude labored in the kitchen, a dour expression pinching her ordinarily pleasant features. Thinking the better of asking for hot chocolate, Lynelle hooked Bobby's arm and pulled him up the servant's stairs.

"And would ye look at those rosy cheeks." Nanny greeted them with quiet tones as they entered the nursery. "Reminds me of bein' a lass back in Rogart, wi' the biting winds whirling off the North Sea." She sat alone in the rocker, a book opened across her lap. "Shh, now, the pair of ye. The wains are still asleep, as well as yer father down below. Hang up yer coats, an' come sit here beside the stove and take off yer chill."

"How is he?" Lynelle asked, moving farther into the room. The dread she'd been carrying throughout the day swelled into fear at Nanny's mention of her father. She hadn't meant to do serious harm with the calomel, but what if she and Bobby *had* poisoned him? What if he died? Catching her brother's gaze, she saw the same dread reflected there.

"I've heard Gertrude has made him some tea an' toast, so he must be feeling better."

"Oh . . . good!" Lynelle's relief rushed forth with her exclamation, making her knees weak. Taking a seat before the radiant heat of the small stove, she extended her chilly toes and fingers, wondering why it always felt as though the ice-cold parts of her were burning as they began to warm.

"Were ye so worried, lass?" Nanny inquired, rocking in a slow, steady tempo.

Flustered, she didn't know how to reply. "Well . . . it's just that Daddy is hardly ever ill . . . and . . ."

"Och, 'twas not a serious matter," the middle-aged widow replied, continuing on in an undertone as she was often wont to do. Her eyebrows went up in an expressive manner, and her short legs pushed the chair back and forth with more gusto. "Leastwise, not till word came down that he'd accused the cook of preparin' spoiled foods."

"He thinks Gertrude gave him rotten food?" Bobby asked, scratching the side of his nose. "Whoo! I bet she's mad! No wonder she was stomping all over the kitchen."

"Aye, she's in fine fettle over the matter. If not for the sake of yer kind mother, I believe she would have packed her bags an' been gone. She was insulted!"

"Oh, dear," Lynelle said quietly, filled with fresh anxiety. Things were getting worse all the time. Daddy hadn't wanted Mother to attend to him at all, and now their cook had been blamed for something she hadn't done. "What do you think is going to happen?" she asked in a quavering voice.

"I bet Gertrude will *really* poison him now!" Bobby interjected with a snicker. "He'd better check his tea."

"Bobby! This is serious!" How could he make a joke while the future of the Colburn family hung in the balance? If something didn't change soon, she was afraid their father would leave for one of his business trips and never come back.

"Hoot! A wee sma' bit o' gripin' in 'is belly an ye'd think the world had come to an end." Nanny shook her graying head and rocked harder. "The mon's gone daft wi' his grief," she muttered, setting her jaw. "Aye, Meg, I say to meself, life is hard. Yer own womb barren an' yer man lyin' in 'is grave. But ye ken fine well the Guid Laird has 'is own plans for yer life, an' ye still go on.

"'Tis true the wee wain Mary Rose died, boot canna the mister see the glorious treasure he 'as before 'im? Four bonnie bairns an' a fair an' gentle wife, but nay, he will na look beyond the end o' his nose. God forbid it would take somethin' happenin' to 'is family to pull 'im out o' the bog he's mired 'imself into."

Lynelle feared her mouth had dropped open. One glance at Bobby confirmed that he was as shocked as she by Nanny's discourse. Never before had their caretaker spoken such a portion of her mind.

"Whisht! Pit yer eyes back in yer heads, dearies, and dinna mind a grieved old *cailleach* an' her loose tongue." Margaret Murray's intense expression faded, and her face melted into a tender smile. Picking up her book, she added, "I love ye so, all of ye. Keep to yer prayin', for the Laird Jesus 'as a special fondness for the prayers of 'is wee bairnies. Perhaps there's a miracle yet to be done this Christmas."

Dinner was a quiet affair. As at breakfast and lunch, they

gathered around the kitchen table for the evening meal, a simple fare of oyster stew, crackers, and spiced pears. Mother did her best to keep up a brave and gracious front, but Lynelle could see the strain the day had taken on her. Though they had many of their dinners in the kitchen while Daddy was away, a strange hollowness persisted in her middle while the family ate. Was it the knowledge that he was home yet apart from them and that things were very, very wrong?

Dejected, she continued to ponder their situation while she and Bobby played checkers in the library that evening. How different last night had been with the whole family gathered, a fire crackling in the hearth. Daddy had clearly enjoyed his pudding, and he'd even smiled when Audrey had showed him Miss Hillary. How she longed for the kind father she remembered, the one who had always made her feel so special.

A fire burned in the grate, but tonight the atmosphere of the comfortable room was devoid of warmth. Nanny had come for Audrey and Kathryn right after dinner, and Mother was in her own world while she sat in her chair and stitched. From time to time she dabbed her eyes with her handkerchief. Was she also comparing the hopeful tone of last evening to the dismalness of this one?

"King me," Bobby spoke in a morose tone, having jumped three of her checkers in one move.

Hope, she thought, dutifully stacking a second red checker on the piece invading her back row. *That's what's missing tonight.*

Last evening things had been promising. Though she and Bobby had no doubt transgressed by putting calomel in Daddy's pudding, they had been buoyed by the anticipation of Mother and Daddy coming together again.

What they needed was another plan. Something more reliable—something that would surely reunite their parents.

Nanny's words from this afternoon came back to her, igniting one thought after another. Of course! How could she have overlooked something so very obvious?

"Bobby?" she whispered, leaning toward him over the checkerboard. Her lips twitched as she tried suppressing her excitement. "You'll never believe it! I just got the most wonderful idea."

CHAPTER FIVE

A sprinkling of stars shone above winter-barren branches. The heavy odor of burning coal carried on the breeze, commingled with the more pleasant tang of wood smoke. In the distance, a chorus of dogs barked. Snow crunched underfoot as Samuel and Joyce walked along Irvine Park Drive to the Forepaugh residence on Exchange Street. The mercury hovered near twenty degrees, mild for a Minnesota winter's evening.

"Is your stomach still a little tender? I noticed you didn't eat much at dinner tonight," Joyce commented, trying to make conversation with the taciturn man beside her. After being laid up all of Tuesday, he had risen early and gone to the office today. "We don't have to go if you're not up to it. I'm sure Joseph and Mary would understand."

"I'm fine," he replied in a distracted tone, taking her elbow to guide her around a patch of slick ice. Once past the hazard, he abruptly let go of her arm.

Thank goodness it's only a bit farther, Joyce thought with hurt and confusion, wondering what thoughts were contained inside her husband's head. Until just two years ago, she would have said she knew his mind as well as her own. Now he was like a stranger, one whose mind she didn't know—nor one whose heart she could claim.

And what of tomorrow, the twins' birthday? she wondered with foreboding. Samuel had been obviously upset when Audrey had mentioned Mary Rose. How could they possibly celebrate Kathryn's birthday without remembering her twin sister? There wasn't a day that had passed since December 23, 1878, that Joyce hadn't thought of her beloved little one and wondered what life would have been like if she'd lived. And the children, especially, liked to talk about their little sister in heaven.

Though Kathryn and Mary Rose had been so different in appearance, Dr. Pfeiffer believed they were identical twins. In her mind's eyes flashed the picture of a pair of sweet, tousle-curled toddlers—two sets of expressive hazel eyes looking to her and calling her "Mama."

Whatever would she do if something happened to Kathryn? Outspoken little Audrey? Or Bobby or Lynelle? The pain of losing a child was something on which she had never reckoned. Living through it had been nearly unbearable. What if God decided to take another?

"Hello, neighbors!" John Matheis called, owner of the Carpet Emporium bearing his name. He walked toward the Forepaugh's from his home on Walnut Street. While Samuel answered, Joyce cleared her throat and blinked back a dam of moisture, wondering in a rather detached way—almost as if she were an observer looking at someone else—at the intensity of pain in her chest.

How long until this hurting stopped? It seemed like every time she stopped to take stock of life and notice that she had gone a day—or even a week—without shedding tears over the loss of her baby, the heartache would return with the force of a hard, unexpected clap on the back. Samuel's aunt Millie had written several letters to her during the past two years, exhorting and encouraging her to continue on, that time and the Lord would indeed heal all wounds. "Perhaps not in the way or at the speed you'd like," she'd penned, "but upon self-examination, I found that progress had been made upon each anniversary of my children's deaths."

"Well, here we are," Mr. Matheis announced, turning up the walk to the elegant, three-story Victorian home. The strains of festive music carried to them as they climbed the steps of the many-columned porch, and Joyce realized she must make an effort to shake the melancholic turn of her thoughts. Thick garlands of fragrant balsam swagged the entrance, and even before they could knock, dark-haired Joseph Forepaugh threw wide the front door, exclaiming, "Come in, come in!"

The parlor contained an assortment of refined merrymakers as well as a five-piece wind and string ensemble. Pulling one hand from her satin muff, Joyce untied the matching, quilted hood and handed both novelties to the Forepaugh's straight-postured manservant. She remembered the day when Samuel would have helped her out of her coat, but he had already moved from the foyer into the parlor. Several acquaintances greeted him, and he was quickly drawn into conversation by a knot of men.

"Good evening, Joyce." Mary Forepaugh smiled kindly. "We're so glad Samuel was home and that you both could come. Please come this way; I don't believe you've ever met . . ."

An hour passed, then two, while Joyce made conversation with neighbors she knew and strangers to whom she was introduced. Several couples danced in the lavishly decorated parlor, swirling and turning beneath the glittering chandelier. Once upon a time she and Samuel would have been one of those laughing pairs. Throughout the evening he did not approach her, but once, glancing up, she found the weight of his stare upon her. His expression, once again, was unfathomable.

"Did you read in the *Evening Dispatch* about the expenses of the president's mansion?" Virginia Rollins queried, giving her bonnet a pat. Ostrich tips and silver ornaments bobbed with the matriarch's movement. Stifling a yawn, Joyce longed to be home, kissing her children good-night. With effort, she refocused her attention on the conversation at hand.

"Why, the president's salary alone is fifty thousand, and the upkeep of the public grounds nears eighty thousand dollars! I don't understand why . . ." On and on the older woman talked, calling the White House's items and expenses to mind as effortlessly as if she'd committed them to memory. Which she probably had, Joyce thought, finding her mind wandering once more.

"We need to leave, Joyce." She hadn't noticed Samuel's approach, but his voice was in her ear, low and urgent. "Right away."

"What is it?" Turning with surprise, she saw worry etched on her husband's features.

He swallowed hard. "Ida just came with a message that the children are violently ill."

"Oh, Samuel," she breathed, reaching for his arm. "Which of the children?"

"She didn't tell me . . . she just said that Nanny wants us home immediately."

"Joyce, Dr. Pfeiffer is right over there," Mrs. Rollins interjected, her ears every bit as sharp as her tongue was purported to be. "Sherman," she summoned, pointing to the silver-haired gentleman helping himself from a tray of candies. Her imperious voice carried without difficulty over the music. "There's trouble over at the Colburns. They're going to need you to go along home with them. The children are ill."

"Be right there," the physician called evenly, popping a candy into his mouth. If he was perturbed at being pulled away from the party, it didn't show. The crowd parted, allowing the three of them passage to the foyer. Towing Joyce through the midst was Samuel, his strong fingers laced through hers. Panic raced throughout every part of her body as he threw on his overcoat and helped her into hers. Never one to be caught without his necessary instruments and supplies, Dr. Pfeiffer claimed his black bag along with his hat and overgarment.

Please, Lord, she pleaded in a silent prayer, hastening down the steps and front walk, *don't take any more of my babies from me. In your wisdom, you know what measure of sorrows each heart can bear . . . O Jesus, please be merciful . . .*

The two blocks' distance home was covered in record time. Samuel shared the details of his illness of the day before with the physician, as well as his suspicion that he'd been served tainted food. Joyce wasn't sure how she knew, but a sense of womanly intuition told her that their comestibles were not the problem. The thought of diphtheria, every mother's dread, coated her heart with a thick, oily layer of fear.

Ida waited for them, peering around the heavy wooden door with wide, frightened eyes. "Oh, good, you've got the doctor. Hurry, they're making a terrible noise up there," she cried out, opening the door to admit them. "Such awful pains. We don't know what they've got."

Indeed, from above came piteous moaning and wailing. Taking the carpeted risers two at a time, Samuel sprinted up the staircase without bothering to remove his hat or coat. Ida hurriedly helped Joyce and Dr. Pfeiffer from their outerwear, filling them in on as many details as she knew.

"There's been no vomiting or diarrhea, leastwise not yet," she addressed the physician. "One minute they were fine, and the next they were like this!" The young servant's words tumbled one over another. "Poor Meg's beside herself, runnin' from one bed to the next. Of the four, Kathryn, the baby, seems to be fine . . . just bewildered at all the goings on. Gertrude's taken her down to her room for the time being."

"Is there a fever?" the physician inquired as they climbed the stairs. "Catarrh? Did the pains come on suddenly, in the back and limbs?"

"Oh, sir," Ida breathed, out of breath with exertion and emotion. "Are you thinking . . . are you thinking it's . . . diphtheria then?"

Joyce's heart raced beneath her bodice of heavy stamped velvet. Oh, her babies. God help her sweet little ones. Lynelle, Bobby, little Audrey. She couldn't lose them, she just couldn't. Every year the dreaded disease claimed the lives of countless little ones.

"A rash, you say, miss? Big red spots?" Dr. Pfeiffer stopped at the landing before ascending the second flight of stairs, wearing a quizzical expression beneath his silvered mane. "Sudden, concurrent onset of pain in three children, accompanied by the appearance of swift-spreading erythema *circinatum*. How curious."

Pouring down from above, in addition to the children's anguished cries, was Samuel's deep voice and a torrent of Scottish brogue. Oh, what was happening to her family? Joyce wondered with despair. Just when she had thought things couldn't get any worse, her troubles had multiplied.

"Mrs. Colburn, I'm going to ask you and your husband to wait outside while I examine the children. Your presence may only upset them more while I do so," the physician explained, shifting his heavy bag from one hand to the other. "Mrs. Murray can assist me while she tells me what she knows of this intriguing illness."

A moment later Samuel exited the nursery and trudged down the stairs, joining her in the hallway of the second story. On his face was an expression of such wretchedness that she was moved to comfort him. Or was it he who comforted her? Into his strong arms she melted, and for what seemed like an eternity, her tears soaked the lapel of his coat while she cried out her sadness, her grief, her fears.

Her husband's embrace was a warm and comfortable haven, making her think of one of the opening verses of the Ninety-first Psalm: *He shall cover thee with his feathers, and under his wings shalt thou trust.* The mental image of being nestled under the wing of the Lord was one that had sustained her through many black hours and days after Mary Rose's death, especially as Samuel grew more and more distant.

"Try not to . . . worry so, Joyce," Samuel comforted with halting words, his fingers tracing the contours of her up-swept hair. The familiar fragrance of his shaving lotion wafted to her nostrils, warm and spicy. "If anyone can . . . Doc Pfeiffer is . . . one of the best." What remained unspoken was that despite Dr. Pfeiffer's skill, one of their daughters now lay in her grave. Were more of their children to follow?

Suddenly, Joyce realized that the noises upstairs had ceased. Only a moment after that awareness struck her, the nursery door opened and Dr. Pfeiffer called out, "Mrs. Colburn? Would you please come up here?"

"What's happening?" Samuel demanded to know, his arms stiffening around her. "What's happened?"

"Things are quite all right," the physician reassured. "We'll call for you in a short time, Samuel."

Things were all right. Oh, thank you, Lord. Relief flooded her eyes with fresh tears, and taking a deep, shaking breath, she disentangled herself from her husband's arms and met his gaze. "Thank you," she spoke aloud, offering him a smile into which she poured the essence of her feelings. *How I love you,* she added silently, still uncertain of her standing with him.

"Oh, Joyce. I wish . . ." He sighed heavily while studying

her face with hazel eyes full of emotion. "I just want you to know—"

"Mrs. Colburn?" the physician repeated.

"Excuse me," she spoke softly, torn between her desire to prolong this long-awaited moment with her spouse, yet needing to see with her own eyes that their children were fine. With another whispered apology, she hurried up the staircase and into the nursery, where she was met by Dr. Pfeiffer just inside the door.

"I'm afraid there is a problem," he began in low tones. "Let's step over this way." He indicated the opposite side of the nursery from the children's partitioned sleep areas. "Mrs. Murray is with them, which will give us a few minutes to talk."

"A problem? But I thought you said they were all right." Like a fountain, fear quickly bubbled up inside her.

"The children are fine," he reassured with a gentle smile. "I fear they will not be so fine, however, a short time from now."

"What . . . what do you mean?"

"Well," he began, stroking his chin. "Let's just say that their pains desisted the moment I discovered their spots could be removed with a damp cloth."

"What?"

"Red watercolor, I'm afraid."

"Oh." She was quiet a long moment, digesting this news.

"You see, Joyce, they falsified their illness to bring you and your husband home from the party in an attempt to . . . ah, reunite the two of you. They also hoped this scheme of theirs would vindicate your cook, whom, I understand, was accused by your husband of serving tainted food." He cleared his throat, a deep noise that sounded suspiciously like a chuckle. "If the dear woman hasn't missed her calomel yet—"

She interrupted the physician with a gasp. "Calomel! Don't tell me they . . . oh no!"

"Calomel," he confirmed, nodding. "Oh yes, indeed. Once the confessions began, they rather rapidly poured forth. The drug was in your husband's pudding, night before last."

"Are they so angry with him then?"

The tender interlude downstairs only moments ago had done nothing to change the fact that her and Samuel's problems were very real . . . and very large. As hard as she'd tried to shield the children from the farce their marriage had become—as well as play the roles of both mother and father—it was now painfully obvious she'd failed.

But had she done such a poor job of things that she'd unwittingly turned the children against their father? She'd never meant for that to happen. To the contrary, she'd always tried to portray him in the best possible light. Thinking of the sad state of affairs their family life had become, her knees grew weak, and she sought a chair.

"No, my dear, they're not angry," the kindly physician clarified, drawing up the chair across from her and patting her hand. "They're not angry at all. They're just frightened of what the future may hold, frightened that their father may walk out the door and never come back. They only wanted to put their family back together again, Joyce. And in not an entirely irrational line of reasoning, they thought that if they made your husband ill, he would need you to take care of him."

"I tried, and he all but threw me out on my ear."

"Yes, well, you know what men can be like in the sickroom." A smile creased his face before his expression grew serious. "I didn't realize how grave your situation was here, my dear. Is there anything I can do to help? Speak to Samuel, perhaps?"

"No . . . I don't think . . ." Sighing, she shrugged her shoulders in a slight, bereft movement. "I don't know what you could say to him. He puts more distance between himself and the children with every passing month."

"And you, too." The words were phrased not as a question, but as a statement.

She nodded, unable to answer. Her children's greatest fear was also her own: that Samuel's remoteness would one day become such that he would simply not come home.

"Mama?" Audrey's voice piped from across the room. "Can you wash me? After Nanny put us to bed, Nell and Bobby painted me, Mama, and they said I had to scream and yell like I was being eaten by cannonballs or they wouldn't like me anymore. That was very, *very* bad, wasn't it, Mama?"

"*Cannibals*, not cannonballs," came Bobby's exasperated retort. "Can't you remember anything?"

"Not another word out of ye, Master Robert. An' you, Audrey, come on back here. Aye, you were all naughty little wains this nicht. Trickin' everyone the way ye did . . ." The weight in Nanny's voice gave testimony to her fatigue and low spirits. "Let yer mother finish talkin' with the good doctor in peace, now, whilst I wash off yer paint."

"Wash off whose paint?" came Samuel's grim voice. His shoes struck hard notes against the smooth, wide-planked floor as he strode into the nursery, the sound deadening once he stepped upon the oilcloth rug and came to a halt. "And what kind of tricks have been played?" he called out into the large room that had suddenly grown as hushed and still as a snow-covered cemetery. "Someone had better give me an answer, and soon."

Lynelle's quiet weeping broke the silence as Joyce stood, her insides quavering. Gone was her husband's loving tenderness; the stony stranger now stood before her. "Samuel, please come sit with us," she entreated. "Dr. Pfeiffer was just explaining—"

"I'd like to hear an explanation from the children themselves, if you don't mind." Turning to the right, he disappeared into the sleeping area. "You're excused for the night, Mrs. Murray," he growled.

With a sad, apologetic expression, the children's caretaker withdrew from the room. Dr. Pfeiffer's gentle hand stayed Joyce's impulse to be at her children's side as well as her instinct to defend their reasons for their actions. "Let him hear it from the children himself," the doctor spoke softly, as two other young voices joined their elder sister's in remorse for their wrongdoings. Dampness flowed down her cheeks at her children's tearful disclosures, followed by her husband's censorious words.

"I am the head of this household. I will leave when I wish, and I will come home when I wish. No one will tell me what to do or when to do it, nor will I be manipulated by my children. It takes a man of *strength* to lead his family, and tonight I see the results of being long neglectful in disciplining your unruly ways."

"It's all my fault, Daddy, not Bobby or Audrey's," Lynelle blurted. "Please don't punish them. I'm so sorry . . . I just thought—"

"You do not have permission to speak right now, Lynelle. And I will do whatever I see fit to correct this reprehensible behavior."

"Oh, Daddy, please don't . . . spank . . . me," Audrey cried, sobbing. "I like you, Daddy, an' I just want you to like me, an' I won't . . . an' I won't be . . . bad no more . . . I promise, Daddy."

A long silence took place, punctuated only by muffled whimpering. "You will keep to the nursery until Christmas Eve," he finally spoke, sounding more weary than angry. "All of you. You older children will write letters of apology to everyone affected by your actions. And nothing of this sort had better happen ever again."

Sparing only a cursory glance at Joyce, standing next to their family physician, he departed the nursery.

"The children have need of your love and reassurance now," Dr. Pfeiffer spoke. "And I will leave you to that. My good woman, I have no doubt that you—and most assuredly your children—have tried just about every means under the sun to soften your husband's heart. It has been my experience that sometimes, however, such accomplishments can be made only by the Lord above."

"What am I to do in the meanwhile?" she whispered in anguish. "And just how long are these children supposed to wait for their father to give them a scrap of his attention? They've been so good and patient . . . and he will hardly even look at them. Do you know, Dr. Pfeiffer," she added, righteous indignation sparking all through her and stiffening her spine, "if I were they, I would have acted up long before now."

The benevolent gentleman nodded, as if deep in thought. "You have to submit this situation to the Father's capable hands, Joyce," he said slowly. "Not part of it and not most of it; all of it."

"But I've done that, over and over again. Nothing changes, except to get worse. I don't know how much longer I can go on like this. I'm getting so tired and so weak . . . I'm just about to the end of myself."

He continued to nod. "Yes . . . good. The end of yourself is the place where Christ can begin his real work. Continue in your prayers, offering him your weakness, and we shall see what happens."

CHAPTER SIX

The ticking of the travel clock in the darkened room seemed as loud as the inner workings of Big Ben. Samuel fidgeted on the couch in his sitting room, causing the undersized wool blanket to fall off his shoulder. With an exasperated sigh, he tried to tuck himself back in, only to pull the cover too high, exposing his lower legs to the chilly air. It would take only a few minutes to get up and build a fire in the small stove across the room, but even that everyday task seemed insurmountable.

Peace would not come. Sleep would not come. Even numbness would not come. Bone-aching fatigue engulfed his body and mind, yet the respite of unconsciousness lay just beyond his grasp. Over and over he studied the shadows of his desk, his bookshelf, his drawing table, remembering how this room had once been a delightful sanctuary.

Tonight these four walls had the feel of a prison cell closing in on him, a dark, echoing chamber in which resounded the pain-filled cries of his children. Not their initial wailing and moaning, during which time he'd been so frightened of their contorted and red-spotted appearance that he'd been nearly out of his mind with worry over losing them.

No, the cries that tortured him were the things they'd said later. Terrible things. True things. Things to which no one had ever given voice. Not that Joyce hadn't tried, in her gentle way, to draw him out with her love. But since failing both her and Mary Rose, he'd felt so unworthy and unlovable that it had been easiest to fall away from the family and allow the distance to grow, all the while pretending nothing was the matter. He'd told himself that he'd get matters straightened out one day, but that day had not yet come.

Now what was he to do? The children had cried out his failings and transgressions for all to hear. Their conviction had shamed him worse than his own guilt, but what awful thing lay inside him, preventing him from giving them reassurance of his love? For he did love them—and Joyce—more than his own life itself.

With an anguished sigh, he threw aside the blanket and sat up, fumbling for a match. After lighting the kerosene lamp on the table beside the couch, he arose and silently padded from the sitting room. The house had been quiet for hours. Up the stairs to the third story he rose, entering the nursery quietly on stocking feet.

To each bed he went, his heart wrenching as he gazed down, one at a time, upon his sleeping children. Lynelle, on the brink of womanhood, her face soft and smooth and beautiful. She lay curled on her side, her covers drawn neatly to her chin. Bobby, sprawled on his back, blankets in disarray at his knees. Pulling the covers back over his only son, a near replica of himself as a boy, he allowed his fingers to caress the already strong line of his jaw.

Audrey, finally quiet in slumber, with only a hint of baby roundness remaining in her cheeks. When had she changed from a toddler to a young girl? *I'm going to be four, Daddy . . . in Febillary . . . do you remember?* With a sigh he moved to

Kathryn, whose second birthday was this very day. Before his youngest daughter he paused the longest, drinking in the details of her angelic appearance. Like her eldest sister, she slept on her side, the small quilt his aunt Millie had sent tucked in around her. As he continued gazing upon her, he noticed that each exhaled breath fanned the soft curls framing her little face.

Would Mary Rose have looked as sweet? he wondered, remembering her round, red face and trusting, dark gaze . . . and her tiny chest, working so hard to draw breath.

Unwelcome memories of that night rushed to the forefront of his mind, filling his eyes with tears. How could he have abandoned his own daughter? The least he could have done was to pick her up and hold her, giving her what comfort he could. But instead he'd acted the coward, running away from his fears.

And still he ran.

Just like you ran away from your mother's deathbed, an inner voice accused. *Remember? Shame on you, Samuel. You were ten years old—more than old enough to walk in and say your farewells. But you were so scared that you ran away. And when you came back, Ma was already gone—no more chances.*

Tears ran down his face as he relived the past, his father's harsh words still burning inside him. *I'm ashamed to say you're my son, Samuel. The world's got no place for sissies, especially weak-livered little cowards who can't even look death in the eye. Death's a part of life, boy, and the sooner you learn that, the better. If you want to get anywhere in this world, you've got to be strong. Now get in there and pay your respects to your mother. Pity you couldn't have done it last night when she was still alive.*

Since then, he'd striven to be strong and successful in everything he did, if for no other reason than to show his father that he wasn't a failure. And still he labored for his father's approval, though John Colburn had lived only ten years beyond his wife, dying suddenly of an unknown ailment. Never had the matter been discussed again, and never had Samuel been granted his father's forgiveness.

Shoulders sagging, he returned to the cold sitting room. If his own father couldn't even forgive him for his weakness, how could his wife, his children? How could God? How *could* God, indeed? Anger surged inside him as he wondered how a good and loving God could take a mother from a ten-year-old boy. Or an infant girl from a couple who had waited with delight to welcome her to their family?

He had always believed in God but had never been quite as assured of his character as Joyce. While his wife looked toward the Lord as the source of her strength and comfort, he was just as certain that there was something to be said for a man's own hard work and vigor. He remembered Joyce speaking of taking up the cross of Christ daily and following him.

Well, right there, that seemed to indicate some sort of strength was needed. Blowing out the lamp, he settled himself on the couch and arranged the blanket evenly over his legs and torso. Strength. More strength would take care of the problems in his life. In a short prayer, he asked the Lord to grant him the strength he needed to put his life in order.

Closing his eyes, he finally found sleep.

About the best thing Joyce could say for Kathryn's birthday was that she got through it. Samuel had worked a long day yesterday, returning home well after the household had retired. Though the children had been restricted to the nursery, she had hoped to make as cheerful a celebration as possible in honor of her youngest daughter.

The affair had been dismal, at best. Samuel's umbrage—and his absence—hung over the third story like a pall. Kathryn was too little to understand what had transpired, but she sensed something was the matter and spent much of the with her thumb in her mouth.

Nanny, too, was uncharacteristically quiet, and Lynelle and Bobby had moped while composing their letters of apology. Audrey had been fretful, asking incessant questions about Mary Rose until Joyce had gone downstairs to fetch the carved wooden box she kept in the back corner of her wardrobe.

She doubted Samuel knew of its existence. And until yesterday, the children hadn't either. With somber faces they'd gathered around as she'd lifted the lid and shown them, one by one, the few humble yet priceless treasures contained in its depths.

A lock of whisper-fine hair, held fast by a knotted thread, tucked lovingly into a small envelope. Tiny footprints of ink, forever preserved upon a sheet of her finest stationery. One ordinary baby blanket, the first in which Mary Rose had been wrapped. During the past two years, it had been unfolded and refolded countless times, its soft weave absorbing a hundred thousand mother's tears.

At the bottom of the box lay the baby quilt Samuel's aunt Millie had sent during her confinement. Each block contained a pattern of triangles and squares known as "Crosses and Losses," only slightly different from the familiar "Anvil." In death, Mary Rose had been laid upon her great aunt's work of love. Once again Joyce had marveled that the elderly woman's arthritic fingers were still able to turn out such perfect stitches.

Remembering how her lifeless daughter had looked against the backdrop of white, evergreen, and cranberry calico, Joyce's eyes had filled with tears. A moment later Nanny had joined her in sorrow for the "poor wee wain," and then the children, too, had wept. What she'd intended to be a day of celebration had turned out to be a gloomy gathering, indeed.

And today, Christmas Eve, was thus far no better for the Colburns. Samuel had gone into work again without having spoken a word to her since the evening of the Forepaugh's party. Would he be home for the sumptuous dinner she had planned? For their traditional after-dinner gathering in the library? Sighing, she walked into the flurry of activity taking place in the kitchen. The temperature in here was warmer than any other room in the house, and a distinctive, sweet smell hung in the air.

"The gizzard took three hours to simmer tender yesterday, so if I add an hour's time to that, the bird should roast for four." Gertrude, her good humor restored, spoke her calculations more to herself than anyone else as she tied trussing cords around the plump turkey she'd just stuffed with oyster dressing. "Ida, check on the almond macaroons, will you? As soon as they're finished, we'll need to stoke up the fire for Mister Tom."

"Oh, hello, Mrs. Colburn," Ida greeted, taking her hands from the sink and wiping them dry on her apron. "I know I told you this yesterday, but I'm sure glad to know the children are well. I was scared out of my wits the other night." She shook her head and smiled, a dimple peeping from the corner of her mouth. "The note they sent down to me was so dear."

"So was the one they sent me, but I still can't believe they had the gumption to put calomel in Mr. Colburn's pudding," Gertrude exclaimed, hoisting the turkey into place on the roasting rack. She nodded, meeting Joyce's gaze. "Your husband apologized to me real early yesterday morning on his way out. Said he was sorry for accusing me of what he had and how much he appreciated my years of service to the family."

"Well, I'm so . . . glad," Joyce replied, both pleased and surprised at the resolution of at least one unpleasant matter.

"We're going to put on the finest meal you've ever had,"

the cook went on, arranging a folded cheesecloth over the poultry, "and I predict that this will be your family's most wonderful Christmas yet."

"Thank you, Gertrude," she spoke softly. "I hope you're right." Walking from the kitchen, she stopped in the dining room and checked her decorations. Running her hand over the smooth, dark wood of a chair back, she remembered Christmas dinners past. Excitement, joy, and laughter once filled this room—as well as every other room in the house—on the commemoration of the Christ child's birth. But for the past two years, the holiday had been as bleak and barren as the landscape of her husband's heart.

Perhaps tonight, as Gertrude predicted, would be the turning point. If Christmas wasn't a time for hope, she didn't know what was. Oh, how she'd prayed since that heartbreaking scene in the nursery. Dr. Pfeiffer's words about submitting the entire situation into the Lord's hands had not left her mind for a moment, and with every prayer she uttered, she asked him to take control of their plight.

On through the rest of the first story she walked, tying a bow here, adjusting a decoration there. In the library she paused a long moment, gazing from the pine-graced mantel to the perfectly adorned spruce across the room. Exquisite. Nothing could be improved. Their lovely home stood in impeccable readiness for the holiday celebration that would soon be upon them.

But would it be a celebration? she wondered, searching her mind for something else, anything else, that she could do to bring healing to her fractured family—for the children if for no other reason. Her love just hadn't been enough.

Even through the blackest hours of grief, she had lavished every last ounce of her love upon her marriage and family. Samuel hadn't responded, but the children had. Still, she and the children, minus Samuel, weren't complete. She owed it to them to keep trying.

When was the last time she'd told Samuel she loved him? she asked herself, unable to remember when she'd had the courage to utter the words she used to speak so freely. After Mary Rose had died, she'd told him several times, but he'd only continued moving farther away from her and the family. Eventually, she stopped trying to tell him what he didn't seem to want to hear. Tonight, she decided with quavering insides, she would tell Samuel of her love for him. Even if he didn't respond in kind, she was long overdue in reassuring him of her feelings. Their embrace, two nights past, made her long afresh for the easy relationship they used to have, as well as being held tenderly in his arms. Yes, she resolved, tonight she would tell Samuel of her love for him.

If he came home.

CHAPTER SEVEN

"Nanny, why doesn't my daddy like us?" Audrey asked in a plaintive voice, edging her way from the sleeping area to where her caretaker sat near the fire. "He didn't come home for Kathryn's birthday an' that made us very, very sad, didn't it? We cried . . . remember? Are we going to cry on my birthday, too?"

"Hush, dearie, an' come here. There will na be cryin' on yer birthday," Nanny reassured, setting her book aside and opening her arms in invitation. "'Twill be a grand day in February, indeed, when we celebrate the fourth anniversary of yer birth. We were a wee bit sad to be missin' yer sister Mary Rose yesterday, is all. 'Twould have been her birthday, as well."

"An' she's dead, Nanny, isn't she?" Audrey replied, clambering into the haven of her nursemaid's lap. "She lives up in heaven with Jesus. Am I going to live in heaven with Jesus pretty soon, too?"

"Och, I pray yer mother forgives me for yer not havin' a nap this afternoon," Nanny muttered before answering. Holding the child close, she stroked her silky hair. "The

Laird Jesus took yer sister to himself because he knew her body wasn't strong enough for this world. Now, you've a fine, strong body, lassie. I should think ye'll be on this earth for many years to come, but ye must always be ready for his call."

"But why did he call Mary Rose first? I'm bigger. I'm going to be four."

"We know," Bobby spoke under his breath to Lynelle. Chafing at their second day of confinement, the pair played an indolent game of cat's cradle at the table near the window.

"Shh, quiet," Lynelle retorted, using her pinkies to quickly pull the string crisscross from her brother's hands, wanting to hear what Nanny had to say. Her glimpse yesterday into their mother's secret box—as well as into the private depths of Mama's sorrow—had evoked a mysterious, more kindred type of grief inside her young breast. It was as if a new place in her heart had opened, expanding wider as each item came out of the box.

Such love Mama had for all of them. Would she love her own children so dearly? Lynelle wondered with a foreign anxiety. Until yesterday, her mind had not conceived of such thoughts. Was this what growing up was about? Thoughts and concepts wonderful and terrifying at the same time?

"The Laird's takin' of Mary Rose was an act of his mercy an' love," Nanny continued, rocking at a steady pace, "just as surely as was his leavin' Kathryn behind to help with the heartache."

The three-year-old was quiet a long moment before asking, "Nanny, does my Daddy have a heartache?"

"Aye, child." The middle-aged woman sighed. "I'd say his heart be achin' most of all."

"More than Mama's?"

"Aye."

"More than Nell's an' Bobby's?"

"Aye."

"More than mine? More than Kathryn's?"

"Aye, dearie."

"But Mama cries and cries, an' I never seen Daddy cry. He doesn't talk, neither."

"Yer father was once a talkin' man, but he's long past due facin' the tragedy of his wee Mary Rose. Imagine him to be a boilin' pot o' water, lassie, wi' a roastin' fire below. What steam is bein' made canna be released, for he's holdin' the lid jammed on so verra tightly."

"Is he going to spill over someday? That happened to our mush one morning, an' it stinked, an' Gertrude had a big, big mess to clean up."

"A clever wain you are, Miss Audrey, indeed. Aye, we've been seein' wee puny sputters here an' there, but a churnin' eruption is on its way, mark my words."

"What kind of eruption? What do you think is going to happen?" Cat's cradle forgotten, Lynelle toyed nervously with the loop of string in her hands. Glancing at her brother, she read the same uneasy expression on his face as was certainly on her own.

"Dinna fash yerself, lass," Nanny replied. "To worrit an' fret only invites the de'il to come make mischief. The good Laird will take care of yer father in his own way. Ours is to be faithful to our prayin'."

Bobby stood suddenly, his chair clattering with the force of his movement. His face had grown red, and moisture glinted in his eyes. "I've said a million prayers! They don't work! They don't keep him home! Why is he gone all the time? How is he supposed to face something he never sees? Mary Rose is dead, but we're still here. He doesn't even look at us anymore!"

An answering anguish arose inside Lynelle as her brother sprinted from the table to the privacy of the sleep area. At the sound of the choking sobs he tried to disguise, tears flooded her eyes as well.

"Here now, lass," Nanny spoke, rising from her rocker. Holding Audrey's hand, the older woman and the younger walked to the table to comfort her. "Take heart. Our Laird works in weal and woe."

"Oh, don't cry, Nell," Audrey consoled, letting loose Nanny's grasp and wriggling into her sister's lap. Small fingers stroked her face. "Jesus will fix Daddy's heartache an' clean up his mush when it spills."

"I'll see to Master Robert, if ye don't mind. A good dose of fresh air would no doubt do ye both a world of good. I'm thinkin' that ye've fulfilled the punishment yer father set forth. 'Keep to the nursery till Christmas Eve,' he said. And Christmas Eve it is. Whisht! Outdoors wi' ye, now, for just a short while. I'll send yer brother right along."

"Thank you, Nanny." Wiping her tears, Lynelle smiled and wound her arms around her sister. "Let's get our coats."

"Do you mean me, Nell? I get to come with you?" Her features showed amazement at being included with her older siblings on an afternoon outing, and she cupped Lynelle's face between her small hands. "Me? Audrey?"

"Yes, I mean you, silly. We'll walk to the park."

"Not too long, now," Nanny admonished, on to her next task of soothing Bobby's distress. She spoke over her shoulder, "It'll soon be time to be gettin' dressed for yer fine dinner. Roast turkey and all the trimmin's, I hear. 'Twill be a miracle if Kathryn hasn't been wakened by all this ballyhoo. A half a nap between the pair of ye wee yins won't do at all. At least ye'll be sound asleep by the time St. Nicholas makes his way through the city."

"Did you know I'm going to stay awake till St. Nich'las comes?" the three-year-old chattered, hopping down from Lynelle's lap and tugging her hand. "Bobby told me we could set a trap for him, an' then we could get all his toys—"

"Hush, Audrey," Lynelle interrupted, feeling a solemn weight pressing on her young shoulders. "Christmas isn't about laying traps for St. Nicholas and stealing his toys. It's about God sending the Christ child to us. Remember what Mama read from the Bible last night? The angel told the shepherds, 'Fear not . . . I bring you good tidings of great joy . . . Ye shall find the babe wrapped in swaddling clothes, lying in a manger.' "

"That means baby Jesus!"

"Yes, Audrey. Baby Jesus, the Savior of this whole world. Isn't it amazing to think that one tiny little baby, wrapped in a blanket, was born to heal the hurts of all men?"

Audrey nodded, suddenly pensive as she pulled her coat from the peg near the door.

Though Lynelle didn't find her younger sister's nonstop jabbering as irritating as Bobby did, she was relieved that this concept had finally given Audrey's voice pause. Reaching for her own coat, she wondered what this year's Christmas would bring . . . and if the Christ child could bring healing to even her father's heart.

Three-thirty. Checking the time for the fifth time in as many minutes, Samuel pushed back his chair and rubbed first his eyes, then the back of his neck. He'd been working hard these past two days getting preliminary drawings completed for a local congregation wishing to build a new church. Projects stood stacked elbow deep on his desk, proof of the great demand for talented draftsmen and architects in the Twin Cities. Frequent requests from other cities came to his firm, as well, and he and his three partners had all they could do to keep up with the workload.

Once upon a time he had struck a balance between his home life and his work time. This equilibrium had foundered with his baby daughter's death to the degree that he could say that he was almost completely immersed in his work.

Almost.

There was still a part of him that could not forget the pleasant and satisfying years of matrimony and fatherhood. Nor could he imagine his present life without Joyce or the children. It was just that things had deteriorated to such an extent that he didn't know what to do anymore. His vibrant and affectionate wife had become timorous. Lynelle and Bobby had not only poisoned him but employed artifice in their attempt to rectify wrongs of which they were innocent. Audrey begged for his attention every chance she got. And Kathryn just sucked her thumb when in his presence, watching him with wary hazel eyes.

"Hey, Sam, when are you going to call it a day?"

"I'm just about finished," he answered automatically, glancing up to see friend and colleague Charles Young in the doorway, already dressed in his overcoat. Instead of moving along, Young continued to regard him with a concerned expression, tapping his hat against his chest.

"You . . . are going home, aren't you?"

"Yes, I'm going home, Charley. Why do you ask?" Nettled, Samuel's reply was clipped. The already tense muscles in the back of his neck stiffened beneath his starched collar.

"You've been putting in some long days since you've been back," Charles spoke, undaunted, "and I wonder how much Joyce and the children have seen of you. Go home, Samuel. It's Christmas Eve. The work will still be here next week."

"Thank you for the reminder," he ground out, thinking of the family dinner and Scripture reading that lay ahead of him this evening. Burdened as he was by the sorry state of his family life, how was he supposed to hold up under hours and hours together with them? He felt so powerless and ineffectual that he could barely hold himself together. In a show of almost vicious force, he kneaded the trail of knotted muscles leading downward from his neck to his shoulders.

"I'm concerned about you, Sam. You just haven't been yourself in a long time."

"I'm fine," he lied, his hand dropping away from his shoulder, limp. Physical and mental exhaustion nearly overwhelmed him. Forcing his features into what he hoped was a semblance of a smile, he added, "I was just leaving, myself."

"Well, good." His friend's serious brown gaze studied his face, and he nodded. "I'll wait and walk out with you, then."

Left with no other option, Samuel slowly rose from his chair and took his hat and coat from the rack standing in the corner.

CHAPTER EIGHT

W hat's for dessert, Mother?" Bobby asked in his most polite voice, wiping his mouth on his napkin and returning the cloth to his lap. His manners and those of his sisters had been impeccable throughout the entire meal.

This was the first time the Colburns had been together as a family since the night of the children's feigned illness, and, despite Joyce's worries to the contrary, dinner had not gone badly. Samuel had been home from the office early, disappearing for a long bath before joining them at the table. His mien this evening was polite but remote, as if nothing had happened.

"Gertrude made charlotte russe," Joyce replied with an encouraging smile, knowing the rich, creamy cold dessert was a favorite of her husband and son alike. Her smile faded when she gazed upon her husband. Though his hair and clothing were as neat as ever, she was disturbed by his lackluster hazel gaze and the drawn appearance of his face. Also, his plate remained more than half filled.

"And you will enjoy the almond macaroons, my darling,"

she spoke to Kathryn, seated in a high chair at her left. Her heart ached for the man at the head of their table. What could she possibly do to help him? During the past two years she'd tried everything she could think of. Would telling him she loved him be as futile as pouring a thimbleful of water on an acre of parched ground?

"Daddy?" Audrey spoke, having restrained her garrulous tongue admirably through the meal. Thanks to a talking-to first by Nanny, then a second by Joyce, all the Colburn children had been on their best behavior. "Daddy?" she repeated. "Did you know that the baby wrapped in the blanket can heal the hurts of all men?"

"Yes, Audrey, I know," he spoke with a deep sigh. "Happy Christmas."

An awkward silence passed. "Mama?" Audrey spoke in a loud whisper, setting down her fork. "Mama, I need to go upstairs. I have to—"

"Shh, darling," Joyce admonished in a gentle tone. "Just excuse yourself from the table. Would you like me or Lynelle to come with you?"

"No, I can go all by myself," the three-year-old replied with a liberal amount of disdain.

"All right, then. We'll wait on dessert until you return."

"Aww-dree," Bobby expressed his impatience at having to wait for his beloved serving of ladyfingers and rich Bavarian cream. "Why didn't you 'go all by yourself' before dinner?"

Having slid from the side of her armless chair, the second-youngest Colburn straightened her lovely holiday dress and walked to where her brother sat. "Just hold yer horses, laddie," she declared in a perfect imitation of their nursemaid, extending her index finger toward him, "I'll be back in four months. . . . I mean, four minutes."

"You don't even know what a minute is," he retorted, his irritation replaced by a glint of mischievousness just a second later. "Hey, Audrey," he challenged, "what were you wearing the day before tomorrow?"

Audrey paused, raising her eyebrows in a lofty manner. "You can't trick me. Lynelle teached me to say, 'What I'm wearing right now.' So there."

Watching her audacious youngster sashay from the dining room, Joyce disguised her smile by dabbing her mouth with her napkin. A quick glance at Samuel showed him seemingly unaffected by his children's raillery. This, to her, was doubly sad, for her husband used to be the instigator of much jesting and horseplay.

Once Audrey returned, the dishes were cleared, dessert was served, and finally the meal was over. While they'd finished eating, Ida had built a snapping blaze in the library's fireplace and lit the ivory-colored candles on the tree. From atop the spruce, the angel garbed in flowing ruby robes smiled her mysterious, faint smile, one hand outstretched as if to bid them entrance.

The library had never looked better, Joyce thought as they retired to its welcoming milieu. Samuel sought the comfort of his chair, looking a bit aggrieved at the prospect of no newspaper within sight. Indeed, the only volume on the table next to his chair was the leather-covered family Bible. Ida's devout faith had apparently precluded the presence of such secular reading material the eve of the Christ child's birth.

"Daddy, are you going to read the story of the baby in the blanket now? The baby that brings healing to all men?" Audrey ran to sit at his feet. "I'm ready. Are you ready?"

Taking her cue, Kathryn, Lynelle, and Bobby took places near the foot of their father's chair. Joyce settled into her chair, her throat growing thick at the sight of the children gathered before Samuel. *O Jesus*, she fervently prayed, *please let this be the night you bring your healing to this man. Please restore him to us—and to yourself.*

Clearing his throat, Samuel picked up the Bible and slowly turned its pages until he found the place he desired. "'And it came to pass in those days,'" he began, "'that there went out a decree from Caesar Augustus . . .'"

Her husband's rich voice washed over her, bringing memories of happy Christmas Eves past as well as mental images of Lynelle and Bobby as infants, toddlers, and growing children. Of Audrey, sticky-fingered and wobbly-legged, bringing delightful chaos to her first Christmas Eve celebration. Since she and Samuel had become parents, it had been a tradition for the family to gather in this room after dinner as well as for Samuel to read the Christmas story from the second chapter of Luke's Gospel. Later, they'd make popcorn, and she would play carols on the piano. . . .

"'And this shall be a sign unto you; ye shall find the babe wrapped in swaddling clothes, lying in a manger. And suddenly there was with the angel—'"

"The baby!" Audrey cried, leaping to her feet.

"Sit down," Bobby whispered loudly as she used his shoulder to steady herself. "He's not done yet."

"Daddy, I have a surprise for you," Audrey averred, tugging at Samuel's trousers.

"A surprise? What kind of surprise?" Setting the open Bible on the table, he studied the excited youngster before him with bemusement.

"Your father wasn't finished reading, Audrey." Joyce leaned forward to correct her impulsive daughter. "You know what poor manners it is to interrupt someone."

"But Mama, I have a wonnerful surprise for Daddy!" she entreated, wriggling in her enthusiasm. "Please, Mama? Please? Please?" Without waiting for a reply, she turned back to her father. "Daddy," she instructed, holding her finger out like a teacher's pointer, "you have to close your eyes and sit very, very still like a mouse. You can't open your eyes, not till I say so."

Instead of showing disapproval, Samuel seemed to brighten at his daughter's directions. With a smile, he reached out to stroke her glossy hair. "All right, Audrey," he granted, "I will close my eyes and wait for my wonderful surprise."

"No peeking," she iterated, scrutinizing Samuel's face to be sure his eyes were indeed tightly closed.

"No peeking," he confirmed.

Joyce's heart filled with hope at this delicate interchange, and she watched her daughter drop to her knees and reach beneath the long table skirt beside Samuel's chair. Grasping a small object between her thumb and forefinger, she climbed into her father's lap and brushed her hand against his cheek.

"Can you guess what this is, Daddy? Don't open your eyes!"

Everyone leaned closer to see what tiny, mysterious item Audrey held. "What is it, Audrey?" Bobby asked, craning his neck for a better view.

Samuel's face broke into a gentle smile while he obediently held his eyes shut. "Hmm, it tickles. Did you find a feather for me, Audrey? That would be a nice surprise in the middle of winter."

"No, Daddy, it's not a feather. You guessed wrong." A giggle accompanied her words. "Now wait. No, no, no! Don't open your eyes! I have 'nother surprise for you."

Nimble as a monkey, she vaulted from Samuel's lap and retrieved another item from her hiding place. The air caught in Joyce's lungs as she watched Audrey pull Miss Hillary from beneath the table and place the doll in her father's arms.

Wrapped around Miss Hillary was the baby quilt used to lay out Mary Rose.

Lynelle and Bobby turned frantic gazes to her while Kathryn chortled, "Ba-by!" Half rising from her chair, Joyce felt her perfect, hope-filled Christmas Eve celebration crash down upon her. "Audrey—," she began helplessly.

"Now you can open your eyes, Daddy," spoke the child, who paid not a whit of attention to her mother.

"You're giving me your doll?" Samuel queried, examining the porcelain face nestled within the folds of the quilt. A chuckle escaped his throat. "I seem to remember her coming to pay a call the other day. . . . Miss Hillary, isn't it? Audrey, dear, you don't have to—"

Stopping midsentence, he pulled a corner of the covering away from the doll. His fair complexion reddened, and his movements grew jerky as he struggled to balance his daughter, hold the doll, and unwrap the quilt.

"I know what this is." Though his voice was strangled, Joyce read open hostility in the gaze he flashed toward her.

"Yes, Daddy, it's Mary Rose's blanket. Mama saved it in a special, special place, an' she saved her hair, too." Unaware of the emotional storm brewing in the man on whose lap she perched, Audrey opened her palm to reveal the tiny bunch of gossamer strands. "I tickled your face so you could feel her touch you." With wide eyes and a sober expression, the three-year-old went on. "Nanny an' Lynelle said the baby in the blanket can heal the hurts of all men, an' they said your heart hurted the most about Mary Rose going to heaven to live with Jesus. So, Daddy, we can pretend Miss Hillary is Mary Rose, an' you can hold her all night long. I don't want your heart to hurt anymore, Daddy, an' I don't want you to spill over and get mush everywhere."

The crackling of the fire was the only sound in the room for what seemed like an endless time. Hurt and confusion were written on Audrey's face as her father pushed doll, blanket, and child from his lap and stood.

"You put her up to this." The accusation shot to Joyce like lead from a rifle.

"No, Samuel, I didn't know—"

Cutting her off, he railed, "I don't need you reminding me of my failures. Any of you!" Steadily, his voice grew in volume. "All these stunts and tricks . . . and Mary Rose's hair? Why don't you just say what you think, Joyce, and be done with it?"

"Wh-what do you mean?" Never had Joyce seen her husband so angry. The children had scuttled to the far side of the room with their father's outburst, the older two protectively holding their younger siblings. On their faces was reflected the fear in their young hearts.

Instead of quaking, Joyce was aware of a queer paralysis creeping over her—a dreamy, floating sensation similar to being in a dream. None of this could possibly be happening. Things like this didn't happen to families like theirs, did they?

"What more do you want?" he shouted, the cords on his neck standing out. "Why don't you just come out with it and tell me you wish you'd never married me?" Samuel's nostrils flared, his chest heaving with emotion.

Wish she'd never married him? Had he really said that? There was nothing farther from the truth. Her arms and legs felt funny, tingly, and it was hard to draw a deep breath. She loved him . . . oh, yes . . . that's what she was going to tell him tonight—that she loved him. On the mantel, candles flickered, creating a halo of light around her husband's head and shoulders.

"Samuel," she began, her voice sounding strange in her ears, "I don't think any of those things, and I . . . I only want to tell you . . . that I love you. We all love you."

There. She'd said it. Whatever happened next was in the Lord's hands.

"You love me?" he spat, sudden moisture shining in his eyes. "How could you? How could you possibly?" He stood silent a long moment, during which Joyce dared not breathe.

"I can't do this anymore," he finally said in a spiritless

voice, a single tear tracing its way down his cheek. "I can't." Shaking his head, he turned stiffly and walked from the room. A minute later the front door opened and closed.

"Mrs. Colburn?" Ida whispered from the doorway. Huddled behind her were Nanny and Gertrude. "Mrs. Colburn, what's happened? We were having our dinner in the kitchen and heard the shouting. . . ."

"Mr. Colburn has . . . left." Joyce was surprised at the calmness of her tone. Where were the tears? The weakness? The hysteria? Her husband had just walked out the door, maybe never to return. From where had such buoying strength come?

"Please go back and finish your dinner. I'd like to be alone with the children. Oh, and Meg, I'll be putting them to bed tonight. You may have the rest of the evening off."

"Aye, ma'am," the nursemaid said with a nod. "Ye know where to find me if ye'll be needin' anything."

"Oh, Mama," Lynelle cried once the servants had cleared the doorway. "Does this mean Daddy's never coming back?" In her arms whimpered Audrey, holding fast to both Miss Hillary and the colorful baby quilt.

"Hush, my darlings," she spoke, walking over and kneeling before them. "Do you see what happens when we take matters into our own hands? This is God's place to work, not ours, and we need to give your father over to him right this minute. I've been as guilty as you by quietly trying to fix things, trying not to cause trouble, trying to make a beautiful home—"

"But those aren't bad things, Mama, not like the naughty things we did." Lynelle sniffed and wiped her eyes with the back of her hand.

"No, they might not seem bad, but my reasons behind them were to accomplish the same thing you children set out to do—bring Daddy back to us. We need to tell the Lord we're sorry for trying to take over for him, and ask him to take good care of our daddy."

"But what if—"

"No more what-ifs, Robert. We either trust in our Savior, or we do not. Do you remember how the eleventh chapter of Hebrews begins?"

"I remember, Mama." Lynelle's voice quavered. "'Now faith is the substance of things hoped for—'"

"And 'the evidence of things not seen,'" Bobby finished.

"Very good, children. If we trust completely in the Lord, our faith is built only stronger during such times as these. Now, I cannot imagine how God can solve a problem so large, so troublesome, so complex as the one plaguing our family. I only know that he can, and that we cannot. Shall we finally tell him so?"

Heads bowed and hands clasped, Joyce led them all in a brief prayer, one in which she asked forgiveness for their lack of trust. "We also give Samuel over to you, totally and completely," she continued, her voice finally breaking. "You know the desire in our hearts to have him restored to us, Father, but he is yours to do with what you will. We pray this in the name of your Son, our Savior, the Lord Jesus, whose birth we celebrate and thank you for this night. Amen."

A soft chorus of amens arose from the children as they engulfed her with tearful hugs and kisses. How very blessed she was, indeed, to have four such healthy, beautiful, and loving children. As difficult as it would be if Samuel never came back, this would be enough, she decided, her heart overflowing with a sudden wash of tranquillity.

Yes, it could be enough.

CHAPTER NINE

Block after block Samuel walked, the rigid control he had worked so hard to maintain over his life slipping from his grasp. How much did Joyce and the children want from him? What did they expect? There wasn't a thing he could do to change the past. He couldn't bring back the dead.

His anger grew when he thought of his family and their manipulations. How could he go back home after what they'd done tonight? Joyce and the children had simply pushed him too far. He might have been able to forgive the calomel-laced pudding and the children's counterfeit illnesses this week, but this evening's stunt was beyond what he could abide.

I tickled her face so you could feel her touch you.

Reflexively, he rubbed his cheek where Audrey had brushed her baby sister's tiny curl. He hadn't even noticed whether or not Mary Rose had had hair. What he remembered was her laborious breathing, the struggle to draw air into her little body. And those dark eyes, fixing on him, seeking from him.

Fresh pain assaulted him, fueling his anger and grief. He'd tried his hardest to be a good husband and father, a good provider. And he *had* been all of those things . . . until . . .

Unbidden, the memory of rolling over on Miss Hillary intruded into the storm of his fury. Audrey, his intrepid and ever-talkative daughter smiled at him in his mind's eye. Somehow the clever three-year-old had escaped Nanny's watchful care the afternoon he'd experienced the ill effects of Lynelle and Bobby's attempt to repair his relationship with Joyce, tucking her precious doll beside him for comfort.

That meant Joyce's denial was probably true, that she didn't have foreknowledge of Audrey's impulsive deed this evening. But what was this business of keeping Mary Rose's hair? Her blanket? Wasn't that unhealthy? Ghoulish, even?

What about your mother's brooch? The image of his mother's cameo pin, tucked deep inside the top desk drawer in his sitting room, came to mind. From time to time he unwrapped the inexpensive but treasured item, remembering the happier days of his childhood before she had fallen ill. Surely it wasn't unnatural for him to keep a small memento by which to remember and honor her memory.

In her brief life, what else did Mary Rose have to offer?

Tears welled in his eyes, and he slowed his pace, for the first time noticing the snowfall. Taking in the fresh, pristine mantle covering the city, he realized his anger had somehow, mysteriously evaporated. In its place were left only pain and weakness, his familiar adversaries.

Hadn't he worked hard enough to overcome his childhood ineptitude and deficiencies? What more was required of him? Hadn't thirteen years of marriage and the establishment of a prosperous career been enough to mature the frightened boy deep inside him to manhood?

A fresh wave of longing washed through him, making him

realize how badly he desired reconciliation with Joyce and the children. His family, his life. How he loved them. Over the years they'd built a household of love and laughter until—until the twins had been born.

Until he'd failed them.

Samuel . . . I love you . . . we all love you.

Joyce's stricken words in the library came back to him. She loved him . . . she *still* loved him? How could she, after what he'd done? He was weak, unworthy.

He realized he'd stopped walking. The snow had grown thicker, causing a hush to fall over the city. Where was he? To his right, in the yard of a small church, was an outdoor crèche. Glancing across the street, he recognized the row of businesses. It hardly seemed possible that he'd covered two miles since walking out his front door.

Now what?

Now where?

He sighed, looking upward. No answer there, just an infinite, dizzying pattern of snowflakes. Aware of frigid hardness pressing against his leg, he glanced down to find himself in contact with the wrought iron fence in front of the church.

He was about to step away when something about the manger scene drew his attention. What was it? The illumination of the corner gaslight barely reached the white-cowled figures. Mary, Joseph. The wise men, the shepherds, the animals. He found it curious that this small house of worship had spared no expense in setting up such an elaborate Christmas display.

At the center of the grouping was a rough wooden cradle stuffed with hay. Still, lonely, and cold lay the white-layered babe upon his crude pallet, the small form all too reminiscent of another motionless child. Samuel shivered in his misery, realizing he had grown chilled while standing.

My strength is made perfect in weakness.

Where had that thought come from? No doubt some Bible verse from long ago. There was nothing perfect about weakness; his own father had taught him that. Why else had he worked so hard, for so long, to be strong?

Thinking of his labor, his trials, his exertion, he sighed with weariness. What good had any of it been? He was on the verge of losing his wife and family. Exhaustion, guilt, and worry had become his constant companions. He just couldn't go on any longer. Shoulders slumping, he leaned forward into the fence, allowing the bars to bear his weight.

A gentle stillness fell upon his spirit as he pondered the helpless infant Christ child in the yard before him, trying to reconcile this Jesus with that of the omnipotent Savior. King of kings. Lord of lords.

Lamb that was slain.

My strength is made perfect in weakness.

The longer he stood contemplating these holy mysteries, the more aware he became of the inner quietness creeping over him, a strange but wonderful weightlessness of being. The sensations of cold and desolation slipped away until he was aware only of peace . . . such peace he had never before known.

A sermon he'd heard shortly after Mary Rose's death came to mind, one in which the pastor had spoken of the power that was found in weakness—weakness submitted to the Almighty. It was a sermon he'd rejected, dismissed as utter ridiculousness. But tonight the words came back with crystalline recall, making him wonder if they were true after all.

And if they were . . . *O Lord, how could I have been so wrong?*

"Please forgive me," he whispered, bowing his head, his beliefs of strength and manliness crumbling beneath the purity of the truth offered him. The enormity of his sin loomed, came sharply into focus, faded and was gone.

Forgiven.

And Samuel Colburn knelt on the snowy sidewalk, sur-rendering himself and his fears to the one who loved him beyond all imagining.

CHAPTER TEN

"Mama, do we get to stay here all night?" Audrey whispered, her small fingers running over Mary Rose's quilt, then caressing her sister's curls. "Look, Mama, Kathryn and Miss Hillary are already sleeping like a bug in a rug. I wanna sleep in your bed, too." Closing her eyes, she collapsed back against the pillows, feigning slumber.

"Faker. Anyway, two people are 'bugs in rugs,'" Bobby scoffed. "Don't you know anything about pluralizing?"

"*Pearl*izing? What are you talking about?" Audrey's nightgown-clad body nearly jackknifed in reaction when he tickled her foot, and she covered her mouth to muffle her giggles.

And Kathryn dreamed on, her thumb tucked securely between her lips.

Despite their earnest prayer in the library, the evening had fallen flat after they'd popped popcorn and drunk hot chocolate. Singing carols just wasn't the same without Samuel's rich baritone to anchor their voices. Where Joyce had gotten the idea to invite all the children to her bedchamber she

didn't know, but their countenances had brightened immediately at the prospect. The race was on to wash faces, brush
teeth, don night wear, and jump into the large carriage bed.

The light burned low, and a small wood fire crackled
behind the screen. A cozy hour had passed, during which
they'd shared stories and reminiscences. No one asked when
Daddy was going to be back—or *if* Daddy was going to be
back; it was as if an unspoken understanding had passed
between them downstairs this evening: Daddy was in God's
hands.

"Tell me the story of when I was born, Mama," Audrey
entreated, wriggling her way beneath the covers. "Were you
so happy?"

"I was delighted, Audrey," Joyce confirmed with a smile.
"You joined our family on the snowiest February day imag-
inable. My goodness, such a storm was raging."

"Was the snow taller than the roof?"

"No, not quite that high, but it was very deep. Do you
remember how excited both of you were to meet your new
sister?" she inquired of Bobby and Lynelle, who shared a
quilt at the foot of the bed. "All Lynelle wanted to do was
hold you," she said to the enthralled nearly four-year-old,
"and your brother couldn't wait to teach you how to walk
and talk."

"He teached me how to walk? And *talk?* Bobby? He
teached me a very lot, didn't he, Mama?"

"Too much!" Bobby covered his face with his hands, shaking his head, while Joyce and Lynelle shared a round of quiet
laughter.

All interest lost in the story of Audrey's birth, the children
continued their banter. As she adjusted the covers and
leaned over to press a kiss against Kathryn's temple, a faint
noise caught her attention, a soft sound such as someone
quietly closing the front door. Had Samuel come home? she

wondered, her heart leaping—only to falter. Maybe it was only Ida, checking the lock.

Or if it *was* Samuel, how did she know he had come home to stay? Perhaps he had only returned to gather his things—in which case, he would be further aggrieved to find all five of them in his bedchamber.

Her gaze flew to the six-panel door when she heard quiet footsteps on the stair. Pulse quickening, she then took in the four beautiful children she and Samuel had created, trying to impress upon her mind a permanent image of them at this moment. So full of life, so trusting, so precious. No matter what happened, whatever their situation was to be, God was sovereign, she told herself, promising never to forsake her.

"I think Daddy's home," whispered Lynelle, head cocked, breaking off her words with her siblings. She turned worried eyes to her mother. "Will he be angry to find us in here? What should we do, Mama?"

"I know . . . let's hide!" Audrey exclaimed, pulling the covers over her head.

"We don't need to hide," Joyce spoke with more reassurance than she felt, reaching over Kathryn and Miss Hillary to pull the coverlet back down, the friction causing Audrey's fine hair to fly all directions.

Despite the tension in the room, a snicker escaped Bobby. "You should see your hair—it's sticking out everywhere! You look like a wild dog, Audrey."

"Wild da-awg?" she replied with a giggle. "I should bite you, then!" Extricating herself from beneath the covers, she leaped at her brother.

"Audrey! Bobby!" Joyce called, just as Samuel opened the bedroom door. He stopped just inside the opening, taking in the scene before him.

"What's going on in here?" he asked sternly, folding his arms across his chest.

"Daddy, Bobby just called me a wild dog," Audrey tattled,

pulling herself off her brother and sitting up primly. The three children sat at attention, moving not a muscle.

"And why would he do such a thing?"

"He said my hair was sticking out everywhere."

Walking to the bed, his features softening into a gentle smile, Samuel reached out and smoothed the flyaway strands. "Your hair *is* sticking out everywhere. Come here, pumpkin," he invited, opening his arms.

Needing no urging, Audrey flew into her father's embrace. Joyce let out the breath she didn't know she was holding and blinked away sudden tears. Samuel. Something had happened to him; she could see it in his expression, his carriage, his smile. Gone was the distant stranger; back was her husband, the father of her children.

"I need to ask your forgiveness, Audrey," he said humbly, taking a seat on the bed. Shifting her to the center of his lap, he spread his arms once more. "Lynelle, Bobby?"

Without hesitation, the older children sought their father's closeness, vying for position. "This includes you, too, little Kathryn," he added, emotion choking his voice, gazing at her sleeping form with an expression of love and longing.

Joy and gratitude flowed through Joyce, her peace made perfect when a hazel gaze brimming with emotion sought her own. "I love you," he whispered, "all of you. And I can only tell you how sorry I am for the way I've treated you." Clearing his throat, he paused before continuing, his voice gaining strength. "You were right, Audrey. My heart was hurting because of Mary Rose dying . . . and because I was trying to be strong on my own. How foolish I was."

"Nanny said your heartache was going to boil over and make a big, big mess," Audrey offered, cupping her father's face in her hands.

Joyce winced at her daughter's words but relaxed when she saw her husband's mouth twitch into a smile.

"A big, big mess? Yes, well . . . Nanny was right. Do you

think you can forgive me for making such a big, big mess of things?"

"I forgive you, Daddy," Lynelle cried, nestled in is left arm. "But can you forgive me for putting calomel in your pudding—"

"And calling you home from your party?" Bobby finished, hanging his head.

"And I tickled you with Mary Rose's hair. I wasn't s'posed to sneak in Mama's wardrobe, but I did," Audrey confessed.

"And will you forgive me, as well, Samuel?" Joyce asked, seeing his gaze focus on her with surprise.

"For what? It was I who wronged you."

"I tried too hard to hold onto you, tried to manage things on my own. I didn't allow God much room to work."

"Nor did I," he replied. "But that's changed. You'd never believe . . ." He shook his head, an incredulous smile breaking over his face like a sunrise upon a long-darkened land. Pressing a kiss upon the head of each child he held, he raised his head and looked at her. "Let me just say that I have the most amazing story to tell you tonight . . . later."

Joyce smiled, her gaze locking with that of her husband's. He was back. Peace shone from his countenance, and in his eyes shone that special warmth reserved for her alone. Joy and completeness swelled within her, pushing aside the painful memories the past two years had held.

"Da-dee?" came a sleepy voice from the head of the bed. "Da-dee home?"

"Yes, Kathryn," she replied, reaching out to take the warm, strong hand her husband offered. "Our daddy is home."

Paths Briefly Crossing

Too many of you have passed through my hands
*   Over the years,*
Passing, pausing, paths briefly crossing
*   On your way from here to there.*
Your brief little lives woven together for a purpose
*   Only our Creator shall know*
And we can only guess at—
*   If we can see past the pain to do any guessing at all.*
But I know, sweet little ones, your lives did have purpose
*   As did your deaths;*
I rest in that; I trust in that—
*   All the while tears stream down my face.*
And I, too, ask,
*   "Why must this be so?"*
So I pause for a time to hold you, to admire you,
*   To love you for a moment as if you were my own.*
I press a little kiss upon your brow
*   And say a prayer,*
Filled with sorrow for how your family will miss you
*   And how the world will never know you.*
"Enough!" I tell myself.
*   "Don't do this anymore!"*
But I will,
*   Yes, I must*
Because, amidst the suffering
*   There is a peace—*
A calm, hushed stillness
*   That I cannot explain.*
Slowly and gently my troubled heart is soothed
*   Until I am restored*
And I am ready
*   For the next one of you to pass through my hands.*

—Peggy Stoks, R.N.

RECIPE

I've made this recipe many times since my girlhood. Rich and flavorful, these cookies are made even better with the addition of freshly grated nutmeg. A small investment (less than five dollars) in a spice grater will more than pay for itself as your family and friends marvel at the exquisite taste of your baked goods.

NUTMEG LOGS

1 cup butter
2 tsp. vanilla extract
2 tsp. rum-flavored extract
¾ cup sugar
1 egg
3 cups flour
½ tsp. salt
1 tsp. nutmeg

Cream together butter and sugar. Add egg, vanilla, and rum-flavored extract; beat well. Add flour, salt, and nutmeg; mix thoroughly. Shape dough on sugared board into long rolls, ½-inch in diameter, then cut into 3-inch pieces (logs). Bake at 350° for 12-14 minutes. Cool, then ice. Sprinkle with freshly grated nutmeg before the icing dries.

For icing, mix together
1 cup powdered sugar
pinch of salt
1 tbsp. butter
½ tsp. vanilla extract
½ tsp. rum-flavored extract
1–2 tbsp. milk

P.S. I almost chose my Grandma Hughs's homemade chocolate pudding recipe to share, but I thought better of it. . . .

A Note from the Author

Dear Reader,
Ideas and inspiration for this story came from many places, and I will never forget the evening my ten-year-old daughter, Allison, and I sat down with a pile of quilting books to decide on a title for this novella. Together we compiled a long list of contenders, the name of nearly every quilt pattern evoking a wealth of plotting possibilities. Our search was over when Allison discovered "Crosses and Losses," and thus the story was born.

About the origin of the pattern name I know very little. Maggie Malone's Classic American Patchwork Quilt Patterns *(Drake Publishers, Inc., 1977) gives brief mention to the pattern, which is also known as "Fox and Geese" or "Double X and X." Forty-two blocks make up a full-sized quilt, each block containing a bold, colorful mix of squares and triangles. It's just the sort of quilt that would look right at home in my family room—if I ever had a few spare moments to devote to one more project!*

So whether you're an expert quilter, a sewing machine hack quilter (like yours truly), or have never sewn a stitch in your life, I pray that this unique collection of Christmas stories blesses your life in some special way this holiday season. Merry Christmas.

Warmly,
Peggy Stoks

About the Author

Peggy Stoks lives in Minnesota with her husband and three daughters. She has worked as a registered nurse for nearly twenty years. She has published two novels as well as numerous magazine articles about child care and pediatrics. In addition to her novella for *A Victorian Christmas Quilt*, she has written novellas for *A Victorian Christmas Tea* and *Reunited*.

You can write to Peggy at P.O. Box 333, Circle Pines, MN 55014.

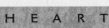
Current HeartQuest Releases

- *Faith*, Lori Copeland
- *Prairie Fire*, Catherine Palmer
- *Prairie Rose*, Catherine Palmer
- *Reunited*, Judy Baer
- *The Treasure of Timbuktu*, Catherine Palmer
- *The Treasure of Zanzibar*, Catherine Palmer
- *A Victorian Christmas Quilt*, Catherine Palmer
- *A Victorian Christmas Tea*, Catherine Palmer

- *With This Ring*, Lori Copeland
- *June*, Lori Copeland—coming soon (Spring 1999)
- *Prairie Storm*, Catherine Palmer—coming soon (Spring 1999)
- *The Treasure of Kilimanjaro*, Catherine Palmer—coming soon (Spring 1999)
- *Finders Keepers*, Catherine Palmer—coming soon (Fall 1999)
- *Hope*, Lori Copeland—coming soon (Fall 1999)

Other Great Tyndale House Fiction

- *The Captive Voice*, B. J. Hoff
- *Dark River Legacy*, B. J. Hoff
- *Embers of Hope*, Sally Laity and Dianna Crawford
- *The Fires of Freedom*, Sally Laity and Dianna Crawford
- *The Gathering Dawn*, Sally Laity and Dianna Crawford
- *Jewels for a Crown*, Lawana Blackwell
- *The Kindled Flame*, Sally Laity and Dianna Crawford

- *Like a River Glorious*, Lawana Blackwell
- *Measures of Grace*, Lawana Blackwell
- *Song of a Soul*, Lawana Blackwell
- *Storm at Daybreak*, B. J. Hoff
- *The Tangled Web*, B. J. Hoff
- *The Tempering Blaze*, Sally Laity and Dianna Crawford
- *The Torch of Triumph*, Sally Laity and Dianna Crawford
- *Vow of Silence*, B. J. Hoff

Heartwarming Anthologies from HeartQuest

A Victorian Christmas Tea—Four novellas about life and love at Christmastime. Stories by Catherine Palmer, Dianna Crawford, Peggy Stoks and Katherine Chute.

A Victorian Christmas Quilt—A patchwork of four novellas about love and joy at Christmastime. Stories by Catherine Palmer, Debra White Smith, Ginny Aiken, and Peggy Stoks.

Reunited—Four stories about reuniting friends, old memories, and new romance. Includes favorite recipes from the authors. Stories by Judy Baer, Jeri O'Dell, Jan Duffy, and Peggy Stoks.

With This Ring—A quartet of charming stories about four very special weddings. Stories by Lori Copeland, Dianna Crawford, Ginny Aiken, and Catherine Palmer.

HeartQuest Books by Catherine Palmer

The Treasure of Timbuktu—Abducted by a treasure hunter, Tillie becomes a pawn in a dangerous game. Desperate and on the run from a fierce nomadic tribe looking to kidnap her, Tillie Thorton finds herself in an uneasy partnership with a daring adventurer.

The Treasure of Zanzibar—An ancient house filled with secrets . . . a sunken treasure . . . an unknown enemy . . . a lost love. They all await her on Zanzibar. Jessica Thorton returns to Africa with her son to claim her inheritance on the island of Zanzibar. Upon her arrival, she is reunited with her estranged husband.

Prairie Rose—Kansas held their future, but only faith could mend their past. Hope and love blossom on the untamed prairie as a young woman, searching for a place to call home, happens upon a Kansas homestead during the 1860s.

Prairie Fire—Will a burning secret extinguish the spark of love between Jack and Catrin? The town of Hope discovers the importance of forgiveness, overcoming prejudice, and the dangers of keeping unhealthy family secrets.

A Victorian Christmas Tea—Four novellas about life and love at Christmastime. Stories by Catherine Palmer, Dianna Crawford, Peggy Stoks and Katherine Chute. In "Angel in the Attic," mistaken identities nearly derail a romance before it can even begin. The prayers of a young widow's child for "A Daddy for Christmas" are answered in a most unusual manner. In "Tea for Marie," love springs unexpectedly from the ashes of disaster in the winter wonderland of Minnesota. And "Going Home" takes you to a plantation where tender hearts must put aside the past before they can embrace the future.

A Victorian Christmas Quilt—A patchwork of four novellas about love and joy at Christmastime. Stories by Catherine Palmer, Debra White Smith, Ginny Aiken, and Peggy Stoks.

H E A R T   Q U E S T

Coming soon from Catherine Palmer

Finders Keepers—The first book in a new contemporary romance series.

Prairie Storm—The third book in the Kansas historical romance series about a town called Hope.

The Treasure of Kilimanjaro—The third book in an exciting romance adventure series.